MAGNUS MERRIMAN

Eric Linklater (1899–1974) was born in Wales and educated in Aberdeen. His family came from the Orkney Islands (his father was a master mariner), and the boy spent much of his childhood there.

Linklater served as a private in the Black Watch at the close of the First World War, surviving a nearly fatal head wound to return to Aberdeen to take a degree in English. A spell in Bombay with the *Times of India* was followed by some university teaching at Aberdeen again, and then a Commonwealth Fellowship which allowed him to travel in America from 1928 to 1930.

Linklater's memories of Orkney and student life informed his first novel, *White Maa's Saga* (1929), while the success of *Poet's Pub* in the same year led him to take up writing as a full-time career. A hilarious satirical novel, *Juan in America* (1931), followed his American trip, while the equally irreverent *Magnus Merriman* (1934) was based on his experiences as Nationalist candidate for a by-election in East Fife.

Linklater joined the army again in the Second World War, to serve in fortress Orkney, and later as a War Office correspondent reporting the Italian campaign, and later writing the official history. The compassionate comedy of *Private Angelo* (1946) was drawn from this Italian experience.

With these and many other books, stories and plays to his name, Linklater enjoyed a long and popular career as a writer. His early creative years were described in *The Man on my Back* (1941), while a fuller autobiography, *Fanfare for a Tin Hat*, appeared in 1970.

Eric Linklater

MAGNUS MERRIMAN

Introduced by Douglas Gifford

CANONGATE
CLASSICS
35

This edition published as a Canongate Classic in 1990 by Canongate Publishing Ltd, 16 Frederick Street, Edinburgh EH2 2HB. Copyright the estate of Eric Linklater. Introduction copyright Douglas Gifford.

The publishers gratefully acknowledge general subsidy from the Scottish Arts Council towards the Canongate Classics series and a specific grant towards the publication of this title.

Set in 10pt Plantin by Hewer Text Composition Services, Edinburgh. Printed and bound in Denmark by Nørhaven Rotation.

Canongate Classics
Series Editor: Roderick Watson
Editorial Board: Tom Crawford, J. B. Pick

British Library Cataloguing in Publication Data is available on request.

ISBN 0-86241-313-3

This is one of the funniest of all twentieth-century Scottish novels, a satire on the movement known as 'the Scottish Renaissance'. It is also an unusual example of the relatively rare *genre* of the political novel, although unlike Disraeli or C.P. Snow, Linklater sets up his political world only in order to knock it down. In the same way, the novel relates to a *genre* developed by D.H. Lawrence, Neil Gunn and Grassic Gibbon, in which it is asserted that an organic relationship exists between man and his natural environment, a relationship which is more important than the superficialities of urban and social life. And then, this relationship in turn is held up to mockery, in a way which locates this novel as the Scottish equivalent of Stella Gibbon's wonderful parody, *Cold Comfort Farm* (1932).

But *Magnus*, like so much of Linklater's work, defies categorization. Indeed, Linklater was to be disappointed all his life about not being taken seriously by critics. In his various autobiographies he typically both deplored the lack of serious consideration given to his books and mocked his 'inability' to impose his own character on his novels. Perhaps, he suggested, 'I have no character positive enough to impress itself on topics of every sort'—hardly a reflection which will ring true to the reader of this novel! A more valid reason for his critical neglect might be his refusal to follow literary trends and fashions in general. His mockery of modernism after the Great War reveals his scorn for what he saw as 'the disruption of language' by writers like Joyce and Eliot, and in *Magnus* he found 'indomitable infantility' amongst most creative writers of the day. But for a full understanding of his apparently contradictory love of and scorn for literature (and even his own work) we must know something of his unusual and restless search for an identity, which perhaps he never really found.

Born in 1899 in Penarth, South Wales, Linklater, son of a sailor from Orkney, and of a Swedish-English mother, was all through his life to encourage the idea that he was the essential Orkneyman. In fact, as his biographer Michael Parnell has revealed, until he was fourteen Linklater had only been to Scotland and Orkney on holiday. When the family moved north it was to Aberdeen, not to Orkney, and Linklater only rooted himself in Orkney on his marriage in 1934. What this reveals is not so much an evasion of truth as the more important pursuit of a dream, comparable to the way Magnus pursues *his* visions. Like Magnus, Linklater had many such dreams, as a soldier, in two world wars, with a career of great distinction (becoming Commander of the Orkney Fortress in 1940), as a politician (like Magnus, he stood for parliament for the SNP in 1933), as a Highland gentleman; and (probably his final dream) as 'an old peasant with a pen'. It is not surprising that there were contradictions and tensions between these dreams, so varied are they in their values, perspectives and *personae*. Linklater's clipped, anglicized army utterance did not speak for the whole man; and perhaps in the end the problem for his writing was that other voices, reductive and mocking, ironic and Rabelaisian, kept undercutting his formally serious and intellectually ambitious self.

The novels reflect this variety, from the light comedy and Anglocentric whimsies of *Poet's Pub*, and *Ripeness is All*, with its Wodehousian frolics in English rectories, to the American and Chinese adventures of his post-Byronic anti-hero, young Juan, to the *Catch*-22-style mockeries of war and 'manliness' in *Private Angelo* (1946), whose peasant anti-hero freely admits that he 'lacks the gift of courage'. This novel alone, set beside Linklater's sympathetic and serious wartime histories (like his moving *apologia* for the surrender of the Highland Division in 1940), shows the contradiction (or as his fellow Scottish Renaissance writer, the poet Hugh MacDiarmid, would have described it) the antisyzygy at the heart of the man's view of life. Linklater's fundamental unwillingness to let himself preach a message, with his preference for lively extremes, may have unsettled critics who wanted consistent development; but it gives his novels a delightful and human unpredictability, which should transcend the vagaries of literary fashion.

Amidst the zigzagging between polar opposites of Scottish-English, flippant and sombre, conservative and sceptical, Linklater's willed Orkney identity acted as a sheet-anchor. Indeed his forebears had been Orkney men for hundreds of years. Something like Jung's 'collective unconscious', the 'great race memory' in the bone, may have been working through him, much as Magnus's memories of Orkney call more insistently to him than soldiering or journalism, or even Scotland itself. This author's relations with his fatherland were ambivalent, to say the least.

At Aberdeen University after the war, Linklater changed from medicine to English. As with Magnus, a profound love of Elizabethan and English literature, its rhythms and linguistic resources, captured him more than the Scottish tradition did (Scottish literature was little taught at that time). Becoming Assistant Editor of the *Times* of India in 1925–7, he travelled back to Britain via Asia and America. *White Maa's Saga* (the *maa* being the northern term for a gull), *Poet's Pub* and *Juan in America* all followed. *The Men of Ness* (1931), is perhaps Linklater's most profound exploration of his Orkney ancestry, for the novel's style and story recreate the traditional Orkney saga. He thought he had revived a fashion of writing characteristic of the great medieval Scottish *makars* like Dunbar and Henryson. The Sagas speak through him, and his empathy with modes of thought over a thousand years old, suggests why Linklater would never quite fit convenient categories of modern literature. The novel's scepticism about the values of humanity, its mordant and understated humour, its genuine sharing of Viking attitudes in an exuberant but essentially pessimistic awareness of the transience and pointlessness of life—all argue that Orkney was a fixed and elemental place in Linklater's heart, whatever temporary illusions or ambitions he might allow himself to enjoy along the way.

All this gives *Magnus Merriman* its themes and its structure. It begins with Linklater's 'Admonition', in which he detaches himself from Magnus, warning that just because his hero contested a by-election he isn't to be taken *for* him. Yet he knows he protests too much. The protagonists of *White Maa's Saga* and *Juan in America do* represent sides of Linklater, and Magnus does, too. The novel is perhaps the closest of all his work to the experiences and feelings of its author in the 1920s and 1930s. Those were the years of the 'Scottish Renaissance' in which the lyrics of Hugh MacDiarmid and his long polemical and philosophical poem *A Drunk Man Looks at the Thistle* (1926), had restored the issues of language, identity and political autonomy to the social and cultural agenda of Scotland. Linklater was to become one of the outstanding writers of this Renaissance, yet his attitude towards it is typically ambivalent. Essentially, he mocks himself *and* the Renaissance: himself as a self-deceiving dreamer, whose bubbles of delusion are burst with monotonous regularity; and the Renaissance as human dreaming writ large, a Scottish collective wishfulness. What disguises the basic simplicity of this design is the way the author identifies with Magnus's thoughts, and the moving and lyrical episodes in which the reader is virtually compelled to share the dream too. Thus Linklater speaks with two voices, for *and* against self- and social deception, with something of Walter Scott's division between the values of the heart and the conclusions of the head.

The character of Magnus is clearly meant to have archetypal significance, but he is something of a parody of those other renaissance heroes—like Gunn's boys, representing their race, or McColla's Murdo Anderson in *The Albannach*, who stands for the spirit of Highland revival, or Chris Guthrie of *A Scots Quair*, who is also 'Chris Caledonia'. But what values, nation or society does Magnus represent? Part of Linklater's cleverness lies in leaving this open to the reader to decide. At one level he can be a kind of 'Great Laughter', Rabelaisian and reductive, that kind of Merry Humanity which trips and stumbles its never-too-serious pilgrimage through life. But the name has deliberate Orkney echoes, reminding us of Earl Magnus, the saint of the twelfth century, whose cathedral in Kirkwall 'rides time', in the words of Orkney poet George Mackay Brown. Less saintly, Magnus can be seen as the essential spirit of Orkney, elementally Viking, making occasional raids out from his island fastness to cock a snook at the ridiculous world at large. Indeed, the progress of the book takes Magnus away from his pretensions as an international Everyman towards another identity, reduced but still essential, as an Orkneyman.

Broadly, the novel moves between these two poles. It's important to see that Magnus's war travels in Mesopotamia and Persia, his London adventures, *and* his Scottish politicking, all belong to the international Everyman phase of his life. Not for nothing do the Orcadians regard Scotland as 'over there'. In the last referendum on Scottish Home Rule in 1979 Orkney and Shetland voted to be neither part of Scotland nor the United Kingdom. This would appear to be Linklater's message too—until the reader recalls those moving passages when Edinburgh's romantic, brooding castle swirls through dark mist, or when Magnus reads of the war's dead in the castle's chapel, or when he has a vision of the varieties of green in Scotland's landscapes. So what *is* the novel's movement northwards telling us?

As far as Magnus is concerned, the movement stems from a common pattern of deflation. Aspiring to military glory, he shoves his bayonet up his Captain's behind. Loving like the world's great lovers Troilus and Romeo, he comes to perceive in his mistress's words—not antelopes in a pale gold morning, but butcher's sheep, and suddenly she seems to him like a fat-bottomed squaw. Dreaming of mastering the mighty torrent of English and of being a poet, Magnus wakes up next day with a crapula. (Linklater mocks the reader by using archaic and specialist words like this at junctures which deflate the reader's sense of sureness— an echo of his central theme.) And the Scottish national dream is simply the biggest self-delusion of all. Note how skilfully and quickly Linklater turns Magnus around from a position of Imperial Conservatism to one where he actually *believes* he's been moving towards Nationalism for some time. Magnus speaks Meiklejohn's words as though they have always been his, when a short while ago he would have had one of his exuberant drunken fistfights on behalf

of the other side! Magnus is embarrassingly fickle, a dreamer
like Scott's Waverley, a born actor like Barrie's Sentimental
Tommy.

Does Linklater therefore think little of the Scottish real-
life characters he mocks? Hugh Skene *is* Hugh MacDiarmid,
and Beatty Bracken *is* Wendy Wood, and Linklater was
taken to court for his description of how she flushed the
Union Jack down the toilet. Meiklejohn is Moray McLaren,
and Melvin McMaster is Ramsay MacDonald, for this is
a *roman à clef*, and unlocking its actuality would seem to
suggest denigration pure and simple. But does it? After
all, Skene *is* allowed the glow of real genius, and it's
only his excesses which are mocked. Consider too that,
for all the marvellous satire of Skene's impenetrable Scots
poetry in 'The Flauchter-spaad', equal if not greater scorn
is reserved for the transatlantic intellectual snobbery and
deceit in English literature. Furthermore, the arguments
Magnus encounters and uses in his election campaign are
genuinely valid, and were seen so by Linklater. It's just that
at the end of the day Linklater doesn't think much of *any*
human comedy, as the descriptions of the empty-coat figure
of Ramsay MacDonald and British politics clearly show; or
consider the later exposure of the world of journalism and
Lady Mercy—a prophetic picture of *folie de grandeur* in a
press baron. Set in this context, the nationalist dreams are
an uneasy mixture of validity and vanity, and Linklater's
novel is a healthy corrective, or perhaps a stringent laxative,
to the national epics and romances of peasant revival which
were to abound in Scotland from 1926 until the Second
World War.

Under all Magnus's activities in love and politics, the
reader should hear the ever-strengthening call of Orkney.
The north called Magnus away from London and his farcical
love-affair there; Fife and its fair shores reminded him again
of the glories of the Highlands; and when Frieda's love and
his election hopes are so typically and ferociously dashed,
the second great movement of the novel begins. Yet even
here Linklater cannot speak with a single voice. After the
initially convincing lyricism of the return to Orkney, we
realize that Magnus is about to fall yet again into visionary

delusion: this time, in his Lawrentian exaltation of ordinary, robust farmers and farming into types of eternal truth, representatives of the earth's underlying rhythms. Here the novel is at its most subtle, in that Linklater knows full well he is being ironic at the expense of his own dearest thoughts on Orkney. Linklater will not allow himself to rest in what he sees as the false anthropological comfort of Edwin Muir, Neil Gunn or Lewis Grassic Gibbon. Instead, his fundamental scepticism must see Magnus stripped of even these consolations. Jupiter, the god-like bull, the great would-be sire of Magnus's envisioned and heroic pedigree beasts, is the ultimate symbol of life's quirky and grotesque refusal to live up to our dreams. Magnus's hopes of being the archetypal crofter, in tune with season and beast, die with his pathetic bull. And the loss of his Orkney idyll is accompanied by the loss of his dreams of a womanly ideal. In this respect the progress of the novel has brought him from a false romance about Margaret Innes, through his earthy but selfish passion for Frieda Forsyth (the raunchy American whose reality is too much for Magnus's spurious notions of female 'purity'), to marriage with his Orkney Rose, whom he sees as a shy country maiden, the essence of her island race, but who turns out to be a selfish, ruthless tyrant in the home.

All this would tend to confirm the early view Magnus had of himself in London: that he was 'Troilus with a cold in his nose, not sighing but sneezing towards the Grecian tents . . . Romeo under the wrong window, Ajax with a boil in his armpit'. After all, his great Renaissance long poem which was to sort out Scotland's ills, first through satire and then through regenerative forward planning, fails because he finds it's easy to satirize but hard to construct. *The Returning Sun*, it was called, and its progress and its fate parallel Magnus's own. Linklater intends us to see the pun, and the bathos. But again, this is to ignore the other voice the author uses. Certainly Magnus is brought down to earth, but after a drunken debauch he is still allowed his equivalent of MacDiarmid's Drunk Man's epiphany. Viewing the whitened landscape of his island after a storm, Magnus perceives a final beauty which this time the sceptical author does not contradict. 'Tears sprang to his eyes to see such loveliness, and perception like a bird in his breast sang that this land was his and he was one with it . . . Patriotism and the waving of flags was an empty pride, but love of one's own country, of the little acres of one's birth, was the navel-string to life.' This is *not* to be confused with other, deceptive, 'epiphanies', such as Magnus's final and most consoling dream, in which he imagines Peter, his son, becoming a great scholar and statesman—on no valid basis whatsoever. By comparison the white truth of Orkney is allowed to stand, against all the other *chimaeras* of the hero's life.

And so, in the end, after laughing gently at more serious Renaissance poets and novelists, Linklater wheels round to join them. Magnus's final perceptions are those of Finn of *The Silver Darlings* or Chris of *Sunset Song*. Nevertheless, Linklater has still warned against finding glib and ever-easy consolation in spurious ideals and delusive identifications with a nature which may or may not care for its creations. His sceptical voice is a vital and healthy one in Scottish and English literature.

Douglas Gifford

The early life of Magnus Merriman was uneventful except for the usual essays and accidents of boyhood which, though they might be magnified into special significance by anyone with a case to prove, were truly of no great interest. The only remarkable feature of his youthful development was a curious change of temper that occurred when he was twelve or thirteen years old. Till then he had been unduly sensitive, sulky, and unhappy. A disorderly imagination had made him cowardly, while a mixture of laziness and false shame induced a constipated habit that naturally affected his temper. But suddenly, as though he had been waiting for his voice to break before he declared his authority, he became a leader of the neighbouring children, and displaying a talent for noise and vulgarity that none had previously suspected, turned the tables on time by bullying the small brothers of the boys who had previously tortured him. At the same time his brain quickened, and he showed abundant cleverness of that youthful kind which so often is regarded as the prelude to a brilliant maturity. But the abruptness with which the costive timidity of his childhood had been overlaid with the truculent inspiration of adolescence gave little promise of stability.

The son of a country schoolmaster in the parish of St Magnus, in the Mainland of Orkney, Magnus was born in 1897. Having acquired from his father and a female assistant teacher in his father's school the useful and customary elements of education, he was sent to the city of Inverdoon, the seat of the most northerly university in Britain and of a school some six hundred years old that was well thought of locally, but whose tradition of classical education had been much impaired by modern commercialism and the resulting importance attached to certain statutory examinations. From his teachers at the Inverdoon Academy, solid unimaginative men, Magnus obtained a moderate amount of information, often accompanied by thrashing with a leather strap, but neither incentive to further scholarship nor stimulus to the creative spirit that was dormant in him.

In 1914, shortly after the outbreak of war, he returned to Inverdoon from his summer vacation in Orkney with the intention of proceeding to the University, but instead of that enlisted in a Territorial Battalion of the Gordon Highlanders and spent the next few months in training in Bedford. He found discipline irksome, and was at first extremely clumsy in performing the simple exercises demanded of a private soldier. At the handling of arms and on the range he became tolerably expert in time, but fatigue duties he constantly endeavoured to escape without the ingenuity necessary to their successful evasion, and such matters as maintaining his equipment in military tidiness, and producing in due form and order the requisite number of articles at the weekly kit-inspection, were for ever beyond his power. In consequence of this he endured a multitude of minor punishments and acquired the habit, on pay-nights, of forgetting the unhappiness of his existence in the canteen. At the age of seventeen a few glasses of beer were sufficient to fortify his spirit with remarkable gaiety, and he discovered under their influence an extravagant improper humour that was greatly to the liking of his companions, who encouraged him to drink more and more when they found that he was able to compose, with sufficient stimulation, witty and slanderous verses about the officers and sergeants of their battalion. These canteen lampoons were Merriman's first experiment in literature.

He went to France with the reputation of a troublesome and unprofitable soldier, but when the formality of army life grew thin, as it did in the trenches, and when dirtiness became a uniform condition rather than a crime, he found fewer difficulties to contend with and was increasingly well-thought-of by his superiors. He was strongly built, but slender, and though above the middle size he was not so tall as to find his height a handicap in troglodyte warfare. He was never notable for bravery, but on occasion showed something like recklessness, that was due either to excitement or to inadequate apprehension of the circumstances: for he became interested in the war, or such a minute portion of it as he was acquainted with, and was inclined to form heterodox opinions about its conduct. He was promoted to the rank of corporal and began to think hungrily of decorations. He decided to win a Distinguished Conduct Medal and some French award before applying for a commission, so that his uniform might be well prepared for the additional glories, in time, of a Military Cross and the Distinguished Service Order. And while his thoughts grew more and more romantic his conduct became increasingly efficient, so that Captain Duguid, his company commander, once said somewhat optimistically, 'Merriman is the best NCO in the battalion'.

Unfortunately an incident occurred soon after this that entirely changed Captain Duguid's opinion and completely destroyed Merriman's ambition, at least for some considerable time. It was an incident of a type that he was to become familiar with later in his life, for in his fortune there seemed, ever and again, to be an element of buffoonery that would trip his heels whenever his head was highest, and lay clownish traps for him in the most serious places. He adventured for a medal and had his stripes cut away; whenever he played Romeo he tripped over the chamber pot; and his political hopes were to be spoiled by a ludicrous combination of circumstances. But in 1916 those catastrophes lay far away in the future, unimagined, almost unimaginable, for the horizon was still occluded by war.

One morning Corporal Merriman was informed that he was to accompany Captain Duguid with four men on a reconnoitring patrol that night. The news at first inspired in him the customary feeling of gloomy foreboding, but in a short while he was cheered by the thought that this might be an opportunity to secure the Distinguished Conduct Medal, for the patrol was to be an important one, and when midnight came, the hour at which they were to start, he was in high spirits. They crowded out of the trench, Captain Duguid slightly in advance, and passed through an opening in the barbed wire to no-man's-land. Slowly and with great circumspection they approached the German line. When a Very light soared over them they lay immobile till the light should die. But Merriman made the mistake of lying on his side and keeping his eyes on the flaring brightness, so that when it sank into the darkness he was momentarily blind. The Captain whispered 'Come on!' Merriman, lurching forward on his belly, thrust his bayonet stiffly ahead of him and heard a muffled cry of pain.

'What's the matter?' he asked.

Another muted whimper answered him first, and a moment later one of the patrol, in the broad untroubled accents of Buchan, said hoarsely, 'Michty God, you've fair ruined the Captain. You've stuck your bayonet clean up his airse!'

Corporal Merriman's response was to roll on his back and let fly a great ringing shout of laughter. The Captain cried petulantly, 'Be quiet, you fool !' The nearest private clapped a muddy hand on his mouth. But the damage was done, and after a brief interval of silence—as though the world were shocked at this noise so irreverent in the midst of war—machine-guns opened their iron stutter, star-shells lit the sky, and grenades burst dully in the neighbouring soil. For half an hour the patrol lay in acute danger and discomfort, and then crept miserably back to their own lines with three men wounded in addition to the Captain.

Corporal Merriman had his stripes removed for conduct prejudicial to the maintenance of order and military discipline, his vision of a bemedalled tunic vanished like a rainbow, and Captain Duguid went home on a stretcher, face-downwards. Some months later, on the Somme, Merriman himself was wounded in the shoulder during a brief but hurried retreat, and having recuperated very pleasantly in a volunteer hospital, applied for and received a commission. He was then sent to Mesopotamia, and after considerable service in conditions of torrid heat, fever, and monotony, was ordered to join the force organized by Major-General Dunsterville for service in Persia. This fortunate adventure had a most important influence on his subsequent career.

He remained with Dunsterville's small army throughout its romantic existence, and journeyed with it into Southern

Russia. In the retreat from Baku he so distinguished himself that he was recommended for the Military Cross, but his perverse fate still unhappily pursued him. In the dull green calm of the Caspian Sea he made his first acquaintance with vodka, and such was its inflammatory influence that he defied all restraint and led a deputation of three to the Commander-in-Chief with an impolitic suggestion to return and launch an immediate counter-attack, that would give him a chance to win a bar for his promised medal. The resulting court martial behaved with laudable clemency, and balanced his impropriety by cancelling the recommendation for the Military Cross.

Peace being at last concluded, Merriman left the army with none of the decorations he had coveted, but only the service medals that indicated an undistinguished though useful capacity to survive or elude the perils and rigours of campaigning in the Twentieth Century.

He returned to Inverdoon and enrolled himself at the University in the Honours School of English Language and Literature. This he did partly in obedience to the impulse which had stirred him to compose improper verses in the army, and partly from a belief that the study of English literature would entail less work than the study of French and German, the classics, pure science, applied science, law, medicine or divinity. The next two years he passed very pleasantly, contentedly occupied with the charming trivialities of University life. He often drank too much, he talked endlessly about the war with other returned soldiers, and he seldom thought seriously for more than a few minutes about any subject whatsoever.

Then, almost simultaneously, the dormant creative spirit in him began to wake and he fell violently in love with a girl called Margaret Innes, a medical student. She was uncommonly good-looking, dark and slender, with a graceful figure, a pretty mouth, and eyes of a gay and lively beauty. She conveyed, moreover, the impression that she possessed some inner reserve of strength and a secret wisdom of some kind, so that her smallest remarks seemed more valuable or significant than other people's conversation, since they were made in the warm shadow of this mysterious hinterland of knowledge or emotional force. She had a large number of male friends, whose attentions she encouraged so far as was consistent with an impregnable chastity, and it was some time before Magnus could obtain her undivided attention. He succeeded at last, and for some eight or ten weeks was supremely happy except for a recurrent feeling that she was in some essential way—other than her continued virginity—untouched by him and remote from his comprehension. That was a winter term. In the spring she laughed at him and divided her time between the captain of the University golf team and a professional violinist in the town. As a result of her virtuous favours the golfer went off his game and the violinist often played with mournful inaccuracy: but Margaret Innes continued to live so competently that she derived nothing but enjoyment from their company, and performed her work in the hospital wards with unimpaired efficiency.

For Magnus the year was productive but ill-managed. He wrote a great deal of flamboyant verse and acquired a reputation for amusing eccentricity when drunk. Stories of his exploits began to circulate, and his more improper *mots* were widely repeated. In the early months of 1923 there was a brief but ardent recrudescence of his affair with Margaret Innes, and in March of that year she took a very respectable degree and almost immediately secured a position as Resident Surgeon in a hospital in Bradleigh in the North of England. They did not meet again for a long time. In the June of the same year Magnus, with some difficulty, took Second Class Honours in English and celebrated his good fortune by drinking so long with the Lecturer in Anglo-Saxon that they quarrelled violently over the rival merits of Beowulf and the Saga of Burn Njal. Continuing their argument in the street, they presently assaulted each other and were both arrested. They found bail, however, without much difficulty—the police were broad-minded and they had many friends—and the brawl had no more consequence than a little quiet scandal.

A month later Magnus was interviewed by the Principal of the United Churches' College in Bombay, himself a graduate of Inverdoon, and obtained an appointment as lecturer in

English Literature recently made vacant by the death from malaria of the previous occupant—he also had been a native of Inverdoon. Magnus had no interest in missionary enterprise, but he had long nursed a romantic desire to see India and the opportunity now offered seemed too good to miss. The dominant motive obscured the minor implications of his decision, and he gave little thought to the nature of his immediate environment and the manner in which he would be required to behave as one of the staff of the Churches' College. He speedily found his obligations irksome, and had not malaria and dysentery made such constant attacks on his colleagues that their number was always under strength his appointment would certainly have terminated long before it did.

During his three years in Bombay he published two books of verse, the first at his own expense. The second, though much better, resulted in his dismissal from the College. It contained a poem entitled *Number Seven* that told, in a spirit of brilliant comedy and galloping Hudibrastic lines, the events of an evening in a house of ill-fame in the neighbourhood of Grant Road; and another, called *The Sahibs*, that described with lively satire a dance at the Yacht Club. The Principal found these verses so distressing to read and so horrible to remember that he was compelled to ask Magnus to resign: that the author of *Number Seven* should teach literature on a Christian basis was manifestly impossible, and Magnus was requested to forego the courtesy of notice and leave at once.

It happened about the same time that a man called Meiklejohn, a gifted but intemperate Scot on the editorial staff of the *Bombay Post*, found it politic to sever his connection with that eminently respectable newspaper. He and Merriman decided to go home together, and to travel by a route more interesting than second class P & O cabins. They made some perfunctory inquiries and haphazard arrangements and set out, through Baluchistan, for Persia. By hired cars that frequently broke down they drove to Meshed in north-eastern Persia, and made an abortive attempt to reach Merv in the Turkoman Republic. Failing to cross the frontier they turned on their tracks and without more difficulty than wayside mishaps arrived in Teheran. From there they travelled north, through Kasvin, across the impressive Elburz mountains, and down their superbly wooded Caspian slope to Pahlevi. Here Magnus was on familiar ground, for he had spent some weeks in the sturgeon port while serving with General Dunsterville; and when they took ship and crossed to Baku he enjoyed the sensation of revisiting Baladjari where, in 1918, he had so nearly won a Military Cross.

From Baku their journey, through Tiflis to Batum and thence by a very dirty coasting vessel to Constantinople, was made anxious by failing resources, and they returned to England in complete poverty aboard a tramp steamer. But this excursion, allied to his war experience, eventually proved very remunerative and gave Magnus material for the novel that established—in a contemporary way—his literary reputation, and made for him a modest fortune of some three or four thousand pounds.

For the next two years he lived thinly by journalism in Manchester, where he tasted but swiftly rejected the principles of Liberalism, and wrote a book called *The Aristocrats*. This was a study of Byron, Shelley, and Swinburne, that defended their aristocratic assumption of social privileges and contempt of social obligations, and discovered in such noble freedom the true source of their poetry's opulent abundance. The book was more anti-social than Byron, Shelley, or Swinburne, and its reception by English critics, with their humane and democratic tendencies, was neither flattering nor hospitable. But it attracted the favourable attention of Mr Julius James Funk, the proprietor of several American newspapers, who was then holiday-making in England, and as the result of his interest Magnus was offered and accepted the literary editorship of the Philadelphia *News-Sentinel*.

He greatly enjoyed his residence in that charming city, whose cultured urbanity was securely established on a solid foundation of political corruption, and he devoted his leisure to a novel inspired by his travels on the western fringe of Central Asia. It was called *The Great Beasts Walk Alone*. It was published in the early autumn of 1930, and in October Magnus returned to England, resigning his post on the *News-Sentinel* for no better reason than a restless desire for change.

By all but one or two critics and a handful of the reading public in England and America the novel was completely misunderstood and vastly enjoyed. It sold in thousands, and the mild, passionless, and commercially disciplined inhabitants of London and Leeds and Birmingham, of Cincinnati and Buffalo and Kansas City, of Sydney and Cape Town and Toronto, thrilled to its recital of wild adventure and back-breaking love without ever seeing or suspecting that all it said was a villainous attack on the trim security and standardized monotony of their daily lives. *The Great Beasts Walk Alone* was the story of Stenka Potocki, a fictitious Cossack who, in revolt against the Soviet Union, endeavoured to establish a principality in Turkestan. His creed was individualism, his military tactics were guerrilla tactics, his morals were those of Casanova, his appetite was the appetite of Falstaff, his humour was Rabelaisian, and his ally was a rascally Chinese, a fat and learned man, sometime Governor of Kashgar, who had been expelled for behaviour too fat and rascally, too anciently absolute, to be permitted even in the Chinese Governor of a Central Asian town.

Warfare, feasting, and love were the staple of their exploits: swords and pillows and mutton-stews were the common furniture of their existence: but the principle of their lives was opposition to the encroaching machinery, the invading tractors and communal discipline, of the Soviets. Their licence was reactionary, their pillage had its philosophy, and every khan their tribesmen burnt reduced to ashes the abominations of the modern world. These implications, however, were generally unremarked by the readers of *The Great Beasts Walk Alone*, who found all the entertainment they desired in the recital of night-marches, sudden evasions, the Chinese Governor's happy impropriety of speech, and the amorous belabouring of women and unwedded maids in Turkestan, Bokhara, Khiva, Khorasan and Khokan.

It was at the height of its success when Merriman returned to London, and for several weeks he enjoyed such popularity as a literary triumph may bring, whether its significance be recognized or not, and he ate many dinners at the expense

of the kindly or curious people who had read or intended
to read a novel so well-esteemed and so widely advertised.
For a little time these attentions pleased him, but he soon
became bored by them. Then, by the intermediacy of a
common friend, he met Margaret Innes again.

Within a year of going from Inverdoon she had married
an elderly and wealthy manufacturer in Bradleigh, and for
four years she had lived in circumstances of great comfort
but no great happiness. Then her husband died, leaving her
with two children and an income very much smaller than
she had expected: for owing to some obscure estrangement
he had revoked an earlier will scarcely a month before his
death, and devised instead a testament that bequeathed
four-fifths of his fortune to local charities. Faced with this
disappointment, Margaret very sensibly decided to make use
of her medical training, and realizing some part of her legacy
bought a practice in Twickenham, where she settled down
to work with all her former competence.

A fortnight after meeting Magnus, and after a very good
dinner, she yielded to his importunity and went to bed
with him in the furnished flat he had taken in Tavistock
Square.

CHAPTER TWO

It would be inaccurate to say that Margaret Innes had been
Merriman's first love, for at the age of fifteen he had been
intemperately moved by a woman of some eight years his
senior, and during the next decade his emotions were exer-
cised with great regularity; and it would be misleading to
imply that during his residence abroad he had been true
to her memory, for he discovered sentimental occasions
both in India and America. Yet in a manner he had been
faithful, since despite the separation of two years he had
remembered her and sometimes, when the company was
small and the wine abundant and the night air melancholy,
he had spoken of her to friends moved in a like manner to
luxuries of recollection; while after a fashion she had priority
to his affections, since she was the first and so far the only
woman with whom he had seriously considered marriage.
When he met her again his love awoke, strong and hungry

as a bear emerging from its winter sleep, and romantically persuading himself that it had never slumbered he drove it to a precipitate consummation.

Wedlock and time had impaired Margaret's chastity. She was, moreover, impressed by the new fame of her old admirer, and touched by his sincere though inaccurate protestations of several years' fidelity to her. She was quite pleased to go to bed with him and accepted his embraces with complaisance and a certain vanity. But she did not provoke embraces, and she contributed to the occasion nothing more valuable than acquiescence and the display of comeliness. She agreed to dine with him again in a few days' time, and in that happy expectation Magnus was hardly aware of any imperfection in the present. The affair lasted for some weeks, and he gradually became depressed by it. Margaret's attractions were less distinguished and more limited than he had found them a few years earlier, and her essential remoteness, her intangible secret power that had once allured him, he now discovered to be merely self-absorption. She had no great interest in anything but herself and her children, and while it was to her credit as a mother that she should postpone embraces to speak of Nigel's talent for drawing, and Rosemary's interest in religion, it did not contribute to her success as a lover. But she appeared quite willing to continue as Merriman's mistress.

One evening in January he was waiting for her somewhat resentfully in a restaurant that she favoured not so much for its food as for its customers, many of whom were well-known theatrical and literary people. She was late. Magnus drank some sherry and began to hope that she would not come. The noise of the restaurant irritated him, and the surrounding laughter and conversation, hard and brittle as the clink of plates and glasses, roused an impatient desire to silence it with some outrageous gesture. He thought how pleasant it would be to hurl his table, with its load of cutlery and crockery, into a neighbouring dinner-party, wine glasses spilling their load on naked and astounded shoulders, knives and forks clattering against the white armour of evening shirts—or to run amok with that wagon of hors d'oeuvres and succulently bespatter the room with a tropical storm of anchovies and olives; here a flutter of red cabbage, there a damp vari-coloured imprint of Russian salad, a miraculous draught of sardines, the chill descent of eggs, and the thick impingement of cold potatoes. His pleasure in this vision mitigated his dislike of the diners who inspired it, and when Margaret arrived he was fairly cheerful.

At the age of twenty-nine she was very nearly as pretty as she had been at twenty-two, and what little she had lost was more than recouped in the smartness of her attire. The provincial gaiety that characterized her dress in Inverdoon had given way to a well-thought-of obedience to fashion, and she had learnt the proper use of cosmetics. She apologized for her lateness without embarrassment.

'I've been terribly busy,' she said. 'Everybody's got influenza, and I've scarcely had time to sit down for days. I nearly rang you up to say that I couldn't come out tonight, but I wanted to, so I hurried through the surgery patients and let Nanny put the children to bed. I told Nigel where I was going, and he asked me if I meant to marry you. He's got very grown-up ideas, and he's fearfully interested in you.'

'Hors d'oeuvres or smoked salmon?' asked Magnus.

'Smoked salmon, I think. What's the matter? Aren't you feeling well? You look terribly gloomy. It's this beastly weather. I need a holiday myself: I'd go abroad if I could, but the practice, of course, ties me down hand and foot.'

'You look fit enough.'

'Well, I'm too busy to be really ill, but I do need a holiday, and if I were as free as you are, I'd take one. Why don't you go away for a while?'

'I'm going to.'

'I'm sure that's the best thing to do. I'll miss you terribly, but you'll be much more cheerful when you come back, and we'll go on having a good time, won't we?'

'I shan't come back,' said Magnus.

Like a flock of sheep in the morning, gently moving in a mist whose fringes are pale gold and briar-pink, Margaret's words travelled with a deceptive grace: but examine them coolly and they were nothing more than butcher's sheep. Once upon a time Magnus had thought them like antelopes. They had seemed to leap from dark coverts and speed with curious significance among innominate flowers. But now he perceived the unmistakable flavour of mutton, and in the instant of recognition he remembered, from a poem called *The Princess of Scotland*, a stanza that read:

> Why do you softly, richly speak
>   Rhythm so sweetly-scanned?
> Poverty hath the Gaelic and Greek
>   In my land.

As in the case of most poetry the assertion was, of course, quite untrue. But the idea was excellent, and confronted with its mellifluous wealth Magnus decided it was foolish to spend more time in exchanging barren thoughts in the bankrupt tongue that not only Margaret used, but the three-score surrounding diners and the farther circumference of London's five or six or seven million inhabitants. He had a sudden vision of Gaelic and Greek in amiable contest among the mountains of Western Scotland or the tall black closes of Edinburgh—Pindaric ode stilling its unlicensed rhythm for the wilder nose of Ossian—and he determined to go northwards. He had not been in Scotland for nearly five years.

Margaret was puzzled and mortified by this resolution, so unexpected and declared so brusquely. Her mouth, opened slightly for a fragment of smoked salmon, remained patent in bewilderment. It was a charming mouth, and the hue of the salmon was precisely that of the outer part of her lips; but the inner part, devoid of cosmetic, was noticeably paler.

'But you said you were going to live in London,' she objected. 'You can't possibly leave it for good. Why, for anyone like you it's the only place in the world to live in.'

'I don't agree with you,' said Magnus. 'It's far too big; it's disgustingly untidy; its amusements are dull and its climate is abominable. 'I've fallen out of love with it—or rather I've discovered that the idea I had of it is not justified by actuality—and so I'm going to leave it. London, I trust, will not be seriously affected by my desertion.'

'Have you fallen out of love with me, too?'

'Are you in love with me? Or are you simply enjoying an adventure?'

'You're part of my life. You have been for years, and I can't bear to let you go. You and Nigel and Rosemary—'

'I should make an abominable step-father.'

'Oh, why do you turn everything into a joke? This isn't a joke to me. I'm terribly upset.'

'Good God! I'm as serious as you are: if I talk lightly it's only for relief. I always seem flippant when I'm really in earnest. Do you know that Aeneas told a dozen bawdy stories to Dido just before he left her? There's no use asking who said so, for I don't think anyone did, but I'm perfectly sure it's true. And don't imagine that Aeneas was a provincial seducer having a bit of greasy fun with a taxi-dancer. There was hell in his heart when he left Carthage. But he had to go, and so have I. Look here, what are we going to drink?'

Magnus's eloquence had always had a slightly bemusing effect on Margaret. She listened to him with a certain remoteness—observing but not sharing the entertainment—in a way that a small boy will watch the conjurer at a party. Her unhappiness and hurt vanity were now mollified by his words as by a poultice, and she controlled her feelings enough to turn the pages of the wine-list. Presently, without reading what she saw, she said, a little sulkily: 'I'd like some Montrachet.'

Magnus leaned forward eagerly. 'Would you really?' he asked. 'It's a magnificent wine: I had no idea that you knew it. I thought your repertory consisted of champagne and Liebfraumilch and Benedictine.'

'You don't know everything about me,' said Margaret crossly. Magnus's estimate of her knowledge of wine had been very nearly correct: she had overheard, in casual conversation, the name Montrachet, and she had asked for it as a gesture of independence, to show that she was not compelled to seek her partner's advice when Liebfraumilch was not to her fancy. But her apparently sapient and certainly unexpected discrimination delighted Magnus, and he began to talk with great gusto and cordiality about the merits of the wine she had chosen. For a little while his old belief in her returned to life; perhaps there really was some secret virtue in her; since, without his knowing it, she had been aware of Montrachet, she might have other wisdom unperceived by him, other wealth of character, and treasures of knowledge. She was undeniably lovely, and to beauty much may be credited.

When the wine came he drank heartily, and Margaret took her share rather as one who thirsts than as a connoisseur. For a little while she talked with wistful reminiscence of their youthful love-making in Inverdoon. Then she spoke of her marriage.

'I married Lawrence for his money,' she said abruptly. 'I'd never had a penny before that: I was desperately poor at University. I hated him really, and the honeymoon was agony. After we got home I didn't sleep with him for months. He was terribly unhappy, but I couldn't do it. Then Nigel was born, and I didn't think of anyone but him. After that I had an affair with another man. I was careless and I found that I was going to have a baby, so I made it up with Lawrence and persuaded him, when the time came, that Rosemary was his. But she wasn't. He didn't suspect anything to begin with, but I quarrelled with him again, and I think he guessed the truth at last. That's why he made a different will and left all his money to those damned charities.'

To Magnus this bald narrative was very exciting. He felt a certain horror as he looked at this mercenary and wanton woman and saw in her, under so little apparent change, the chaste and elusive Margaret of his University days. But he admired her, after a fashion, for the cold straightforward way in which she had told her story—it was so much better than her usual chattering—and he also admired, with the kind of admiration a good play compels, the competence, save in one particular, with which she had arranged her life. He was conscious, too, of an irrational jealousy of Rosemary's unknown father.

'Have you had any other lovers?' he asked.

'One other,' said Margaret.

Self-pity came noisily into his mind. He felt betrayed. It seemed to him that he had been true to her for years while she had been faithless and incontinent. He forgot his own dalliance with other women in the surge of so exquisite a misery: he forgot the months and quarters during which he had never given Margaret a thought.

She had deceived him and made naught of his devotion. But accompanying this misery there arose a more combative thought: he warmly desired to take yet more advantage of her incontinence, and with his own image he wanted to obliterate her memories of his predecessors in love. By sleeping with her once again he could forget his sorrow and at the same time revenge himself on the unknowns who had, it seemed, so cruelly cuckolded him.

His voice deepened. 'So I'm merely one in the procession, but you're the only woman I've ever loved,' he said, and believed most truly his own veracity. 'I came home from the war and you took me captive, and I'll never be free of you. I've scattered memories of you over half the world. I've thought of you in temples in Benares, in New Orleans, and in Oregon in the snow. I took you over the Elburz mountains with me, and across the Caspian. I've loved you in three continents and a dozen seas, Meg.'

'And now, when you could love me quite simply, without needing a map to help you, you're going to go away and leave me?'

'Oh, I don't know. I was angry and wretched when I said that. Let's have some brandy, and then we'll go back to my flat.'

In the taxi, on the way to Tavistock Square, Margaret carefully eluded an embrace and said: 'You know, Nigel is really an astonishing child. He reads the papers now, and he's so serious about the news. He came to me the other day and said: "Mummy, what is the League of Nations, and what is it *for*?"'

'I hope you told him,' said Magnus, a trifle bitterly.

'Well, I said that he wasn't old enough to understand yet, and that he'd better go away and play with his soldiers. He's really fond of playing at soldiers.'

An hour later Margaret sat up in bed, patted the pillow, and said in an interested voice: 'Your ears are quite hot now. A little while ago they were as cold as ice.'

Magnus stretched himself luxuriously and quoted to the ceiling:

Tollite, o pueri, faces:
Flammeum video venire.
Ite, concinite in modum
Io Hymen Hymenaee io,
Io Hymen Hymenaee.

'I'm going to see that Nigel starts Latin quite soon,' said Margaret, 'and I think Rosemary should learn it too, so that they can help each other. I'm rather worried about her at present: she's terribly interested in religion. Nanny says that she'll sit in the bathroom singing "Jesus loves me" for hours at a time.'

CHAPTER THREE

Margaret left the flat about one o'clock, indignant and lately recovered from tears. She had concluded another embrace with the remark: 'Wasn't it clever of Nigel to ask if we were going to get married? Children have curious intuitions, don't you think?'

Magnus, with a cold and sudden volubility, answered: 'I've discovered the truth about you at last, Meg. You're simply a squaw. No, don't interrupt me: I haven't nearly finished. You've got a lovely caressing voice, a very good figure, a handsome chin, the most delicate and alluring of nostrils, a complexion almost as good as it used to be, really beautiful ears, and well-brushed hair: but under all that there's a squat, square-faced, beady-eyed squaw with a baby at her breast and her bottom on the earth, and nothing in her heart but perpetual hunger and the will to survive. You're the eternal squaw, and since I've realized that I've become genuinely fond of you, though not in a romantic way, I'm afraid. But for God's sake don't say another word about your confounded children: I heartily disliked them when I saw them, and I'm tired to death by your stories of them.'

With righteous vexation and a tinge of fear—for she had never heard Magnus speak in this manner—Margaret scrambled out of bed, and catching her foot in the blanket fell heavily on her knees. She burst into tears.

'I don't know what you mean,' she cried. 'I let you make love to me—I didn't specially want you to, but you talked such a lot about it, and said you had loved me for ten years or something, and now you tell me I'm a squaw! And you've no right to talk like that about Nigel and Rosemary. They're darlings and I love them more than anything on earth, and I don't care a damn what you think of them. And I've hurt my knee, and I'm not a squaw—go away, I hate you!'

Magnus made vain gestures of comfort and reconciliation. He had yielded to impulse in uttering his thoughts aloud, and when he saw Margaret struggling to control her sobs and thrusting her hair, usually so tidy and now all unruly, away from her face that was flushed and miserable, he was filled with remorse.

He said unhappily: 'Meg, I didn't mean it in the way you think I meant it. I talk a lot, you know, and words simply come out and make astonishing suggestions before I know what they're doing. I didn't mean to hurt you. I think Nigel's a splendid youngster, and Rosemary is a dear.'

'You're sitting on my stockings,' she cried, and pushed him away.

'Come back to bed and I'll explain exactly what I meant.'

Margaret, dressing speedily and imprecisely, said viciously: 'If I had talked about your books instead of my children you wouldn't have grown tired to death of listening to me. But it happens that I've never read your damned novel, though I said I had, because the first chapter was so stupid and pretentious that I couldn't go on with it.'

The circumstances in which this judgment was delivered prevented Magnus from taking it too seriously—a critic struggling to bridge the gap between her stocking-top and knickers with a revulsive suspender cannot be held to be speaking *ex cathedra*—but it aggravated his depression, and he grew still more contrite to think that Margaret had, to some extent, spoken the truth. She was correct in believing that discussion of *The Great Beasts Walk Alone* would have bored him less than anecdotes about her children. He had often known a desire to hear her talk about it, and he had several times, by leading questions and more subtle means, tried to elicit her detailed opinion of it. But she had always hidden her views in misty generalities, or offered some strong superlative when he asked for the bread of nice perception. It was probably true that she had never read the book. It made him genuinely unhappy to realize this, but he had not the heart to upbraid her for such unkind neglect when he himself had lately been much less than kind. He made instead another move to console her and restore good-will, but again she repulsed him, and declared her intention of immediately going home.

'Then let me get you a taxi,' he said.

Margaret tilted a mirror, knocked down a pair of brushes, and pouted her mouth for lipstick. 'You can't go out like that,' she said.

In a gloomy silence Magnus began to dress himself. When he had reached the point of knotting his tie Margaret said coldly: 'You needn't bother. My car's just outside in the square—I drove it here and took a taxi to the restaurant.'

All trace of emotion gone she walked firmly downstairs, and disdaining his help opened the door and left without more words than a decided 'Never!' in reply to his ill-judged query: 'When shall I see you again?'

Magnus returned to his flat and sat down to consider, with the help of a whisky and soda, the events of the evening. His criticism of Margaret's character now seemed mere ill-natured abuse. He recalled his words and they combined with a picture of their catastrophic sequel to stand, in vivid opposition, against all his memories of her in her lovely youth. He groaned and damned his soul for such cruelty and misfortune. Then he remembered telling her at dinner that he had borne his love for her, intact and bright, from Persia to the Pacific, and was woefully ashamed of such bombast and mendacity. 'I'm a fool and a liar,' he said aloud and stood up to look at himself in a glass that hung on the wall.

His eyes, a greyish-blue beneath dark brows uplifted at the outer corners, stared back at him with mournful intensity. Under the disorder of his hair, and in the brightness of reflected light, his face was pale and his expression a settled melancholy. In solitude he generally wore this appearance, and as he found considerable pleasure—exercising curiosity rather than vanity—in looking into mirrors, he believed it to be his true aspect. But in conversation the restless force of his imagination and the vigorous interest that argument roused in him gave his features animation so lively that their very shape appeared to change when scorn gave place to warm agreement, when indignation followed laughter. He looked like a satyr when the topic was bawdy, like a rustic at a fair when he more loudly laughed, and often he had an air of solid worth and even benignity that was somewhat misleading.

'God forgive me, I'm a liar,' he repeated, and took his whisky from a table and watched himself drink it. 'A liar and a lover gone bad, and drink is one of the elements in which I live.'

His self-distaste became somewhat more remote, and he came gradually to contemplate his unhappiness, if not with satisfaction, at least with resignation. He saw himself as the tragic wooer, the prey of hope ever resurgent and a hostile universe. But tragedy had run its course and the life in him was still undefeated. He decided, quite definitely, that he was out of love with Margaret as well as himself, and he resolved anew to leave London, partly for the reasons he had already stated and partly because it was associated with his present misfortune, and to seek recreation in his native Orkney.

He thought of the Islands with sudden affection. For several years he had not troubled to revisit them, but he had often remembered them and not seldom spoken of them with enthusiasm that, to his listeners, seemed immoderate and unreasonable: for in the ignorant opinion of the majority Orkney was a group of boreal atolls, storm-swept, primitively inhabited, so unimportant and so perilously near the shadow of the Arctic that room for them could hardly be found on the map. But to the mild astonishment of a casual audience Magnus would speak of them as the home of Viking earls who had sat there and ruled all the islands of the north and the west and all the seas they could reach; and sometimes in high-flown mood he would claim descent on the distaff side from Magnus, that earl of Orkney who, in the year 1116, was murdered on the island of Egilsay. And he would say that his family had been lairds in Orkney, though of the smallest kind, from the twelfth century, and that the Merrimans were, with some few other families—Fletts, Cloustons, Paplays, Linklaters, Heddles, Scarths, and so on—the true heirs and remnants of the old Norsemen. But neither of these statements was strictly true, for he was not descended from Earl Magnus, and the Merrimans had scarcely been four hundred years in Orkney. But despite this brevity his affection for the islands was well-founded, and the idea of returning to them was very comforting.

Before going, however, he would see Margaret once more, and after a discussion that should be kindly and cool and wise he would say good-bye to her, and as lovers they would never meet again. Hardly aware of what he did he then found paper and pen and began to write. An hour later he had composed a sonnet that gave him much satisfaction at the time, though on the following day he could find little merit in it:

> Come then, for God's sake let us kiss and part,
> And keep our eyes insensible as stone,
> Our casual lips too politic to own
> A word of all the words within each heart—
> Your dull relief, your desolated greed
> That I, who baited you with alien thought,
> Am gone at last—my desert-peace, that's bought
> By what must live and is too weak to bleed.
>
> We shall not say that honour's been maintained,
> Your chastity, or my pretence of strength;
> Neither be honest nor propound at length
> Excuses for our titles being stained—
> But we'll preserve appearance, be polite,
> And all the world can watch our last *Goodnight*.

It was a bad sonnet, but it served its purpose and sensibly relieved Magnus's feelings.—The mingled curse and blessing of all poets, good or bad, is that their emotions can be taken out and pinned to paper like butterflies in a collection-case. And there, however pretty they seem, with whatever hues of the celandine or the sunset or bitter blood they may be dyed, there's no more life in their wings, or perception of April and autumn in their bodies. Poets would soon die of exhaustion were their responses not prolific as a spawning salmon is of eggs.—The bravado of the concluding couplet especially was restorative, and Magnus was comparatively cheerful when he went into the bedroom to look for cigarettes. But there he saw something that caused a new discomfiture.

In the precipitation of her dressing Margaret had forgotten her brassière, and it lay half under a chair like a puppy that has misbehaved. Its shape was vaguely pathetic but unhappily ridiculous. It suggested grape-skins discarded on the rim of a plate. Its wistful abatement produced in Magnus a corresponding collapse, and now he perceived in his defiant sonnet something that resembled, not a soldier's plume, but a mental brassière, a lace bandage for a sagging mind.

It is a proud thing to be the undefeated hero of a tragedy, but the victim of farce can find no comfort. That his love for Margaret should be destroyed with dust and tears was not incongruous in a world so thickly peopled with calamity; but it was intolerable that disaster should be mocked by this scrap of silk and ribbon, this cynical revelation of the falsity of women and the nature of their lying beauty. It struck him like a fool's bladder, and he saw himself again, as he had often seen himself before, the prey of a clowning destiny. Destructive laughter rang in his ears, and fate lay before him treacherous as a banana-skin.

I'm a buffoon, he thought: 'I'm Troilus with a cold in his nose, not sighing but sneezing towards the Grecian tents. I'm Romeo under the wrong window, Ajax with a boil in his armpit, Priam with a hundred hare-lipped daughters, Roland with a pair of horns. But before God I'm a poet too, and I've weapons to defend myself. I can use words. I can make and mend what I please, I can plait words into whips, and like moles they'll burrow into the ground. I'm a poet. I can live in my own mind, as if it were a Border keep, and raid where I will. But I'll have no women in the house. I'll live alone and write alone till the whole country sees my strength.'

Like an explorer who travels through mountainous and wooded country with the noise of a giant waterfall in his ears, ever growing louder, and sees at last the feathery precipitation of a lofty river, and hears that soft and falling whiteness magically make thunder on the rocks below, so Magnus in a vision saw the torrent of the English language flung down before him, with sunlight in its hair and the trapped strength of long centuries in its limbs, and heard alike the liquid melody of its verse and the clatter of its common little words and the sonorous fulmination of its most imperial majesty and Miltonic measure. He longed to throw himself into the stream below and battle in its strongest current and dive in the deepest pools for pearls. To master that river, that language! He would strive like an athlete for perfection, he would learn to be native in that element as a sea-Dyak, as an Eskimo in his frail canoe, as an albatross sleeping in the slow magniloquence of the Atlantic swell. He saw the river out-flood its banks and grow to an ocean that Shakespeare ruled in Neptune's place, and where, dyed like the dolphin for their death, Marlowe and Keats and Shelley spent their bright strength and sank beneath its waves.

'By God, I'll be a poet!' said Magnus; and, still in his clothes, fell asleep on the tumbled bed from which Margaret had so lately fallen. In the next room the gas-fire poisoned the air, and sluggish wisps of fog crept through the window.

CHAPTER FOUR

Magnus woke with a crapula and spent the morning packing and paying bills. He had rashly signed a year's lease of the flat, but he hoped, without much reason, to be able to sub-let it, and he made suitable arrangements for watch and ward with the caretaker who sustained a twilit and beetle-haunted existence in the basement. Then he telephoned to Margaret to request a last interview at which, to justify his sonnet, they would both behave with admirable composure, aware of sadness but showing nothing of it unless, perhaps, in the gentleness of their temper or in some phrase of slightest irony. Margaret, however, was not at home. A maid replied that she had been called out to a consultation.

Magnus found it a little strange that she should be able to conduct her life and her profession as though nothing had happened while he, unshaved and queasy, his half-packed belongings scattered in awful confusion on the floor, showed so clearly the effects of disaster. He sat in a muddle of shirts and books; a dispatch-case full of press-cuttings and unanswered letters had spilled its contents upon a table where last night's glasses stood; a bowl of withered chrysanthemums drooped over a pair of evening trousers that lay limp and awry... And at this same moment Margaret, neat as a packet of pins and smart as new paint, would be discussing with a colleague—her voice calm and cool, her mind single, her knowledge all in trim array—some distemper of the colon, or cardiac lesion, as impersonally and efficiently as though she herself possessed neither heart nor bowels. There was something inhuman about women. They indeed were of the earth and as indomitably pursued the seasons. They, far more than men, were at home in the world, and moved with the cold certainty of a hostess from room to familiar room. Magnus reassured himself that for the future he would live celibate and strong in the inviolable tower of his mind— and busied himself with unimportant tasks until such time as he could again telephone to Margaret.

In the pocket of an old coat he discovered a forgotten letter from Francis Meiklejohn, the man with whom he had journeyed through Persia and the Caucasus on his way home from India. Meiklejohn was now a journalist in Edinburgh. He had written to Magnus: 'Why the hell do you stay in London when there's room for you in Edinburgh? Come to Scotland. A renascence is on the way—political and literary—so come and be its midwife. You are, I suppose, a Nationalist? If you are not one already, you will be. There's a wind in the trees and a muttering in the heather. We talk of liberty when we're sober, and dream of it when drunk. Come to Scotland, you pestilent renegade.'

Magnus had a large affection for Francis Meiklejohn, who was an amiable talkative man, a great liar, and given to hearty enthusiasms. He now thought it would be a pleasant and convenient thing to spend a few days in Edinburgh before going farther north, for he would be glad to see Meiklejohn again, and it occurred to him that as he had not written to his people in Orkney for some considerable time he would be well-advised to warn them of his intended visit. The reference to a Nationalist movement in Scotland did not interest him, though he was vaguely aware of its existence. There had been so many loud expressions of nationalism in post-war Europe that the muttering in Scottish heather had been almost inaudible. Such people as the Latvians and the Esthonians and the Czechs might well have good cause to fight for independence; but what freedom could Scots imagine that they did not already enjoy? Magnus concluded that the mutterers were simply cranks and oddities and splenetic seceders of the kind that fomented so much obscure disruption in the Church, and finally retired, in self-righteous defeat, to the moors where only whaups and lapwings could contradict them. Nationalism won't find a recruit in me, he thought; but I should like to see Frank again, and find out how many lies he's told about his travels abroad.

In the late afternoon he telephoned to Margaret, and again she was out; and in the early evening he was told that she was busy with postponed surgery patients. In a great hurry he turned to finish his packing, and made a feverish effort to catch the night train to Edinburgh. But his taxi was slow and he missed it by several minutes. He returned to Tavistock Square and slept once more in his disillusioned bed. In the morning he coldly refrained from any further attempt to communicate with Margaret, and arrived at King's Cross in ample time to secure a seat.

As they emerged, with gathering swiftness, from the far-reaching tentacles of London, Magnus felt a growing relief. A damp and sluggish air swathed the shapeless suburbs, and in its chill torpor the train grumbled as though impatient for the freedom of the grass-lands beyond. Then through winter fields, wet underfoot and flagrant with hideous advertisements for linoleum and quack lenitive and soapy purge—but aconite and hemlock were the only remedies for those who so beplastered the world—they ran at speed. Presently they came to more gracious country, and fields whose quietness the thieving metropolis had not yet robbed of dignity. The train rocked and swayed on its bright steel lines, and raced for the approaching north. Elated by speed and the illusion of escape Magnus went to the restaurant car and drank with a new delight to think that Bacardi rum should trickle down his gullet while his gullet was hurled from county to county at seventy splendid miles an hour.

Two girls sat near him. They were well-groomed, smartly clad, and they spoke of nothing in particular in clear high-pitched confident voices. They looked at Magnus with cool appraisement. For a moment he cast about for some phrase or contrivance with which to enter into conversation with them, but he remembered instead his resolution to have nothing to do with women. He asked for another cocktail and plumed himself on this high indifference. This was freedom. Whereas he had lately thought of woman occupying the world like the mistress of her own house, he now beheld her earth-bound and woefully situated between the horns of an eternal dilemma. He alone, by virtue of the poetry in him, was free of the world. But women were condemned for ever to the wearisome burden of love or to celibate starvation. These girls, uneasily aware of their position, were meanwhile, precarious as a tight-rope walker, balancing between the horns. But he, in the solitude of poetry—doubly safe because most of it was unwritten—was gloriously independent. His mind, exultant, quickened with an idea, with rhythm and a phrase, and he began to write on the back of the menu card.

'Un peu cabotin,' said one of the girls.

The other shrugged her shoulders and lit a cigarette.

Unaware of these disparaging comments Magnus continued to write, and had presently composed, with buoyant cynicism, some verses which he called *Miss Wyatt and Mrs Leggatt*:

> Poor Mrs Leggatt with a drunken husband—
>   Beer was a red-gold snow-capped nectar,
>   Song-raising, bitter-cool Nepenthe to him—
> Poor Mrs Leggatt with nine pale children—
>   Gladys was chlorotic and May had goitre,
>   Others had adenoids and Bright's disease—
> Poor Mrs Leggatt with her varicose veins
> Hated her neighbour with hatred's pains,

Who was poor Miss Wyatt of the corner shop:
For poor Miss Wyatt had once said: 'Stop!'
To the fumbling hot young man who would woo:
'Stop!' she had said, and she meant it too.

For poor Miss Wyatt had shrilly said
   To her hoarse young lover, no, no, she wouldn't;
And poor Mrs Leggatt had also denied,
   But keep to her word the poor thing couldn't.
And poor Miss Wyatt was a withered virgin—
   Vinegar brewed in that thin bosom,
   Acid returns of repression arose—
Poor Miss Wyatt with none to live for—
   Loneliness frighted her wakeful night-time
   Horrible desires took shape in her sleep—
Poor Miss Wyatt with her sunken breast
Hated her neighbour with a dreadful zest,
Who was poor Mrs Leggatt the drunkard's wife:
For poor Mrs Leggatt knew all about life-
She had learnt on the grass, she had learnt in her bed,
She had learnt and learnt till she wished she was dead.

For poor Mrs Leggatt had weakly denied,
   But stick to her word the poor thing couldn't:
And poor Miss Wyatt had shrilly said: 'No!'
   And though her lover pleaded the silly thing wouldn't.

The composition of this poem and the enchanted delight
that an author may feel in the first flush of creation—but
never again—occupied a large part of the journey. Racing
against the coming night, the train roared through the
northern marches and crossed the bridge at Berwick. Colder
air blew through an open window. Scotland lay hidden in the
early dusk of winter.

A tearing robustious wind greeted Magnus in Edinburgh.
He drove to an hotel in George Street and after a little while
went out again to look for Francis Meiklejohn.

The wind hurried him along Princes Street. It blew with
a bellow and a buffet on his stern and half-lifted his feet from
the pavement. It beat his ears with a fistful of snow, and
clasped his ribs with icy fingers. It tore the clouds from the
sky, and laid bare, as if beyond the darkness, the cold grey
envelope of outer space. Heads bent and shoulder thrusting
like Rugby forwards in a scrum, east-bound pedestrians

struggled against it, and westward travellers flew before it with prodigious strides. To the left, towering blackly, like iron upon the indomitable rock, was the Castle. To it also the storm seemed to have given movement, for as the clouds fled behind its walls the bulk of its ancient towers and battlements appeared to ride slowly in the wind's eye, as though meditating a journey down the cavernous channel of the High Street to Holyroodhouse, its deserted sister.

Magnus tingled to the heart with cold and his spirit soared in pride. He was in Scotland again. He had come home after far voyaging, and the ghosts of his own country thronged about him. Out of its bloody history came figures armour-clad and tartan-breeched. Now the wind carried a noise of swords, and now its speed was the naked charging of the clans down a bare hillside. It slackened for a moment to sing a dirge in the chimney-tops, and cry in a stony coign the dolorous rhyme of Flodden and Culloden. It roared against high walls as though against the sails of a great ship. Far to the north and the west the islands of Scotland lay like the lost galleys of the Norsemen, and like them were lashed by the ceaseless waves. Pine-forests bent to the storm, and the mountains divided the blast to shout over frozen corries the wildness of their Gaelic names.

It is no niggard welcome that winter finds in Scotland, but every room is opened to its bitter violence as freely, as generously, as later they are opened to the daedal beauty and soft airs of spring.

CHAPTER FIVE

Francis Meiklejohn received Magnus with all the enthusiasm that was his most engaging characteristic. He was dressed, for the moment, only in a shirt, and when Magnus entered he was in the midst of a lively argument with his landlady about the disappearance of a pair of trousers. She, a thickset, dark-haired woman, with animated gestures and a Highland accent, had just declared: 'I lent them to Mr McVicar last Tuesday, for he has no evening trousers of his own, poor man, and seeing he was a friend of yours I thought you wouldn't mind him taking them for a night. He's a quiet man who wouldn't get them torn or destroyed in any way

like young Buchanan did to your others. And he promised
to bring them back, so I hope to God he hasn't pawned them
instead.'

'I swear to God I'll leave this house for ever if you lend so
much as a handkerchief to anyone again!' said Meiklejohn
warmly.

'Oh, they can get on well enough without a handkerchief,'
said the landlady, 'but it's hard for a young man who wants to
go out and hasn't a pair of trousers to wear. But you're quite
right in being firm, Mr Meiklejohn, and Mr McVicar should
have brought them back, for it's not as if they had been old
ones. It was the new pair that fitted him best, he said.'

At this moment the door opened and Magnus was shown
in. Meiklejohn, thrusting his landlady aside, uttered a loud
shout of welcome.

'Magnus Merriman!' he cried, 'the only poet of our age,
and blood-brother with the town-drunkards of Teheran,
Tiflis, and Tuscaloosa! Mrs Dolphin, it's a great man who's
come to your house, and we're going to make a night of it.
There's a bottle of vodka in the cupboard—never mind my
trousers: get the vodka—and ring up the Café de Bordeaux
and tell them to reserve a table for two.'

Meiklejohn's shirt was long enough to cover his plump
body, but his very sturdy legs were quite unconcealed by
it. Careless of nakedness, however, he pranced about the
room, helped Magnus to remove his overcoat, smacked him
on the back, pushed him into a chair and snatched from Mrs
Dolphin the bottle she had quickly discovered.

'Get a glass for yourself,' he said to her.

'I have one here,' she answered. Her expression was earnest and alert. 'If there isn't enough vodka to go round, I
have some whisky of my own, and I'll drink Mr Merriman's
health in that. I've often heard Mr Meiklejohn talking about
you,' she told Magnus, 'and we're always glad to see another
Nationalist here. You'll be a member of the Party?'

'Of course he is,' said Meiklejohn, and poured for his
guest a noble dram of vodka. 'Slainte!' he said, and drank
his own tot with back-flung head and a libationary casting
away of the scanty drops that remained.

'Slainte math!' Mrs Dolphin piously responded.

'Happy days,' said Magnus.

Mrs Dolphin finished her drink with a sigh. 'I like something that you can taste all the way down. My God! I wouldn't be a teetotaller for anything! You won't be wanting dinner tonight?' she asked Meiklejohn.

'No, we're going out.'

'It's just as well,' said Mrs Dolphin, 'for there's not much in the house, and I think Johnstone and young Buchanan are coming round, and they're always glad of a bite. They're both members of the Party,' she explained to Magnus.

'I'm going to get dressed now, Mrs Dolphin,' said Meiklejohn, and held open the door for her.

'And high time, too,' she answered. 'The only other man I ever knew who'd be going about the house half-naked all the time was Lord Moidart, but he was so thin you hardly noticed it.'

'What's this Party that she talks about?' asked Magnus when she had gone.

'The National Party of Scotland, of course.'

'I never heard of it.'

Meiklejohn was horrified. 'My dear fellow,' he said earnestly, 'it's the biggest thing that's happened in Scotland for generations. It means the re-creation of a people, the re-birth of the nation of Scotland. It's the only topic of the day. The whole country's talking about it.'

'And who belongs to the Party except you and Mrs Dolphin?'

'You do, for one,' said Meiklejohn promptly.

'I'm damned if I do,' said Magnus.

'I sent your name in a week ago, and paid your half-crown for membership. I got a badge for you, too, but I think Mrs Dolphin's wearing it.'

'But what's the idea of the Party? What is it trying to do?'

Meiklejohn gave Magnus some more vodka. 'We're going to re-create Scotland as an independent sovereign state. We want self-government, a Scottish parliament with complete control of Scottish affairs, and no more English domination. Don't you realize that the status of Scotland today is hardly greater than that of an English county? We've got no national life. We're ruled from Westminster by a lot of constipated Saxons. Scottish industries are being ruined, rural life is becoming extinct, and the very idea of Scotland is going to fade out of existence unless we preserve and re-fashion it.'

Magnus drank his vodka thoughtfully. The room was dimly lighted, and from the window-seat he could distinguish, against the moving darkness of the sky, the dark shape of the Castle. He felt in his blood a rippling sensation, as when a catspaw of wind blows contrary to the quiet current of a stream. Quickened by the patriotism that his return to Scotland had evoked, he perceived, though faintly as yet, the possibility of taking an active part in the affairs of his country, and exhilarated by vodka he considered with growing interest the intoxication of politics, that alluring perversion of patriotism.

Meiklejohn brought an armful of garments from an adjoining bedroom and began to dress himself. He continued to talk about the grievances and aims of young Scotland.

'It wouldn't be easy to cut ourselves adrift from England,' said Magnus.

'Norway cut herself adrift from Sweden,' answered Meiklejohn.

'But how many people in Scotland want self-government?'

'The whole land's seething with discontent, and the Party's growing every day. It's sweeping the country. It's a youth movement, and practically all the younger men you'll meet believe in it. But they can't do much till they find a leader. That's why I told you to come back to Scotland, because you can speak, and write, and you have the proper ideas—or you had when you wrote *The Great Beasts Walk Alone*.'

'I think a certain amount of reaction throughout the world would be a good thing,' said Magnus.

'Of course you do! No one but a fool wants more progress when progress means only standardization and sterility.'

'London's a dull town,' said Magnus, diverging from the main line of the conversation with a sudden recollection of his recent unhappiness with Margaret. His new-found delight in Scotland encouraged him to take a pessimistic view of the metropolis, and he felt some righteous anger against

the city that had witnessed so deplorable a collapse of his
romantic love. Misanthropy assailed him when he thought of
those too-many millions who apparently found life tolerable
and even agreeable in an atmosphere that had been so hostile
to him, and he stretched southwards a denunciatory finger
in the attitude of one confronting the cities of the plain. 'It's
easy to live in,' he said, 'but the air's flat and stale and the
people are half-hearted. There's nothing to do there. You
can make love without trouble or meaning, or get mildly
drunk, or extract second-hand emotions from the cinema,
or put your mind to sleep on a dance-floor, or play bridge,
or throw yourself in front of a train on the Underground.
There are forty ways of escaping from consciousness. But
I want something more exciting than that.'

'You want something to believe in,' said Meiklejohn earnestly. 'There's nothing more exciting than belief. And as
you're a Scot you should believe in Scotland first.'

Meiklejohn had now finished dressing. He tied round
his throat a red scarf with white spots, put on a thick
dark overcoat, and a black hat that he pulled down on
his forehead. He had a round ingenuous countenance, a
right eye wide open and dancing with life, and a left one
partially occluded by a drooping lid that gave half his
face an expression of engaging debauchery. Politics was
no burden to him, and revolutionary conversation of the
most alarming kind filled him with glee and encouraged
him to celebrate with generous potations his possession of
such noble aspirations.

'We're going to make a night of it, my boy,' he promised
and, calling to his landlady, whispered with muted enthusiasm, 'I may be drunk tonight, Mrs Dolphin.'

'Well, you're only young once,' she answered, 'and there's
old sheets on the bed, so there won't be much damage done
though you forget to take your shoes off. Good-night, Mr
Merriman. We'll be seeing a lot of you, I suppose, and Mr
Meiklejohn will be glad of your company, for there's too
many gentlemen nowadays who think of nothing but dancing and golf, and haven't a head for politics or drinking.'

The Café de Bordeaux, where Meiklejohn took Magnus
to dine, was in essence an oyster-bar. It had established its

reputation on excellent fare and sound vintages, and in a city where only railway hotels disputed with unimaginative restaurants for the privilege of catering to impercipient palates it had acquired a certain Bohemian flavour. Meiklejohn and his guest dined simply but well on oysters and a cold grouse, and having drunk some Chablis with the former, shared a bottle of claret with the latter. Their conversation ranged the world from India to America. Meiklejohn spoke with gusto about the indignities of editing, without proper authority, an evening paper in Edinburgh, and Magnus mentioned the more picturesque aspects of journalism in Philadelphia. Meiklejohn made some apt and generous comments on *The Great Beasts Walk Alone*, and Magnus listened with pleasure vitiated only in the smallest degree by embarrassment. Then they reverted to their adventures on the road from Meshed to Constantinople, and Magnus found that Meiklejohn had introduced some very interesting and romantic additions to the tale of their travels.

'You're a variegated liar, aren't you, Frank?' he said thoughtfully.

'On the contrary, I'm frequently and spaciously truthful,' said Meiklejohn, and taking a large pinch of snuff he wiped the surplus from his nose with a grandiloquent flourish of his bright yellow handkerchief. He offered his box to Magnus. 'It's better for you than tobacco. Smoking impairs virility, but snuff clears the brain without ill-effects lower down.' His drooping eyelid dropped lower in a significant wink. 'When did women start to assert themselves? When did they begin to stick their heads out of the blankets and lay down the law? Not till men took to smoking and lost the power to keep their wives and wenches quiet. The Mormons weren't allowed to smoke because Brigham Young knew that pipes and polygamy couldn't exist together. Every woman doctor, every woman lawyer, every woman in Parliament absolutely owes her position to tobacco. But snuff won't do you any harm. Try this.'

Magnus took a pinch, sniffed vigorously, and felt throughout his head a profound disturbance, as though innumerable springs were about to gush forth and unknown fiery chambers of air were all at bursting point. He gasped for breath, his head nodded helplessly to and fro, and then, in successive explosions, he loudly sneezed. A wine-glass was blown from the table and a thin silver flower-vase fell before the storm. Attracted by this genial noise four young men who sat at a neighbouring table joined in the conversation for some minutes. They knew Meiklejohn, and as at one time or another they had all fallen victims to his snuff-box they viewed Merriman's discomfiture with sympathy. They were tall well-built young men of prosperous appearance and notably athletic in their bearing.

When the interchange of civilities had terminated, Magnus asked, confidentially, 'Are they members of the Party?'

'What party?' said Meiklejohn.

'The National Party.'

Meiklejohn took snuff again with an elaborately casual air. 'No,' he said, 'they're not members.'

'Why not? You said the younger men were all in it.'

'Oh, yes, but not people like that. Two of them play for the Academicals or some such team and the others have been golfing. You can't expect a revolution or a renascence to start among footballers and golfers. They'll come in later, of course, but it's very difficult to get people who play games seriously to be serious about anything else.'

As though guessing at the nature of this dialogue—for it was muted and had an air of conspiracy—one of the golfers called to Meiklejohn: 'How many recruits have you found this week, Frank?'

'When are you going to declare war?' asked another.

'As soon as you join, and others who'll do for cannon-fodder and for nothing else,' said Meiklejohn. His voice was good-humoured though his words were not, but his face grew pale and his mouth tightened with hidden anger. He drank his brandy without regard for its quality.

'No more wars for me,' said one of the golfers. 'Think of getting up at five o'clock on a winter morning to go out and be shot to hell! I'm neutral from now till the cows come home.'

Meiklejohn called impatiently for his bill. 'Neutral,' he

muttered. 'They're neuter as well as neutral. Half the country's sitting on the fence like a gib-cat howling in the rain for a female he couldn't match though he caught her. They make me angry! Let's go somewhere else.'

Magnus was impressed by this display of temper and the sincerity of feeling that it indicated, but the attitude towards Nationalism of their athletic acquaintances led him to wonder if Meiklejohn's conception of the general situation were not more imaginative than actual. While they were in Bombay, he remembered, Frank had become a supporter of Indian Nationalism, and had once declared that Mahatma Gandi was making many converts even in the Yacht Club. This assertion was subsequently disproved to the satisfaction of everyone but its author.

'You weren't exaggerating when you said that Nationalism was sweeping the country?' he asked.

'That's the simple truth,' said Meiklejohn earnestly. 'Of course you'll find a lot of people who don't believe in it, but that's because they don't believe in anything but sitting still and keeping their bottoms warm. There are bottom-warmers in every country on earth, and there always have been. You needn't pay any attention to them. But all the people in Scotland who think for themselves are Nationalists, and all the people who feel they're really different from the English: the men you meet in the Highlands, and the Outer Isles, and in low pubs. Let's go to a pub in the High Street. There'll be nothing half-hearted or English or respectable about it. Or shall we look for Hugh Skene? He's probably in the Cosmopolitan just round the corner.'

Hugh Skene was a poet whose work had excited more controversy than any Scottish author had been flattered by for many years. Those who admired his writing declared him to be a genius of the highest order, and those who disliked it, or could not understand it, said that he was a pretentious versifier who concealed his lack of talent by a ponderous ornamentation of words so archaic that nobody knew their meaning: for Skene's theory was that the English language, having become devitalized by time, was incapable of sustaining any vigorous or truly poetic meaning, and that the proper material for Scottish writers was Gaelic or the ancient language of Henryson and Dunbar. But whatever his merits he had roused much argument, and Magnus was eager to meet him.

The Cosmopolitan was noisier and more populous than the Café de Bordeaux and Meiklejohn failed to find Skene in the crowd. He made his way with difficulty to the bar and asked the barman if he had seen him.

'He was here a while back,' said the barman, 'but he wasna looking very weel, and he went early. He said the beer had upset his stomach.'

Somewhat saddened by this discovery of frailty in the constitution of a fellow-Scot, Meiklejohn and Magnus left the clamorous bar and walked towards the High Street. The weather had moderated. Having completed its *allegro* movement, the storm had passed with diminished vigour to an *andante* of pleasing melancholy. The wind no longer leapt from wall to pavement, lifting with a shout and cold finger protesting skirts, but in the farther purlieus the sky debated with fleeing clouds a serious and more gentle theme. Pale stars came into view, against a lighter background and the old tall houses of the High Street showed in solid darkness. From Holyroodhouse to the Castle the ridge runs, hard and high, like the rough spine of Edinburgh, and the tall houses are its vertebrae, and in its marrow is a wilder life than that which animates the dignified terraces and sedate Georgian crescents below. Those lofty houses are not an aristocracy decayed and subdued, but an aristocracy debauched and ruined, sprawling in rags and dirt where it once flaunted itself in threadbare finery and three-piled pride, and lived in the high perfume of insolence and treachery and blood. As a wounded eagle, scabby and fly-infected, is a nobler and more tragic spectacle than a sick barnyard fowl, so are those houses, once turbulent with all the nobility of Scotland, more tragic and nobler than houses of the solid citizenry abandoned in the dull ebb of fashion. And as an eagle, even in its last hours, will shake from its feathers the buzzing flies, and rise in its excrement to fight, so do those houses seem fiercer than shop-keeping brick and mortar, and those who inhabit them, breathing the spirit of their dead greatness, have more vitality than their more respectable neighbours.

Magnus, who had been unusually quiet, was still disinclined for conversation. He was conscious of opposing arguments in his mind. On the one hand there was a romantic urging to believe all Meiklejohn said and to throw himself into the task of re-fashioning on prouder lines his native country—how splendid, how intoxicating, to assist in the rebirth of a nation!—and on the other hand there was a colder and more rational inclination to discount Meiklejohn's assertions and to pursue his original plan of securing happiness and fame for himself in the solitude of poetry. He had intended to retreat from life, and now he was tempted to advance into its liveliest activity. He thought with regret of the peace he had contemplated, but the prospect of action grew more and more alluring. He still tried to convince himself of the wisdom of selfishness and regression, but his natural inclinations depreciated his arguments and beckoned him forward.

Meiklejohn, now silent also, was somewhat ill-tempered. The irritation caused by the golfers' mockery of Nationalist aspirations had been aggravated by disappointment at not finding Hugh Skene, and his pride as a host was hurt by the failure of the evening to achieve the high degree of conviviality that he desired. Down his throat and his guest's had gone generous draughts of vodka and Chablis, of claret and brandy, and yet both were disappointingly sober. They should have been shouting to the stars. But wine is a fickle thing.

Like a great battlement the north side of the High Street confronted them. From their lower level a long flight of steps led upwards, a narrow passage between black walls whose farther end was invisible, and on whose middle distance a lamp shone dimly. Here and there on the steps, obscurely seen, were vague figures. Under the lamp, with harsh voice and combative gesture, two men were quarrelling. Another, oblivious to them and perhaps to all the world, leaned against the wall with drooping head. From the high remote darkness of the passage came the shrill sound of a woman laughing, and from the tavern whose door the lamp lighted there issued, muffled by the walls, the multifarious sound of talk and argument and rival songs.

Meiklejohn grew more cheerful as they climbed the steps, and he pushed his way impatiently past the men at the door. One of them turned indignantly and asked him where the hell he thought he was going. Meiklejohn paid no attention, and the man followed him into the crowded bar, his temper ruffled, bent on pursuing this new quarrel.

'Hey!' he said, and took Meiklejohn by the shoulder, 'did you no hear me? Or are you deaf as well as blind?'

'That's all right,' said Meiklejohn.

'Oh, that's all right, is it?' said the man with an offensive parody of Meiklejohn's voice.

Magnus spoke soothingly: 'He hasn't done you any harm. If he pushed you it was only by accident.'

'And what the hell's it got to do with you?' asked the quarrelsome man. 'It's him I'm talking to. Can he no answer for himself?' He glared fiercely at Magnus. He was a square-shouldered fellow, very shabbily dressed, but nimble and soldierly, and his face was red and bony and truculent. Then, slowly, his expression altered. Pugnacity gave place to surprise, to recognition, and finally to beaming pleasure. 'Christ!' he said, 'it's Merriman, the beggar that stuck his bayonet up the Captain's airse at Festubert!' He turned and called to the companion with whom he had been arguing outside. 'Here's a bloke that'll tell you the truth! I said the war was a bloody picnic in '15, and so it was. We had a bloody picnic for three weeks at Bécourt.'

Magnus had now remembered the red-faced man as a former comrade in the Gordon Highlanders. 'Sergeant Denny,' he exclaimed, and shook hands with him enthusiastically. Denny introduced his companion. 'He was a bloody conscript,' he said, 'and didn't come out till '17. And now he starts telling me what the war was like.'

The other man, whose name was McRuvie, muttered: 'It wasna a picnic for the Black Watch, onyway.'

'It would have been if you'd come out soon enough,' said Denny. 'Three bloody weeks at Bécourt and a hot dinner every day, and the officers sleeping in real beds, and every bloody morning I picked a bunch of flowers on the parados and put 'em in a jam-pot on the fire-step!'

'Ach, to hell! Who shot the cheese?' said McRuvie.

Magnus hurriedly ordered three pints of beer, before his reference to an old regimental scandal could aggravate the quarrel to violence: for the Gordons were sensitive about the allegation that they had once opened fire on a ration cheese, mistaking its pallor in the dusk for the pale face of an enemy.

It was difficult to maintain a conversation in the bar, for there was a great deal of noise and the customers stood so close to each other that a man might easily drink out of his neighbour's glass did not the latter keep good watch on it. Tobacco, the smell of beer and whisky, and a heavy odour of dirty clothes made the air so thick as almost to be visible. Cigarette smoke floated in thick whorls that were disturbed by the vibration of the floor above, where apparently a reel was being danced. Meiklejohn had fallen into talk with a little old shrivelled man in ragged trousers and more ragged coat whose face, unshaved and grey, wore a look of half-witted cunning. Meiklejohn shouted through the crowd to Magnus.

'Come and listen to this,' he said. 'I've found a minstrel, a ballad-singer. He's got the finest song I've heard for years.'

The little man winked lewdly. Each hand held a glass of beer that Meiklejohn had bought for him. In a thin husky voice he began to sing:

> O, Jenny she's ta'en a deep surprise,
>> And she's spewed a' her crowdie,
> Her minnie she ran to bring her a dram,
>> But she stood more need o' the howdie.

At Magnus's other elbow McRuvie had just referred to Sergeant Denny's regiment as the Kaiser's Bodyguard.

'Away and play at Broken Squares!' replied Denny ferociously.

These twin vilifications—the former a bitter reference to a stain on the Gordons' honour, the latter recalling an unhappy incident in the history of the Black Watch—brought the argument to a head. McRuvie hit Denny on the nose, and Denny knocked McRuvie down with a right hook to the jaw. The noise increased with this sudden excitement and a great deal of beer was spilled as everyone turned to so violent a centre of interest. Two barmen forced their way through the crowd, and without waste of time seized hold of Denny and flung him out of doors. Then they returned, and finding McRuvie preparing to follow his enemy they sternly warned him of the consequences, and by a timely reference to the police persuaded him to stay where he was.

Meiklejohn was annoyed by this interruption of the little man's ballad, but when on all sides, awakened by the regimental breeze, reminiscences of the war rose to the surface of men's memories and into the thick yellow-lighted air fell the names of Givenchy and Sanctuary Wood and Poperinghe—half these ragged fellows, these slouching dole-men, these pot-bellied deformities, had once stood rigid and magnificent on parade, and marched behind the pipes with kilts swinging, and eaten their food under storm-clouds of death—when these memories found tongue Magnus was engaged in conversation by an ill-formed and evil-smelling lump of a man who proudly pulled up his trouser-leg and showed on his grimy skin a long and puckered scar.

High Wood disputed with the Labyrinth, the mud at Louvencourt rivalled as a topic of humour and delight the carnage at Mont St Eloi. In red leather volumes in the Memorial on the Castle Rock were the myriad names of the Scottish dead, and here in the lively squalor of a lousy tavern were their comrades who had survived, and whose names were nowhere written—unless perhaps on the wall of a jakes. But they were alive and, for the moment, rich with their memories. They had marched on foreign soil and killed their country's enemies. Thin-ribbed with hunger, or gross with civilian fat they might be, shambling in their gait and dismal in their dress they were, but once their buttons had shone bright, and their shoulders were square, and they were Gordons and Seaforths and Camerons. They had worn the Red Hackle, and ridden on jolting limbers, and swallowed with their ration beef the acrid taste of danger. Here, with foul shirts and fouler breath, were Mars's heroes. Kings had fallen and nations perished, armies had withered and cities been ruined for this and this alone:

that poor men in stinking pubs might have great wealth
of memory.

Magnus, perceiving this irony, was delighted by it, but
Meiklejohn, with no military recollections of his own, was
merely upset by the loss of his ballad-singer, who had disappeared in the commotion.

'What debased pleasure do you find in looking at that
filthy sore?' he asked Magnus, who was examining with
interest the wound on the dirty man's skin.

Magnus answered:

> Then will he strip his sleeve and show his scars
> And say: 'These wounds I had on Crispin's day'.

'Don't quote that sentimental barbarian to me,' said
Meiklejohn irritably. 'You miss the chance of hearing a
damn fine Scots song and then you recite Shakespeare.
This is a pub, not a girls' school matinée.'

'What the hell has a girls' school got to do with
Shakespeare?' asked Magnus.

Meiklejohn ignored him. 'Let's go upstairs. Perhaps the
little man's there.'

On the upper floor of the tavern were another bar and
a small dingy lounge. Following Meiklejohn up the stairs
Magnus quoted, somewhat contentiously:

> And many a man there is, even at this present,
> Now, while I speak, holds his wife by the arm,
> That little thinks she has been sluiced in's absence
> And his pond fished by his next neighbour, by
> Sir Smile, his neighbour,

and asked: 'Is that stuff for girls?'

'Certainly, if they're nasty girls,' said Meiklejohn.

The upper floor was even noisier than the lower one, for
on the latter had been nothing but men, but here there were
women also. A few were elderly, pouchy-faced, wide in the
hips, with over-flowing contours, but most were young. A
cocksure strutting little creature with pointed breasts, black
eyes, a loose mouth and oiled black hair took Magnus by
the coat and said: 'Hey! are you sleeping with me or am I
sleeping with you tonight?'

'Neither,' said Magnus.

'Och! Be a man! I'll no tell your mother, if that's what you're thinking. Gie's a drink, anyway.'

'What do you want?'

'Whisky, and a big one. And you needna bother about soda. There's no guts in the drink here, and there's no guts in the men either.'

She took the drink and swallowed it at a gulp. 'Come on,' she pleaded, 'it won't cost you much.'

'No,' said Magnus.

'Oh, well,' said the slut, 'there's a kiss for your drink. It wasna worth more than that.' And she reached up and kissed Magnus noisily.

'An honest little whore,' said Meiklejohn.

Magnus, with wicked intent, answered:

> Those milk-paps
> That through the window-bars bore at men's eyes,
> Are not within the leaf of pity writ.

'For God's sake keep your tongue out of that plate,' shouted Meiklejohn. 'I take you to a good Scotch pub and you quote a noisy, dirty-minded, untidy, romantical Englishman to me! I detest Shakespeare, and I'm damned if I'll listen to him for you or anyone else.'

Meiklejohn was dogmatic in his tastes, and professing a large enthusiasm for Latin poetry of the Augustan age, for classical French literature, for Viennese music, for the bothy ballads and ruder verse of Scotland, he would recognize no merit in what was written outside those areas. Essentially a romantic himself, he hotly denounced all romantic writing, and confessed his passion for Johann Strauss only because those rosy melodies brought to his eyes such fond and copious tears that his weakness was immediately discernible. But to Magnus, as to many other people, depreciation of Shakespeare was dangerously near to blasphemy, and Meiklejohn's scandalous denigration of England's most mellifluous and triumphant voice roused in him hot anger and resentment. For his new-come patriotism was not yet exclusive.

'Forgive me for uttering so naked a commonplace,' he

said offensively, 'but you drive me to it. Shakespeare is the greatest poet of all time,

'A fustian, long-winded, turgid, slovenly ranter who never missed the opportunity to make a dirty joke,' retorted Meiklejohn.

'Name a better poet,' said Magnus.

'Racine,' said Meiklejohn promptly.

'That dull, pedantical schoolroom exercise! That prosy, plodding, weary, unimaginative padding for a deserted library! That's not poetry: that's route-marching to Parnassus with full pack and a sergeant alongside to see that you keep step.'

Meiklejohn took Magnus by the lapel of his coat and shouted very loudly: 'Listen to this, you chuff!'

> Le ciel de leurs soupirs approuvait l'innocence;
> Ils suivaient sans remords leur penchant amoureux;
> Tous les jours se levaient clairs et sereins pour eux.

'Is that poetry, you poor simpleton, you Boeotian, you country slab?'

Magnus shook off the detaining hand, and in his turn shouted: 'No, it's costive as you are, and flat as this beer you've given me, and colourless as an old hen's rump blown bare by the wind. Listen to this, you rattle in a tin can, you wind in a sheep's belly, you varicose puff!—

> We two, that with so many thousand sighs
> Did buy each other, must poorly sell ourselves
> With the rude brevity and discharge of one.
> Injurious Time, now with a robber's haste
> Crams his rich thievery up, he knows not how,
> And scants us with a single famished kiss,
> Distasting with the salt of broken tears.

Meiklejohn interrupted, bellowing a single line:

> C'est Vénus toute entière a sa proie attachée!

By this time they had attracted the attention of the whole room. The pianist who had been playing for two or three pairs of dancers fell silent. The dancers came to a standstill. The drinkers took firmer hold of their glasses to keep them safe should trouble arise. An old man with a pendulous red nose and a silver watch-chain across his greasy waistcoat, shocked by the sound of a foreign tongue, shouted: 'They're Bolsheviks! Pit them oot!' His neighbour, a pallid man with red hair and no teeth, gobbled like a turkey and cried: 'I'm a Bolshie masel! Pit me oot, if you can!' Two sailors, on leave from a destroyer lying in the Forth, set their girls down from their knees, stood, and hitched up their trousers in preparation for anything that might happen. And a tall barman came threateningly to Meiklejohn and asked: 'Is that language for a gentleman like you to be using? Are you no ashamed of yourself?'

'I was quoting a line of pure poetry,' said Meiklejohn.

'Pure stite,' said the old man with the red nose.

'Shut up!' said the barman, 'it's got damn-all to do with you, anyway.'

'They're Bolsheviks!' said the old man.

The barman ignored him and spoke sternly to Magnus and Meiklejohn: 'Don't let me here another word from you! If there's any more of that dirty talk, out you go on your bloody dowps, the pair o' you!'

'And now, will you give me two pints of beer?' said Magnus stiffly.

He and Meiklejohn sat together without speaking. Meiklejohn's drooping eyelid had fallen far down, and his left profile wore a sleepy look, while his right was set in haughty indignation. Magnus maintained an air of remote dignity, impaired though by no means ruined by a convulsive hiccup when he drank his beer.

The other occupants of the room returned to their previous amusements, and as closing time was imminent the barmen were kept busy pouring glasses of whisky and pulling beer-handles to fill those last cups that would sustain, for as long as might be, the Dionysiac euphrasy of the week-end—and would also ensure, when the traditional glory of Saturday had departed, a Sabbath morning queasy and grey and a mood most apt for piety and repentance.

The girls who had been sitting on the sailors' knees and had now returned to those warm seats, began to sing:

> Morning never comes too soon,
> I can face the afternoon,
> But oh! those lonely nights!

Then the sailors laughed loudly, and tickled the girls till they squealed, and one of them said: 'There ain't going to be no lonely night tonight, Jenny.'

'My name's no Jenny, it's Jeannie,' said the girl.

'Jenny or Jeannie, Polly or Molly, what the hell do I care?' said the sailor.

'Time, gentlemen, please!' shouted the barmen, and began to hustle those customers who were slow in finishing their drinks and to collect the empty beer-glasses, and to rebuke those ever-thirsty souls who pleaded in vain for a deoch-an-doris, a snifter, a valedictory nip, a homeward cup.

The girls stood up and laid on their captive sailors hands that were compulsive to follow. One of the girls sang in a voice of vulgar but cogent allurement:

> If you could care for me
> As I could care for you!
> Oh, what a place this world would be,
> A paradise for two!

Her voice rose and fell on the rhyming diphthongs with the exaggerated undulation of an Alpine yodel, and the cacology of the streets informed her pronunciation. But her voice was melodious.

'Is that another Scotch song?' asked Magnus with urbane malice.

Meiklejohn made no reply, but took snuff with a gesture that seemed to dissociate him from the pervading Englishness that could corrupt even a tavern in the High Street. Reluctantly the crowd staggered from the bar, and down the rickety stairs met those emerging from the lower rooms. The sailors, firmly clipping their girls, marched purposefully away. A decrepit old man with dirty white hair and a drop at his nose stood in a corner mournfully contemplating a halfpenny that lay in the palm of his hand. It was worn smooth and bright, and he had thought for one blessed moment it was a shilling. Now, discovering its insignificance, he cursed it slowly and carefully, dropping on its smooth surface abominable words that yet seemed, in his quavering tones, to lose their foulness and become the reasoned criticism of Job-in-the-gutter.

Magnus, still combatively inclined, saw the opportunity for another quotation, and aptly remarked:

> You taught me language, and my profit on't
> Is, I know how to curse.

'Who said that?' asked Meiklejohn suspiciously.

'The greatest poet of all time.'

Meiklejohn, with a temperate and judicious air, said: 'It's better than most of his stuff.'

Magnus grew earnest. 'My dear fellow,' he said, and paused to summon words so forceful and conclusive that his friend would of necessity repent his aesthetic blasphemy. Being now somewhat drunk—but solemnly, not riotously drunk—it seemed to him imperative and important beyond all else that Meiklejohn should confess the poetic supremacy of Shakespeare, and he strove with the fuddled resources of his memory for phrase and argument that would compel the admission from him. They were now on the dark corridor of steps outside the pub, and the crowd was fast disappearing, up or down, except for some in whom desire to journey anywhere had become inoperative; and they, idle as Stylites, leaned against the walls and contemplated in a puddle at their feet the black reflexion of the sky, and, in that dim mirror, the minute starring of tiny water-drops. For the rain had gone, and the clouds had settled lower, and small rain fell silently.

'My dear fellow,' Magnus repeated, 'think of the profundity of Shakespeare, and the enormity of his invention. The range of his understanding . . .'

Meiklejohn, equally in earnest and stammering in the speed of his desire to refute Magnus's assertions, said: 'But think of Racine!'

'Racine is a bore,' said Magnus.

'Shakespeare's a periphrastic, platitudinous peacock,' said Meiklejohn.

Magnus began to recite Clarence's dream from *Richard III*, and Meiklejohn attempted to over-shout him with the passage from *Roxane* beginning: 'Ah! je respire enfin, et ma joie est extrême,' but unfortunately, owing to the disorder of their minds, neither could remember more than a line or two, and their quotations expired in a common silence of defeat. They tried new pastures.

'Quoi! pour noyer les Grecs et leurs mille vaisseaux,' Meiklejohn began, with less assurance than before.

> Then of thy beauty do I question make
> That thou among the wastes of time must go,

said Magnus fiercely.

'L'Aulide aura vomi leur flotte criminelle,' shouted Meiklejohn.

'Will you listen to me?' said Magnus, and took Meiklejohn by the throat.

'I'm damned if I will,' said Meiklejohn, and struck Magnus on the side of the head. It was a clumsy blow, but sufficient to unbalance him, and falling, he fell down several steps before he could recover himself.

In the meanwhile Meiklejohn had taken off his coat and hat and given them to one of the several nearby loafers, who happened to be Private McRuvie, late of the Black Watch. He had found Sergeant Denny waiting for him in a pacific mood and they were now on friendly terms.

Magnus, stripping in turn, gave his coat to the Sergeant, who encouraged him to go in and win. Meiklejohn, though somewhat unsteadily, stood in an attitude of defence, but Magnus hesitated to begin the fight.

'I'll give you a last chance,' he said, 'if you admit that Shakespeare's a better poet than Racine . . .'

'*Merde!*' answered Meiklejohn rudely. Whereupon Magnus hit him lightly on the face, and Meiklejohn countered heavily to the body. Then they sparred for another opening.

'Up the Gordons!' cried Sergeant Denny, and officiously thrust back the several spectators.

'Mind where you're going,' said Private McRuvie, whose toes had been trodden on.

'Away and take a running jump at yourself,' said the Sergeant.

'There's no bloody Gordon with a white strip in his kilt

can tell me to take a running jump,' answered McRuvie indignantly.

Then by common accord McRuvie and the Sergeant threw down the coats they carried for the other combatants and began, with great gusto, to punch and pummel for themselves.

The yellow lamp outside the tavern grotesquely lighted the swaying figures of Magnus and Meiklejohn. They had drunk too much to be either strong or accurate in their hitting, and for some time they fought without inflicting much damage. Presently for lack of wind they fell into a clinch, and Magnus, with no regard for orthodoxy, seized Meiklejohn by the hair and pulled back his head till, panting, he gaped at the lamplight like a dying fish.

Magnus, himself almost breathless, had just enough strength and animosity to gasp—as though setting his flag on a conquered town—

Leading him prisoner in a red-rose chain!

At this moment two tall and robust figures, helmeted, dark, a glisten of rain on their black capes, silent and portentous, ponderous but alert, came into the lamplight, and seeing them the spectators fled, one turning as he ran to say: 'Look out, boys, it's the polis!'

But Magnus, still regardless, though a heavy hand fell on his shoulder, continued to recite:

The moon's an arrant thief,
And her pale fire she snatches from the sun;
The sea's a thief whose liquid surge resolves
The moon into salt tears; the earth's a thief
That feeds and breeds by a composture stolen
From general excrement.

Now Meiklejohn, with a last effort, kicked his opponent's legs from under him, and they fell together, breaking the policeman's grip, and rolled down some dozen steps, locked in each other's arms till they came to a flat landing. Bruised and bewildered, Magnus rose, and immediately a policeman had him by the neck and arm, and a moment later his wrists were handcuffed. But Meiklejohn lay where he had fallen.

'Now stand there quietly, if you don't want to get hurt,' said the policeman, and knelt to examine Meiklejohn.

'Ay,' he said, 'this'll be a bad night's work for you, my man. Your pal's clean knocked out, and maybe worse. We'll need to get the ambulance.'

But Meiklejohn, not yet defeated, opened his eyes and struggled to get up. Leaning on one elbow he said, very slowly and distinctly:

C'était pendant l'horreur d'une profonde nuit.

Then, with the quotation of this ample and sonorous line for a last defiance, he collapsed and fell backwards on the stone.

CHAPTER SIX

Under the protection of alcohol a man may confront the most appalling fortune with equanimity, and while he walked with his escort to the Central Police Station, Magnus was unperturbed by the fact of his arrest and the possibility that Meiklejohn was seriously hurt. Like a cloudy nimbus the fumes of all he had drunk now veiled his mind, and within that delicate circumvallation he felt calm as an Oriental philosopher contemplating the whimsical illusion of the world from the exquisitely poised foundation of his own unreality. The very act of walking was performed without any sense of physical effort. He seemed rather to float by the policeman's side, as though indeed he were sitting on a lotus-flower, air-borne like Gautama. Smoothly and gravely—but not too much—he talked with the constable as he was wafted along, and the constable, a good friendly fellow, was charmed by his manner and expressed his belief that Meiklejohn was not seriously hurt after all.

'A dunt on the heid's no great matter when a man's drunk,' he said consolingly. 'It's damned easy to kill a man when he's sober, but it takes time and forethought to do it when he's fou'.'

The other policeman had taken McRuvie and Sergeant Denny in charge. They also were now quiet and contemplative, and they meekly carried to the police-station the coats which Magnus and Meiklejohn had discarded. They had already been charged when Magnus and his escort arrived, for the latter had waited till the ambulance came for Meiklejohn.

The station sergeant was a benign little man with spectacles and he listened with sorrowful disapproval while the nature of Magnus's breach of the peace and assault upon Meiklejohn was described to him.

'A person like you shouldn't be found brawling in the streets,' he said, 'for if you want to get drunk you can do it quietly and decently in your own house.'

Magnus bowed under the rebuke. 'I can only apologize,' he said with rather ponderous courtesy. 'I'm afraid that I lost my temper. My friend and I were discussing a literary problem, and literature, if you take it seriously, is a great breeder of quarrels. I once knew a man who was shot for describing another's verses as catalectic, which they were. But the author thought he had said "cataleptic".'

'That may be,' said the sergeant. 'But the constable says you were using very filthy language.'

'I was quoting Shakespeare.'

The sergeant scratched his chin. 'There was a man brought in on the same charge last week, and he said he had been quoting the Bible.'

'It may be that all great literature is anti-social in its effects,' Magnus suggested.

'Then there's your friend,' said the sergeant, 'who may be very badly hurt. I might overlook the swearing, considering the circumstances, but I can't overlook a fractured skull.'

At this moment, however, the door opened and Meiklejohn, very dirty from rolling down the steps, came in with a policeman close behind him. On the way to the hospital he had suddenly recovered consciousness, and the constable in attendance, finding there was nothing seriously wrong with him, had decided a doctor's attention would be wasted on him and that he had better be charged with the others.

The sergeant now decided that there was nothing very serious in the case, and offered to release the prisoners on security of two pounds apiece if they promised to indulge in no more literary discussion that night.

'And if you don't find it convenient to appear before the

magistrate on Monday morning you'll forfeit your bail and justice will be satisfied without troubling you further,' he explained. He mentioned that Denny and McRuvie might also be liberated on security, and Magnus paid a pound each for their freedom. Then the police bade them all goodnight with great cordiality, and they parted outside the station to go their several ways home.

Magnus and Meiklejohn walked together downhill to the Mound, exchanging mutual apologies for their mutual assault, in which the amiability of their sentiments was made abundantly evident by prolixity and repeated assurance.

Meiklejohn especially was remorseful, in that he had outraged hospitality by insulting and thereafter striking his guest. He insisted on accompanying Magnus to his hotel, and there were tears in his eyes when, with a last freshet of words, he at length said good-night.

Magnus slept heavily and woke feeling so fresh and healthy as to be quite impenitent for the previous night's excesses. He was, indeed, so far from regret that he lay on his pillow and recalled the events of the evening with immoderate pleasure. An exquisite sensation of well-being suffused him as he stretched his legs and turned this way and that, feeling his muscles extend and contract, and gathering in the fold of memory one image after another from the rude comedy that had begun with Scottish Nationalism, passed through the temperate luxury of the Café de Bordeaux to the riotous delight of the High Street pub, included in its elastic form the inter-regimental rivalry of the Gordon Highlanders and the Black Watch, and concluded with the translation of Gautama to the police-station.

If this is Scotland, he thought, then Scotland is worth living in. And again the intoxicating idea returned that here in truth was a nation worth refashioning, and that might be the very moment dictated by some strange conjunction of the stars for its second birth, and that he, Magnus Merriman, would win a place in history not as a poet, but under the prouder title of patriot. He considered from what rank in life the liberators of the world, the leaders of new nations, had come; and a score of misty figures—soldiers, a country gentleman, a shabby professional Marxian, a Polish pianist, a Cossack trooper—moved in his memory as if upon a screen. They were various as flowers in a cottage-garden, though hardly smelling so sweet. There was no reason why he, sometime a soldier, lately a journalist, and always a poet, should not do as they had done. So far as he could see, in the optimism of his present mood, there was only one factor that could possibly hinder him from becoming a patriot and the maker—at least in some degree—of a new nation: Scotland, as a whole, might not be inclined for re-making, or disposed to welcome patriots whose unruly ambition would bring upon her the pangs of renascence and commit her to a new gamble with fate and time. Despite the invigorating example of the new nations that, since the War, had sprung up like green crops and re-coloured the whole earth, Scotland might prefer to remain comfortably obscure in the broad shadow of England and console herself for national insignificance by counting the material advantages that accrued from her junior partnership in the Commonwealth. What chance for patriots then? It was true that Meiklejohn had said the whole country was restless and eager for change, but later events had compelled him to exclude all footballers and golfers from his potential revolutionaries. And that was a serious handicap to Nationalism.

But Magnus's spirit was too robust and buoyant to admit to difficulties for long. If Scotland did not yet want independence it should be made to want it. From a sentimental aspect the plea for it would be irresistible—and who but a libbed accountant, a gelded intellectual, could decry sentiment?—and though he was not yet aware of any material arguments in favour of political freedom, there were doubtless plenty, and Meiklejohn and Mrs Dolphin would know them all. The world was full of arguments, and the general condition of humanity was so unsatisfactory that one needed but little wit to elaborate a case for altering it, whether locally or all across the map. Magnus felt sure that there would be no difficulty in showing cause why Scotland should immediately assert her independence, and in all probability it could be shown that she would benefit from the change. Statistics were notoriously elastic and could bend both ways like any gymnast. During his residence in America he had argued, time and again, that the British Empire was the most beneficent factor in world equations, and that the world's peace, the world's progress, and the world's prosperity all depended on the continued existence, strength, and prestige of the Empire. After that colossal task it would surely be simple to find arguments for the continued existence of so small a country as Scotland.

Elated by the prospect of activity so largely if not wholly altruistic, Magnus rose and dressed himself rapidly. After breakfast he seriously considered his financial position, for clearly, if he was to engage in politics, he must defer his visit to Orkney and settle himself in Edinburgh—and to live in Edinburgh would cost him a great deal more than living in Orkney. But he was secretly glad of the excuse to postpone his return to the islands, for after residing very comfortably in America and very warmly in India the prospect of a small house in Orkney under the boisterous winds and the pervading ocean-salted coldness of winter appealed to him less and less the more he thought of it. And, he reflected, he had not yet written to his people to warn them of his return. It would be better, on all counts, to stay for some time in Edinburgh.

He began to calculate his resources. He had saved £340 while he was in America, and in London he had earned £180 by casual journalism: in the flush of his novel's success his name had acquired a certain transient value, and various newspapers had commissioned him to write articles of no importance on such topics of scanty and ephemeral interest as were, in their editors' opinion, suitable for readers in suburban trains and provincial breakfast-rooms. But in London Magnus had lived somewhat extravagantly, and spent, in rather less than three months, rather more than £400. His earlier books had never earned anything but a little pocket money, and though now they were enjoying a slight increase in popularity, his income from royalties from them would not, in all probability, exceed another fifty pounds. And that was not due till June. His wealth lay almost entirely in *The Great Beasts Walk Alone*. A few days before leaving London his publishers had told him they had sold thirty-one thousand copies. His royalties on that large sale would, he calculated, amount to something over £1,800. The book, moreover, was still selling two or three hundred copies a week; he had signed an agreement for an American edition by which he would receive an advance of £250 on account of royalties; and negotiations were in progress for its translation into Swedish, Norwegian, Dutch and German. He felt comfortably well off and perfectly able to enter upon a political career.

He wrote to his publishers asking for an advance of £200 and, stating the calculation he had made, requested them to check its accuracy. Then he went out for a walk to inspect the capital city of the new sovereign state, and to see some of its soon-to-be independent burgesses.

But as it was Sunday the streets were empty, for those of its citizens who were not lying abed had gone to church. And in the morning light the Castle appeared somewhat flat and diminished in size from the vague grandeur of its darkling look.

CHAPTER SEVEN

Ten days later Magnus had settled himself in a small furnished flat in Queen Street, a row of tall flat-fronted houses whose residential dignity had been somewhat impaired by the invasion of offices and a few shops of a superior kind. His flat was at the top of the house and its windows looked north across gardens and a descending terrace of intersecting streets to a mistiness that in fine weather dissolved and revealed the steely brightness of the Forth. Beyond that were the ancient kingdom of Fife, soberly coloured, and the rising blue shadow of the Ochil hills, that outpost of the Highlands and a promise of farther heights.

In common with the ancient Athenians and the modern Americans, Magnus had a great liking for novelty, and would adopt a new fashion—in thought, in clothes or in behaviour—not only with enthusiasm but with such conviction that often it appeared to have been his own discovery. Already, following the example of Meiklejohn, he had abandoned smoking and taken to snuff, and his reasoning in favour of the latter commodity was more copious and incisive than his preceptor's; while his conversion to

Scottish Nationalism had been so complete that he could now remember perceiving its benefits, and formulating a programme for its attainment, some three years previously. He had spent several days in close study of the case for it, and many of the arguments were so cogent that he could not believe he had ever been ignorant of them. From that impression to the more positive one that he had himself enunciated them—and indeed he had enunciated so many arguments in favour or dispraise of so many things that he could not possibly remember them all—was a short and easy step, and he now regarded himself as one of the earliest apostles of the Scottish political renascence.

He had seen Meiklejohn several times, and he was at present reading a book called *The Flauchter-spaad* in preparation for meeting, in Meiklejohn's rooms, the poet Hugh Skene and the latter's less distinguished friend Padraig McVicar. *The Flauchter-spaad* was Skene's latest volume of poems, and the critics were, as usual, divided into two factions, one party calling it a work of superlative genius, the other declaring it, quite simply, to be gibberish. The general public, being ignorant of its very existence, reserved their opinion.

Among the disruptive phenomena that followed the Great War, not the least remarkable was the disruption, or threatened disruption, of language. In most of the so-called civilized countries of the world a group of writers had appeared who stated their belief that existing literary forms were no longer of significance or value, and that to express themselves fully serious writers must rediscover some prime vitality in the roots of language. This belief had shown itself in varying degrees. Many authors contented themselves with writing ungrammatically, some acquiring the art and others possessing it by nature: in America especially did illiteracy come to be encouraged and recognized for some little while as the distinguishing feature of the new literature. Other writers, by virtue, it may be, of some indomitable infantility in themselves—perhaps a mere hypothyroidism, or thymal persistence—reverted to nursery modes, and by the infinite repetition of simple sounds created for themselves the illusion of primordial meanings, but in less biased critics fortified the conviction that compulsory education was by no means so efficacious as many people thought it. The poets of the post-war world were fairly united in their belief that poetry, to be poetical, must be unrhythmical, unrhymed and unintelligible: and by these standards their output was of a high order. Their leader was the American Eliot, who by incorporating in his verse, with frolic wilfulness, tags from half the literatures of the world, had become popular in more than strictly intellectual circles for the likeness of his work to a superior parlour-game called 'Spot the Allusion' or 'Favourite Quotations'. His protagonist in prose was the Irishman Joyce, and Joyce, with the genius of his people for destruction, had treated the English language as Irish tenants had not seldom treated the cattle, fields, and houses of an absentee English landlord, and built on the ruins an edifice far beyond normal comprehension and incomprehensibly charming. Faced with these attacks the English language withdrew into its shell, and conventional writing became somewhat pale and nerveless indeed.

In Scotland the chief exponent of literal revolution was Hugh Skene, and he, as has already been noticed, attempted to revive the ancient Scottish forms of speech. They had this advantage, at least, that they were fully as obscure as Joyce's neologisms or the asyntactical compressions of the young English poets. But as Skene's genius matured he discovered that the Scots of Dunbar and Henryson was insufficient to contain both his emotion and his meaning, and he began to draw occasional buckets from the fountains of other tongues. At this time it was not uncommon to find in his verse, besides ancient Scots, an occasional Gaelic, German, or Russian phrase. The title-poem of his new volume, *The Flauchter-spaad*, was strikingly polyglot, and after three hours' study Magnus was unable to decide whether it was a plea for Communism, a tribute to William Wallace, or a poetical rendering of certain prehistoric fertility rites. The opening stanza read:

> The fleggaring fleichours moregeown on our manheid,
>   And jaipit fenyeours wap our bandaged eyes:
> *Progress!* they skirle with sempiternë gluderie—
>   The sowkand myten papingyes!

> But Lenin's corp ligs i' the Kremlin still,
> Though Wallace's was quartered like the mune
> By the Crankand English for their coclinkis' gam—
> *Kennst du das land wo die citronen blühn?*

This was fairly straightforward and the meaning was clear enough with the help of a glossary, but owing to a large infiltration of Russian and Gaelic the ensuing stanzas were extremely difficult, and Magnus put down the book feeling that should *The Flauchter-spaad* be discussed that evening he would need to be very discreet in giving his opinion of it.

Skene and McVicar were already there when Magnus arrived in Meiklejohn's rooms. He had some conversation with Mrs Dolphin before going in.

'Take a look at McVicar's trousers,' she said. 'You remember that business about Mr Meiklejohn's best evening pair going astray? Well, McVicar's wearing them now, and Mr Meiklejohn can't take them off him because he hasn't another pair to put on. He got his own torn to bits at a meeting at the Mound the other night. He was talking about Nationalism, but he speaks in a very solemn way and the crowd thought he was a Mormon, and rushed him.'

McVicar was indeed wearing a pair of black evening trousers, and only a dignified demeanour saved their companionship with a light tweed jacket from being ludicrous. But he was a young man so solemn, so grimly handsome, of so darkly fanatical a glance, that his clothes were of no importance. Sackcloth or the mantle of a prophet might have matched his bearing, but failing those his attire had no significance. It was merely a concession to the exigencies of a northern climate and to the prevailing mode that prescribed concealment for the human frame.

Skene, however, had gone to some trouble in selecting his raiment. His suit was unremarkably grey, but he wore a purple collar and shirt and a yellow tie with red spots. Apart from his clothes his appearance was sufficiently striking to suggest genius. He had a smooth white face, dwarfed by a great bush of hair, and in brisk, delicate, rather terrier-like features his eyes shone bright and steady. His hands were beautifully shaped and somewhat dirty. He greeted Magnus very cordially, and made some kindly references

not only to *The Great Beasts Walk Alone*, but to his earlier
books of verse. Magnus took a liking to him and sat down
beside him.

Meiklejohn, excellently cast in the character of a host, pro-
vided everyone with drinks, talked with abundant vivacity
about French wines and French politics, and played on his
gramophone, in rapid succession, excerpts from *Fledermaus*
and *Figaro*.

'Have you any modern music?' Skene asked.

'I'm afraid not,' said Meiklejohn. 'Don't you like
Mozart?'

'It doesn't mean much.'

'Nothing written before 1920 has any great depth of meaning,' said McVicar gloomily.

Skene turned to Magnus and said: 'So you've become a
Nationalist, have you?'

'Yes,' said Magnus. 'But I didn't become converted in
the usual way. There's nothing sentimental in my brand of
nationalism. I'm quite cold about it. I've been abroad for
the last few years, and some time ago I came to the conclusion—a fairly obvious one—that what is mainly wrong
with the world is that there are too many great nations
in it. Both Britain and the United States, for instance,
are too big to be run efficiently. In countries of their
size there's too much opportunity for abuse, and abuses
become too widespread and complicated to be reformed.
The only way to improve conditions in the great nations
is to split them up and let each segment reform and control its own affairs. I believe in small nationalism because
it would mean reducing the world to manageable areas.
And, of course, small nations are safer to live in than big
ones.'

'I'm not interested in safety,' said Skene, 'and I don't
believe, as an ultimate thing, in small nationalism. I want to
see the creation of a world state. I'm a Communist. And I'm
a Scottish Nationalist because I believe that if Scotland were
independent we could do a great deal towards establishing a
central state in Western Europe.'

'To hell with Communism!' said Magnus warmly.

'Do you know what Communism is?'

'It's a damned Oriental perversion, a funk-hole for weak-lings, an attempt to turn the world into an ant-hill!'

Magnus stopped suddenly in his catalogue, though a dozen other definitions, equally offensive, had already occurred to him. He perceived that he was unnecessarily rude to a fellow-guest, and apologized for being so dogmatic in the utterance of personal opinions.

'But still,' he concluded, 'I'm perfectly convinced that my opinion is correct.'

'Communism liberates the individual from himself,' said McVicar.

'So does castration,' said Magnus more rudely than ever.

Meiklejohn attempted to create a diversion by telling the story of his arrest for brawling in defence of Racine, but Skene, making a gesture for silence, asked Magnus if he drank heavily.

'I'm fond of drinking, and sometimes I get drunk,' said Magnus.

'I drink a great deal,' said Skene. 'I'm a philosophical drunkard. I drink because I like drink, and I like the good fellowship that goes with drinking. But there's a more important reason.—What was the social argument for classical drama? By rousing emotion it purged the mind of emotion. It excited pity and fear, and by exciting them it cleared them out of the system. It was a cathartic. Well, drink is a better cathartic than anything that Aeschylus or Euripides ever wrote, and when I'm tired by poetry, weary with the loveliness and the height of poetic thought, drinking washes out the poetry and brings me back to the ordinary common world. I come back to common life and its dirt and rest myself there. I touch these things with the common touch and relieve my overwrought senses. I find comfort again. Drink does that for a man, and Communism would, in some ways, have the same effect. I could be free of myself in a Communist state.'

'But I don't want to be free of myself,' said Magnus.

'Then you've never felt the burden of poetry,' said Skene.

There was such conviction in Skene's voice that Magnus could find no answer or objection that did not seem trivial. A nervous triumph irradiated the poet. His hands trembled, his eyes shone brightly. On the edge of the light that escaped from a shaded lamp his great bush of hair seemed like a burning bush. His political opinions, thought Magnus, are the waste products of his genius.

Meanwhile McVicar was talking very earnestly to Meiklejohn. Magnus overheard a fragment of his conversation: 'I certainly don't believe in marriage, and I'm not in favour of birth control. There would be no need for contraceptives if people could be persuaded to abandon their romantic interest in love and content themselves with biological selection. I want the girl with whom I mate simply to regard me as a suitable father for her child.'

Skene said: 'You're a successful novelist, Merriman. But what are you aiming at? What do you think the future of writing is going to be?'

Magnus, who had never given much thought to the matter, promptly declared that he was a traditionalist. He was beginning to enunciate a conservative policy for literature when Skene interrupted him.

As if it were a pistol he aimed his slender and rather dirty forefinger at Magnus and said, with cold and deliberate ferocity: 'You're feeding on corpse-meat. In all its traditional forms English literature is dead, and to depend on the past for inspiration is a necrophagous perversion. We've got to start again, and the great literary problem confronting us today is to discover how far we must retract the horizontal before erecting a perpendicular.'

The solemnity with which Skene enunciated his last sentence persuaded Magnus of its importance, but as it was also somewhat obscure he hesitated to reply until he had elucidated its meaning. Skene took advantage of his silence to continue.

'I don't write prose myself,' he said, 'but if I did I should consider a story as an exercise in pure thought. I should write a story like this, for example: There's a man sitting at a window with a tray on his knees, and on the tray there are six insects running about. He's watching them. They're all exactly alike and indistinguishable from one another. Presently his wife comes in and looks over his shoulder and says: "There's a new one among them. There's a new insect on the tray." He looks again, and though the insects are all so alike as to be absolutely indistinguishable, he knows that his wife is right and that one of them is a newcomer. Now how did she know that? And how, eventually, did he know the truth for himself?—There's a theme I should like to elaborate, and I could make quite a long story out of it.'

'Would there be any climax or solution?'

'Yes. After considerable speculation the woman would say: "Now they've changed again. Those are the original six insects." The man would see that she was right, and I would examine the thought processes by which she knew and he knew that they had changed, and by tracing the involutions and convolutions of their thoughts and cognition-tracks in a reverse direction I would complete the story.'

'Are the insects of any particular kind? Beetles, for instance?' Magnus asked thoughtfully.

'No, just insects. I couldn't particularize them without distracting attention from the main theme,' said Skene.

Meiklejohn and McVicar had both joined Skene's audience, and after the recital of his insect story there was a short silence. Skene's manner had passed from ferocity to a very gentle earnestness, and Magnus, though his brain was confused by its pursuit of six isometrical and equivocal beetles, felt warmly attracted to him. Presently McVicar smoked the last cigarette in the room, and Magnus offered to go out and get some more from a near-by automatic machine. He was glad of the opportunity to escape, for the beetles were worrying him, and his attempts to isolate the metamorphosing member of the bewilderingly homogeneous sextet were distracted by the ebb and flow of conversation.

He stood for a moment on the pavement and made a last endeavour to immobilize at least one beetle of the six. But at the very moment when he had successfully visualized the tray and cornered the nearest insect, a motor car swerved across the street and halted abruptly a few yards from him. A door was thrown open and a girl came out. She walked round to the back of the car and proceeded to kick, with great violence and ill-temper, a punctured tyre. She was unusually dressed for that hour and that urban neighbourhood, for she wore Jodhpur trousers, a hunting coat and a neatly-tied scarf. She was bare-headed, and in the light wind that puffed and played about the street her light-hued, curling hair was dancingly dishevelled. Without hesitation Magnus abandoned his beetle-hunting and asked if he could help in any way.

'You can tell me a few dirty words to throw at this damned tyre,' she answered, and leaning against the back of the car considered him with a somewhat dazed expression.

She spoke with a drawling American accent, not the hard Northern tone or the strident voice of the Middle-West, but the rich cadence of the South. She had large and beautiful blue eyes, set wide apart and now somewhat obscured by the heaviness of their lids; a short pugnacious nose; a broad, square jaw; and a streak of dirt on one cheek. She was sufficiently tall, conventionally slender, glowing even in the darkness with rose and tawny hues, and her legs were long. And clearly she was not quite sober.

Magnus said: 'You're tired, aren't you? I have a friend who lives in this house here: come in and rest for a while and have some coffee.'

'Sure I'll come in,' she answered, 'but you needn't hope for fun and games when you get me on the sofa. I'm tight all right, but I can look after myself. There was a guy tried to get fresh with me this evening already, and I busted him on the jaw. Look at that!'

She showed him the back of her right hand, and Magnus observed with pleasure that the knuckles were indeed bruised and swollen.

'It must have been a good punch,' he said. 'But don't worry; you won't have to use the other hand. I promise that we'll behave with perfect decorum.'

'Well, I've heard that tale before, but I guess I'll risk it once again for a cup of coffee.'

Meiklejohn's flat was at the top of the house, and, climbing the first long flight of stairs, the girl staggered slightly. She offered no objection when Magnus put his arm round her waist to steady her.

On the top landing Magnus suddenly realized that Skene and McVicar were unlikely to think this girl a welcome addition to the party, and that she might find them no

more congenial to her than she was to them. He paused
in some perplexity, and wondered whether Mrs Dolphin
had another sitting-room into which he could take her.

'What's the matter?' asked the girl.

'I've just remembered that Meiklejohn—the man who
lives here—has a couple of guests, and. . .'

'Well, if you think I'm not respectable enough for them
I'll go: and to hell with you and your friends and your
coffee too!'

'That's a bad guess,' said Magnus. 'I only meant that you
mightn't find them very interesting—they're talking about
politics and literature and that sort of thing . . .'

'And you think that I'm too dumb to sit-in on a high-brow
party? You've got me diagnosed already, have you? Well
you're smart.'

Magnus ignored this provocation and continued: 'I'm
going to tell the landlady you're tired, and ask her to bring
you some coffee in another room. Now will you wait here
for a minute while I go in and speak to her?'

'Sure I'll wait,' said the girl, and sat down on the top
step.

Magnus found Mrs Dolphin in the kitchen.

'Mrs Dolphin,' he said, 'there's a girl outside who isn't
feeling very well—she's had a drink too much—and I
thought you might perhaps make some coffee for her. Can
I take her into your other sitting-room?'

'Indeed you can't,' she answered, 'for there's two men
sleeping there. They came this morning, from Skye, and
what they want in Edinburgh God only knows, but young
Buchanan came with them and said they were Nationalists,
and could I put them up for a night or two. So I said I would
give them a shake-down, and there they are, snoring away.'

'And Skene and McVicar are still in Mr Meiklejohn's
room.'

'What's the young lady like? Is she respectable?'

'Oh, perfectly,' said Magnus.

'Well, I'll take your word for it, though I wouldn't take
Mr Meiklejohn's where women were concerned. Not when
he's had a drink or two, at any rate. He'd kiss a pig when
he's drunk.'

'But how can we get rid of Skene and McVicar?'

Mrs Dolphin answered promptly: 'Take her into Mr Meiklejohn's room and they'll clear out fast enough. McVicar's frightened to death of women, and when he goes Skene will go with him, for they live near to each other.'

Magnus found the girl still sitting outside, and she followed him into the flat readily enough. In the sitting-room conversation suddenly died when they entered. McVicar stood with a haughty embarrassed look, and Skene's expression lost its animation. But Meiklejohn sprang forward with a cry of delight. Magnus thought he knew the young woman, such was his pleasure at seeing her, but he was in fact merely welcoming her femininity, for he had grown tired of travelling hither and thither on the arid plains of male conversation.

Magnus found the task of introduction easier than he had expected, for while he was tactfully explaining that her car had met with an accident she took charge of the situation and exclaimed: 'I've had a bum day with the Duke of Buccleugh—anyway, chasing his darned foxhounds—and then a guy took me home with him and gave me all the liquor in the wine-list. So I'm suffering from a touch of the sun. Then I hit the pike for home and got a puncture just round the corner. That's where your friend found me, and he thought it best to bring me in to recuperate. My name's Frieda Forsyth, if you want to know.'

'Whatever your name is we're charmed to see you,' said Meiklejohn gallantly, and found a cushion for her chair, and asked her what she would drink, and stood before her with an engaging smile to which his drooping eyelid gave a peculiar distinction.

'Mrs Dolphin's going to bring in some coffee,' said Magnus.

'I certainly need it,' said Miss Forsyth. 'I'm sore all over, and my fist aches like hell after socking that guy on the jaw—but I'll tell you that story later—and I'm half-blind through trying to keep the headlights and the road in the same place. I only went in the ditch once, though, and that was when a lump of grit about the size of a roc's egg got in my eye. I thought I was never going to see blue sky again. But I got it out. I pulled my top eyelid over my bottom, and that did it.'

Magnus laughed loudly and abruptly, and suddenly was silent again.

'Where's the egg?' demanded Miss Forsyth. Then, with immoderate enjoyment, she also laughed, throwing back her head and opening her mouth so wide that its pink roof was disclosed. She wiped away tears of mirth with the back of her hand, and the grimy mark on her cheek was much enlarged. With her voice still at the mercy of laughter she said: 'Well, I certainly laid it myself. Pulled my eyelid— say, am I a contortionist or am I not?'

Without shame or embarrassment Magnus and Meiklejohn laughed with her, but Skene showed no amusement, and McVicar was patently ill-at-ease. Before the joke had properly been dismissed the latter stood up and nervously said that he must go. Skene also rose to say good-bye. Miss Forsyth shook hands very cordially, but they showed no great friendliness in reply.

While Meiklejohn was showing them out Mrs Dolphin brought in the coffee. She regarded Miss Forsyth with evident suspicion, and made an excuse of attending to the fire in order to get a full view of her. Then Meiklejohn introduced her and the frown vanished.

'I wanted to get a good look at you,' she explained, 'for I've known girls who wore riding-breeches for no more than the show of them. But I see by the marks on yours that you've been on a horse, so stay as long as you like and get a good rest. Mr Merriman and Mr Meiklejohn will look after you.'

'I've been on a horse all right. There's marks on me as well as on my pants.'

'Well, we'll not ask you to prove that,' said Mrs Dolphin affably, and bade them good-night.

A new vitality had entered the room with Frieda Forsyth. It would be untrue to say that hitherto the conversation had been dull, for both politics and literature are subjects of perennial interest and superlative importance. But except for a few combative moments the atmosphere had been heavy, and once or twice, his mind wandering, Magnus had found himself contemplating the phenomenon of speech with a detached and semi-hostile wonder. All over the world, from human lips and teeth and tongue, from palate and throat, words were issuing—and to what purpose? Simply because speech was a human attribute? Had words any more significance than the drumming of snipe, the creaking of a swan's wings, the saltation of March lambs, the thumb-stain on a haddock's side? Once, while he listened to some sentence of inordinate length, he had almost believed that the walls and roof of the room were receding in a gradual seismic yawn. But now the walls came close, eager and friendly, and the air was lively as he and Meiklejohn competed for the attention of their new guest. Now words had a meaning indeed, for they were flies cast on the waters of conversation to attract her smiles, her favour and her interest. And now when Meiklejohn replayed his *Fledermaus* records—because Magnus and Miss Forsyth were finding too much common ground in reminiscences of America—that jocund music had the success it deserved, and their minds reflected its gaiety and warmth.

It appeared that Frieda Forsyth had led an adventurous life. Without boasting of strange experiences, she inferred them by familiar reference to undisciplined modes of existence, and by the rapid scene-shifting in her conversation it was clear that for some time she had enjoyed a nomadic life. She appeared to live with gusto, and she talked with great vitality: that American vitality which, like shot-silk, is interwoven with the colour of wit. But she was Scotch by inheritance, she told them, and now— she said it with a shrug and a grimace—she had come home. She was living with an aunt in Edinburgh. Her father and mother were dead. Her father had been the black sheep of his family, and burdened with that hue had gone in early life to the United States, hoping that there the moral colour-line was not so sharply drawn as in his native land.

'There's a hell of a lot of dark sheep bred in these respectable Scotch families,' she said. 'I've heard quite a bit of talk since I've been back living with Aunt Elizabeth, and it seems there's a black lamb in every second family at least, though the rest are so white and blameless you'd never suspect it. Say, do the men in this town sleep in stiff collars? They look like it.'

'The trouble is that all the black sheep are sent abroad,' said Magnus. 'Scotland would be a lot better off if they were kept at home and some of the white ones were deported instead.'

'Don't get too bitter about respectability,' she said. 'It's a dull quality, but it's comfortable, and if you'd seen as much of the other side of life as I have you wouldn't be so quick to sneer at it.'

Stung by the suggestion that their lives had been spent in virtuous security, both Magnus and Meiklejohn hotly replied that they also were acquainted with poverty, adventure and turpitude.

Meiklejohn rose from his seat, so great was his agitation, and with indignant gestures said: 'My dear Miss Forsyth! I admit that anyone so lovely and attractive as you are must have encountered temptations to which we have never been subject, but our lives have not been uneventful. We haven't spent all our days in Edinburgh. I could tell you some astonishing stories about India, and my God! when we were in Russia we took our lives in our hands!'

'That's a bedtime story,' said Miss Forsyth. She had finished her coffee and was drinking a mild whisky and soda. Suddenly her expression grew sullen and her voice harsh. 'Ever been a stenographer in New York and held down your job by sleeping with the boss?' she demanded. 'Ever gone through the Mojave Desert in a 1916 Ford with two cracked cylinders? Ever washed dishes in a company town in North Carolina, or run three blocks from a tubercular Bohunk trying to rape you? Ever pawned your mother's rings to pay for an abortion?'

The ugly violence of these rhetorical questions startled and shocked both Magnus and Meiklejohn. They had not regarded their vision as a tragic figure, for though she had implied her close acquaintance with hardship she had seemed to possess the seagull's aptitude for navigating with unruffled feathers the darkness and unruly depths of tempestuous waters. But now the marks of stormy voyaging showed clearly on her, and Meiklejohn's volubility was silenced, while to Magnus there came irrelevant thoughts about his native Orkney. Her face was hard, and her eyes cold as a seagull's indeed. He remembered white gulls sailing, cliff-high, on widespread wings and regarding with chill cruelty in their gaze the watcher on the headland. Perhaps the cold brightness of their eyes came from acquaintance with the gulfs of the sea and the ragged edge of a devouring wave. Perhaps that lonely bitterness—he remembered a fulmar sailing three yards from him, insolent and graceful and unwinking eye—perhaps that brumal solitude derived from knowledge of hunger in December and thrashing gales in March. The wren from southward meadowlands had no such black and bitter a gaze. It was an eye familiar with the sea's elements of ruin.

Magnus roused himself from these thoughts. They were growing too pretentious. And, on colder consideration, Frieda Forsyth's rhetorical questions also appeared melodramatic; but then the brutalities of life always seemed forced and unreal when brought into personal conjunction with the occupants of a safe and comfortable and friendly room. That this gaily attractive girl should have played the harlot, not from desire but from necessity, was an abominable thought, and to imagine those long legs, so smart in their Jodhpur trousers, running from the terror of rape, was frankly impossible. Had they, in truth, ever run in such fashion, or was she embroidering a fictitious occasion with lurid colours?

As though aware that she committed an indiscretion, and as if anxious to erase it, Frieda Forsyth sat up and returned to her former tone of boisterous amiability.

'Hell!' she said. 'What's the use of talking like that? This high-ball of yours must have gone to my head. Say, let me tell you about socking my suitor on the jaw today— or was it yesterday? Well, I fell off my horse. He was shaped like a hen behind—the horse, not the suitor; he'd a fanny like the end of a scow—and when he stood up I just slid. I could ride pretty well in Wyoming, but I'm not too good on a darned English saddle that's no bigger than a pocket handkerchief. I've been taking an odd day

with these blue-blooded fox-hunters of yours, down on the
Borders and over in Fife, but I haven't seen a fox yet. I
fall off too soon. This is the first time anyone's stopped
to pick me up, though. Does fox-hunting make you kind
of unfriendly? Anyway, there's been no one dying to make
my acquaintance till today, when Sir Edward fell for my
girlish charms. That isn't his name, but if you want to
identify him go down and look for a guy with a fat white
face and a big blue lump on his jaw. I'll say this, that his
boots were lovely, and his tailor's a genius, but the rest of
him was cheap and ordinary. Well, he stayed alongside,
and after the fun was over—and there wasn't any high
mortality among the foxes so far as I could see—he said
would I go home and have a drink with him? There didn't
seem any reason why his wine merchant shouldn't be as
good as his tailor, so I said yes. We got rid of our horses
and into his car, and I ought to have known by the way
his near-hand was straying that I wasn't safe, but hell, I
wanted that drink. And we had it, and several more. Then
he said he was dining all alone that night, and would I eat?
Now food's got an uncommon appeal for me, so again I
shrank from wounding his feelings by saying no, and we
sat down to the soup and fish. Sir Edward does himself
well. But when he started telling the old, old story his
style didn't draw me to him, and those feminine responses
that he hoped for just wouldn't come. So he fell into a
clinch and I picked one off the ground and hung it on
his chin, and ran like hell. His car was waiting to take
me home, so I climbed into it, meditating on the fate
that is worse than death, and drove away at considerable
speed.'

'It's his car that's outside now?' asked Magnus.

'Sure it is, and what the hell am I going to do with it?'

'You'd better take it to a garage and write to tell him
where it is.'

This recital did something to alleviate the discomfort
caused by her previous outburst, but her vivacity was forced
and could not wholly delete that oppressive memory. Slowly,
however, its quality changed. The feeling of revulsion, as
from contagious disaster, that Magnus and Meiklejohn at

first experienced, became in time a contrary impulse, and the revelation of a more pungent flavour in her character attracted them with increasing urgency. She had knowledge to give, as well as gaiety and boisterous charm, and that knowledge was of a seductive kind that may not be acquired in the smooth intercourse of society's conventional traffic. She drew them with the compulsion of a tale of piracy when the recital of honest voyaging but mildly draws. This became evident when, some while later, she looked at the clock and exclaimed with dismay at the lateness of the hour.

'Why didn't you tell me what time it was?' she demanded. 'Say, I'm scared to go home. My Aunt Elizabeth and my Uncle Henry have got the darndest ideas about late hours, and they won't give me a key. I guess they don't trust me too much either. I'm here on probation. I'll have to knock someone up, and there'll be hell to pay. I'm real scared.'

'Why not spend the night here?' said Meiklejohn thoughtfully. 'Then you can go home in the morning and tell your people that you missed the last train from Selkirk.'

'Don't be crazy,' said Frieda Forsyth.

'It's not a bad idea,' said Magnus, 'but you would be more comfortable in my flat. I have a spare bedroom.'

'My dear fellow,' exclaimed Meiklejohn, 'there's no point in her going to your flat when there's a perfectly good bed here.'

'I was only thinking of Mrs Dolphin,' Magnus explained. 'She might not be too pleased; but in my flat. . .'

'I don't care what Mrs Dolphin says!'

'No, but Miss Forsyth might. There would be no possible embarrassment if she came home with me.'

'I can absolutely guarantee that nothing would happen here to make her feel uncomfortable, and if. . .'

'But my flat is only a few hundred yards away, and. . .'

Frieda Forsyth interrupted them. 'There's no need to get feverish, for I'm going home. I know you're just being big-hearted, but I don't trust any big-hearted man at two o'clock in the morning. I'm going right now. Will either of you look after that stolen automobile for me?'

'Why, certainly,' said Meiklejohn. 'I'll ring up a garage and see that it's taken away at once.'

'Then I'll get a taxi and take you home,' said Magnus promptly.

Meiklejohn glared fiercely at Magnus, who opened the door with an air of calm authority.

'Will you have lunch with me tomorrow, Miss Forsyth?' asked Meiklejohn.

'Hell! No!' she answered. 'I won't be allowed out for a week after this. But I'll ring you up sometime. And thanks a lot for the drinks.'

Magnus called to a passing taxi, and they left Meiklejohn on the pavement contemplating with obvious ill-pleasure the purloined car.

'Your people sound rather unreasonable,' said Magnus. 'Why should they worry you with these nonsensical restrictions and treat you like child? Can't you talk to them and tell them how absurd they are?'

'I haven't got a nickel except what they give me. They paid my passage from New York, and when I arrived I had just two of everything: two vests, two pairs of pants, two dresses, and two dollars, and only the dollars were fit to be seen by daylight. If I said: "Uncle Henry, I think your way of living is absurd and nonsensical," he'd answer: "Niece Frieda, on the other side of that wall is the street. If you like the street better than my house, go to it!" But I don't, see? Uncle Henry's house is none too warm, but it's warmer than the sidewalk, and a wardrobe full of clothes, even though they were bought in Scotland, looks better to me than a couple of vests so full of holes that any respectable laundry would think they were fish-nets. So now you know.'

The taxi stopped in Rothesay Crescent, a semi-lune of tall houses, solemn in mien, dignified, wealthy in fact and implication. Here was respectability achieved in such perfection as to be magnificent indeed. Here was dignity wrought by endeavour and most zealously preserved. Here were roofs that covered success, and though that success might seem incomplete to an impartial observer—like a wall-pear that may grow no higher than its wall, nor stretch its branches north and south to contemplate its shadow at afternoon, but must be content to live in two dimensions only— yet the occupants of the houses showed in their bearing no trace of doubt, and obviously had made of their rich circumscription a cosmos that contented them. But that Frieda should live here seemed unnecessarily incongruous: as though a flying-fish should come to a goldfish bowl, a merlin dwell in the canary's cage, a Barbary sheep consort with a fat flock of Southdowns. Before Magnus could find the exact comparison she was saying good-night.

'Shall I wait to see that you get in all right?' he asked.

'Not on your life.'

'Then when shall I see you again? Will you dine with me sometime soon?'

Frieda looked at him thoughtfully. 'Come round on Saturday,' she said. 'Now scram!'

Magnus paid off the taxi and walked to Queen Street. It was not till the following morning that he remembered his solemn decision to concern himself no more with women, but to live in self-sufficiency with poetry for his sole companion. The lure of politics had already made a breach in that delectable isolation, and here he was foolishly offering hospitality to Frieda. But he consoled himself with the thought that poetry must be nourished by experience, and that when he did retreat to his ivory tower his writing would be strengthened by any casual harvest of knowledge he might in the meanwhile reap.

CHAPTER EIGHT

Except in its literal connotation the assertion that no man by taking thought can add a cubit to his stature, is clearly fallacious. Even when interpreted with a most narrow regard for meaning it comes dangerously near contradicting the more optimistic and equally authoritative view that faith will move mountains; while if one regards it as a generalized statement of mankind's inability to alter its mortal size, shape or constitution—and surely that is the meaning intended—it is immediately seen to be as inaccurate as a blind man's idea of Venice by moonlight. Within living memory the shape of civilized humanity has very materially changed: the paunch of middle-age follows to extinction dodo and dinosaur, the opulence of the female bosom has shrunk, and the philanthropic vastitude of the haunches has become a little thing. The corset that was wont to make of woman's waist an isthmus of Panama—a tropic narrowness between the North America of her breasts, the Argentine, the Braziliance, of her hips—the corset, like the cod-piece, has become a museum piece, for the female continent has dwindled to a tube that has no place for stays. The vanishing of man's tail when he came down from the trees and went into a hole in the ground, is no stranger a miracle than the diminishment of their backsides when women came out of the nineteenth century and into the twentieth. And so also, by arcane process, does woman change her tallness according to the seasons of fashion. At one time there is a plenitude of tiny creatures, the height, as they say, of a man's heart; at another time the streets are filled with the daughters of Anak, and the height of a man's heart is his boots. So far from being able to believe that human height, breadth, and thickness are predetermined and unchanging things, it seems more likely they are simply the manifestation of a mass intention to achieve certain measurements in those directions.

Considering, then, humanity's gross ability to change its appearance—especially marked, as it is, in the female of the species—there was little cause for surprise in the metamorphosis of Frieda Forsyth when she dined with Magnus in the grill-room of the Albyn Hotel. She was admirably dressed in laurel-green velvet, and her manner had undergone a change corresponding to that from breeches to a dark evening gown. Her demeanour was composed—there was even a touch of haughtiness in it—and her American accent was muted to the smallest intonation. She brushed aside a casual reference to the evening spent in Meiklejohn's flat, and talked with polite disinterest of Edinburgh's shops, of current events, and contemporary newspaper topics. But Magnus chose a dinner of beneficent variety and discovered a Burgundy of supernacular virtue, and presently, in that warm current, her reserve melted away and the conversation grew more cordial.

'I've just read your book,' she said, 'and I like it tremendously. It's a wonderful idea, and you certainly can write.'

Magnus was on the point of complaining that he had

written more than one book, and of asking to which she referred, but the generosity of her commendation changed his mind, and he wisely accepted her tribute to *The Great Beasts Walk Alone* without pretending dubiety as to the object of her praise. He began to explain the inner meaning of his novel, but she interrupted him with the assurance that she had fully understood it.

Magnus said: 'It was, in its way, an argument for reaction, and now I'm translating my views into practice. I've become a Scottish Nationalist. I've believed, as a general idea, in small nationalism for a long time, of course, but I've only recently joined the Party. I suppose Nationalism is discussed a good deal in your uncle's house?'

'They've never so much as mentioned it, to my knowledge,' said Frieda. 'What's it all about?'

Magnus briefly outlined the case for the independent sovereignty of Scotland, while Frieda listened without any remarkable interest.

'It sounds crazy to me,' she said. 'Why, your whole country's only the size of a game reserve, and why you should want to split it into two I just can't understand.'

'It would make life more interesting,' said Magnus. 'The world is getting monotonous, people are bored by the sameness of things, and the best tonic for boredom is variety. From a therapeutic point of view two countries are certainly better than one.'

'Then perhaps you would like to see the United States split up, and each of the forty-eight become independent with a president of its own?'

'I think that is a very good idea,' said Magnus.

'Why, now you *are* being crazy! What would happen to big business if that happened? All the corporations and newspapers and national banks and railways would go bankrupt, the dollar would slump, and life would be just impossible.'

With the zeal of a new-made reformer Magnus demanded: 'What do you mean by life?'

'I'll tell you right away. I once had a beau who came from Iowa, and he'd done some tall thinking and come to some handsome conclusions. He knew darned little about it in practice, but he was strong in theories of life, and he said it was a name for the physico-chemical qualities of protoplasm, and protoplasm was a kind of formaldehyde generated by lightning in wet weather, such as you generally get in this country. Now does that help you any?'

'No,' said Magnus. 'But just tell me again, will you? I'd like to remember your definition.'

The subject of politics was not further pursued. It seemed unlikely to foster that accordant spirit which is the principal objective in dining *à deux*, and Magnus abandoned it in favour of personal topics.

'What were you doing in America immediately before you left it?' he asked, and divided the remaining Burgundy fairly between his glass and Frieda's.

'Do you want me to go into the confessional? I suppose I was talking rather freely the other night, and I may have said more than I intended and more than was strictly accurate.'

'Then start again and tell me the true history of your life. Autobiography is fashionable.'

'You want a lot for the price of your dinner, don't you?'

'I'm frankly curious. You arrive from nowhere in the middle of the night, most unsuitably dressed, and your conversation is full of allusions to an exciting and, I must say, improbable career: the natural effect of that is curiosity, and curiosity is the mother of questions. And if you inspire curiosity it's only fair to answer the questions.'

'I'm not proud of everything I've done. I've been down on my luck for the last three years, and a girl can't be master of her fate in New York City when she hasn't the price of a Club sandwich in her bag. But I've lived! Oh, I'm not talking of protoplasm now, but of adult men and women, and I've learned more than you'll find in the text-books. Some of it was god-awful, but some of it was lovely, and there's times when I don't regret anything. But I'm not going back. I've had enough of the rough stuff, and now I'm Miss Forsyth of Rothesay Crescent, Edinburgh, and my life is ordered and comfortable and generally dull as ditchwater. And I like it.'

'Go on,' said Magnus. 'I want to hear more.'

'I'll bet you do!'

Magnus regarded her calmly. 'When did your father die?' he asked.

Gradually certain facts emerged, but parts of her story remained obscure; there were allusions that she did not stay to explain, and a tangle of times and places that she would not unravel. Her father, her Aunt Elizabeth's brother, had at one time been prosperous and a successful speculator in real estate in Florida and California. But he left very little money when he died, and shortly afterwards his widow fell in love and went to live with an aeroplane-pilot who had made some reputation by long-distance and endurance flights. Frieda disliked him—he was apparently a vulgar man, and, moreover, already married—and refused to join her mother's air-minded ménage. After learning shorthand and typewriting she discovered that her legs would earn more money than her fingers, and she obtained a place in the chorus-ranks of a Broadway theatre. But her engagement there terminated for some reason that she did not explain, and thereafter her fortunes declined. In bewildering succession she had been a stenographer, a school-teacher in some awful sun-shocked hamlet on the Mexican border, an artist's model, and a pedlar of subscription forms for a popular magazine. Some of these occupations had been forced upon her by the necessity to earn a living, but others she had wilfully entered through a restless desire to explore strange places and encounter unfamiliar people. For three months she had starved and washed dishes in a cheap restaurant in a North Carolina mill-town, hoping to obtain material for magazine or newspaper articles. But she had no aptitude for journalism, and her experience had been productive of little more than nausea and swollen hands. She said little of any personal connections she had formed, but now and again she mentioned a man's name with admiration, now and again spoke of one with strong distaste. It was fairly obvious that her odyssey had not been virginal, but she said nothing to confirm her experience of those unhappy depths to which she had referred in Meiklejohn's flat. Nor was her recital always chronological, for she travelled to and fro in time as erratically as she had done in place. But presently she spoke of her last weeks in New York, when apparently she had lived in almost complete destitution in the vicinity of Sheridan Square, dependent for most of her meals on the charity of strange casual acquaintances, and driven at last to claim help from her relations in Scotland. She heard of her mother's death some weeks before she wrote, and her appeal had been strengthened by this bereavement, though she was really too old to complain of being orphaned.

'How old are you?' Magnus asked.

'Twenty-six. Well, twenty-seven—just.'

Her aunt and uncle had responded generously and treated her with much kindness, though she found their domestic discipline irksome and was constrained to modify her language and devitalize her criticism to ensure a favourable reception for them in her new home. Her uncle, Henry Wishart, was a Writer to the Signet and senior partner in the old-established, wealthy and dignified firm of Graham, Coldstream, & Wishart, Writers to the Signet. His profession, however, had not brought him into contact with anything sordid in life—conveyancing was more profitable than crime—and he and his wife were protected by pachydermatous innocence from too suspicious inquiry into their niece's antecedents. She had satisfied their unimaginative curiosity by a very simple story of hard luck, she said.

'It would only make them unhappy if they knew all I've told you,' she continued, 'and if they heard the full story of my life, unexpurgated and with notes, they'd throw fits all over the house and me out of it. So I thought discretion was the better part and told them the children's version of my travel-tale.'

Magnus had listened to Frieda's narrative with attention, diverted only by the recurrent thought that, interesting though it was, he would rather be her present lover than gather allusions to his predecessors. He had been immediately attracted to her—as indeed had Meiklejohn—and now he was also aware of a certain jealousy, a competitive male instinct, that urged him to erase from her memory these antecedent bed-fellows by implanting himself in full possession of her consciousness. She was eminently desirable. She was long-limbed, quick in movement, fleet in appearance. Her throat was white and round, her eyes were bright with abundant vitality, and there was in her face such evidence of strength that she would never yield from folly or feebleness. She was worth conquering, and in a dozen ways her manner was provocative of conquest. But Magnus hesitated to say what was in his mind lest she should think he had offered her dinner merely as a bribe for going to bed. He did not want to seduce, and he had still less desire to appear as a seducer. He had a vanity that inclined him to value love only when it was an offering in freewill, when it appeared to be unearned increment, and how to achieve it in this guise, without the manifest arts of seduction, had often set him a pretty problem.

'What's on your mind?' said Frieda.

Magnus was tempted to speak the truth, but he remembered in time how people were offended by the spectacle of nakedness, and he decided on guile instead.

'I was thinking how much I would dislike going to bed with you,' he said.

'You needn't worry, you won't get the chance.'

Magnus waited. In a moment or two Frieda asked: 'What's wrong with me? You're the first man I ever met who went backwards if I gave him a chance to come forward.'

'I should be miserably jealous of all the others who had preceded me.'

Frieda, her elbows on the table, leaned forward and asked indignantly, 'Are you trying to insult me, or is that your ham-handed idea of a compliment? Because if so, I don't like it.'

'It was something between a critical observation and a confession.'

'Well, I'm not interested in your confessions. Anyway, it's time we were moving. You said you were going to take me to a music-hall, didn't you?'

They arrived at the theatre in time to see some part of a variety performance, and then returned to Rothesay Crescent. As the taxi drew to a standstill Magnus put his arm round Frieda's shoulders and kissed her. She drew back, grimacing, looked at him for a moment in the dusk, and suddenly returned his kiss.

'Now that's enough,' she said, and with no more delay, no backward looks, got out of the taxi and went indoors.

CHAPTER NINE

The nationalist movement into which Magnus had been drawn by the solicitations of his friend Meiklejohn and by the impetuosity of his own nature, suffered from an unusual handicap. The normal preamble to a revolution or separatist movement is a phase of violent oppression by some foreign power or social minority, and the Scottish Nationalists were unfortunate in not being able to point to any gross or overt ill-use at the hands of England. Except for a few surviving Jacobites they had no passionate red embers to fan to a certainty of flame, and the stolid temper of lowland Scotland was not inclined to waive the material advantages of stability for the gambler's increment of change. The Nationalists' arguments were many, and many of them were sound, but they had small chance of influencing people who had forgotten or not yet learned or were by nature disinclined to think for themselves. Economic reasons and valid patriotic sentiment are both insufficient, without assistance from some sensational train of incidents, to overcome the inertia of a modern democracy, and so the Scottish Independents consisted mainly of spirits congenitally factious, of a small minority, mostly young, who had read history and considered the economic problem in some detail and with an open mind, of remaining Jacobites, of a few Liberals who remembered the early doctrines of their party, of some eccentric ladies, and of an insecure working-class element, more susceptible to sentiment than their bourgeois neighbours, and who further believed that any change from the existing order of society would of necessity be for the better. Vested interests were openly hostile to the movement, and the great majority of middle-class people were indifferent to it with the calm indifference of ignorance.

Magnus soon discovered that Meiklejohn's estimate of the situation was quite erroneous, but to counter this he developed a firm conviction that the Nationalist cause was justified, and presently his conversation assumed the very tone and colour of Meiklejohn's optimism, and he would assure casual acquaintances and passing friends that the country was ripe for independence, and they, did they not

join the Party immediately, would be left with the laggards
and the slaves far in the rear of a triumphant nation marching
to the goal of its assured destiny.

He met Skene again, and argued with him hotly but
amicably. He was introduced to other Nationalists, and in
return for his, heard their perfervid views. His novel was
still selling, and the modest fame he had won by it assured
him, among friends, of a respectful hearing and persuaded
his fellow-members of the Party that his accession to it was
of unusual value. He wrote several times for the obscure
periodicals that favoured the cause, and Meiklejohn, braving
the proprietors' wrath, asked him to contribute a series of
articles on the general aspects of small nationalism to the
evening paper which he edited. He addressed two or three
small outdoor meetings, but his arguments were too remote
and his language too learned to rouse excitement in a street
audience. In a very short time, however, all the Nationalists
in Scotland had heard of their new recruit, and many of
them were gratified by the conversion of so distinguished
a person.

In the flush of this political excitement Magnus discovered
the subject for a poem. It was to be called *The Returning Sun*,
and it was to picture a Scotland glorious in the revisiting of
its ancient pride. But the first part was to satirize, very pun-
gently, the existing Scotland of commercialism and dullard
resignation to a dwindling name, and he was already taking
great pleasure in the composition of this prelude.

Being so strenuously occupied he did not see Frieda again
for rather more than a fortnight. He telephoned her once
or twice, but owing to his other engagements they were
unable to arrange a meeting. Then, late one afternoon, she
rang him up and asked if she might come to see him that
evening. It happened that Magnus was going to a soirée
given by one of the few wealthy Nationalist supporters,
a genial, enthusiastic, elderly Jacobite named Sutherland,
whose acquaintance many members of the Party were glad
to foster and whose hospitality they accepted with great
willingness. The soirée was not meant as idle entertainment,
for a political discussion had been arranged, but in spite of
this Magnus invited Frieda to dine and afterwards go with

him to Mr Sutherland's. He hoped, incidentally, to impress
her with the reality and importance of their aims, for that
afternoon he had been talking to a Mr Newlands, whose
duty it was to open the discussion, and Mr Newlands had
promised him fireworks.

He was a solid-seeming man, black-haired and dark of
complexion, whose manner of speech gave to every word the
semblance of deep significance. He spoke in a quiet voice
with ever and anon a sidelong glance of the eyes as though
to make sure that no English spy was listening. Then he
would thrust forward his head, tap his listener with a strong
forefinger, and speak in yet more thrilling tones.

He had said to Magnus, 'When Sutherland asked me to
speak tonight, I refused. It's a dilettantish crowd he gathers
there, not ripe for the real stuff, and I was afraid there
would be unpleasant scenes if I told them the truth. I don't
want women screaming in the middle of my speech. But he
assured me that he would back up all I cared to say, and
that all the people he had invited for tonight could stand
anything. So then I agreed to speak. I don't know what
the others mean to say, but there'll be no milk-and-water
about my address. There'll be no namby-pambyism from
me'.—He looked round cautiously to see if the English
Government had a spy in the vicinity.—'I'm going to detail
a plan for immediate action! I tell you, Merriman, there'll
be fireworks tonight!'

In high expectation Magnus warned Frieda to pay close
attention to what Mr Newlands would have to say: 'I know
you haven't a very great opinion of Nationalism, but you'll
change your mind when you've heard Newlands. There's
nothing dilettantish or impractical about him. His plans
are complete, and he's going to explain how to attain independence immediately.'

Mr Sutherland welcomed them with exuberant kindliness. He was wearing full Highland dress, and his plump
figure was of such noble circumference that his kilt might
almost have served as a tent. His face shone like an October
moon. His guests, of whom there were about thirty, were
already being pressed, not merely invited, to eat sandwiches
and drink whisky, cocktails, claret-cup, or several liqueurs,

and the atmosphere was already lively enough for the birth
of revolution, though many of the guests appeared hardly
suitable witnesses for so violent an accouchement. There
were several ladies of advancing years who spoke very
loudly to various mild-looking young men who listened
in gloomy silence. Hugh Skene was there, and so were
McVicar, Francis Meiklejohn, and Mrs Dolphin. A hearty
and excitable young man in a kilt was talking about vice
and other modern topics to a girl with a blank expression
and a long cigarette-holder. A pleasant motherly woman
was listening with commendable patience to a Breton separatist who knew but little English, and McVicar, still in
Meiklejohn's best evening trousers, was arguing under circumstances of equal difficulty with a polyglot Czech who had
learned all his languages in prison, and was handicapped by
a purely theoretical knowledge of their pronunciation.

Presently Mr Sutherland intimated that the formal discussion was about to commence, and ushered his guests
into another room where seats had been arranged for an
audience—an audience of potential speakers, that is.

Mr Newlands rose to open the debate. He stood beside
a window concealed by high curtains, and before saying
anything he looked rapidly behind them to make sure that
no hostile agent was concealed there. Then he inclined his
body forward, thrust at the air with a stiff forefinger, and
spoke in low conspiratorial tones.

'The time has come,' he said through clenched teeth, 'the
time has come to take *the next step!* We have talked long
enough about Scotland's grievances, and now the fateful
hour has arrived when we must redress them. Mere talk
is not enough. Talk has served its purpose, and now we
require action. What we must immediately decide is this:
the proper mode of action, and the proper hour for the
attack! But before explaining my plan of campaign—and
my plan is complete—I should like to review, as rapidly as
possible, the existing situation.'

Mr Newlands then proceeded to catalogue the Scottish
grievances and to reveal, with the help of copious notes,
the statistical plight of the shipbuilding industry, the textile
industries, of farming and fishing, of the railways and the

coal-mines. The figures he quoted were known, in varying degrees of accuracy, to everyone in the room, and though some listened with great pleasure as to a familiar and accepted creed, there were others who revealed a certain impatience. Among these was Magnus. While Mr Newlands had stood waiting for silence in which to begin his epochal speech, Magnus had whispered to Frieda: 'Now listen to this! We may make history tonight.' But as the monotonous recital of figures grew longer and longer, and the procession of accepted facts stretched its weary length through time, he became restless and finally dismayed. Beside him Frieda yawned widely.

Mr Sutherland fidgeted with his watch. Presently, in the politest and most genial way, he interrupted Mr Newlands and said he had already exceeded the time allotted for his speech, and he must call on Mr Skene to continue the discussion. There was some altercation at this decision, for as yet Mr Newlands had revealed nothing of his revolutionary plan, and many people wanted to know what it was. Magnus got up and suggested that in consideration of the importance of Mr Newlands's promised announcement he be allowed to continue his speech for another five minutes.

'I should require more time than that,' said Mr Newlands. 'I can't say exactly how long I need, for the speech I have prepared is, as you say, an important one, and there's nothing I could conscientiously leave out or even cut short.'

At this there woke a babel of talk, for nearly everybody had prepared a speech at least as important, in his or her estimation, as Mr Newlands's, and while no one desired to prohibit that gentleman from speaking, everyone naturally wished for an opportunity to air his or her views. Gradually the confusion of tongues subsided, not so much in voluntary abandonment of argument as under compulsion, for now a clear female voice was dominating the storm, and before its authority the others fell mute.

The floor had been taken by a young woman who bore a striking resemblance to popular pictures of Joan of Arc, and she was talking with evangelical earnestness about Ireland. Her fluency was remarkable but her meaning was somewhat obscure, for though it was obvious that she had a great admiration for Ireland and thought that Scotland should follow its political example *vi et armis*, it also appeared that she was a fervent pacificist and desired to abolish all weapons from howitzers to rook-rifles. She concluded her speech with a rhetorical gesture and a tangle exordium in which Scotland was commanded to be true to herself.

Then Mr Sutherland introduced Hugh Skene, and the poet, with burning intensity, declared that he was a Communist. But he also referred, with dark elusive details, to some private economic policy of his own that was, apparently neither communistic nor capitalistic, but ideally suited to modern conditions. He refused to explain the system because, as he logically declared, an explanation would be wasted on people still ignorant of its fundamental hypotheses. Those hypotheses they must discover for themselves. His advocacy of nationalism, he said, was mainly due to his desire to see this system established, at first in Scotland and then throughout the world. Lest his hearers should consider him a materialist, however, he hotly denied any concern with the increase of wealth that might be expected to accrue from his policy. 'I have no interest whatsoever in prosperity,' he declared, and left the uncommon impression that here was a man who advanced an economic theory for purely aesthetic reasons.

He was followed by McVicar, who quoted a few equations from Karl Marx, a recondite excerpt from *The Golden Bough*, and a long sentence from *Ulysses*. He created a strong feeling that Scotland was in the throes, if not of renascence, at least of some experience equally shattering. After his address the action became general, and it was hardly possible to distinguish one speech from another. Most of them referred to deer-forests, Bannockburn, rationalization, and Robert Burns, and every third sentence began with the first-person singular pronoun. When the fray grew scattered Mr Sutherland rose and said they were all pleased to have with them, that evening, the Party's distinguished new recruit, Mr Merriman, and now would Mr Merriman continue the discussion?

By this time Magnus was in a somewhat contentious ill-humour, and he spoke with unnecessary vehemence.

'I am a Scottish Nationalist,' he said, 'because I am a Conservative. I believe in the conservation of what is best in a country, and what is truly and desirably typical of it, and I believe that small nations are generally more interesting, more efficiently managed, and more soundly established than big ones. I am not a Communist, a Socialist or a Pacifist and I strongly protest against the association with Scottish Nationalism of any tenets of Communism, Socialism or Pacifism. Communism is an Oriental perversion, Pacifism is a vegetarian perversion, and Socialism is a blind man's perversion. There are two essential factors in any national movement: a leader or leaders of a suitable kind, and a sufficient number of people who can be persuaded or compelled to follow them. At present Scotland possesses neither of these factors, and our first task is to find them.'

This speech was received with great indignation, and half the audience rose to protest publicly while half looked round for suitable confidants to receive their private resentment. But Mr Sutherland quelled the disturbance by loudly announcing that the time was opportune for more refreshment, and began to shepherd his guests into the former room, where the supply of sandwiches had been renewed and still more bottles stood close-ranked on the vast sideboard.

Magnus found himself buttonholed by the young woman who looked like Joan of Arc. She introduced herself as Beaty Bracken. Magnus had heard a good deal about her, and he was interested to meet her, for she had recently achieved fame by removing a Union Jack from the Castle and placing it in a public urinal. She began to speak familiarly of war and peace, and said that another great war was surely imminent, for on all sides people were talking of it and it was well known that there was no such breeder of war as talk of war.

Magnus said, 'Then surely it would be wise of you to stop talking about it.'

'But women must talk about it, because women can do so much to prevent it,' said Miss Bracken earnestly.

'Is woman's influence always pacific? I seem to remember historical examples of rather warlike women.'

'Ah, but not women who were mothers!'

'In the last war there were plenty who boasted of having "given their sons to Britain". From Sparta onwards history is full of belligerent mothers.'

'But they went into battle beside their sons.'

'Who did?' asked Magnus, 'and when?'

'There was Dechtire for one.'

'Who was she?'

'She was the mother of Cuchullin. She was also an ancestress of mine.'

By this time Magnus had quite forgotten the subject of the argument, and it was clear that Miss Bracken had never known. He told her, in reply to her claim on Cuchullin's blood, that he himself was descended from St Magnus of Orkney, and then he was extricated from the fog of Irish mythology and Norse genealogy by a vivacious lady with heavy ear-rings, an eager vulpine look, and a voice like a macaw's.

'Mr Merriman!' she cried, 'I've been dying to meet you! I've read your book. Such a terribly naughty book! Such a terribly naughty man you must be! It frightens me to death to talk to you really, but I feel I must. I told my husband I was going to meet you tonight, and he told me I'd better take care. Ha-ha-ha! What a lot you must know to write a book like that! However did you learn it all? No, don't tell me, don't tell me. I couldn't bear to hear it. *Too* naughty! But I love to read about it. And now you're a Nationalist, too. Isn't that splendid? I think we're all splendid, all we young people who believe in Scotland's future and are prepared to work for it and fight for it if necessary. I should love another war, though I couldn't bear to see people killed, of course. But I think I could do anything for Scotland, I'm *so* enthusiastic about Nationalism, though my husband says it's all rubbish.

At this point Magnus felt a heavy hand on his arm and Mrs Dolphin said to him, 'There's a gentleman here who's very anxious to meet you, and he's got to go in a few minutes to catch a train. So will you come and talk to him now?'

As soon as they were out of earshot of the vulpine lady she said: 'I heard that creature shouting away at you and I knew you couldn't stand her blethering much longer, so I just came to rescue you. But it's true enough there's a man wanting to talk to you, and that's Mr Macdonell, who's a Vice-President of the Party, and a good man too. He's got his head screwed on the right way. He's not like some of these others who talk as if they'd taken a dose of castor-oil and couldn't help it.'

George Macdonell was a short, red, freckled young man on whose very youthful features sat a premature look of statesmanship. He had a serious manner and a deep ringing voice. He said, 'You made the only sensible speech this evening, Mr Merriman, but you mustn't say things like that again if you're going to be a politician. You must learn tact. You can't afford to alienate people if your primary aim is to obtain their votes. You can frighten them or flatter them, but you shouldn't tell them the simple truth unless you've calculated its effect.'

'I'll be damned if I turn Socialist or pacifist for any quantity of votes.'

'If you were contesting an election you would have a large number of Socialists in your electorate, and it would be foolish to offend them.'

'You're not one of them are you?'

Macdonell laughed shortly. 'No!' he said.

Magnus began to feel that this young man was a new Machiavelli, and his admiration grew large. He asked several questions, and Macdonell's answers were all very satisfactory. Magnus's spirits rose, and when the guests began to go he shook hands warmly with his new acquaintance and swore they would stir Scotland yet.

He looked for Frieda and found her listening, though without sympathy, to Meiklejohn, who was trying to persuade her of the benefits of Nationalism.

'Take me out of this crazy joint,' she said, 'and for God's sake, don't say another word about politics. I'm sick to death of them.'

They said good-bye to their host, but found it difficult to tell him how much they had enjoyed his party because of the vigorous music played by a piper at his very elbow. Magnus asked Meiklejohn to come with them to his flat for a last drink, but Meiklejohn, with the excuse that he had work to do, refused. Such rejection of conviviality was unusual in him.

Frieda explained: 'I suppose I wasn't too polite to him about this darned Nationalism. He will talk about it. I've been out with him a couple of times, and he'll talk of nothing else, and the whole sad story just gives me a pain.'

'That depreciates you, not Nationalism.'

'Now I ask you, how can a movement be worth anything that depends for its existence on a crowd of nuts and bums and high-brow poets and side-show exhibits like we saw tonight?'

'Every revolution, from Christianity downwards, has begun by attracting the more volatile elements of society.'

Frieda said with considerable surprise, 'Now that's the very thing that Meiklejohn said when I asked him the same question. What do you make of that?'

Magnus thought it unnecessary to tell her that he himself had first heard this plausible explanation from Meiklejohn and answered, 'There's nothing to prevent a problem being correctly solved by more than one person.'

'Say, are you religious as well as Scotch?'

'No, just superstitious.'

'Honest to God? You really are? Do you believe in witches and that sort of thing?'

'Certainly I do. My great-grandmother, in Orkney, was a rather well-known witch.'

'No, I'm serious, because I was once scared out of my life, or darned near it, by a witch. That was in York County, Pennsylvania. I'd been hitch-hiking, and I'd got a lift from a drummer who was going to see his girl. Well, it was about ten o'clock of a pitch-black night when we reached the village where she lived, and the wonder is we didn't go right past without seeing it, for there weren't more than five houses on one side of the street and three on the other. It was the darned-loneliest place I ever struck, and the wind was howling like a wolf and lifting the snow off the road—it was in January when this happened—and the whole country seemed empty except for those five houses. And there wasn't so much as a light in any of them. But the drummer was a good guy and he went with me and knocked on the door of one of them, and presently a woman came down. She didn't seem too pleased to see us. She was Pennsylvania Dutch, and kind of stupid. But after a while she agreed to let me come in and to give me a bed for the night, and then the drummer went off to his girl's home across the street. He didn't want to take me there till he'd had a chance to explain about me, and tell his girl I was only someone he was giving a lift to. So he said good-night and promised he'd come and see me in the morning, and bring his girl with him. But he was back long before that. Well, the old Dutch woman began to make up a bed for me in the parlour, and while she was fixing it she asked me who I was and where I was going, and so on. She asked me who was the guy I was with, and where he was going. So I told her he'd come to see his girl. 'What girl is that?' she said. She spoke pretty bad English. It sounded as though she was grumbling at something all the time. I said the girl's name was Elsa, and that gave the old woman a surprise. You could see she was upset. She stood still for quite a while, with a blanket in her hands and her mouth half open. Then she said, 'Elsa, Elsa!' and something in German, I don't know what. So I asked her if anything was wrong with Elsa, and if she had a nice home, and if the family were nice. The old woman got all excited at that, angry, and yet kind of scared as well. Oh, they were a very nice family, she said, but the way she said it you just didn't believe it. "Her father is a carpenter," she said. "He makes coffins, but he don't make them too good." Well, just then there was the hell of a knocking at the door, and there was my drummer back again. He was white as cheese, and he was so frightened he couldn't speak. I guess his mouth was too dry. He was shaking all over, and when he tried to say something he just made funny noises. Then he sagged at the knees and slumped down, dead-out in a faint.'

The story was interrupted by their arrival at Magnus's flat, and Frieda postponed its conclusion till Magnus should have found decanter and glasses and they might be comfortably settled. She took off her hat and coat and stood before a mirror, patting her hair.

'Aren't you going to light the fire?' she asked.

'I can't find any matches.'

'Look in my bag: there's some there.'

Magnus opened the bag that she had laid on a table and discovered a magpie's nest of small articles: there were two keys, a powder-box, some loose change, a cigarette case, a lipstick in a metal container, a pocket-comb, several letters and, most remarkable of all, a tooth brush. It was not a new brush that she had just bought, for the bristle tips were faintly tinged with some pink dentifrice. The reason for its presence among articles of strictly daytime use was not immediately apparent, but after no more than a moment's thought Magnus, with characteristic optimism, came to a feasible conclusion.

Frieda, turning away from the mirror, spoke sharply: 'Here, give me that bag! I'll find the matches.'

'I've got them,' said Magnus, and put the bag down. Frieda looked at him suspiciously. He wasted no time but clipped her in muscular arms, kissed her enthusiastically, and pulled her on to a sofa. She resisted with a brisk display of energy, wriggled in his grasp, turned her head this way and that, gasped fiercely a command to let go, an adjuration to stop, and then relaxed, and then grew fierce again—but not now to thrust away, for now she drew him to her, holding as strong as he did, nor waited passive to be kissed, but foraged on her behalf.

Presently Magnus said: 'You're going to be late tonight.'

'You bet I am,' she answered.

'What will Uncle Henry say?'

'Uncle Henry's gone to London, and Aunt Elizabeth's gone with him, and they won't be back for a week.'

Two or three hours later Magnus woke from dreaming of a large Dutchwoman who was spreading bedclothes in an empty coffin. He turned over, remembering Frieda's unfinished story, and immediately the terror of the dream vanished beneath the occursion of pleasure. Like rocks before a flooding tide it disappeared, and over his senses an army of delight marched with music. Frieda, still sleeping, lay beside him. They had left a table-lamp burning, for she had none of that modesty which blemish and physical imperfection so respectably beget. She had undressed with as much pleasure as the owner of one of Rembrandt's great pictures will draw a curtain and show to a chosen visitor that masterly drawing, that magical light, the gleam as indescribable as that which glorified the visible form of the gods:

οἷα Θεοὺζ ἐπενήνοθεν αἰὲν ἐόνταζ

And as use makes perfectness, so Frieda had achieved it by implementing her beauty with the grace, dexterity, and cordiality of her love-making. Here, thought Magnus, is the perfect mistress, and suddenly he chanted:

Io Hymen Hymenaee io,
Io Hymen Hymenaee!

But then he frowned and muttered a rude objurgation, and grew unquiet with vexation to remember he had once quoted that marriage-hymn while Margaret Innes lay beside him: and he had deliberately thrust Margaret out of his memory, for she had disappointed him and made a fool of him by spoiling a fine romantic image with the disclosure of reality. In a variety of ways it was unpleasant to be reminded of Margaret, for he was uncomfortably aware that he had not treated her very well, and to recall the extravagant protestations he had made to her caused him exquisite embarrassment.

Frieda stirred in her sleep, stretched, and woke.

'Heartsease!' said Magnus. 'Honeyheart, beatitude! Wake up and tell me the story about the witch.'

'The hell I will! I want to go to sleep.'

'Wake up! I want to hear about the witch.'

'Because you've got a family interest in them? I bet your grandmother didn't behave like this one in Pennsylvania.'

'It was my great-grandmother. She was my great-grandfather's third wife, and she ill-wished the first two so that they died in childbirth. Then she married him.'

'Don't put ideas into my head, or I'll marry you.'

'You'll do no such thing. I'll cosset you and comfort you and bewilder you with love, but I'm damned if I'll marry you. I've got Blake's ideas about marriage: "Whoso touches a joy as he flies, lives in Eternity's sunrise, but whoso binds to his heart a joy doth the winged life destroy." Besides, I think you're a witch yourself: they milk from the moon a shining white liquor, as white as you, and sometimes a pool of it is found in high moorland places, and to touch it will drive a man mad.'

Magnus invariably grew loquacious when he was in high spirits, and he continued to talk enthusiastically about witch-craft and to relate several Orkney superstitions, one or two authentic, but the rest of which were his own invention. By and by Frieda said, 'Say, did you wake me up to hear your stories, or to hear mine?'

'I'm sorry! I was only filling in time till you were ready.'

'Well, if you want to know what happened, I'll tell you. But it's no joke: remember that! I was scared to death at the time, and I'm still scared when I think about it. Well, I told you about the guy coming back, and then fainting? The old Dutchwoman undid his collar and I rubbed his hands, and presently he got better, and as soon as he could sit up he wanted us to go back with him to his girl's house. The old woman said no, she wouldn't move a step outside the door, not at that time of night. But Hyson—that was the drummer's name—he was just about frantic to go, though he could hardly stand by himself. So we talked some more to the old woman, and by and by she got a shawl, grumbling all the time and kind of frightened too, and out we went. The wind was blowing the snow up in a little vortex, and it was so cold it took your breath away. I don't know if it was owing to that or to something else, but just outside the other house I got a feeling as though I couldn't go in, no, not for anything. The old woman walked right in, though, and I thought I'd better follow her. Then we found the girl. She was lying on her bed, with the covers rumpled back and her nightgown torn, and she'd queer torn marks, some of them like tooth-marks, on her arms and breast. She was dead all right. Hyson just put his head in the covers and began to cry, and the old woman stood there shaking all over. Well, I thought I'd better see if we couldn't get some help, but there wasn't another soul in the house. So I asked the old woman what we should do, but she'd only speak German and I don't know what she said, till she began to talk about the girl's father, who was a carpenter. She seemed to think it was all his fault because he didn't make his coffins out of good wood or screw down the lids properly. I didn't see what that had got to do with it, but Hyson looked up and screamed, 'Witches, you fool! If a witch hears of a corpse that isn't properly buried she'll come and tear it to bits with her teeth. They're witch's marks on Elsa!" Then he cried again, sobbing and kind of holding his breath. It made you feel cold all over, and sick, too, to look at those marks after hearing that. I asked the old woman where Elsa's father was now, but she wouldn't answer. Hyson stopped crying, too, and just sat quiet. We all sat there, saying nothing. We sat there till morning, and we were so stiff with cold we could hardly move then.'

Magnus felt a pricking of the flesh and his blood seemed to run more chilly in his veins as he listened to this unpleasant story, and when Frieda spoke of that frozen room and the witch-marks on Elsa's body he even grew a little frightened of her—though he would indignantly have denied this— for she had sat there and seen the strangely torn flesh and carried as if by infection some tinge of the horror with her. But he made an effort to judge the story with common-sense scepticism and asked, as casually as he could, 'And what happened the next day? What was the explanation of the girl's death?'

'God knows,' said Frieda. 'I didn't stay to hear. I said good-bye to them as soon as it was light and went out and stopped a car that was going to Harrisburg, and I got a ride as far as that. I'd had enough of that darned village. Wild horses wouldn't have drawn me back.'

'But what do you think was the explanation?'

'Say, I thought you *believed* in witches? And now when I tell you a story about them you ask me to explain it away. That doesn't seem reasonable to me.'

Magnus was very unhappy. His exultation, that had risen like a wave, had fallen like a wave, and when Frieda's voice grew sharp to rebuke his scepticism he felt a small but definite tremor of fear. He remembered inopportunely a verse about strange women whose feet go down to death and whose steps take hold on hell, and he recalled a story about a succubus, and he wished that he had lived more virtuously and thought hopefully of the rectitude he would henceforth pursue. The lamplight shone white on Frieda's shoulder, and the discomforting thought returned of the witches' virus, that pale and shining fluid which is sometimes found on high heaths and is poison. All the tales of horror he had ever heard, and even those that he himself had confected, assailed his imagination, and in his ears the old Dutchwoman muttered rumours of hex-men.

Presently Frieda, wearying of inactivity, said, 'Well, there's no use worrying about something that happened three thousand miles away,' and approached him with tentative caresses. But Magnus could not strengthen his spirit nor rouse himself to respond, and the night, unflowering, dwindled bleakly to the dawn.

CHAPTER TEN

Henry Wishart had gone to London on business, and his wife had accompanied him partly for pleasure and partly from domestic habit, for she and her husband had rarely been separated for more than a day or two during the thirty years of their marriage. A matter of disputed inheritance in which the firm of Graham, Coldstream, and Wishart was interested had gone to the House of Lords on appeal, and Henry Wishart had accompanied it to explain to their lordships the difficulties they were required to unravel. In one way and another the case was delayed and judgment deferred, and two weeks elapsed before he could return to Edinburgh. During that interval of unguarded liberty Frieda fell seriously in love with Magnus, and Magnus was gravely hindered in the prosecution of his political studies and in the composition of his new poem.

He had found inspiration for the first part—that which should deal satirically with the existing order of society—in the National War Memorial in the Castle. This building, the most distinguished piece of recent architecture in Scotland, was of curious interest in that, without shame or concealment, it glorified the martial spirit while all elsewhere in the land it was considered fashionable and proper to exalt the name of peace. The Memorial contained, in addition to the names of the dead, trophies of the Scottish regiments and catalogues of their battle honours. Considering these

far-flung names that smelt of Indian temples and desert
sand, of fields in France and roads in the Peninsula, of
China and the islands of the sea, Magnus perceived that
Pericles' praise of the dead—*All the earth is the grave of gallant men*—might, with but little exaggeration, be rewritten
as *All the earth is the grave of Scottish men*. And dwelling on
the sound and savour of these names he began to compare
them with the nomenclature of Scotland itself, and found the
latter trivial beside them: he set Ramillies, Blenheim, and
Malplaquet against Falkirk, Peebles and Troon; he balanced
Chitral, Delhi, and Mysore with Motherwell, Galashiels,
and Dundee; he contrasted Balaclava and Waterloo, Anzac
and Coronel, with Forfar and Paisley and Cowdenbeath; and
always the chorus of battle names, of the names of the places
where men had died in bravery, was louder, more melodious,
and apparelled in more glorious associations than the trios
of peaceful names, of the names of the places where men
merely lived. As it was absurd to believe that the reason for
this difference was the superiority of death to life—his very
bowels found blasphemy in the suggestion—Magnus was led
to believe that Blenheim and Waterloo and Chitral rang in his
mind with prouder euphony than Peebles and Paisley merely
because Death, that distasteful creature, had in the former
places worn brighter vestments, a more glorious bearing,
than Life, that lovable thing, was encouraged to wear in the
latter. With this incongruity in his mind he walked about till
he came to a great bronze panel on which were sculptured in
high relief representations of the different kinds of men who
had served in the last war. There were soldiers laden with
the panoply of battle, so thickly thewed and tall they could
without stumbling carry rifle and three hundred cartridges,
a great pack, a steel helmet, and a cartload of Picardy mud;
there were sailors, severe of gaze to watch for periscope and
reef and mine, and wrapped in oilskins against the bitterness
of the North Sea; there were subalterns whose youth was
grim, not gay; young airmen who had lived like hawks and
poets and paladins and died the quick death of dragon-flies;
there were solid stubborn ploughmen transformed by discipline to grandeur; there were nurses of gentle gallantry and
grave beauty—and leading them in their unplanned path to

the laurel-grove a piper marched—O glory and grave of the McCrimmons!—whose pibroch like an evening wave lipped all the gleaming bronze.

Standing before the strong heroism of these figures Magnus began to think of living men, and imagined a panel that should represent, not his countrymen who had died, but his countrymen who still existed. Piety, reverence, and glory ran from his mind, and so violent was their outgoing that the inrush of contrary emotions was savage, and he filled his imagined frieze with the ignoblest spawning of the time: weaklings, fools, and knaves; dullards, fat profiteers, and starving dole men; the chatterers, the rushers to and fro, the self-doubters and the self-satisfied; with snivelling piety and supercilious unbelief; with empty heads and full bellies; with ossified Tories and rattle-brained Socialists; with pimping prettiness and ugliness too mean to hide itself; with cowardice, hypocrisy, greed, stupidity, and all the other ailments and emblems and deformities that satirists, from the earliest time, have discovered to be the characteristic features of humanity. Excited by this revelation he hurried home and worked on his poem with pious indignation and a fierce desire to cleanse and reform his degenerate country.

But though his brain was able to see visions and conceive a high poetic purpose, his flesh was irrepressible flesh, his blood had a stronger flow than the pale ichor of his mind, and his bone was simply the rude salts of the earth. When Frieda became his lover his fury dwindled and the zest departed from his hunting of iniquity. He was still convinced that the times were corrupt and men were base—with the possible exception of a few Nationalists—but in her company, as though she came attended by a moral thaw, this reformative indignation melted like an iceberg before the erosion of summer seas. And even when he sat alone his larger thoughts were likely to be interrupted by small thoughts of her, if not by the ringing of the telephone or her actual appearance at his door. He pursued his love-making with increasing interest and some uneasiness.

Frieda spent a part of every day with him, and often betrayed discretion by extending her visits far into the night.

She frankly confessed that her first surrender had been premeditated and inspired by nothing more than unruly appetite. Magnus, who thought she had already fallen in love with him, was somewhat perturbed by this admission.

'The truth is that celibacy doesn't suit me' said Frieda. 'I'd lived a pure life, unspotted by the world, for six months, and purity had gotten a taste like stale bread. I was tired of it. And as I'd seen a kind of dewy look in your eye, once or twice, I thought I could tap at your door without being treated as if I were trying to sell summer frocks to a colony of nudists.'

'But you don't mean that you were ready to go to bed with anyone at all?'

'Not anyone, perhaps, but I can think of a whole lot of men who'd have suited me pretty well.'

Magnus, his pride hurt, said warmly, 'I'm not narrow-minded, and I'm not a Puritan, but I think that's a detestable statement. You're admitting yourself to be shamelessly wanton and completely immoral.'

'Well, you slept in the same bed, so the same bad words apply to you.'

'Not at all. I thought you were in love with me.'

'And were you in love with me?'

'I was very fond of you, and very interested in you.'

'And that's quite enough to excuse a man playing happy families under the blanket, is it?'

'A man's conduct can't be judged in the same way as a woman's,' said Magnus patiently. 'There are many things that a man can do quite naturally and quite properly that would be improper and undesirable if a woman did them.'

'Say, there's more whiskers on your ideas than the world has seen since the Hairy Ainus disappeared. Your morals are something that an archaeologist would be interested in, but nobody else. You want women to be pure and unattainable, but you like to have a good time with them just the same. Well, I'm going to teach you a thing or two before I've done with you.'

Magnus began to expose the flaws in her argument: 'All I implied was that I dislike the idea of promiscuity. And I do dislike it. I don't approve of general looseness and the complete abandonment of impulse that you apparently would agree to.'

'How many women have you made love to in your young life?' Frieda interrupted.

'That's got nothing to do with the question. I was discussing general principles.'

'Yes, you would! And so long as your principles are all right you can act just as you please.'

'Principles are very important and useful even though you don't always live up to them.'

'Now you're putting hypocrisy on the programme.'

Magnus stood up and shouted: 'I'm doing nothing of the sort! And if you haven't the wit to distinguish between the possession of principles and a pretence to principles then you ought to consult an alienist, though I don't suppose he could do anything for you. You're one of those people who want to abolish all the rules in the world because you're too damned lazy and incompetent to learn them. But I say the more rules the better, because then life would be more difficult and more interesting: there would be more rules to break. And that's not hypocrisy! You want to bring everything to a dead level, so that no one can be reproached with going downhill, and no one may be tempted to sweat and lose his breath climbing uphill. There used to be two sorts of women at least—good and bad—but you'd like to abolish the difference and make one kind only: automatic!'

'To hell with you!' said Frieda. 'I'm bad anyway.'

She picked up her skirts and danced an agile mimicry of the age's tarantism, a rapid, knee-slapping, haunch-wagging, shaking and shivering nimbleness that flattered the Creator's ingenuity in devising joints and muscles.

'You just hate the sound of your own voice, don't you?' she asked. Then she threw a couple of cushions at Magnus, who threw them back, and the debate finished in a wrestling-match, that presently grew gentler. Arm-locks became embraces, a head-hold the prelude to a caress. Argument vanished like cream in the cat's saucer, and disagreement was obliterated by the emollience of love's amiable gossip.

Within three or four days Frieda had expiated her immorality by very seriously falling in love. In the excitement of earliest intimacy she had talked with greater detail than before, and with a certain boastfulness, about her previous liaisons, but now when Magnus, still curious, asked further questions, she grew sulky and taciturn.

One day she exclaimed, with heat and unhappiness, 'I never want to speak again about anything that happened to me in America. I never want to think about it. I used to be proud of having lived as I have, and done everything I wanted to without fear of the consequences, and I used to despise people who had lived easy, sheltered, virtuous lives. I never regretted anything till now. But now there's a hundred things I hate to think of, and I wish . . .'

'What?' said Magnus.

'That I had never loved anyone but you.'

Magnus experienced a variety of emotions. He was in truth very fond of Frieda, and even in love with her if to be in love does not necessarily connote resignation to love's continuance, but may exist in satisfaction with the moment only. He was flattered by her complete surrender, and slightly perturbed by the responsibility that it put upon him. And he was distressed by the sight of her distress. He did his best to comfort her with a variety of casuistical arguments, telling her that what would disfigure one person might well leave another healthy and whole; that innocency's loss was gain to experience; that remorse for sins of commission was less bitter than regret for omitted sins; that what had happened yesterday was dead as Nineveh and all its deeds; and that her recital of misadventure, so far from making a distasteful impression, had filled him with admiration for the courage with which she had oversailed adversity.

Frieda suddenly stood up, thrust back her hair with impatient fingers, pulled her dress straight, and said: 'Hell! I'm getting soft. I didn't mean what I was saying then. There's no man on earth can dominate me, and I'm not dependent on any man. I can look after myself. I'm going now; I want to get some air.'

'It's raining.'

'Then I'll get wet too. Give me my hat.'

But when Frieda came back on the following afternoon she brought an old silver snuff-box that she had bought

for Magnus in a second-hand shop in the High Street, and
on succeeding occasions she presented him with a book,
a silk muffler, and a pair of cuff-links. These presents
Magnus accepted with more embarrassment than pleasure,
for though a young man may bestow gifts in a mood of
lightest dalliance, a young woman seldom gives anything
away except under the compulsion of serious intentions.
Woman's nature is conservative, and her presents to a
man are tainted with a suspicion that they are ultimately
destined for the enrichment of her own household. Magnus,
however, put this disturbing thought from him, and restored
his self-respect by purchasing a hand-bag and a handsomely
illustrated edition of *Candide* that together cost, according to
his calculations, some ten shillings more than the aggregate
price of Frieda's gifts.

   She was delighted to receive them, and showed a pleasure
in possessing them that was childish in its extravagance.
She thanked him so warmly, so enthusiastically, that he
was touched by her joy and used her with a somewhat
elderly fashion of affection that she appeared to welcome.
Presently they sat together turning the pages of *Candide*,
while Magnus talked volubly about the charm of irony
and condemned the English habit of mind that could not
appreciate it. 'For,' he said, 'they cannot stand ridicule.
The whole policy of their lives is designed to ensure comfort of mind and body, and though they pride themselves
on their sense of humour, their humour consists of little
gobbets of laughter stuck in the chinks of their walls to
keep out the wind of criticism or contrary opinion. Irony
is one of the chief graces of literature, but the English will
have none of it, because it makes them feel uncomfortable.
They won't allow tragedy on their stage or in their novels,
because tragedy makes them think; though sometimes they
accept it in translations from a foreign tongue, as then the
tragedy obviously occurred too far from home to be of any
importance to them. And they won't take a serious view of
comedy because when comedy is taken seriously it becomes
as disturbing as tragedy. All they want and all they will
pay to see or read are aphrodisiacs, hobbledehoy farces,
multifarious peacocking pageants, and something that will

curdle the blood for twenty hectic minutes in the benign assurance of an ultimate happy ending.'

Frieda would now let Magnus talk as long as he liked, and she could be happy in listening to him no matter what he said. But at this point Magnus remembered the noble Pococurante—that man of so prodigious a genius that nothing would please him—and discovering that he himself had been talking in Pococurantist manner grew elated to find that Voltaire's satire was still living, and began to search the volume in front of him for the description of Candide's visit to the learned Venetian. In the unfamiliar edition, however, he could not readily discover it, so he went to look for an older copy that was among the eighty or a hundred books he had brought with him from America or acquired since his return to Britain. Frieda joined him in the search.

Some of his books stood disorderly on shelves in his sitting-room, others lay on a table in the bedroom, and a shabby *Candide* was at last discovered in a trunk, together with a vast untidy pile of manuscript, a bundle of letters, a passport, a revolver, a sheaf of newspaper cuttings, a copy of *Ulysses*, an odd volume of the Greek Anthology, the Koran, two American detective novels, and three dress-shirts.

Frieda made female noises of disgust at the sight of this disarray and proceeded to pull out drawers and examine wardrobe and cupboards for further evidence of domestic confusion. She professed dismay at what she found, and with expostulation, with odium and reproach, held out for Magnus's inspection shirts that had no buttons on them, socks that required darning, and a medley of articles that lay together without form or order wherever temporary convenience had decided they should be concealed.

Magnus watched her activities with mild interest. 'Time is too valuable to waste on the elaboration of a routine, on compiling laundry lists, card-indexes, or systems of life,' he said.

'Whenever you find people who keep everything orderly and docketed and filed for reference you can be sure that they have so much time to waste, that they have to pretend they are busy by constantly tidying things up. And all labour-saving systems are like machinery that requires continual attention to keep it in running order. The man whose brain is always busy is opportunistic in his life: he has no time to be anything else.'

'Who darns your socks for you?' Frieda demanded.

'Nobody. I buy new ones.'

'You need someone to look after you.'

'Nonsense! I look after myself perfectly well, and I can't bear people fussing over me.'

'In a few years' time you'll be a permanent bachelor with odd habits and nasty manners, whom people will entertain only as a curiosity, and only once at that, and you'll get lonelier and lonelier, and then you'll begin to get dirty, and you'll finish up by hating everybody and yourself worst of all.'

'My God, Frieda, you talk a lot of rubbish! Do you think, simply because I don't keep my socks in one drawer and my shirts in another, and because I don't want to get married, that I'm going to be a hermit, a heteroclite, a freak, a cave-dweller, a Stylite sitting in a privy on a pole with my lap for a parlour and my beard for a blanket and my shoulders a perch for rooks? I'm one of the few people now alive who maintain a free, pleasant, and reasonable existence, and because of that you prophesy for me not the beatitude which I deserve, but some ghastly future of eccentric misery. I call that damned unreasonable.'

Frieda ignored all but a fragment of this entangled remonstrance.

'Why don't you want to get married?' she asked, and sat beside him on the bed. 'You'd be able to work far better if you had someone to look after things for you, and you'd be a lot happier than you are now.'

'I'm perfectly happy as I am.'

'You said the other night that you were discontented five days out of seven, and that loneliness was the worst thing a human being had to suffer.'

Magnus wished that he had not given her so expensive a hand-bag, so sumptuous an edition of *Candide*. His presents had obviously encouraged her affection for him, and love, augmented by repetition, now in her female heart clamoured to become a habit; a legalized habit, moreover, for

Frieda was tired of outland ways and the paths of society's exiles, and desired conformity to polite usage, security, and a settled estate. But Magnus, who had suffered little or nothing among the mavericks, was by no means ready to retreat within the walls of convention. He began to talk about the history and philosophy of marriage, and discussed polygamy, polyandry, temple prostitutes, Polynesian rites, the royal incest of Egypt, the teaching of the Christian Church, the influence of property, the *ius primae noctis*, the curious sterility of the Parthians, Demeter, the Salic law, and primitive matriarchates until even Frieda grew tired of his voice.

But after she had gone Magnus considered his dilemma and hers with growing uneasiness: for he sympathized with her desire but could not encourage it, and while he had no wish to acquire a wife he had no will to lose his mistress. He remembered his vow to remain celibate and pursue with Artemis's chastity the milk-white hind of poetry, and for some minutes regretted his breaking it. But quickly he thought of Frieda again, and was most unhappy to think that she was not happy, and decided that he must see her again at the earliest opportunity to persuade her that their present relations were pleasant as they could be, and more suitable to both their natures than any more binding union.

CHAPTER ELEVEN

Henry Wishart and his wife returned from London on a Tuesday evening. At six o'clock, when their train arrived, Frieda was sitting in Magnus's flat yawning over a pamphlet on Scottish Nationalism. She was still unable to find any great interest in the subject, but partly out of curiosity, partly out of a desire to please Magnus, she had consented to read the views of some of the apostles. She was so far under his influence that she was now inclined to believe him when he spoke of its advantages, though when other people put forward the same opinions she was as sceptical of them as she had ever been. She turned over several pages and came to the conclusion that the author was making a great fuss about nothing and doing it in a very tiresome way. She threw the pamphlet down with a gesture of impatience.

Magnus, who was writing an article for Meiklejohn's newspaper, looked up and said, 'That's an interesting little essay, isn't it?'

'Yes,' said Frieda, and, getting up, reached over the table to stroke his hair.

'What's the time?' he asked.

Frieda looked at her watch. It was ten minutes past six. 'My God!' she said, 'I had to meet Aunt Elizabeth and Uncle Henry ten minutes ago! I've got to run. You're taking me out to dinner tomorrow, aren't you? Well, don't be late.'

She hurriedly put on her hat, flourished a powder-puff over her nose and cheeks, pursed her mouth and with a lipstick drew on it two or three strokes that she rubbed to a smoother and more equal colour with a vigorous finger-tip, and fled with the noise and precipitation of children coming out of school on a summer afternoon. Without considering the uselessness of her errand she walked swiftly to the station, and having discovered from a porter that the train had arrived at its proper time, she was greatly astonished and much perturbed. She took a taxi back to Rothesay Crescent and found her aunt conversing with an elderly maid called Thomson, who, perhaps from having been in Mrs Wishart's service for nearly twenty-three years, had acquired an expression of repressed irritation resembling that of her mistress.

Frieda ran to embrace her aunt and cried excitedly: 'Gee, I'm sorry I was late! I got all balled-up over the time. I must be going nuts or something. But it feels like a million dollars to see you again, Aunt Elizabeth. Say, you've got a new suit! That'll give 'em an eyeful on princes Street. Your girl-friends'll need to go into a huddle to think up something to beat that one.'

Mrs Wishart was a lady of nearly sixty years, not so much dignified by nature as by ill-nature. She wore a sombre costume that scarcely merited Frieda's praise, and was certainly of insufficient attraction to induce her elderly friends to go into a football-huddle to discuss it. She escaped with difficulty from Frieda's affectionate arms, and patted herself into tidiness before she spoke.

'Really, Frieda,' she said at last, 'I thought I had broken you of those disgusting American expressions, but apparently you were only waiting for me to go away to start using them again. I will not have you talking like that. Give Princes Street an eyeful, indeed! And in any case my costume isn't new. I've had it for several years. I shouldn't dream of travelling in a new costume.'

Frieda's exhilaration collapsed. 'I'm sorry, Aunt Elizabeth,' she said. 'I was so excited at seeing you I just didn't think what I was saying. But that suit . . .'

'Costume!'

'Well, that costume *looks* new, no matter how old it is. I guess you'd make anything you liked to wear look nice and new.'

'There's nothing to be gained by flattery, Frieda. I've told you that before. Perhaps in America you found that compliments were valuable, but here, among sensible people, truth and honesty will create a much more valuable opinion. Now what were you doing that prevented you from coming to the station in time to meet us?'

'Oh, I was just having tea with someone. Where's Uncle Henry? Did he win his case? And what did you do in London? Did you go to the theatre a lot?'

'Your uncle is resting, because train-journeys tire him. He won his case, of course. We always knew he would. And if you have read my letters you must know that we went to the theatre on three occasions, and each time wished we had stayed at home. But you are evading my question: with whom were you having tea this afternoon?'

'Oh, with a man I know. His name's Magnus Merriman.'

'Is he the young man who, so Thomson tells me, has called here several times during our absence?'

'Yes, he's been here once or twice. He's a writer. He wrote a swell novel called *The Great Beasts Walk Alone*. He's written poetry, too.'

'I may have heard his name, but I don't think so. Where and when did you meet him?'

'The day I went fox-hunting with the Duke of Buccleugh.'

'The Duke himself wasn't out, Frieda. You know that perfectly well. You merely followed his hounds. And this Mr Merriman was there, was he? Does he hunt regularly?'

Frieda's reply to the previous question had not been a premeditated attempt to give her aunt the impression that Magnus was a fox-hunter, and in consequence a person socially desirable. She had merely been unable to think of a better answer and had hoped with time to be able to improvise on her true but elliptical statement. But when she saw something like amiability, a relaxation of the facial muscles and a glance less frosty, in her aunt's expression, she hastily decided that the hunting *motif* was too good to be discarded. She was unwilling to tell lies, but despite Mrs Wishart's recommendation of the truth she knew that a truthful explanation would not be welcome. She therefore combined a little truth with a lot of tact, and answered: 'No, I don't think he hunts regularly. I guess he's too busy. He's writing a poem— a long poem—and he's pretty interested in politics, too.'

Mrs Wishart moved about the room, nervously altered the arrangement of some flowers, and lifted a few ornaments to see whether the maids had been dusting with sufficient zeal during her absence. She made one or two little exclamations of dissatisfaction, and having taken a cushion from one chair to put it on another, sat down and began to speak in a voice whose natural severity was thinly overlaid with conscious forbearance.

'I'm very tired,' she said, 'and I must go and lie down before dinner. One can get no proper rest on these long journeys. But I can't go without saying that I have been very upset by what Thomson has told me. It appears that you have taken advantage of our absence, your uncle's and mine, to behave without regard for the comfort of the servants or even for your own reputation. You have not helped with the housekeeping as you promised. You have constantly been late for meals, and often you have ordered dinner and then not come home at all: at any rate, not till very late at night. Naturally the servants are displeased. And I, knowing nothing of your movements, am very worried indeed. Is it this young man Merriman with whom you have been spending so much time?'

'Yes, I've been seeing him a lot. He's interesting. He's different from the other men I've seen here.'

'I've no doubt that he is an estimable young man, but I know nothing about him except what you have told me. Who are his people? Have you met them? No? Well, I must find out. He doesn't belong to Edinburgh, of course, or I should have heard of him. But, quite apart from that, you have evidently been very indiscreet. You have spent a great deal of time in his company—I do not want to know exactly how much—and though in America you may have learnt to think carelessly of such matters, you are living in Edinburgh now, and your Uncle Henry's house is not to be abused. I needn't remind you of his generosity towards you, for I am sure you are not likely to forget it. Now I don't know how serious your friendship for this young man is. . .'

'I like him better than anyone I've ever known.'

'I was going to say that you can hardly treat this friendship seriously until your uncle and I have met Mr Merriman. But if you care to invite him here we shall be very glad to see him.'

'He's coming round tomorrow night to take me out to dinner,' said Frieda somewhat unhappily.

'There is no need for you to go to a restaurant when there is plenty for you here. You can ask Mr Merriman to dine with us, and that will give your uncle and me a chance to talk to him. And now I shall go and lie down. But I must take some aspirin first. All this talking has given me a nervous headache.'

The following day Frieda made two unsuccessful attempts to telephone to Magnus to warn him of what he might expect when he called. She found him at last and spoke hurriedly to convey appropriate instructions before she was interrupted.

'Oh, Magnus,' she said, 'do you know one end of a horse from another? Well, you've got to pretend to. And you first met me that day we were both fox-hunting with the Duke of Buccleugh: remember that. No, I haven't time to explain. And you'd better wear a tuxedo tonight, because you're dining here. Yes, that's what I said: you're eating a family dinner here, and you're a hell of a guy for chasing foxes. Get a hold of that.'

While Magnus was impotently protesting and still asking vain questions, Frieda rang off in time to evade inopportune discussion with her aunt, who at this moment entered the room with a fretful expression and a paper-knife.

'I'm reading a book,' she said, 'and I've lost it. I have the paper-knife all ready to cut the leaves, but the book itself has disappeared. I mislaid it while I was looking for the knife. Do try to find it, Frieda.'

When Magnus arrived he was shown into the drawing-room where, in a heavy silence, Uncle Henry was reading a volume of Lockhart's *Life of Sir Walter Scott*, while Aunt Elizabeth and Frieda also sat with books in their hands. In obedience to Frieda's request Magnus had put on a dinner-jacket, but the somewhat brusque manner with which he permitted himself to be introduced showed that he had not received her instructions with any great complaisance.

'I believe you're going to dine with us,' said Mrs Wishart. 'It's very kind of you to accept such an informal invitation.'

'I'm afraid I can't,' said Magnus. 'I'm entertaining a friend of mine and his wife tonight.'

'Oh, what a pity! But perhaps you could put them off?'

'He's leaving for Paraguay tomorrow to investigate the Bolivian frontier question for the League of Nations, so this is my last chance to see him.'

'How annoying! And is his wife going with him?'

'Yes. Her father was Blasco Irigena, the authority on Indian dialects, and she is supposed to have, as far as a white person can, the confidence of the tribes.'

'I see,' said Mrs Wishart thoughtfully. She sighed. 'Well, perhaps you will come some other time.'

Henry Wishart was a lean and solemn man with reddish complexion, high cheek-bones, and thin sandy hair. He spoke little, but followed the conversation with quick glances and a disconcerting upward jerk of his eyebrows. He pronounced his words with deliberation and the trace of a Scots accent. Now he cleared his throat and said: 'I believe you met my niece in the hunting-field, Mr Merriman?'

'Yes,' said Magnus. 'It was a poor day. We didn't kill.'

'Do you hunt regularly?' asked Mrs Wishart.

'Not now. Unfortunately I've got a semi-lunar cartilage that isn't very trustworthy.'

Uncle Henry's eyebrows shot up alarmingly, and Magnus, who was by no means certain that his semi-lunar cartilages were of any importance in riding, hastily added, 'I took a bad toss in India. I hunted with the Bombay Jackal Club for a couple of years. Very rough going, you know. Very rough indeed. It was quite a regular thing to take a toss and land in a cactus-bush and come out looking like a porcupine.'

Nobody laughed. Mrs Wishart said, 'You don't belong to Edinburgh, do you, Mr Merriman?'

'No, my home's in Orkney,' Magnus answered.

'Really—I suppose you know the So-and-so's of Such-and-such, and the What's-their-names of Such-a-place?' asked Uncle Henry, mentioning the two families socially most eminent in the islands.

'Oh, very well,' said Magnus. 'Do you know the Macafees of Harray and the Newlands of Wideford?'

'No, I don't think I do.'

'Charming people,' said Magnus, and rose to go.

'As you can't stay tonight, perhaps you will come to lunch on Saturday?' asked Mrs Wishart.

Magnus looked at her thoughtfully. 'I had thought of asking Frieda to come to the Rugby International with me that afternoon,' he said, having thought of no such thing.

'Some of our party may be going there, too,' said Mrs Wishart, 'so that will be quite convenient.'

'Have you got any tickets?' Frieda asked.

'Not yet.'

'Then you won't be able to get any now,' said Uncle Henry.

'Stephen Lorimer can always get them,' said Mrs Wishart, 'and you'll see him at the Club tomorrow. Ask him for two then: I'm sure Frieda would like to see the game.'

'Why, that's splendid,' said Frieda. 'Isn't it, Magnus?'

Magnus, by no means pleased, said, 'It's very kind indeed of you,' and hastened their departure. When he and Frieda were outside, he said, 'What the hell do you mean by letting me in for that?'

'I couldn't help it, Magnus! Aunt Elizabeth just about

gave me the third degree to find out who you were and what we'd been doing. Thomson, that damned snooping maid of hers, has been talking, and she was hopping like a flea on hot sand to know all the dirty details.'

'But there was no need to drag me into it.'

'But you were just splendid! She's taken a liking to you. I know she has. All that stuff about hunting in India was grand. They swallowed it and asked for more. But say, who are these folk we're meeting tonight: this guy that's going out to Bolivia?'

'We're meeting nobody. I didn't want to dine with your uncle and aunt, so I made a simple excuse to get away.'

Frieda stopped in the street, laughed aloud and, paying no attention to a passer-by, threw her arms round Magnus and kissed him heartily. 'Well, it was a darned good story,' she said. 'I believed it myself.'

Mollified by the compliment, Magnus began to outline a theory of lying that depended for success on the addition of circumstantial details to an improbable premiss, and was still talking about it when they sat down to dine. It was with much diminished rancour that presently he recalled his embarrassing entrance into the Wishart family circle, but he was still annoyed and he explained to Frieda, very firmly, that he disliked interference, above all domestic interference, in his personal affairs, and that he had no desire to see the Wisharts again.

'But everything will be so much easier if you get friendly with them,' said Frieda. 'You can come in whenever you like, and I won't have to make excuses to get out and see you. Please, Magnus! It's going to be very uncomfortable for me if you won't be agreeable.'

Magnus argued in a contrary direction for some time longer, but Frieda so skilfully attacked his general propositions with personal and specific objection, not disdaining an occasional *ad captandum* plea, a feminine-unfair translation to him of responsibility for her happiness—these round-the-corner appeals, however, she interspersed with jest and good humour, so that compliance should not be squeezed out like a tear, but tickled to emergence like laughter—that Magnus at last consented to behave with due politeness to

Uncle Henry and Aunt Elizabeth, to lunch with them on the following Saturday, and to take advantage of the tickets which Uncle Henry would obtain to escort Frieda to the Rugby match.

But when, late in the evening Magnus was alone—Frieda, tactfully early, had gone home shortly after ten o'clock— he felt ruefully that he had committed himself beyond the frontier of bachelor discretion, and that by accepting the Wishart's hospitality he was regularizing his association with Frieda in a fashion he had never contemplated nor now thought desirable, but that she—an uncomfortable thought—quite clearly approved and most evidently desired. A sticky sensation, as of fly-paper, assailed his misogamous idiosyncrasy.

Meanwhile, in Rothesay Crescent, Uncle Henry and Aunt Elizabeth discussed his eligibility in guarded terms.

'If Frieda were my daughter,' said Mrs Wishart, 'I should certainly discourage her friendship with him. I was *not* very favourably impressed by his manner.'

'Too overbearing,' said Uncle Henry.

'And, of course, we don't know who he is. His people may be anything. But Frieda—well, we can't overlook the fact that she has lived, on her own admission, in a very curious way in America. I've sometimes wondered if she has told us the whole truth about her wanderings there.'

Uncle Henry cleared his throat. For the sake of his own peace of mind he had always refrained from speculating on Frieda's past, and he greatly disliked any reference to it. In deliberate tones he said: 'I want to hear no insinuations against Frieda. The girl is your own niece and you have no cause to suspect her of impropriety.'

'I was suspecting nothing!' said Mrs Wishart indignantly. 'I was merely wondering. One can't help *wondering* with a girl like that.'

For some minutes she made a pretence of reading. Then she said, apparently at random, 'I suppose novelists are often quite well-to-do?'

'I have never known any,' said Uncle Henry.

There was another period of silence. Then Mrs Wishart said, 'I think I shall write to Mrs So-and-so in Orkney. It would be interesting to hear if she knew anything of Mr Merriman's people.'

Uncle Henry's eyebrows rose violently and he was evidently about to expostulate when Mrs Wishart hurriedly explained: 'Her daughter Kitty has been ill—I forget who told me, but I'm sure it was Kitty—and I have intended for several weeks to write and ask how she is. But our trip to London put it out of my mind. There can be no harm in my saying that we have met Mr Merriman, and then she is sure to tell me if she knows anything about him.'

Uncle Henry made no reply. With the air of one who turns his back upon an unpleasing spectacle he turned a page of Lockhart's *Life of Scott*, and the conversation died.

CHAPTER TWELVE

It is customary to praise the appearance of Edinburgh, and a custom that has more excuse than some, for in certain aspects the city has indeed a noble countenance, and by some trick of light or situation an illusion of supplementary grandeur, a sublime superfoetation, is not seldom added to that which already possesses a dignity and a beauty of its own. The precipitous small hills that rise about Arthur's Seat, for example, often appear to be of mountainous size and seem to fill the sky with shadowy vastness, so that one thinks of Asian peaks, and a panorama of the world's high tablelands—plastered as if by glaciers with the shining names of Kanchenjunga and Demavend, of Aconcagua and Kilimanjaro—unrolls in the confusion of one's mind. Then from the Castle that slow declivity, criss-crossed with mild grey streets, to the veiled lustre of the Forth and the pale gold lands beyond, may under certain skies be revealed in such kindliness that urbanity puts on a pastoral light and one can almost hear the bleating of sheep, and yet be not moved to cry *Absit omen*. Or, from the Craigs, where the smoke of a thousand chimneys blows like a banner, or flaunts itself like a blue forest, or dances like snakes, or grows like dim tide-waving seaweed to an upper calm, then the roofs below might be the houses in a town that Hans Andersen built, and witches live there, and broomsticks have a moonward bent, and children go hand-in-hand by the signpost of Three

Wishes to fantastic adventure. And stranger than all else, more haunted by the beauty of the air, is the Castle, that now looks straight of side, severe as a child's castle cut in cardboard, and now recedes from the eye and is draped with mist, so that walls grow beyond walls and the battlements are endless, and a watch-tower, out-thrust, impends not only on the plain beneath but on Time's abyss and caverns of the past. It is a castle of moods, now merely antiquated, now impregnable, now the work of giants and now of dreams; a fairy castle, a haunted castle, a castle in Spain, a castle you may enter with a twopenny guide book in your hand; it has heard the cry of Flodden, the travail of queens, the iron scuffle of armour, and, no more than a handful of years ago, the roaring of forty Australians, seven feet high and drunk enough to rip the stars from heaven, penned in its guardroom; it is Scotland's castle, Queen Mary's castle, and the castle of fifty thousand annual visitors who walk through it with rain on their boots and bewilderment in their hearts. To be final—and, finally, to be brief—it is a good castle, and the people who walk Princes Street below are, as Magnus discovered, not always of a mien that deserves so dignified a neighbour.

But once in alternate years there is a Saturday morning when Edinburgh is filled with men and women who truly may call the Castle their own and in their bearing not shame its ancient walls. It is not devotion to the gods that calls them in, not some blazing heyday of the Trinity that brings them to worship, nor the inception of a crusade, nor memory, like a phoenix feathered and flowered again, of elder glory that comes in every second year to proper ripeness for a festival. It is not to worship they come, nor to exalt themselves, nor in tears of humility to taste the saltness of the earth, but, very sensibly, to be entertained. And the source of their entertainment is a football match between Scotland and England.

On the morning of that day, in bright blustery March weather, Princes Street is full of tall men from the Borders, brave men from the North, and burly men from the West who have made their names famous in school or university, in county and burgh, for prowess in athletic games. It is not footballers only who come, for on this day all other games do homage to Rugby and admit its headship over them, so that cricketers and tennis players, players of hockey and racquets and fives and golf, boxing men and rowing men and swimmers and cross-country runners, putters of the weight and throwers of the hammer, hurdlers, high and low jumpers, pole vaulters and runners on skis, as well as mountaineers and men who shoot grouse and stalk the red stag and fish for salmon—all these come to see Scotland's team match brawn and wit against the wit and brawn of England. To see them walking in clear spring weather is almost as exhilarating as the game itself, for their shoulders are straight, they are tall and lithe, they are square and strong, their eyes are bright, and their skin is toughened and tanned by the weather.

But not the men only walk proudly, for the women with them are also swimmers and hockey players, golfers and moorland striders, and they are often as tall as the men, and their complexions are lovelier and their bearing is free. Here is Diana, here is Atalanta, there, with gay scarf and a blackcock's feather in her cap, goes Hippolyte with a troop of Amazons—God be praised, not mutilated for the bow but supple and whole for the more lenient brassy—and there is one who, wrestling with Spartan youths, might bring to earth twelve at a time. It is no muslin prettiness that walks here with the fleet-limbed barrel-chested youth of Scotland, but strong loveliness that can face the wind and keep its colour in the rain. They would not allure the delicate mind, the feeble-luxurious mind, the petty sensual mind that desires soft flesh, provocative warmth, and the titter of prurience; they would frighten the epicene, the pallid tribe of catamites and ingles and lisping nancies; but raiding Vikings would roar with joy and straightway seize them and carry them, scratching like tigers, to their ships.

Now in the morning the crowd goes to and fro on Princes Street, but in the early afternoon it heads westward, all one way, to the football ground. And on this particular afternoon it was joined by a second crowd, different in appearance, manner and speech, that was also bent on seeing a football match. But this match was another kind of football, played by professional players, and the spectators hurrying to it, though far more excited and livelier in their conversation than those who were going to the international game, had not the athletic look of the latter. They were another order, socially inferior to the devotees of Rugby, and they had not been seen on Princes Street in the morning sunlight because they had been at work. To look at them it seemed obvious that work was a perversion, for it had not given them the upright bearing and the swinging stride that play had bestowed on the others, but rather it had kept their faces pale, and though it had toughened them it had not given them grace. But also it seemed that they had a larger gift of enthusiasm, for already they were hotly arguing about the prospects of the game—the Rugby people discussed their afternoon's entertainment in tones of calmness and with easy comment—though the professional match had not the spur of international rivalry, but was merely a competition between two Edinburgh clubs known as the Hibernians and the Heart of Midlothian.

While the fore-runners of these crowds were already marching westward—or being conveyed thither in tramcar or motor bus—Magnus sat at lunch with Henry Wishart. There were also present, besides Mrs Wishart and Frieda, Miss Mary Wishart, an aunt of Uncle Henry's who had arrived on a visit of some duration; Mr Simon Anstruther, a Writer to the Signet; a thin colourless lady who lived with Miss Mary and seldom contributed to the conversation; Colonel Gowrie-Blair, late of the Indian Army, and Mrs Gowrie-Blair, who was Mrs Wishart's sister; their son, who was about to enter Sandhurst; and a Miss Barleycorn, who, despite her name and the high colour of her cheeks, was interested in the cause of Temperance as well as in country dancing and the Women Citizens' Movement.

Of this company Magnus and Frieda, the Gowrie-Blairs, Mr Anstruther and Miss Barleycorn were all going to the football match, and the Colonel, Mr Anstruther, and Miss Barleycorn had some unfavourable comments to make on the Selection Committee that had chosen Scotland's team. Observing, however, that his host was not particularly interested in this topic, the Colonel, who like many soldiers was a disciplined church-goer, made some remark on the threatened *rapprochement* between the Episcopalian Church and the Established Church of Scotland. Uncle Henry and Mr Anstruther were both members of one of the most respectable congregations in Edinburgh—Uncle Henry was an elder—and the subject bore fruit for some ten minutes. It was not doctrine or creed they discussed, but management and ecclesiastical politics. From their conversation indeed it was not apparent that any difference in faith or dogma existed between the Anglican and the Scottish foundations, but the question of control was evidently of great importance, and there were some contemptuous references to Canterbury and a very telling gibe at Rome that showed the continued existence of the old Covenanting spirit— though neither Mr Anstruther nor Uncle Henry would have fared very well on the moors on a diet of heather-tops and whaups' eggs.

Then the conversation turned to music, for Mr Anstruther was a member of the Bach Society, and his funereal aspect— he closely resembled an undertaker's assistant—suggested that in his care the fugue would preserve a solemnity sufficient to attract none but grave and even moribund audiences. It seemed to Magnus, who listened attentively, that it was the politics of the Bach Society, not the music, that concerned the party, even as in the previous discussion it was the politics of religion, not the ideology of the Athanasian Creed or the virtuosity of the Sermon on the Mount, that had excited their interest. And he was about to comment, very unwisely, on this apperception when Aunt Mary leaned over the table and said loudly: 'You wrote *The Great Beasts Walk Alone*, didn't you, Mr Merriman?'

'I did,' said Magnus.

Miss Mary Wishart was a very old lady who sat perfectly upright in her chair and ate with a hearty appetite. Her hair was white, and the aged pallor of her face was dominated by a high-ridged imperious nose. She spoke slowly and deliberately, like her nephew, but her intonation was more noticeably Scottish than his. There was complete silence after she had spoken, partly out of respect for her years, partly due to a slight uneasiness, for none of the others except young Harry Gowrie-Blair had read the novel and most of them doubted the propriety of literary discussion.

Miss Mary continued, 'I thought it was clever but coarse. I read a great deal, and all you young men are coarse nowadays, and the young women who write are worse still.'

Harry Gowrie-Blair said, 'I've read it, and I thought it was fearfully good.' His father and mother from their several positions darted twin glances of reproof at him, and he relapsed into silence.

'If you shrink from occasional coarseness you are forced to leave out a great deal that is important and significant in life,' said Magnus. 'You can't make a steak and kidney pie without kidneys.'

'I'm not very interested in pies until they are cooked,' said Aunt Mary, 'and what I complain of is that you young authors don't cook your kidneys sufficiently. You serve them up half-raw, and I don't like them raw.'

'I seldom read modern novels myself,' said Uncle Henry, and there was a general murmur of assent.

'You never do anything, Henry,' said Aunt Mary sharply, 'so your statement's not worth much.'

Mrs Wishart, bridling, said, 'Henry has just won a very important case before the House of Lords, so you can hardly say he does *nothing*.'

Aunt Mary snorted. 'The House of Lords, indeed! Fiddle-faddle! Nothing but Socialists and Pacifists. I don't call *them* Lords!'

There was a medley of comments on this assertion, and the Colonel was heard to say that Melvin McMaster, the Prime Minister, was ruining the country; Miss Barleycorn briskly remarked that the world would be a better place if everybody signed the pledge, renounced war, and learned to dance *The Dashing White Sergeant*; and Mrs Gowrie-Blair plaintively asked, 'What will become of poor Harry's profession if you all turn pacifist?'

Magnus said, 'It's absurd to be an absolute pacifist, but to be a pacifist about wars like the last one is reasonable enough. The solution lies in small nationalism, which would reduce wars to decent proportions. Are you a Nationalist, Miss Wishart?'

'I'm a Jacobite,' she said, 'and always have been.'

Mr Anstruther leaned forward and very gravely asked: 'Can you tell me anything about Scottish Nationalism, Mr Merriman? I hear it mentioned now and then, but none of my friends seem to know much about it, and I'm rather at a loss to discover who are the Nationalists and what they want to do.'

'The fundamental idea is to obtain independent sovereignty for Scotland,' said Magnus.

Again there was a confused chorus of protest. Mr Anstruther said 'Oh!' with a slow sound like a groan, and sat with slowly nodding head, pondering the whole import of this explanation. Uncle Henry said 'Nonsense!' Mrs Wishart sniffed loudly and told a table-maid to offer some more cauliflower to Miss Wishart. Miss Wishart said, 'There are too many Socialists and silly young women in the country to do anything of that sort nowadays,' and her silent companion looked round the table with a vaguely happy smile. Frieda said to Harry, 'Will you wear a kilt at Sandhurst?' and he answered, 'No, not till I get to my regiment.' The Colonel said, 'And I suppose you're going to break up the Empire to get your confounded independence?' His wife said, 'Hush, my dear, hush!' and Miss Barleycorn said, 'Would you be in favour of closing the public-houses if we were to get Home Rule, Mr Merriman?'

'No,' said Magnus.

'Then I shall have nothing to do with Nationalism. I don't believe in it, anyhow. How on earth could we get on without England? It's absurd to think of it.'

Miss Mary asked, 'Would you be prepared to fight for independence, Mr Merriman?'

'I don't think there's any need for that,' said Magnus. 'If Scotland were united in its demand we could get all we want by constitutional means.'

'But Scotland isn't united,' said Uncle Henry, 'and it never will be united for any foolhardy nonsensical project like that.'

The Colonel and Mr Anstruther muttered their agreement.

Miss Mary said, 'There is such a lot about killing people in your novel that I thought you might prefer going to war.

You should read Mr Merriman's book, Colonel. It's about fighting in Central Asia; at least the more proper parts are about fighting.'

'Central Asia?' said the Colonel. 'H'm. Have you been there?'

'I've been to Teheran and on the border of the Turkoman Republic, and I was in Baku with Dunsterville during the war.'

The Colonel grew more friendly. Asia was a bond of interest. He knew all Northern India; he had been in Gilgit and the Hunza Valley, he had been on a mission to Kabul, he had guarded the Khyber Pass; he had soldiered with the levies in Persia, and he was familiar with all the gossip from Trebizond to Turkestan of the little warlike nations who in the post-war years had been betrayed by Britain's facile promises. He was a hard-shelled Conservative, narrow-headed, but in his narrow head there was a vast deal of knowledge, hot sympathy for the tribes and people he knew, enthusiasm for the ideals he had served. He said, 'The more I hear of English politicians the more I love my Punjabi Mussulmans.'

Magnus said, 'The Punjab is not all India. The Mahrathas have as good a war record as the Punjabis.'

'Then you admit your liking for India?' said the Colonel.

Magnus, with a second glass of port before him, said, 'India is the most fascinating country in the world.'

'And what is going to happen to India if you split the Empire by separating Scotland from England? You're not one of those arm-chair optimists who believe that India could look after herself? What do you think would happen if we cleared out and said to the Swarajists, "Now carry on by yourselves"?'

'There would be internecine warfare on a large and unpleasant scale. There's a Punjabi proverb that says, "The day after the British leave India. . ."'

'You can't quote that one here,' said the Colonel, 'but it's quite correct. And worse than internal trouble would be external invasion. The Russians would come in from the north, Japan would come in by sea, the Germans would penetrate with trading concessions, the French and

Italians would follow them—no, Italy would probably precede them—and you'd turn the clock back to the eighteenth century and make India the cockpit of the world.'

'No, we can't abandon India,' said Magnus decidedly.

'But how are you going to avoid abandoning it if you carve Britain in two?'

'If Scotland were independent we could press forward the idea of an Imperial Federation, which is the logical conclusion, in modern terms, of our eighteenth-century colonization. We wouldn't weaken the Empire; we would strengthen it by adding to it a new and forceful nation.'

The Colonel looked sceptical. Most of the other members of the party considered their coffee-cups with that air of abstract speculation which is the polite disguise of boredom, but Aunt Mary had followed the discussion with interest and Frieda looked at Magnus with fond admiration. Mrs Wishart rose and with some acerbity reminded them of the time. The ladies followed her out of the room.

Magnus and the Colonel drew their chairs together, and in three minutes had agreed that Britain must be infused with new pride, new determination, and a new Imperialist spirit, though the Colonel was by no means willing to admit that that end could be attained by a path leading from Scottish Nationalism to Federation. With difficulty they were eventually separated, and each proceeded to the football match with the conviction that he had made a convert of the other.

CHAPTER THIRTEEN

The bastard Faulconbridge, having discovered that the world was mad, came to a very sensible decision and declared:

> Well, whiles I am a beggar I will rail
> And say there is no sin but to be rich;
> And being rich, my virtue then shall be
> To say there is no vice but beggary.

Without having precisely formulated such a code, Magnus was not insusceptible to this chameleon philosophy, and frequently found himself in happy agreement with his surroundings—though there were occasions when he yielded to an anti-chameleon ethic and, in the midst of white, proclaimed himself all black. It was rather in this latter mood that he went to the football ground at Murrayfield, and after Uncle Henry's port and his discussion with the Colonel he felt superior to, and impatient with people who had in their minds no thought but to be entertained by an idle game. Five minutes after the match started, however, he was at one with the vast throng about him, a very chameleon on that pounding field, coloured like eighty thousand others with the fierce hues of enthusiasm.

There is a kind of Rugby that is no more than dull squabbling in the mud, a drenched and witless wrangling punctuated by a fretful whistle. But, at its best, Rugby is a game that all the gods of Greece might crowd the northern skies to see, and, benched on our cold clouds, be not restrained either by frozen bottoms or the crowd's chill sceptic hearts from plunging to the aid of stronger Myrmidons, of plucking from the scrimmage some Hector trodden in the mire and nursing him to strength again. Well might the Thunderer send fleet Mercury, swooping from the heights, to pick from the empty air Achilles' mis-flung pass and with it race—dog-rose and buttercup fast springing in his track—to the eternal goal.

And that square Ajax—dirtier than his namesake and more brave—would Hera not guard his brow from flying boots as, dauntless, down he hurls himself to stop a forward rush? Is there in all that crowd a Helen not quick-breathing, tip-toed and ready to leave dull Menelaus in his office chair and flee with Paris there, who runs so lightning-swift on the left wing?—on the left wing only? Eagles would need two to fly so fast.

Rugby can be a game for gods to see and poets to describe, and such a match was this. *L'audace, encore l'audace, et toujours l'audace* was both sides' motto, and which was more gallant—England, taller and bulkier-seeming because clad in white: Scotland, running like stags and tackling like thunderbolts in blue—no one can truthfully say and none would care to know. If Tallent for England was magnificent, Simmers for Scotland was superb. Did Tallent run the whole length of the field and score? Then Simmers, leaping like a leopard, snatched from the air a high cross-kick of Macpherson's and scored from that. Did Black for England kick like a giant, long, true and hard? Then see what Logan at the scrum, Smith on the wing, did like giants for Scotland. And each side in turn, tireless and full of devil, came to the attack and ranged the field to score. Pace never slackened from start to finish, and every minute thrilled with excitement till, at the end, wisps of fog came down—perhaps the gods indeed, hiding their brightness in the mist—and in that haze the players still battled with unwearied zeal.

Judge, then, of the fervour of the crowd, poised as it were on the broad rim of a saucer, and as thick together as if the saucer had been smeared with treacle and black sand thrown on it. But they were more mobile than sand, and ever and again a movement would pass through them as when a wave of the wind goes through a cornfield. Ever and again, as when walls in an earthquake fall asunder, some twelve or fourteen thousand would shiver and drift away from their neighbouring twelve thousand and then, stability reasserted, fall slowly into place again. And now, like a monstrous and unheralded flowering of dark tulip-beds, the crowd would open to its heart and fling aloft, as countless petals, hats, sticks, and arms, and pretty handkerchiefs, and threaten to burst the sky with cheers. Now they were wild as their poorer neighbours who, some mile or two away, were cheering their paid teams with coarser tongues. Now all Scotland was at one, united in its heat, and only the most sour of moralists would decry that heat because it had been lighted by a trivial game.

Magnus carried his excitement with him, through the voluminous outpouring of the crowd, all the way to Francis Meiklejohn's flat, and Frieda, walking beside him, was as fervid as he, and willing even to admit that Rugby such as this transcended the staccato violence of American football. But Meiklejohn, who had not been to the match, was sceptical of its virtues and scoffed at their enthusiasm. Mrs Dolphin, who entered the room with them to hear the news, rejoiced to learn that Scotland had won, but was disinclined to believe that such a game was worthy to show off her country's virility.

'Was there any blood?' she asked, and on being told that injuries had been few, said, 'It's shinty they should have been playing. I remember seeing a game of shinty at Kingussie, and half the men there had bloody heads before it was over. Every other crack of the ball there was a man carried off the field, for if it wasn't the ball that hit him it was the stick, and a shinty-stick is a fine weapon. There was a man called Alistair Mhor, and he stopped at one time and said, "What's this on my stick?" And then he saw it was a man's eyebrow he had knocked off. Alistair was a Macdonald and the man who had lost his eyebrow was a Campbell, so Alistair wasn't as sorry as he would have been otherwise. Oh, shinty's a fine game if you don't mind it being a little bit rough. It pleased them well enough in Kingussie, for the people there said they hadn't had such a treat for years.'

Though Meiklejohn was not sympathetic with his guests' enthusiasm, his zeal for hospitality was unimpaired. Several other people arrived, and presently the room was full of the familiar sounds of *Figaro*, glass and bottle music, loud conversation, and Meiklejohn's detonating laughter. Among the newcomers was a very pretty girl whom Meiklejohn greeted with a flourish of welcome and introduced as Miss Beauly. He gathered her and Magnus and Frieda into a corner and said, 'We're dining at the Tarascon tonight. I've got a table for four. Now I don't want any argument or hard-luck stories of previous engagements. We're going—so there's no more to be said.'

Magnus alone, however, found no difficulty in tacit agreement. Miss Beauly said a great deal about the difficulty of getting dressed in time and the breaking of earlier promises that would be incidental to the acceptance of this new invitation, and made a fine show of reluctance before consenting to join them. Frieda was anxious to go, but was doubtful of her aunt's compliance, and would not say yes till she had telephoned Mrs Wishart for permission. After that the party continued with such agreeable hilarity as to put them in danger of forgetting the subsequent engagement, and indeed they did not remember it till so late an hour that neither Miss

Beauly nor anyone else had time to go home and change into evening dress. But fortified by Meiklejohn's vodka they then found themselves ready to flaunt the conventions and dare the invasion of Edinburgh's most distinguished restaurant in the permeable armour of ordinary clothes.

The Tarascon Restaurant was in the Albyn Hotel. It gave facilities for dancing and dining at approximately the same time: one could rise from one's turbot *maître d'hôtel*, that is, and while forgetting its flavour in the polite amusement of a waltz, find diversion—if such were one's nature—in the thought that all around one were agitated couples whose ears were full of music and whose stomachs were full of newly ingurgitated fragments of cutlet, potato salad, partridge and rum soufflé. In a mechanical age the mechanism of the human body is of universal interest, and the spectacle of mortality overcoming so many difficulties at once was enthralling: here was a brain zealously receiving afferent impulse from the American orchestration of an African melody, analysing it, and transmitting a hundred instructions to all the muscles from trouser-top to toe; and there were the muscles, huge fellows like the quadriceps extensor and tiny pink slips like the flexon digiti quinti— or some such thing—co-ordinating these instructions and obeying them with more than the discipline of a Guards' battalion. And immediately above the trouser-line was a digestive system revolving the mixed bag of an eight-course dinner, sorting its contents with the care of a stamp collector before a tray of new specimens, telegraphing to the brain for hepatic aid and pancreatic reinforcements, and notifying its descending tracts of their imminent burden. Meanwhile the lungs were filtering oxygen from a bewildering indraught of cigarette smoke, perfume, and the odours of food; the ever-versatile brain was putting a score of facial and glottal muscles through their drill of social conversation, and still navigating its owner down the crowded fairway of the floor; and a host of tactile sensations were informing various parts of the body that of all God's creatures there were only two kinds, and male and female created He them. Nor does this catalogue comprise more than half the activities of these dancers—whom many people would foolishly call idle—

but of other physiological business and cortical traffic there is no need to speak, for enough has been said to account for the popularity of the Tarascon Restaurant in those classes of people that could afford to frequent it.

On this particular evening it was full as a hive in the honey months, and as busy, with people who had been to the football match and were unwilling to stay quietly at home after the excitement. As though disgorged by the teeming dance-and-dining room, tables lined the foyer and corridor outside, whose occupants might hear the muted music from within, and people were still coming and going on the stairs, greeting friends and blocking the way with fortuitous assembly. The table that Meiklejohn had reserved was in the restaurant itself. It cowered beneath the orchestra and was overshadowed, almost overgrown, by surrounding diners like a Mayan temple in the jungle.

Meiklejohn and his friends, dressed for daytime purposes, were received by the waiters with obvious displeasure; for tweed and flannel had a raffish, disrespectful look among the elegances of evening wear. The head waiter indeed was unwilling to admit them, but yielded when Magnus said loudly, 'The law of the land declares that an inn, tavern, pub, pot-house, coffee-stall, brothel or posada shall not refuse admission to customers able to pay for what they eat and drink, and that such refusal is a criminal offence. If you don't believe me send for the manager and I'll argue with him.' They were then allowed to proceed to their table, and the slow sequence of dishes began.

Owing to the contiguous noise of the orchestra they were compelled to speak at the top of their voices. Meiklejohn said, 'The last time Magnus and I dined together we were arrested,' and he told the tale of their visit to the High Street pub and the subsequent interposition of the police. Frieda had heard the story before. In the early days of her acquaintance with Magnus she had thought it amusing, but now, when she saw him in a graver light and love had made her both sensitive and practical, she deprecated such wildness and did not like to be reminded of it.

She said, 'Well, I hope you're not going to argue about Shakespeare and Racine tonight.'

'Goodness, I hope not,' said Miss Beauly. 'I came here to be amused.'

'Anyhow, we shan't quarrel about them,' said Magnus, and Meiklejohn agreed.

Now later in the evening it happened that Meiklejohn himself quoted Shakespeare and the topic was reborn. They had danced several times, Magnus with Frieda, Meiklejohn with Miss Beauly, on each occasion Meiklejohn complained of the crowded floor. Magnus, who was a bad dancer and moreover in a mood of benign contentment with the world, did not object to being crushed by mortal shoulders, impeded by mortal legs, and blown upon by mortal breath in the intimacy common to a herd of sheep; he held Frieda closely to him, talked to her with boisterous and extravagant affection, and happily pranced or limped in accordance with the prevailing density of the multitude. But Meiklejohn was a good dancer, and could not find room to exercise his skill; and Miss Beauly got kicked on the heel by some high-stepping Boeotian, and so they returned to their seats with tempers rather ruffled.

Filling his glass from a new-come bottle of champagne, Meiklejohn drank it off, still creaming, and said: 'I hate the mutable rank-scented many.'

'You hear that?' said Magnus. 'Even the Devil can't get on without Scripture.'

'What do you mean?' asked Frieda.

'He quoted Shakespeare. He pretends to despise him, and yet he can't do without him.'

'My dear fellow!' said Meiklejohn, 'that's an absurd thing to say. I happened to use a perfectly ordinary phrase. . .'

'That you couldn't have used if Shakespeare hadn't invented it. And every day we use his inventions. English speech is full of them. Fat men from Glasgow and Manchester, tax-collectors and commercial travellers and sellers of soap and debentures and second-hand motor cars, and priggish old maids from Cheltenham, all make their speech glorious by talking about Triton of the minnows, and my prophetic soul! my uncle! and all the world's a stage, and cakes and ale, and a lion among ladies, and the lunatic, the lover, and the poet, and maiden meditation fancy-free, and the hundred other things that Shakespeare said first. You talk about Racine, but did Racine create a whole speech? Shakespeare did. Shakespeare shines. . .'

At this point the music reached an unpleasant degree of loudness as all instruments blended in vulgar encouragement to the dancers, and Magnus, now very excited, found this opposition to his harangue utterly intolerable.

He jumped from his chair and confronting the orchestra shouted in tremendous tones: 'Shut up!'

The music wavered through involuntary discords to half-silence. The agitated conductor looked round to see who had interrupted him, and, they also shaken and now released from the spell of the commanding baton, the remaining players put down their instruments.

For half a minute there was a comparative silence, and Magnus, now facing his own companions but still speaking in a very loud voice, said decisively, 'Shakespeare shines through the shoddy of everyday speech like the body of Cophetua's beggar maid through her rags.'

This remark was audible to some sixty or eighty people who were very astonished by it. Some were moved to laughter and others, thinking that the speaker was drunk—he was in truth not sober—made haughty motions of disgust. With some show of temper the orchestra recommenced, and several waiters drew in to Meiklejohn's table. The senior of them spoke severely to Magnus. They were, he said, prepared to allow a certain freedom of behaviour on such a night—this was indisputable: decorum now fingered a paper cap and soon might even wear it. Staid citizens carolled to the band. Here was a lady laughing in a way that would appal her mother's drawing-room, and there was a stout gentleman in evening dress, glazed of eye and sprinkling his words like a flower-pot, going from table to table with invitations to come and drink in Room Number 334, where, he said, there were bottles and bottles of fine liquor: 'I've lost all my friends,' he said, 'but I've lots and lots to drink. Dozens and dozens of bottles. Come and have a drink with me! Room 334. Three-three-four! Don't forget the number!'— reasonable licence, said the waiter, was permitted on such a night, but neither conduct so outrageous as an interruption of the band nor speech so improper as to mention a young woman's body. If there was any further disturbance from this table they would all be asked to leave the hotel.

Magnus, in his usual manner, ignored the rebuke and ordered another bottle of champagne.

Frieda and Miss Beauly had been alarmed by Magnus's interruption of the orchestra and embarrassed by the consequent reprimand. They were very relieved when the waiter went away, and what was left of their anxiety they vented on Magnus, telling him that his behaviour had indeed been reprehensible, and that neither a lecture on Shakespeare nor a display of rowdyism were proper to entertain young women who had come out for an evening of polite amusement.

Meiklejohn waited impatiently till they had finished. During the waiter's admonition he had sat tapping with his fingers, testily interjecting 'Yes, yes, that's all right,' and then he had been interrupted by Frieda and Miss Beauly and compelled to listen to their strictures while on his own tongue a whole troop of controversial opinions waited the opportunity to gallop into action. His chance came at last. 'Shakespeare and Racine are as night and day,' he said. Frieda groaned.

'Shakespeare is a cloudy sky, Racine is a clear sky,' he asserted. 'Who cares?' said Miss Beauly, and helped herself to a little more champagne.

Meiklejohn was in fine voice. He quoted *Phèdre*, he quoted *Iphigénie*, he made bull-headed assertions and astonishing generalizations. Magnus grew warm and replied with lavish excerpts from *Lear*, *Timon*, *Henry IV*, and *Twelfth Night*. Often they quoted against each other simultaneously, and with a great shock the French lines, glittering like cuirassiers in their silver breastplates, met the plumed and plunging chivalry of England in the middle of the table. Magnus and Meiklejohn forgot their surroundings and, declaiming splendid fragments, enjoyed themselves thoroughly. Sometimes, such was their emotion, their eyes were bright with tears, and their voices shivered like lances that have struck home. But Miss Beauly was very bored.

She was normally a girl of no imagination, and of perfect propriety, at any rate in public. But now the champagne

she had drunk made her inclined to giggle, and she felt
a keen desire to do something foolish and unusual. She
looked behind her and saw two saxophones balanced near
the edge of the platform. The smaller one was quite close
to her. For a minute she fiercely desired to take it and blow
down its silver throat a furious unorchestrated medley of fun
and egotism. But she had not drunk enough to be so brave
as that, and wistfully she put away the temptation. Another
took its place when Meiklejohn, having taken snuff, put
down his box on the table and forgot it in the continued
heat of argument.

Miss Beauly picked up the box and examined it. It was
nearly full. She fingered the powder and almost yielded to
curiosity by sniffing it. Anything must be better than listening
to Meiklejohn's unintelligible French and—Magnus spouting
in reply—English that was as meaningless as a foreign tongue.
But in the very immediacy of snuffing a superior project
occurred to her. With a quick and tiny giggle she turned and
emptied the box into the mouth of the near-by saxophone.
Then, a little overcome by her daring, she masked her emotion
with a front of too-candid innocence and pretended to pay
attention to the interminable literary discussion.

The next dance was one of those sentimental pieces that,
oozing like a sleepy python through a grove of sugar-canes,
fill the air with abdominal colloquialism and an almost
diabetic sweetness. To fortify the intentions of the dance
the lights were turned low, and a sophisticated blue darkness descended on the room. Languorous now, but still
close-packed as moonlit elvers in their homing stream,
the dancers drifted on the warm and honeyed tide. The
saxophone-player took his smallest instrument and came on
to the floor to wander through the crowd and play, now into
this ear, now into that, the dulcet accidents of the melody.

Presently a woman sneezed. It was a high-pitched sneeze,
a most delicate sternutation, the merest zephyr tangled in
a pretty, powdered, finger-tip of a nose. But then came a
very blizzard of a sneeze that roared and burst in thunder
as though its owner's nose were a fore-topsail carried away
off Cape Horn. While that still echoed round the room three
others followed: one that was no more than a draught, one

a kind of winter squall, and the third like the north-east Trade, it blew so steadily and long. Now the orchestra grew vexed with these interruptions and, sacrificing sweetness for strength, played somewhat louder. But wherever he went the saxophone-player spread more sneezes. When he had passed them a couple would halt, look at each other with a puzzled expression, see lips tremble, mouth open like a new-caught fish, eyes grow moist, nose redden, agitation spread quick and quicker, and then the hurricane before which all yields or is broken and flung aside. As palms in the Bermudas bend and houses shake when the ocean tempest hurls itself at them, so men wilted and women shrank away when some strong sneezer let fly his loud *Atishoo*—yet even as they turned themselves gave birth to storm, sternutation bred in their noses, and *Atishoo!* cried they all. And as in hurricanes, dull amid their large noises, there is the sombre thudding of falling coconuts, so on all hands was the little thudding noise of other sneezes caught at birth and smothered in the nose.

Now on the periphery epicentres of new storms appeared among the diners, and chaos increased when every squall blew flower-vases down or lifted a port-glass to the ground. But still, unscathed himself, the saxophone-player meandered down the decimated floor and puffed abroad his fatal tune. As he passed beneath them, the orchestra shuddered, caught their breath, and amidst a clatter of falling instruments sneezed in awful unison.

The lights were turned on and the ravages of the storm made visible. The dancers, dishevelled, weather-beaten, stood all awry, still twitching, still wet-eyed and haggard. Ties were askew, here was a shirt-front riven asunder and there a shoulder blown bare of its nosegay. Faces most carefully cosmeticked were streaked and plain, and the red strong faces of the men wore a startled, nervous look. Many dancers, and diners too, cowered like starlings in an August gale, and others shied like yearling horses whenever a sneeze rang out. The head waiter, himself weakened by successive paroxysms, strove to avert a panic and, valiant as a ship's officer when his vessel rams an iceberg, bade his customers be calm and return quietly to their own tables.

Meanwhile Miss Beauly, sneezing violently, was very frightened by the success of her trick, and Magnus, Meiklejohn, and Frieda laughed uproariously at it. Magnus quoted some lines describing the storm in *King Lear*, and when convulsions louder than usual startled the room cried: 'Blow, winds, and crack your cheeks!'

Both Magnus and Meiklejohn offered to take the blame for Miss Beauly's misbehaviour if need should arise. Indeed, they began to quarrel as to who should have the privilege of taking the blame. Magnus maintained that as he had been quoting Shakespeare so liberally he had a special claim, for was there not a Shakespearean character, one Lance, a clown, who had taken the blame for his dog's misbehaviour?

'What had the dog done?' asked Meiklejohn.

Magnus, screening his voice from Miss Beauly, whispered, 'Piddled under the table.'

'That's not a parallel case,' said Meiklejohn firmly, and maintained the contrary thesis that he, as champion of Racine and France, that was the birthplace of courtesy and the home of fine manners, had now clearly the right to defend Miss Beauly. And while they were still arguing the head waiter came to their table and asked if either of them was responsible for the storm that had not yet subsided.

'Yes,' said Magnus.

'I am,' said Meiklejohn, and they frowned irately, not at him, but at each other.

The waiter suggested they should discuss the matter outside, and they followed him willingly. But at the door of the restaurant Meiklejohn, who was in front, turned to wave good-bye to Miss Beauly, and being uncertain both as to equilibrium and direction, unfortunately with his valedictory hand slapped Magnus on the cheek. Magnus promptly slapped in return. Meiklejohn hit back, retreated, trod on someone's toe, and became embroiled in a general scrimmage. Magnus, following him up, perceived that several people were apparently hindering him, and engaged them all. He succeeded in hitting Meiklejohn on the nose, and then both of them were hurried and bustled, tripped and tumbled, and finally thrown downstairs. At the bottom they were held securely, now in a semi-conscious state, till a telephone message brought speedily a Black Maria to a rearward door of the hotel, and into that they were thrust and borne to a small divisional Police Station a few hundred yards away.

CHAPTER FOURTEEN

Magnus and Meiklejohn made an unhandsome spectacle in the Police Station. The violence to which they had been subjected had stirred up their huge potations, and the rising fumes had so smothered their wits that now they had barely strength to stand and listen to the charges made against them. They made no protest, but, sagging at the knees, limply acquiesced in whatever was said. They were taken to a small cell, and there fell instantly asleep.

An hour or two later they were roused again. The Black Maria had called to take them to the Central Police Station, and in company with several other prisoners they made a miserable journey thither.

The small spectacled sergeant who had received them on a previous occasion was again on duty, and he appeared genuinely distressed to see them.

'Well?' he asked, 'have you been arguing about literature again?'

A policeman in attendance said they had gravely disturbed the peace of the Albyn Hotel by committing a variety of assaults there, and the sergeant sighed and said, 'Drink is a terrible thing.'

Meiklejohn, making an effort to defend himself, said in uncertain tones, 'Just an accident, sergeant. Highly respectable party—but met with an accident.'

Magnus, however, made full confession. 'We're drunk,' he said. 'Irremediably drunk. Irremediably.' And he supported himself on a neighbouring policeman's arm.

'You'll need to go to the cells,' said the sergeant, and consulted his book to see what accommodation was available. The police station was somewhat crowded, for in addition to the usual temptations of Saturday there had been the International game and a particularly thrilling match between the Hibernians and the Heart of Midlothian.

'There isn't a vacant cell left,' said the sergeant, 'but I won't put you in with strangers.' And he took a large key from a hook.

A massive gate was opened. Magnus and Meiklejohn were led down a stone passage. A confusion of small sounds issued from the peep-holes in narrow doors. There was a good deal of snoring, and someone recited, in a quiet monotone, the story of his wrongs. Another of the invisible prisoners was crooning a song of dismal sentimentality, and another was suffering from resonant hiccups. The passage was well lighted. They turned into a side corridor and the sergeant unlocked a door.

In a fair-sized cell two men were sleeping. Their boots had been taken off, and they lay, unblanketed, on a gently sloping platform against the far wall.

'You won't feel the need of conversation tonight,' said the sergeant, 'but you'll have company for tomorrow.'

The door closed, the loud lock was turned. Meiklejohn, with a final effort to greet destiny with a gesture, tried to pronounce 'All hope abandon ye who enter here.' Had he been content to say it in English he might have succeeded, but a Latin spirit still flickered in him and he essayed the original Italian form. The sonorous sibilation of *lasciate* was too difficult, and a mere susurration escaped his lips. He sat on the floor and dolefully shook his head. Magnus lay down without pretence that he desired anything but rest, and instantly fell asleep.

Early in the morning they were half-awakened by the rattling of the little barred opening in the door. One of the original occupants of the cell, who had been asleep when Magnus and Meiklejohn were admitted, got up and took from the warder outside four cups of cocoa and four slices of dry bread. He turned to rouse the newcomers.

'Come along, my lucky lads,' he said. 'Rise and shine! You can't lie there till the sun burns a hole—God A'mighty, it's Mr Merriman!'

Magnus, groaning for his stiffness and his headache, sat up and rubbed his eyes. 'Hallo, Denny,' he said. 'You here, too?'

It was indeed Sergeant Denny, with whom they had been

associated in their previous encounter with the police, and the fourth man in the cell was none other than Private McRuvie, late of the Black Watch. Denny was very surprised to see Magnus, and, when his surprise had worn off, over-joyed to meet an old friend again. But Magnus was suffering too keenly, both in mind and body, to be susceptible either to surprise or pleasure. Meiklejohn was also taciturn, and McRuvie was frankly surly. Denny alone seemed immune to remorse and unaffected by imprisonment, and for a long time his endeavours to promote a happy family atmosphere were unsuccessful.

After drinking their cocoa Magnus and Meiklejohn sat side by side in dismal silence, broken only by the inter-jection, first from one and then from the other, 'My God, what fools we were!'

An appalling unhappiness possessed them both. Not only were their stomachs queasy, their heads aching, and their mouths most sourly flavoured, but their minds were full of shame and foreboding. At first they could scarcely remem-ber what had happened, but then incident after incident came back to memory, and as each one returned their souls withered within them. That vain wounding wish, that time would turn back, assailed them, and they thought how easily they could have evaded this horrible occurrence. Meiklejohn had the additional misery of realizing that his job as editor of the *Evening Star* was imperilled.

'Oh, why do we get drunk?' he exclaimed.

Sergeant Denny looked round in a lively interested way. 'Man,' he said, 'its a grand feeling to be fou'! It's like climbing a mountain: you get a rare view of the world, and everything looks bonnier than you ever dreamt it would be. If I were a millionaire I'd never be sober.'

'What about your job?' asked Meiklejohn. 'You'll get the sack if you don't turn up in time on Monday morning.'

'I havena been in work for three years,' said Denny. 'And McRuvie's the same, or worse. Hey, McRuvie! How long is it since you've had a job?'

'Four years,' said McRuvie, 'or maybe five. I canna remember.'

'You're living on the dole?' asked Magnus.

'He is,' said Denny, 'but no me. I had it for a while, but och, they're too particular with all their questions and the like, so I just gave it up.'

Magnus threw off some of his private cares and began to question Denny about his manner of life since leaving the army. Denny had had a varied career and was ready enough to talk. After the orthodox part of the war was over he had served in the North Russian force. Then he had come home, and for a year he had been a policeman. But the discipline was too exacting. He had worked for a while in the fish market at Inverdoon, and after that, for some eighteen months, he had been cook aboard a trawler. While he was at sea his wife had run away with a friend of his, and after a period of idleness in which he had dissipated his sorrow in drink he had occupied himself in the collection of street-corner bets for a bookie in a small way of business. But the police warned him off, and he took advantage of an offer of employment from an uncle in Leith, who had just bought a small greengrocer-shop. In the course of selling potatoes he had met a young woman and fallen in love with her. To avoid the misdemeanour of bigamy they had lived in sin, as the saying is. When his uncle went bankrupt Denny supported himself and his wife on the dole for some months, but presently the authorities, prying here and there and asking inconvenient questions, discovered that though his wife might be his helpmate in the eyes of God she was not his spouse in the sight of men, and charging Denny with perjury, fraud, and misrepresentation, mulcted him of his dole and sent him to prison for six weeks. On his release he had put ten shillings, which was all he possessed, on a greyhound called Idle Sam, and winning thereby the sum of two pounds, had since lived in reasonable comfort by betting on horses, dogs, and football teams.

Magnus was greatly cheered by this recital, for he was always delighted to meet a man who had fought the hardships and injustice of life with a series of pretty shifts and dependence on his own wit. So long as a man could maintain existence by his own strength he had no cause to worry about the opinions or the criticism of the rest of the world, and even the folly of drunkenness, the stain of imprisonment, could by such a one be forgotten in a night's sleep. Magnus, with his moral opportunism, became aware, through his discomfort, of the freedom that pertains to the underdog, the gipsy, the outlaws of society. His expression grew happier. He slapped Denny on the shoulder, laughed, and said, 'The Gay Gordons, what? Once a Gordon, aye a Gordon.'

'That's the word,' said Denny.

McRuvie snorted.

'And what about McRuvie?' asked Magnus, 'has he lived as variously as you?'

But McRuvie, it appeared, had monotonously supported himself and his family on the dole ever since the yards at Rosyth had been closed in the interests of economy and their workers discharged *pour encourager les autres*. McRuvie had cause to be somewhat surly.

'And what were you doing last night to get run in?'

'Fighting,' said Denny simply, and related the whole story. He and McRuvie had gone to the football match between the Hibernians and the Heart of Midlothian. He supported the Hearts, McRuvie the Hibs, and there was some argument between them over a disputed goal and the dubious award of a penalty kick. But Denny had been magnanimous, and being in funds—he had won four pounds as the result of his week's betting—he had taken McRuvie to a pub and treated him to a large number of drinks. Then the discussion about the penalty kick had reawakened, and from hot debate about the rival merits of Hibs and Hearts they had progressed by stages which Denny could not clearly remember, but which at the time had seemed quite natural, to even warmer dispute about the emulous virtues of the Black Watch and the Gordon Highlanders. They had been thrown out of the pub, and while punching conviction into each other outside the police had come upon the scene and arrested them. It was a simple story, plainly told and easy to comprehend.

It suddenly occurred to Magnus that Scotland was full of contending elements, and that the possibility of two Scotsmen living together in peace was regrettably small. If one were a Catholic and the other a Presbyterian then there would certainly be enmity and suspicion between their houses; if one came from Glasgow and the other from Edinburgh then they would assuredly hate and despise each other; if one were a Campbell and the other a Macdonald they would have a fine bitter store of ancestral memories to feed their mutual execrations; the Black Watch and the Gordon Highlanders, it seemed, could not be neighbours without a taunting interchange of references to Broken Squares and the Kaiser's Bodyguard; scarcely a village but called its proximate village dirty, drunken, or thievish; and even peaceful literary men, admirers of Shakespeare and Racine, were in danger of a punch on the nose if they made known their admiration.

It was indeed a combative land, and if the Nationalists succeeded in making it independent they would have a pretty task to reconcile all the contentious parts. Magnus grew thoughtful at the prospect of this difficulty, but presently consoled himself by pretending that local rivalries were a sign of national vitality. He turned to engage Meiklejohn in conversation, who was still sitting mute and unhappy because he might soon cease to be editor of the *Evening Star*.

The hours ebbed slowly. At midday a warder brought them each a bowl of soup and another slice of bread. No one but Denny had much appetite, and he cleaned the bowls and finished every crust. They sat for a long time in silence broken only by a rumbling belch from McRuvie.

Then the office-sergeant, the little spectacled man, came in and looked at them over the top of his spectacles, and said how sorry he was to have them all here. Meiklejohn asked if they could be released on bail, but the sergeant said that was impossible. They had done a certain amount of damage in the Albyn Hotel, it seemed, and they would have to go before the magistrate and take their punishment.

'I let you out on bail once before,' said the sergeant, 'and the warning should have been enough for you if, as they say, it's only a fool who can't learn by experience. I'm very sorry indeed to see you in here, but I can't do anything to help you now. You'd better plead guilty in the morning. It'll save you trouble.'

He paused and cleared his throat. 'There's a scripture reader outside,' he said. 'If any of you would like to hear a chapter read I can tell him to come in.'

No one appeared to want this consolation, and the sergeant said, 'Well, I thought it might pass the time for you, but it's for yourselves to say. You'll be finding the day wearisome, I doubt.'

'Very,' said Magnus.

The sergeant put something in his hand and whispered, 'I'll come back for that later.' Then, with a solemn shaking of his head, he left them and closed the door hard behind him.

It was a pack of cards he had given Magnus, and everyone grew a little more cheerful to see them. Denny in particular praised the sergeant loudly for his clemency and kindness. 'He's a grand wee man,' he said, 'if there was more like him it would be a pleasure to be putten in gaol.'

Neither Denny nor McRuvie could play bridge, and there was some difficulty in deciding what other game would be suitable. They played a few hands of vingt-et-un, and made a trial of brag, but their lack of money—for all their possessions except their clothes had been taken from them—made these games uninteresting, and the keeping of a score without markers was soon found to be impracticable. Then Denny, having shuffled the cards with expert fingers, showed them how to cut the pack for banker and be reasonably sure of winning. 'Do you mind the Crown and Anchor board I used to run?' he asked Magnus. 'That's a fine game. Sometimes I made seven or eight pounds on a pay-night. Man, it wasna so bad a war as some folk try to make out.'

Meiklejohn, fearing a spate of wartime reminiscences, hurriedly suggested a game of solo whist, and they played that for several hours.

In the early evening the warder reappeared with bowls of thin gruel and more bread. Denny suggested they should play banker for the bread, and because the others had seen him demonstrate the way of it they thought they could beat him, and agreed. He won all four slices.

Time grew tedious again. The cell was warm enough,

but the air was sour and stuffy, charged with their breath and still heavy with the beery exhalations of the night. Meiklejohn had said little all day. Magnus and Denny kept conversation going, but towards night even Denny grew somewhat depressed, and Magnus became aware that all the miserable thoughts of the morning were again crowding in upon him.

He lay down to sleep on the sloping wooden platform, and could find no comfort on it. The cell grew darker and the pink-washed walls turned to a dull maroon. He was oppressed by the nearness of the others and the smallness of the room. His mouth was still sour, and his head ached. He felt a passionate desire for the cleanliness of an ascetic life, the hard decency of strenuous work in the lamp-lit severity of a scholar's library, of strenuous exercise in the open air that should be the only relief to study. He promised himself to lead a better, harder, cleaner life, and in this pious expectation fell into troubled sleep.

CHAPTER FIFTEEN

On the following morning the dull lethargic air of Sunday was replaced by an atmosphere of bustle and trepidation. The stone corridors of the Police Station were loud with the passing of official feet, and the brusque tones of official gossip were constantly heard. As the time approached for their removal to the Police Court both Magnus and Meiklejohn were conscious of a growing nervousness. They were permitted to wash, but soap and water could not remove their two days' growth of beard, and their collars were regrettably soiled. Despite all their efforts to smarten their appearance they wore a look of weary dissipation, and Meiklejohn's drooping eyelid hung so low as to give him a peculiarly rakish air.

To their consternation they were handcuffed for the journey, and their dismay increased when they learnt that they must walk, thus manacled, to the Court. They had no more than a hundred yards to go—out into the High Street and round the corner into Parliament Square—but a score of spectators, natives of the High Street and unkempt children, observed their progress, and the very daylight seemed of a piercing hawk-eyed kind that scrutinized their inmost being. The day was cold and its brightness was exaggerated by their week-end's confinement. The policeman escorting them spoke cheerfully to them and seemed well-disposed, but they were unable to share his humorous view of their situation.

They were taken through a narrow doorway and down a stone stair to wait for the arrival of the magistrates. There were many policemen and Court officials walking about, chatting genially among themselves. They wore an Olympian air. They seemed remote from the sins and frailties of their prisoners, and their rubicund benignity proclaimed them a race apart. Magnus grew envious of their self-esteem, their power, their semblance of beatitude.

By and by the prisoners were marched upstairs again and into the Court room. Their handcuffs had been removed. They filled three rows of benches in front of the Court, and behind them sat relatives and other interested spectators. Policemen stood in the doorways. A couple of agents spoke to their clients. Meiklejohn signalled to a reporter whom he knew and told him to keep his name and Magnus's out of the papers.

The magistrates came in. They wore their dignity less composedly, less authoritatively than the policemen. It was not so deeply ingrown, so conclusively and inevitably a part of their nature. But the senior magistrate set about his work with proficiency and dispatch.

There were several classes of drunken disorder that a minute or two's examination disposed of. Then a woman was called and charged with attempted suicide: she had drunk a bottle of spirits of lemon for no other reason, it seemed, than to attract the waning attention of her husband, and her neighbours. She was bound over to keep the peace and released under her husband's recognizances. She had succeeded in arousing his interest.

Then an old man, handsome in a Roman way, white-haired and dignified, was accused of cruelly ill-treating his grandchildren: he was remanded for further examination. Magnus and Meiklejohn followed the sadistic old man and stood together to hear the charges read against them. They were accused of assault, and breach of the peace, and committing five pounds' worth of malicious damage in the Albyn Hotel.

Meiklejohn immediately pleaded guilty. Magnus said, 'I plead guilty, but with reservations: we didn't commit damage to that extent. I don't believe we committed any damage at all.'

The magistrate, after consulting with a police sergeant, said, 'There is a representative of the Albyn Hotel here prepared to give evidence to the effect that you committed damage to glass and cutlery, furniture, and to a stair carpet, to the extent estimated. If you plead not guilty you can, of course, contest that assertion.'

Meiklejohn muttered, 'Guilty, you fool!' Magnus said, 'I plead guilty, sir,' and glared fiercely at the head waiter who had come to bear witness against him.

The magistrate said, 'It is very shocking to see people of your class brought here and charged with such offences. If you can afford to dine in such an hotel you ought to know how to behave yourselves. But apparently you conducted yourselves with great disorder, persistently annoyed your fellow-guests, and when you were requested to leave the hotel you committed the said assault. Have you any excuse for such behaviour?'

'We were rather excited,' said Magnus, 'I had been to the International in the afternoon, and I grew very excited there, and—well, we had rather a lot to drink and we continued to be excited. Then we had an argument . . .'

'About the match, I suppose?'

'No,' said Magnus.

'Then what was it about?'

'About Shakespeare,' said Magnus.

'*Shakespeare?*' said the magistrate.

'Well, Shakespeare and Racine.'

'Who?'

'Racine, the French dramatist.'

'I know, I know,' said the magistrate testily. 'I know who Racine is. You needn't tell me that. But what do you want to argue about him for?'

'My friend Meiklejohn says that he is a better poet than Shakespeare.'

By this time there was a sound of ill-suppressed merriment in several parts of the Court, and the magistrate and the law agents were regarding Magnus and Meiklejohn with that air of mild astonishment which well-bred people bestow upon an exhibition—of acrobatics, for example—that is sufficiently remarkable but not in the best of taste.

The senior magistrate, in a temper, said, 'Be careful, or I shall commit you for contempt of court.'

Magnus said, 'I assure you that I am speaking with all respect for the Court. We had an argument about the respective merits of Shakespeare and Racine, and we grew somewhat heated over it.'

The magistrate blew his nose. 'I can't understand you,' he said. 'If you had been arguing about the football match I should have been ready to take a more lenient view of the case—it is natural that young men should grow excited over such a topic—but for the puerile excuse that you have offered I have no sympathy whatsoever. However, you have been in prison since Saturday night, so I shall take that into consideration and fine you three pounds each. You will also have to pay five pounds damage. And I hope this will be a lesson to you: if you can't think about literature in a reasonable way, as reasonable people do, then don't think about it at all.'

When their possessions had been restored to them Magnus and Meiklejohn were just able, by pooling their money, to pay the eleven pounds required of them. Meiklejohn spoke to the reporter again, who promised to make no mention of the case, but in spite of this assurance he was still nervous and said he must go at once to his office, whence, by the tactful dissemination of personal explanations, he hoped completely to safeguard himself and Magnus against the unpleasantness of further publicity. He was also depressed by having to pay such heavy damages, for he was already in debt to Mrs Dolphin and now the prospect of paying his rent was indefinitely postponed.

'The only comforting feature of the whole business,' he

said, 'is that we didn't pay for our dinner. In the confusion they've probably forgotten all about the bill.'

But unfortunately for this lonely gleam of optimism the head waiter, very sprucely dressed, met them as they left the Police Court and presented a bill for £6 17s.0d.

'There's no ill-will, gentlemen,' he said, and smiled most amiably. 'We shall be pleased to see you in the Tarascon Restaurant any time you care to come.'

'A soup kitchen will be all I can afford to go to now,' said Meiklejohn gloomily. But Magnus took the bill and promised to pay it immediately.

They parted without more delay. Meiklejohn went to his office, and Magnus, head down to conceal his beard, hurried back to his flat in Queen Street. He desired one thing only: to escape the scene of his humiliation and avoid the glances of his fellow-men. He thought once more of taking refuge in Orkney, and though to flee thither would mean the abandonment of his political ambitions and desertion from the vanguard of Scottish Nationalism, he debated even those contingencies.

He found several letters waiting for him. One was from Frieda. It was a long rambling letter full of upbraiding that was mitigated, in a way, by the assurance that she still loved him. She said: 'I blame you—I must blame you—for getting drunk and behaving so badly, but I blame myself too, for I feel that I could have stopped you from drinking too much if only I had guessed what was going to happen. I meant to look after you—for I know your weakness now—but I failed. That's why I blame myself as well as you.'

Magnus felt that this was an unwarrantable impertinence. He had no wish to be looked after, and he could not see that Frieda had any right to consider herself as his guardian. And though he had criticized himself far more bitterly than she did, he did not, because of that, feel inclined to accept her strictures. He threw the letter down impatiently, without finishing it, and opened another. But in a minute or two curiosity supervened on impatience, and he picked it up again.

Frieda continued: 'It would have been bad enough if such a thing had happened at any time, but on Saturday it was especially hard to bear after what you had said to me while we were dancing. That made me so happy, and because I was happy then I grew more miserable than you can imagine afterwards. Oh, Magnus, you *did* mean what you said, didn't you? Call me as soon as you can, and I'll come and see you.'

Magnus read this in great embarrassment, for he could remember nothing of what he had said to Frieda while he was dancing with her. He knew that he had talked a great deal and that his volubility had often been affectionate. It might even have been extravagantly affectionate, for when he protested his admiration for a girl he liked to do it well, and words were such charming playthings that often he used them more for the pretty patterns they would make than for the stark conveyance of information. 'My God!' he muttered, 'what did I say to her?' But to save his life— had it been in danger—he could not remember, and he put down the letter very unhappily, fearing the worst.

The remaining letter was even more surprising. It was from Mr Macdonell, the Vice-President of the National Party, whom Magnus had met at Mr Sutherland's soirée. And Mr Macdonell wrote as follows:

'We have information that there will be a parliamentary by-election in Kinluce in the near future. Will you accept nomination as the Nationalist candidate? We have as yet no organization in Kinluce, but the whole strength of the Party would be behind you, and, as you know, such an extra-ordinary wave of enthusiasm for our cause is sweeping the country that I believe you would have a magnificent chance of success. From our point of view you would be an excellent candidate. Your name is already known, you are an able speaker—your few remarks at Sutherland's party greatly impressed me, and I have heard from various sources that in your University days you were a very skilful debater—and your articles in the *Evening Star* have been widely read and widely approved. You will be doing the Party the greatest service if you consent to fight this by-election.'

Mr Macdonell went on to remark that the old political parties had served their day, were now suspect on all sides, that Scotland was waiting for a new voice, and so forth. He concluded by saying that Magnus would be—had he said an excellent candidate? He had under-estimated him. He would be the ideal candidate. And Mr Macdonell earnestly hoped that Magnus would accept this invitation forthwith.

Magnus immediately forgot his humiliation in the Police Court, his subsequent desire to escape the world and live in solitude, and the acute embarrassment which Frieda's letter had caused him. He was enchanted by this sudden prospect of patriotic activity, and already the vague but shining vista of a great political career was unfolding in his imagination. The idea of declining the invitation, even of hesitating to accept it until he knew more about his constituency and the nature of the support which he was promised, never occurred to him. Nor did he suppose that his recent escapade would diminish his parliamentary value or impair Mr Macdonell's conception of him as the ideal candidate for Kinluce: for many patriotic people had been in prison for some period of their lives, and though their offences had generally been more explicitly political than his, yet to be arrested for arguing about Shakespeare and Racine had at least a flavour of political crime, for it closely resembled the disputing of the rival merits of England and France. Magnus almost felt that he could claim to have been a political prisoner, and without more ado sat down to reply to Mr Macdonell's letter and state that he was prepared to contest the forthcoming by-election in the interests of Scottish Nationalism.

CHAPTER SIXTEEN

When Frieda came to see him in the afternoon Magnus was in the pearly depths of a day-dream in which he saw himself entering Westminister as Scottish champion and heard himself thundering to those stricken benches the tale of Scotland's wrongs and Scotland's future. With the speed of light the dream pierced still farther into time, and he saw, as the end of his campaign, a consecration service at which all Scotland knelt to receive back into the midst the Stone of her Destiny, that rude block which the first Edward stole, whereon so many alien kings had been unjustly crowned. He was so moved by this dream that there were tears in his eyes when Frieda came in.

She, seeing him thus bedewed, thought he was repenting his sins and melted too. She threw her arms about his neck and murmured, 'Magnus, you won't ever behave like that again, will you? I do love you. Have you had a terrible time? Tell me about it and I'll help you to forget it all.'

'I've already forgotten,' said Magnus, and put away her encircling arms. 'Things are moving too fast for me to waste time on remorse. Look at this letter I've got. My dear, I'm going to stand for Parliament in a few weeks' time. There are tremendous events in the offing, and I've been extremely busy all day working out my plan of campaign. I'm going to put before the electors a plain straightforward programme, and insist that no remedy for Scotland's distress can be obtained until we have secured our independence. It's perfectly obvious . . .'

'All right, all right,' said Frieda, 'you're not elected yet and I'm not going to elect you. There's no need to make speeches at me. Give me a chance to read this letter.'

She was offended by her rebuff. She read the letter, and asked, 'Well, are you going to accept this kind invitation?'

'I've already accepted it. Don't you see what a marvellous opportunity it will be to preach Nationalism openly, to put our cause to the test of public approval, and possibly— probably even—to demonstrate that Scotland is at last determined to be free and independent? If I win I shall be the first Scottish Nationalist in Parliament.'

'And if you lose?'

'I'll have had the satisfaction of fighting for what I believe in.'

'What's this election going to cost you?'

'I don't know yet.'

'And what will happen to your poem and your other work?'

'I'll have to give up writing for some time, of course.'

'And sacrifice yourself in the sweet name of patriotism?'

'There's no need to put it like that. I don't want to

posture and prance and talk highfalutin' nonsense, but the fact remains that I do believe in Nationalism and I do know it's important. It's all-important.'

'So you're ready to let all your other interests go to hell or look after themselves?'

'For the immediate future, yes.'

'And that includes me, I suppose?' said Frieda.

'What do you mean?'

'Well, on Saturday night you asked me to marry you. But I suppose you'll be too busy now.'

Had the solid floor turned into quicksands—had the walls tumbled and revealed a hideous precipice before him—had time with a roar reversed its aim and revealed all history's backsides rushing towards him, Magnus could hardly have felt much more aghast. True, he had suspected this earlier in the day, but suspicion is only a pale shadow of fact, and even suspicion had been forgotten in his excited contemplations of a political future. He stared dumbly at Frieda. His lips felt dry. He licked them, and his throat made a nervous movement of swallowing.

'Well?' she asked.

'On Saturday, of course, I didn't know that this was going to happen,' he said. 'The invitation came as a great surprise to me, but it was impossible to refuse, and I think you'll admit . . .'

'Do you love me?' she interrupted.

'Most certainly I do.'

'And do you want to marry me?'

'Well, at present it's hardly a question of what I want to do. My own inclinations . . .'

'I see,' said Frieda. 'Duty before decency is your watchword, and I get the air. Well, you needn't worry. I never pleaded with any man to marry me yet, and I don't intend to start now. You've changed your mind, haven't you? I guess your opinions just naturally alter when you sober up. You wouldn't have asked me to marry you if you hadn't been cock-eyed at the time: is that so? Well, I wouldn't have said yes if I hadn't been cock-eyed too. So now you know. I'll say this, that you've got a swell line of talk when you're properly lit—and after the liquor's burnt out there's nothing left but cinders and dust. You're a piker! Hell! What's the use of talking?'

She had never looked lovelier. Her anger, like a lamp, lighted her tawny beauty. Vituperation expanded her lungs and her breasts thrust out their firm contours like haycocks on a summer field. Her throat was a white column, and her chin was square, truculent, and delicious. For a moment she stood, tall as a soldier, lovely as yellow roses, and wild as a Fury. Then, turning abruptly, she stalked out of the room and slammed the door behind her.

A feeling of relief, that he recognized as cowardly and undesirable, was Magnus's first sensation after she had gone. But it was a negative feeling, a poor substitute for the exhilaration of his political dreams that this stormy interlude had banished. Even relief was short-lived, for his conscience, tattling like an old maid, began to tell him that Frieda was justified in all she had said, and that he was indeed a poor specimen of manhood, a false hero who flaunted himself in fine colours when he was drunk and dwindled to a shabby twit when sober. And then another of those inward voices that keep mankind from happiness spoke up to say that Frieda was the finest girl he had ever known. Very brave and most lovely, and that he was a fool to let her go. Marry the girl, this voice adjured, and let politics go hang.—But marriage, said a more thoughtful voice, marriage is a dull estate, a thing of chains and fetters, and Frieda, for all her loveliness, is not altogether desirable as a wife. Other men have been there before you, and that thought will worry you. She's wild, moreover, and you would have no peace with her.—Be ruthless, said another voice. Fame is the only good worth fighting for. Love is a paltry thing, pity a slavish thing. Forget her, let her go, and, being ruthless, become famous. That's all very well, said Magnus himself, but I'm not sure that I'm really made that way.

Then these familiar voices took up the argument again, tearing it to shreds, knotting it and cutting the knots, and for the rest of the day Magnus was the unhappy auditor of their conflicting theories.

But in the morning he went to see Meiklejohn, whose enthusiasm on hearing the news was very comforting.

Meiklejohn borrowed a couple of pounds from Magnus and took him to lunch at the Café de Bordeaux.

'I'm devilish hard up,' he said, 'and I've got no appetite. Order what you like, old fellow. I'm going to have some caviare and half a bottle of champagne. Nothing else. I always cut my meals to a minimum when I'm on the rocks. But you go ahead: there's some very good cold roast beef there. Have some of that, won't you? And now tell me all about Kinluce.'

After a long and exhilarating conversation, in which Scotland's independence came appreciably nearer, Magnus returned to his flat and found Frieda waiting for him. She had come to apologize for her rudeness and to admit that he had been right in declaring that his career was more important than her happiness.—Magnus tried to interrupt, but she continued in the tones of sweet reason.—She had been impulsive: love had made her so: but now she was resigned to wait. She was not going to be a hindrance to him. If, for the meantime, Magnus was disinclined to commit himself to a formal engagement, then she would not demand one. They could still be friends, and she would be contented with that relationship.

She stayed with him till nearly dinner-time, and encouraged him to talk of the situation in Kinluce and to explain the lines on which he proposed to fight the election. She showed such perfect sympathy that Magnus warmed to her again and allowed the conversation to include topics more intimate than political matters. It became evident that her understanding of friendship was somewhat proprietorial, and that the harmless relationship which she had proposed might well be described as an unofficial engagement. Her demeanour was so charming, however, that they parted not only with affection but with reluctance.

For the next week Magnus was very busy. He had interviews with Mr Macdonell and other important members of the National Party, and he was given a great deal of advice and information about the state of affairs in Kinluce. The present Member was seriously ill and was expected to resign at any moment. It appeared that financially the Party was not very well off, but Mr Macdonell was sure that for so important an occasion their members would contribute handsomely, and that sufficient funds would be forthcoming to meet all the election expenses. He had secured an ideal person for Magnus's election agent, he said, a Captain Archibald Smellie, a gentleman who had much experience of political organization and was a perfervid Nationalist. Captain Smellie was a tall thin man with black hair and a pronounced squint. He had a confident and ingratiating manner. He immediately referred to Magnus as 'The Candidate', and took advantage of every occasion to recite passages from Blue Books and Year Books and similar publications.

In addition to these official conversations Magnus was visited by Hugh Skene, McVicar, Mrs Dolphin, Mr Newlands, Miss Beaty Bracken and other people whom he had first met at Mr Sutherland's soirée. They all promised to come and help him in Kinluce, and though their diverse enthusiasm for Communism, pacifism, vegetarianism, poet nonconformity, and economic heresy might impair their presentation of a united front, Magnus was very glad to accept their offers of assistance.

Frieda came to see him every day. She made herself perfectly at home in his flat, and acquired a number of habits that indicated her increasingly domestic view of their association. She would, for instance, borrow his handkerchief when she had forgotten her own. As she was a strong healthy girl with few affectations she blew her nose very vigorously, and when she returned the handkerchief Magnus often felt that it was really hers and that it was he who was borrowing it. But his mind was so occupied that he gave little thought to what was happening, and let her darn his socks without perceiving the significance of such benevolence.

News came at last that the Member for Kinluce had applied for the Chiltern Hundreds. Two days later Magnus visited his constituency, accompanied by Mr Macdonell, Captain Smellie, and other prominent members of the Party, and in a draughty, ill-lit Temperance Hall addressed some eighteen or twenty apathetic electors, who were subsequently declared to have unanimously adopted him as the Nationalist candidate.

CHAPTER SEVENTEEN

Kinluce is an East Coast constituency. Predominantly an agricultural district, it contains two little towns, one of which, called Kingshouse, is the market-town of the surrounding neighbourhood, and has also a few small industrial interests: the other, called Kinlawton, is a health-resort and the home in their retirement of many officers in His Majesty's service, Civil Servants, and elderly ladies. North of Kinlawton there are several fishing-villages, and on the western border of the county, that abuts on a mining area, there is a fringe of colliers' hamlets.

The constituency has a reputation for keen thinking and a fierce interest in politics. At this time, however, there was such confusion in the general situation that even the most ardent of political amateurs were handicapped by a certain dubiety as to what their parties stood for. There were many critics, indeed, who maintained that politics had lost reality, and that it was impossible to tell one party from another except by the accent of their speakers: and even this difference was rapidly vanishing owing to the number of wealthy and aristocratic people who, during the Socialist Party's tenure of power, had announced their conversion to its principles.

The Socialist Prime Minister, Mr Melvin McMaster, had held office for some two years. During that time the policy of his government had travelled so far to the right that now only the most bigoted Tories could discern the red hue of Socialism in its complexion, and not a few people declared that it was more Conservative than the Conservatives. Having completely failed to do what it set out to do it had much in common with all other post-war governments, and so orthodox a record of unachievement had given it a certain dignity. Its prime task had been to reduce unemployment, for the progress of civilization had brought into existence this curious state of affairs: that the world's work, which used to be of such huge proportions that no one could hope to do all that was required of him, had now so shrunk and dwindled as to be a rare and elusive treasure. Work, that was once a curse to mankind, blinding him with sweat and

torturing him with aches and pains, had now become a boon
to be sought for and not found. And though the granaries
and warehouses of the world were packed full of food and
all kinds of commodities—owing to the benign progress of
civilization—the world had grown so poor that it could not
afford to buy them. Unemployment was therefore not that
paradisal state which it might have been had provision been
made—in the progress of civilization—for the distribution
as well as production of commodities, and all the governments of the world were pledged to reduce it. Some, by
methods considered unamiable in this country, had made a
partial success of their endeavours, but all British governments had come to the conclusion that unemployment
was due to cosmic embarrassments, planetary influence,
the delayed invention of contraceptives, God's providence,
and other matters over which they had no control. And
therefore, the problem being insoluble, their only duty was
to maintain the unemployed by charitable contributions
until their *morale* had gone, after which it would be safe to
neglect them.—It was found that three years on the dole was
generally sufficient to break a man's spirit, so three years was
declared the period for which the unemployed were entitled
to relief.—The conversion of Mr McMaster's government to
this theory was hailed as a triumph for Conservatism, and
there were rumours on the wing that he intended, before
long, to go to the country with a programme illuminating
such a view, and plead with the electors to return, with
him at its head, a National-Constitutionalist government
prepared to maintain, against any odds, this truly wise and
conservative policy.

Faced, then, with the prospect of a general election before
the year was out, and also with the emergence of a new party,
the political associations in Kinluce were taken aback by
their sudden by-election, and found it difficult to decide
what to do. For several days Magnus, who had taken up
residence in the Grant Hotel in Kinlawton, was the only
candidate in the field, and Captain Smellie was already
prophesying that the election would be a walk-over.

By virtue of his greater political experience the Captain
adopted a somewhat patronizing manner towards Magnus.

Their first few meetings were ill-attended, and Magnus said, 'I'm afraid the electors aren't very enthusiastic about Nationalism.'

Captain Smellie smiled in a superior fashion and answered, 'Now don't you worry about that. I've sized-up this constituency pretty well, and I understand the mentality of the people. They're not giving anything away, but I happen to know that you've made a very favourable impression. I've tapped a great many sources of information, and I *know* that the whole county is well-disposed to you.'

Captain Smellie had a rich purring voice, and he spoke with such confidence that Magnus was compelled to believe him, though so far as he was aware the Captain spent every day smoking a large pipe in the Committee Rooms and had not met a dozen electors all told. He carried with him a brief-case and a huge leather portfolio full of documents, pamphlets, Blue Books, and official forms, and these he would examine with frowning intentness, squinting so hard that he appeared to be reading two pages at once. Whenever Magnus asked what he was doing he would answer, 'Planning the campaign, Merriman, planning the campaign. To work without a plan is mere waste of time. I've had considerable experience in business of this kind, and I know what I'm talking about. Now I think you'll find this little book on electoral law and procedure well worth your attention, and if you'll go away and study it I'll get on with *my* work. I must co-ordinate my sources of information.'

When a week had passed and still no other candidates had been adopted, Captain Smellie, purring contentedly, said, 'You'll find my prophecy is coming true. You're going to have a walk-over, Merriman. I've been in touch with all the local organizations, and I have it on good authority that none of them can find a suitable candidate.'

Unfortunately for the Captain's reputation as a prophet, the Socialists, on the very next day, announced their adoption of Mr Robert Nimmo as a candidate, and two days later the Conservative Association chose as their nominee a Mr Gatwick Buchanan.

Captain Smellie said, 'I thought as much. They were trying to pull the wool over my eyes. They're frightened

of us, Merriman! But they can't deceive me. I had a very
good idea of what was going on all the time—and I don't
think that either of their candidates will cut much ice in
Kinluce.'

It was true that neither Mr Buchanan nor Mr Nimmo
were ideal candidates. The former was a recently converted
Liberal—the Liberal Party was so diminished in numbers
and authority that many truly patriotic people, realizing the
folly of adhering to its principles when there was no chance
either of putting their principles into practice or themselves
into office, had resigned from it to join either the Conservatives or the Socialists, sacrificing their personal inclinations
with the cheerful alacrity of patriots and practical men—and
though a majority of the Kinluce Conservative Association
was satisfied with Mr Buchanan's newly-acquired probity,
there was a minority that shook their heads over his Liberal
past, and suspected that his Conservatism was lukewarm.
And all the remaining Liberals in Kinluce naturally detested
him for his recusancy.

Mr Nimmo, on the other hand, was a lifelong Socialist,
but his creed was far too extreme to have the approval of
Mr McMaster and his Cabinet, and Mr Nimmo was hard
put to it to reconcile his own interpretation of Socialism with
the practice of a Socialist Government. He suffered a further
handicap in that he had previously worked as a miner in West
Kinluce, and many of his early associates were so jealous of
his advancement that they would certainly refuse to vote for
him although he preached the creed which they protested.

With three candidates in the field the political atmosphere became fairly lively, and the county was already well
sprinkled with bills and posters, in a variety of colours,
that exhorted the electors to vote for Nimmo, Buchanan,
or Merriman. Magnus toured the constituency in a hired
motor car, addressing small outdoor meetings by day and
small indoor meetings at night. Perhaps it would be more
accurate to say that he toured the county with the intention
of addressing such meetings, for it often happened that when
they arrived at a village they discovered that the meeting had
been advertised for the following night, or the preceding
night, or not advertised at all. For these mistakes Captain

Smellie blamed his sub-agents, Mr Boden and Mr Bird, and protested that no one, not even Napoleon, could efficiently conduct a campaign if he were unable to rely upon his subordinates. But he was not shaken by these reverses. He would say that Mr Boden and Mr Bird required discipline: that was all: and when they had been sufficiently disciplined they would do their work very well indeed.

'And I know something about discipline,' he said with a hoarse laugh. 'Ha-ha-ha! Leave them to me. I'll make them jump. As soon as my plans are complete this campaign will go like clockwork.'

It happened one night that they went to a village called Pitsharnie with great anticipation of a successful meeting, for Captain Smellie had reported that the villagers were already addicted to the principles of Nationalism and would undoubtedly be there in force to welcome their candidate. Magnus was in high fettle, moreover, because on the previous day he had addressed a large and attentive meeting in Kinlawton, and had dealt in excellent manner with half a dozen determined hecklers. He was accompanied to Pitsharnie by Miss Bracken from Edinburgh and by a Mr McCunn from Glasgow, and on the way he talked to them in tones almost as optimistic as Captain Smellie's.

But when they arrived at Pitsharnie they discovered that not a single poster adorned the village, not a handbill had been distributed, and the school in which the meeting was to be held was occupied only by the caretaker.

'By God,' said Captain Smellie, 'this is Bird's fault—or it may be Boden's. But I think it's Bird's. I'll give him hell for this. I'll give them both hell. This is the last piece of muddling I'll put up with. There'll be no more muddling after this, Merriman. Take that from me. I'll stand no more of it, and Bird won't readily forget what I'm going to tell him tonight.'

They returned to Kinlawton in some gloom. Miss Bracken and Mr McCunn were very annoyed at not being able to deliver the speeches which they had prepared, and they made many invidious remarks about the efficient manner in which other elections, at which they had assisted, had been conducted. Captain Smellie agreed with everything they said, assured them that so small a disaster as this would not impair the chances of their candidate—which were excellent, he said—and reiterated his promise to deal in exemplary fashion with Mr Bird and Mr Boden.

Mr Bird and Mr Boden were drinking stout and tonic water in the Commercial Room of the small hotel where they lodged. Mr Bird was a wizened little man with a red nose and a thin straggle of black hair: Mr Boden was a hale and hearty fat man with false teeth which he usually kept in a little tin box, where he found them more comfortable than in his mouth.

Captain Smellie came in with an air of great determination and fixing Mr Bird with a converging stare—the angle of his squint grew more acute under the stress of anger—said brusquely, 'Look here, Bird, how many bills and posters did you have distributed for the meeting tonight?'

'Oh, quite a number,' said Mr Bird.

'I asked you *how many*?'

'Well, I think there were six posters and some handbills.'

'But there were twenty-five posters and a hundred handbills in the parcel I sent you.'

'There weren't nearly as many as that,' said Mr Boden in a loud bluff way.

Captain Smellie grew polite and ingratiating before his opposition, and his masterful frown gave place to a winning smile.

'Oh, come,' he said, 'I think you're making a mistake. They go into very small bulk, you know.'

'Maybe,' said Mr Boden, 'but there were only six all the same. And you were late in sending them as well.'

The Captain turned to Magnus. 'You see what I have to contend with,' he said. 'This is a very difficult constituency to organize, but when my plans are complete . . .'

'But I saw no bills at all at Pitsharnie,' Magnus interrupted. 'What happened to the six you did send?'

'We put them up at Pitmidden,' said Mr Bird.

'At Pitmidden?' exclaimed the Captain. 'What the hell did you take them there for?'

'Because you told me that you had a meeting there tonight, as well as at Pitsharnie,' said Mr Boden.

'Good God!' said Captain Smellie. 'Why wasn't I informed of this earlier? Merriman, I've never had to work with such a faulty organization before. How can my plans be carried out in face of such incompetence as this? I must go back to the Committee Rooms at once and set to work to repair this damage. But don't be disheartened, Merriman. You're winning! I have it on the best authority that wherever you go you make a most favourable impression. You're doing very well indeed. *Mine* is the harder part; I must go and make new plans immediately.'

'Plans!' said Mr Boden contemptuously, and finished his stout and tonic-water.

His growing perception that Captain Smellie was hardly so competent as he pretended to be gave Magnus a lot of worry, but fortunately Mr Boden was both able and energetic, and the task of organization fell more and more on his shoulders. They were severely handicapped by lack of funds, but Mr Macdonell had written several times saying that Lord Sandune, an aged and wealthy peer who had dabbled in politics in the latter years of Queen Victoria's reign, was a recent convert to Scottish Nationalism and would shortly be appearing in person in Kinluce, not only to support Magnus on the platform, but to contribute handsomely to Party funds. Now came another letter from Mr Macdonell in which he stated that Lord Sandune would definitely be in the constituency early in the following week.

But before his lordship appeared there came a surprise that all the more sensational newspapers referred to, not inaptly, as a bombshell. This was caused by the intervention of Lady Mercy Cotton, who suddenly put forward a candidate of her own choosing, and by exerting a mite of her enormous influence secured his nomination by a fairly representative meeting of electors.

CHAPTER EIGHTEEN

Lady Mercy [some account of her activities may be found in a novel called *Poet's Pub*] was a power in the land, though it would be difficult to make an exact assessment of her strength. It was more than her enemies pretended, but less than she herself believed. She commanded an audience of

several million people, but as there are limits even to the
gullibility of a great democracy she was not always able
to persuade her audience to do what she wanted. She
could, however, make herself extremely objectionable to
her political opponents, and her destructive criticism might
have been more effective had it been more stable. But its
habit of veering from one point of the compass to another—
now blowing hotly against the Conservatives, now rudely
buffeting the remainder Liberals, and anon whistling icy
derision at the Socialists—tended to diminish its potency
though greatly increasing its value as entertainment.

Her fortune had been founded on Cotton's Breweries. Her
growing wealth had nourished a growing ambition, and by
sacrificing the amiability that previously had characterized
even her professional activities she had become a truly
conquering figure. After the death of Sewald Cotton, her
mild and dignified husband, she had assumed full control
of the business, and presently added to her possession a
couple of provincial newspapers. The intoxicating power of
the press—even of such a comparatively small draught as
this—had tempted her into greater extravagance, and in a
little while she had also acquired a London daily paper, the
Morning Call, and its subsidiary organ, the *Evening Bolus*.

But her commercial genius stood her in good stead: so
far from losing money in this venture, she made it, and
her fortune mounted to bewildering heights. For some
years it had been the practice of certain newspapers to
win new readers by offering gifts, or free life insurance,
or free household insurance, to regular subscribers. Lady
Mercy immediately discerned the full possibilities of this
custom, and after negotiations with a building society, a
well-known firm that specialized in the supply of furniture
on the instalment system, and an insurance company, she
elaborated a scheme by which readers of the *Morning Call*
might acquire, with no further expense than their subscrip-
tions, an artistic freehold dwelling and elegant appointments
for every apartment from the drawing-room to the scullery.
The purchase of a single copy of the *Call* entitled you to
the free gift of a chamber pot; a year's subscription, paid
in advance, brought you a handsome suite of drawing-room

furniture; and if you could persuade five hundred of your friends each to pay a five years's subscription you at once became the owner of a half-timbered semi-detached villa built in the Elizabethan style so far as that was consistent with single-brick walls.

A week after the announcement of this scheme the circulation of the *Call* had risen to three and a half million, and Lady Mercy had quadrupled her advertising rates. She was able, then, to appeal to an enormous public, and it was a source of real sorrow to her that these people, many of them living as they were in her half-timbered villas and more of them using her chamber pots, could not yet be relied upon to believe all the news with which she supplied them, or to obey her numerous behests to write at once to the Prime Minister and demand his adoption of a firmer attitude towards America.

But she was not dismayed by this popular ineptitude: she determined to save the country in spite of its predilection for *laissez-faire* and the road to ruin. Because of the Socialists' two years in office, and because they seemed likely to be replaced by a set of lukewarm, milk-and-watery Constitutionalists, she was at this time well-inclined towards the Conservatives—but only to those Conservatives of the true two-bottle, penal-flogging, forty-shillings-on-wheat, hands-off-the-Navy complexion. Mr Gatwick Buchanan, that new and suspect convert to Conservatism, was not at all to her liking. She therefore instituted inquiries in Kinluce and discovered that there was an excellent candidate in the person of a gentleman there called Hammerson. He was a prosperous farmer who had political ambitions, was the kind of Tory she favoured, and being of a generous and open-hearted nature he was extremely popular throughout the county. She decided that with her support he could easily win the election and she promptly established connection with Major Muir-Macbeth, the secretary of the Kinluce Conservative Association, who was known to be dissatisfied with the candidature of Mr Gatwick Buchanan.

Major Muir-Macbeth was instructed, by telephone, to go and see Mr Hammerson and to tell him that if he would agree to stand he would be assured of Lady Mercy's personal assistance, of the support of her newspapers, of her political organization, and of the most generous financial backing. The Major seemed somewhat surprised by this commission, but having accepted it he very soon reported, again by telephone, that the offer had been accepted with great pleasure, and that he would immediately arrange a nomination meeting for the Cotton-Conservative candidate.

Lady Mercy thereupon sent Nelly Bly [a previous adventure of Nelly Bly is also told in *Poet's Pub*], the most brilliant of her special correspondents, to Kinluce in order to report the meeting and also to prepare the way for the advent of further Cotton auxiliaries.

On the following day the *Morning Call* described, with great enthusiasm and prominent type, the adoption of a fourth candidate in Kinluce, and already prophesied his success at the polls. But his name, by some curious mistake apparently, was said to be Emerson, not Hammerson. Lady Mercy angrily demanded an explanation. She was informed that there had been no mistake, but that Mr Emerson—a prosperous gentleman-farmer, a Conservative, and a man with political ambitions—was in truth the candidate.

'Then where is Hammerson?' she demanded.

Mr Hammerson, it appeared, was sitting quietly at home, and the dilucidation of this unfortunate error was only made when Lady Mercy interviewed the assistant news-editor of the *Morning Call*, who had conducted the telephone negotiations with Major Muir-Macbeth.

'It was you who spoke to Major Muir-Macbeth?' she asked.

'Yes, your ladyship,' said the assistant news-editor.

'And you told him to get in touch with Mr Hammerson?'

'Yes, your ladyship.'

'And what happened then?'

'He rang up again and told me that Mr Emerson would be very pleased to stand.'

'*Who* would be pleased to stand?'

'Mr Emerson, your ladyship.'

'Hammerson, I told you, not Emerson.'

'Yes, your ladyship, Mr Emerson. That's what I said.'

'Give this fool a week's wages and tell him to get out of

here,' shouted Lady Mercy, and strode up and down the room in a stupendous rage.

The unfortunate assistant news-editor was therefore sacked for no more grievous a fault than the possession of a Cockney accent, and for the same slight phonetic reason Lady Mercy found herself committed to a large public gamble with the wrong cards in her hand.—Also the electors of Kinluce were saddled with a candidate whom neither they nor anyone else wanted; but that, after all, was a matter of small importance.—Lady Mercy, being a great woman, quickly decided that any man who stood with her support was better than any other without that help, and resolved to prosecute Mr Emerson's candidature with all her energy. She announced her own early arrival in the constituency, and sent ahead of her a small army of supporting speakers, canvassers, handbill-distributors, reporters, photographers, agents and organizers. Kinluce was filled with the sound and fury of her campaign, and even the phlegmatic countenances of the dour east-wind-hardy electors began to show occasional traces of excitement.

The announcement of the Cotton candidate affected Magnus with some dismay, for the election now appeared to be taking on the likeness of a raree-show, and he grew painfully aware of the indignity of competitive shouting. But Captain Smellie was unperturbed.

'I've been expecting something like this,' he said. 'I was talking to a man who's in Muir-Macbeth's confidence a few days ago, and I got an inkling of what might happen. But I said nothing about it because I didn't want to cause you unnecessary worry. And you mustn't worry now, Merriman. It was clear from the beginning—at least it was clear to me—that this was going to be no ordinary election. From the very first day I knew that we had to be prepared for anything. And I was prepared! That's why I left my plans in a somewhat fluid state, so that I could adapt them to meet an emergency. On the whole I'm very glad of this Cotton intervention. It will split the Conservative vote, and your chances will be much improved. We're doing very well indeed. I was talking to an errand-boy yesterday, and he assured me that if he had a vote—unfortunately he hasn't—

he would certainly give it to you. But every straw shows how the wind blows.'

Magnus said idly, 'What regiment were you in during the war, Smellie?'

Captain Smellie coughed and turned to look out of the window. 'I was unattached during most of my service,' he said. 'I was on the General List.'

'What were you doing there?'

'I had special duties. At the War Office, you know.'

'Intelligence?'

'Yes,' said Captain Smellie.

'I thought as much,' said Magnus bitterly. But Captain Smellie was pleased by the compliment.

Magnus said, 'Well, I'm going for a walk. I want to think out a couple of speeches for tonight.'

The Captain purred sympathetically. 'I have a score of things to do,' he said. 'There's a very busy morning ahead of me. Bird and Boden must be kept up to scratch, you know, and owing to this Cotton complication my plans will need a certain amount of revision. It's lucky that I'm an old hand at the game and was prepared for it.'

Magnus walked moodily out of the town, across a golf-course, and down to the sea-shore. Firm yellow sands stretched southwards. In cold sunlight the sea shone azure-bright, and white gulls wheeled above its crumbling edge. The gorse on the links was breaking into golden bloom, a lark rose singing on its invisible ladder, and far-off hills smudged the oyster sky with blue. Suddenly Magnus felt his heart fill with passionate love for the very soil of Scotland, for the sea that broke on its coasts, and the mountain airs that filled its sky with music. Why should he waste his time talking of statistics, in the counting of dead chimneys, in the unearthing of political scandals, in the dull reiteration of economic facts? Was it not better to open blind eyes to the beauty of Scotland, to waken sleeping minds to pride, and trust to pride for strength to leap all obstacles?

He thought of all the counties of Scotland he had never seen: of the Highlands, of the islands of the north and the west: and the beauty of his own country cried like trumpets in his blood and woke in him such desire and love that a

weakness came on him, and tears broke saltily in his eyes . . .
He saw the granite and the grace of the Western Highlands,
the stark hills and the multitude of small bright flowers that
enamelled all the summer fields. Here in a dark pool grew
water-lilies with hearts of gold and cool white petals: that
water-lilies should grow in flat English ponds was nothing,
but here, where birch trees made a curtain for the tarn and
the stony grandeur of the mountains made under heaven a
wall for the birches, here water-lilies were a sign of grace
indeed, as though, not silver-footed Thetis, but some white-
foot girl of Ossian's or Freyja from the northern snows, had
walked in loveliness and painted flowers where she trod.
Now to the white shore came with green banners an army of
young trees, and stooped upon the sand, and gazed beyond
it to still water more deeply green than they. Where in the
world was greenness so multi-hued and various as here?—
the green of young larches, the pallid green of winter fields,
the tender gaiety of young corn, the peacock tones of the sea
past Eriskay, the black-heart green of pine-forests, the soft
green of old and faded tartan, the darkly-gleaming holly-
green, bracken-green and heather-green, reeds in the lake
and peewit's wings, and the emerald heart of Atlantic waves
that reared like horses in the sun and broke like thunder on
the shore? And this was the abiding magic of the land, that
wherever you looked closely you saw loveliness in delicate
and tiny shapes, and whenever you raised your eyes to far-off
things you beheld beauty tall and severe, the stony ribs of
the mountains, the cloud-capped sublimity of their peaks.
Kneel on that white sand and behold the infinite variety
of its colour: stoop to orchis and heartsease, heather and
hare-bell, and discover the minute perfection of their design:
then stand and see Braeriach in the storm, or the towering
heights of Rum, savage and blue, crowning a golden sea.

In such guise did Scotland appear to Magnus as he walked
by the sea-shore, and over its mountains and its glens, its
lochs and islands, flew like wild sea-gulls the shrill voices
of their Gaelic names. In his exalted mood it seemed to him
infinitely more desirable to speak in grave and lofty terms
of these aspects of his country than to argue irately about
unemployment, shipyards on the Clyde, and injustices that

were killing the textile industry. Surely politics were false, were mere huckstering and trading in a clipped coinage, unless based on patriotism? And surely patriotism might be given a voice even in a Parliamentary election.

Magnus resolved to speak that night on larger issues, in a nobler key, and driving to Pitsharnie, where a meeting had been arranged to take the place of that which had been mis-arranged, he preserved a somewhat gloomy silence despite the provocative chatter of Captain Smellie and a talkative young man from Glasgow who had recently arrived to display, in the name of Nationalism, a truly remarkable power of oratory.

At Pitsharnie, however, Magnus found an atmosphere and an audience ill-suited to an exposition of lofty patriotism. A little fat man, who had opened the meeting, was speaking to an audience of some twenty or thirty oafish rustics. He was quoting the poet Burns—whom with greasy unction he referred to as *Rabbie*—and he was distorting the utterance of that sweet singer, that boisterous satirist, into something as mealy-mouthed, as nauseatingly sentimental, as his own saps-and-treacle habit of thought. Magnus listened to him with sour distaste—there had been no applause when the candidate entered—and looked at the audience.

There was an ill-washed, ill-favoured boy sitting beside a rat-mouthed mother. There was a coarse lumpy woman, dressed in the dark, who showed eight of her badly-assorted yellow teeth when she yawned. There was a brace of loutish hobbledehoys, and an old man with a dribbling nose, an ear-trumpet, a dirty beard, and a noisy habit of breathing. There was a rough sneering red-faced slit-eyed cattle-dealer, all whisky and lechery, and a plump blouse-full of girl hotly aware of him in the seat in front. There was a smug trim smooth little minister, making three hundred a year pimping for a God in whom his heart was too small to believe; an angry impotent schoolmaster who made rather less by petty sadism and failing to educate children whom—in his favour be it said—no power on earth could educate: and a rickle of rural inanity behind.

In face of such an audience the noble sentences, the passionate high thoughts, the lofty hortations that were in

Magnus's mind crumbled like dreams in the grey light of a November morning, and his mouth was filled with dust.

The little fat man concluded his speech by assuring these dismal electors that a man was a man for a' that, and they were a' Jock Tamson's bairns. He sat down in a mutter of apathetic applause.

Magnus rose to speak, and throwing aside all thought of Atlantic islands and sunbright lochs, recited so dull a string of facts and figures that even the Calvinised Boeotians in front of him were bored. Half an hour later he drove to the neighbouring village of Pitmidden and made an even worse speech, for he forgot his figures, began—after an interruption—to talk about India instead of Scotland, and was led into an angry defence of Imperialist policy that ill-accorded with the peaceful aims of small nationalism.

He returned to Kinlawton in a very bad temper, and found waiting for him another letter from Frieda. She had written to him every day since he left Edinburgh, sometimes twice a day, and often at great length. Her letters were overflowing with endearments, voluble, full of vitality, and fat with solicitude for his welfare. There was so much of them and so many of them that, despite their warmth, they seemed like a snowstorm so heavy that it was impossible to breath without inhaling the fleecy thick flakes. Sometimes, such was their enfolding care, they seemed like a feather-bed. And Magnus, already tried and troubled by his political campaign, found them an added weariness from which he would be glad to escape.

This latest letter held new cause for worry. Frieda reported that her aunt had received a letter from a friend of hers in Orkney, to whom she had apparently written for information, in which it was stated that people called Macafee and Newlands, with whom Magnus had claimed acquaintance during his first brief conversation with Aunt Elizabeth—in response to her assertion of friendship with the best families in Orkney—were by no means people with whom respectable citizens would choose to associate, but well-known tinkers or gipsies. On top of this her Uncle Henry had heard rumours of Magnus's escapade on the night of the Rugby International, and nosing along their trail had presently learnt the full story of his week-end in prison. This tale had filled a whole evening in Rothesay Crescent with hideous conversation, till at length, partly with the brave idea of openly taking sides with him, partly to shock her aunt and uncle, Frieda had announced that she and Magnus were engaged to be married. The news had had the desired effect of shocking them, but not into acquiescence. It had on the contrary doubled their hostility towards him and stimulated them to fresh commands that she should have nothing to do with him. But that, said Frieda, was an impossible prohibition. No power on earth could make her give him up. And now her chief hope was that Magnus would win the election—from the beginning, for his sake, she had hoped for that, but now for her own sake as well—because success in such dimensions would surely influence the Wisharts. To Members of Parliament much may be forgiven, even occasional drunkenness and a week-end in prison, and as Member for Kinluce Magnus might yet reinstate himself as a desirable suitor in the Wishart household.

This suggestion proved less comforting to Magnus than it had to Frieda. But the fear which had lately been assailing him, that he had small chance of success in the election, now seemed less unkind. He wanted to win, and he still hoped to win: with the vote split between so many candidates a small majority would be sufficient to elect any one of them: but now, should he lose, a kind of consolation prize was offered him in that his shadowy yet close-clinging engagement to Frieda would apparently be broken off. For he was now assured that he did not want to marry her. The voluminous solicitude and the undiminishing liveliness of her letters had been too much for him. Marriage to her, he thought, would be an occupation that permitted no other activities. Had she been content to remain his mistress he would have been delighted, for she was lovely to look at, charming to fondle, and her vitality was indeed engaging so long as it was curtailed by social expediency. But since the idea of marriage had taken root in her mind all other qualities had been obscured by, or had come to subserve, an alarming possessiveness. And no matter how alluring the bait, Magnus still shrank from being thus possessed.

CHAPTER NINETEEN

The meeting at which Lord Sandune was to make his reappearance in politics—and where, it was hoped, he would present the Party with a handsome cheque for their campaign expenses—was to be held in a mining village called Crullan. It was the centre of the coal district, and a large audience might be expected. That morning Magnus was greatly cheered by the arrival of Sergeant Denny and McRuvie, who said they had come to help him. Denny had won eighteen pounds on a horse named *Scotland Yet* that chanced to be running at Kempton Park, and thereupon he had conceived the idea of assisting the Nationalist candidate and had generously paid McRuvie's expenses so that he would have company. They were both flattered by the thought of having been in prison with a potential Member of Parliament, and they offered to do anything from bill-sticking to the man-handling of hecklers. They were immediately sent to Crullan to distribute handbills.

That evening began inauspiciously, for Magnus and his party arrived at Crullan, where they were to meet Lord Sandune, at seven o'clock, and found that the meeting was advertised for eight. Captain Smellie made his usual excuses and blamed Mr Bird, who was not there. Lord Sandune, however, proved unexpectedly amiable, and merely suggested they should find somewhere to wait, for it was raining and the Crullan Public Hall was cold as a barn. There was a public house, that called itself an hotel, in the village, and they went there. The landlord said there was a fire in the coffee-room and led the way upstairs.

It was a shabby stuffy little room with a table laid for high-tea at which a corpulent piggish-looking man with small mean eyes and a large wet mouth sat eating ham and eggs. From his complexion and from the untidy way in which he ate it was clear that he was drunk. Lord Sandune looked at him with some distaste, and the piggish man stared back in a stupid way, snorted, and then, as though to assert his independence, lavishly poured tomato-sauce over his ham and eggs and the neighbouring parts of the tablecloth.

Lord Sandune was a tall old man, very slow and portentous of speech, who leaned on his aged dignity as though it were a crutch. Magnus had been accompanied from Kinlawton by Captain Smellie, Mr Boden, Mr Macdonell, and Hugh Skene, who had already spoken several times in Kinluce with great vigour but commendable restraint. Now they talked together in quiet tones and behaved deferentially towards Lord Sandune in expectation of his cheque.

Presently the piggish man said, 'Hey! Who are you? Are you more of these bloody politicians?'

Captain Smellie whispered to Magnus, 'Never waste a vote! I'll have this fellow's promised before we leave here'; and answered, 'Yes, we're politicians, and I hope you're going to support our party.'

'What party's that?'

'The honest party,' said Captain Smellie.

'Sh—!' said the piggish man, and sucked half a fried egg into his mouth.

'Oh, really,' began Captain Smellie, but the piggish man interrupted him.

'Shut up!' he said, and rose unsteadily from the table. 'You're only an under-strapper, and I want nothing to do with you. I'm going to talk to the high heid yin.'

He advanced on Lord Sandune, hovered in front of him, blew in his face, and suddenly demanded, 'Here! Can you sing?'

'I have no intention of singing now, if that is your meaning,' answered his lordship.

'I've got the finest bloody voice in Kinluce,' said the piggish man. 'I should have been a professional. Harry Lauder, Caruso, Madam What's-her-name—none of the bloody lot of them can hold a candle to me. Would you like to hear me?'

He shook himself, coughed, loosened his collar, tilted his porcine face to the fly-blown ceiling, closed his eyes, and suddenly bellowed in a piercing tenor,

Bonny wee thing, canny wee thing.

Then he stopped to clear his throat again, and finding that

the obstruction still lingered thrust a dirty forefinger into his mouth and presently dug from some interstice in his gullet a large piece of ham.

'Look at that,' he said. 'There's no wonder I couldna sing.' And he flicked the offending morsel into the fire.

He began again, shriller than ever, 'Bonny wee thing, canny wee thing.'

Magnus took him by the shoulders and thrust him into his chair at the table. 'Sit down and be quiet,' he said.

'You're a Conservative,' said the piggish man indignantly. 'You're a bloody Conservative and you don't give a damn for the working man. You'll no get my vote, onyway.'

'You see,' whispered Captain Smellie. 'We've practically got his vote already. At least Buchanan won't get it.'

Conversation proceeded in a desultory way. It was interrupted by the piggish man who sang defiantly, 'I'll sing thee songs of Araby', but no one paid any attention to him. Hugh Skene drank several glasses of whisky and waited moodily for the meeting.

At eight o'clock they went to the hall and found it full of noisy, hearty miners, their eyes made bright by coal-dust, their clothes dark and shabby. Lord Sandune spoke first, and his slow, egotistical speech was listened to with respectful attention. Then Skene spoke, and in an instant had his audience afire. A lamp behind him lit his flaming bush of hair, his thin and lovely hands beat the air. He was more than a little drunk, and he spoke of revolution as though man were made only to break through barricades and run with torches down a ruined street. Whether the revolution he advocated was Communist or Nationalist was not very clear, but it was exciting, and the miners cheered him loudly.

Magnus spoke more soberly. His speech was closely argued. He threw some bitter criticism at his opponents and concluded by saying: 'They speak to you of political parties: I speak to you of a nation. Their parties must dwindle and die, and be blown out like a candle in the wind: but the nation of Scotland, if such is your will, can live for ever.'

A scraggy young man with a raucous voice and a pimply neck rose at the back of the hall and shouted, 'Comrade Merriman, are you a Communist?'

'No,' said Magnus, 'and I'm not your comrade either, so don't pretend I am.'

'Do you believe that work is the only thing that entitles a man to respect and his daily bread?'

'On the whole, yes,' said Magnus.

'Then what are you doing on the same platform with a bloody Capitalist?' And the young man pointed a scornful finger at Lord Sandune, who sat, very large and dignified, wrapped up in a large fur coat.

Magnus rose to answer, but the young man shouted again, 'Is Comrade Skene a Communist?'

'Yes, I am,' said Skene.

Magnus began to say that in the common cause of Nationalism men of many parties were united, but now a great uproar had risen in the hall, for the pimply young man and his friends were singing *The Red Flag*, and on the other side of the room an equally noisy party was struggling over the seats to come to close quarters with them and assault them. This second party was led by Denny and McRuvie. The battle joined, and there was a fine scene of confusion. With the exception of Hugh Skene the platform party kept their seats, but Skene appeared to be meditating a descent into the body of the hall to join in the fray. Magnus dissuaded him, and they argued hotly together, reproducing in miniature on the platform the violent dissent on the floor.

Because, in a little while, the more numerous disputants left the hall to fight on more spacious ground outside, the floor grew quiet before the platform did, and the remaining audience were treated to the spectacle of Magnus and Skene fiercely gesticulating at each other and vainly endeavouring to shout each other down.

Skene was the first to perceive this anomaly. He faced the interested electors and cried, 'Ladies and gentlemen! The vigour with which my friend Magnus Merriman was arguing is typical of the vigour that animates all Scotland, and it is on that vigour that we rely for the victory of our cause!'

Magnus, gallantly following, said loudly, 'Ladies and gentlemen! Hugh Skene is Scotland's foremost poet. The National Party is the only party that poets are proud to join.

If you prefer politicians, vote for Conservatives, Cotton-Tories, or Socialists: but if you are wise, join the poets and vote for the independence of Scotland!'

Lord Sandune was heard to mutter 'Rubbish!' but the audience, already excited, cheered loudly, and the confusion of noise could easily be construed as a vote of confidence.

The platform became busy with little acts of courtesy towards Lord Sandune, but his lordship retired to his waiting motor car without mentioning the cheque that he had been expected to offer. Nor was he seen again in the constituency, and whether he fled in fear of so rowdy and vulgar an election, or in disgust—being a practical business man—at Magnus's references to poets, was never ascertained. But he contributed nothing to Party funds.

Sergeant Denny and McRuvie, however, were perfectly satisfied with the evening's entertainment. Each had knocked down half a dozen opponents, and occasionally been knocked down in return, and both, when rescued, were in a state of bruised and blissful contentment.

Meanwhile, in Kinlawton, a smaller but more important meeting had been held in Lady Mercy's private suite in the Royal Standard Hotel.

Lady Mercy had addressed two meetings on behalf of her candidate Mr Emerson. Her platform manner was peculiar but arresting. She would stand up, and, as though she were a Lewis gun, fire off a hundred short, striking, and often irrelevant statements at her stricken audience. Then she would point to Mr Emerson, and say, 'Here is the man whom you trust, whom I trust, and who *must* be elected!' Mr Emerson would thereafter speak in a solid, blustering way, and the hecklers would rejoice and pepper him with questions.

Owing to the genius of Nelly Bly, that charming and most able of reporters, all Mr Emerson's meetings, as described in the *Morning Call*, appeared to be triumphal occasions. But Lady Mercy and her regiment of agents, canvassers, and subsidiary speakers, knew better. It had not taken them long to discover that the assistant news-editor's mistake had been a serious one, and that though Mr Hammerson would have been a very good candidate, Mr Emerson was a very bad one, for he was one of the most unpopular men in Kinluce. He had been far too successful in his career to enjoy the favour of his neighbours, and despite the loud and persistent advocacy of Lady Mercy's regiment, and the constant trumpeting of his virtues in the *Morning Call*, it was feared that only a small minority would vote for him.

'Well, what are we going to do about it?' said Lady Mercy. 'I don't intend to be beaten in a trumpery constituency like this, so you'd better think of something quickly.'

Her audience consisted of Quentin Cotton, her son, who acted as her private secretary; Nelly Bly; and the Earl of Faloon, who wrote acid and vivacious society gossip for the *Morning Call* and assisted her in the financial direction of her newspapers.

Quentin Cotton said, 'Do you know, a most curious thing has happened: Hammerson, who's been a lifelong Conservative, had turned Liberal.'

'*What?*' said Lady Mercy.

'It's perfectly true,' said Nelly Bly. 'He's going all over the country denouncing the Conservative Association and saying that old-fashioned Liberalism is the only honest policy left. I suppose he's jealous of Emerson and wants a bit of publicity for himself.'

'Perhaps he's like St Paul,' said Lord Faloon, 'and has been convinced by a vision of Mr Gladstone.'

'He's got a lot of influence in the county, hasn't he?' said Lady Mercy.

'He would have made a better candidate than Emerson,' said Quentin.

'I know that. How many Liberals, regular die-hard Gladstone and Asquith men, are there in Kinluce?'

'Six to eight thousand,' said Nelly Bly.

Lady Mercy said, 'Some of them will vote for Buchanan to keep Emerson out; some will vote for Nimmo; and I suppose a dozen or two will vote for that fool Merriman. Now if their votes could be detached from Buchanan and Nimmo—Merriman doesn't count—Emerson would still have a chance. With four candidates, an odd thousand votes subtracted here and there might leave him with a majority.

'But how are you going to subtract them?' said Quentin.

'By putting up a Liberal Candidate,' said Lady Mercy.

'You mean . . . ?'

'Hammerson.'

Lord Faloon whistled a few bars of *The Wearing of the Green* and begged permission to light a cigar.

Quentin said, 'You can't do that. Your name would be mud if it were found out that you were backing two candidates; and in any case Hammerson wouldn't accept your support: he's pig-headedly honest.'

'I have no intention of supporting him,' said Lady Mercy. 'But your Aunt Agatha will. She has been fanatically Liberal ever since she spoke to Mr Asquith at a garden-party—I cannot imagine what he replied—and she's as full of plots as a White Russian. Now you'll go and tell her that there's a marvellous opportunity for a Liberal revival in Kinluce, and that Hammerson is the man to lead it. She can afford to put up a thousand pounds quite easily, and as she knows all the young Liberals still in existence she can send up a good deal of support. If you play your cards properly—you can say that I've sacked you if you like, and that will explain your apparent anxiety to put a spoke in Emerson's wheel—she'll jump at the chance, and Hammerson will be led out as a very useful red herring.'

'That sounds feasible,' said Quentin slowly.

'Feasible! It's dyed in the wool, copper-bottomed, jewelled in every hole, guaranteed against wear and tear, and will keep its colour in any climate,' said Nelly Bly. 'It's a marvellous plan, and you must get busy at once. If you hurry you can catch the night train to London, and fix everything up tomorrow.'

'Yes,' said Lady Mercy, 'speed is essential now.' She turned to Lord Faloon: 'What do you think of the plan, Tony?'

'I'm afraid I wasn't listening to it,' he answered. 'Where ignorance is wise, 'tis folly to be wiser.'

'That's good advice,' said Lady Mercy. 'Well, Quentin, you're no longer my private secretary: there's a cheque for a month's salary in lieu of notice. Anything you do hereafter you do on your own responsibility. But God help you if you don't make a good job of it.'

Quentin worked quickly and well, however, and three days later the second bombshell exploded in the constituency when it was announced that Mr Hammerson, that well-known Conservative, had been adopted as an Independent Liberal Candidate. Mr Hammerson set to work immediately, attended by a small but energetic company of young Liberals who, suspecting that their faith was dead, preached it with all the passionate enthusiasm that befits a lost cause. The ghostly voice of Mr Gladstone was heard again; the gospel of Free Trade was cried in evangelical earnestness; the olive branch of disarmament was held aloft like a monstrance on White Sunday. The young Liberals ran through the land like a flame, but for all their heat they set very little on fire.

For now the electors were puzzled indeed and suspicious of everyone. They felt uneasily that someone was making fools of them, and they resented the multitude of candidates and canvassers who were plaguing them for their votes. They had been brought up to believe that their votes had a certain value, and they were naturally averse from throwing valuable things away. But which of so motley a five deserved their confidence? They were asked to elect a Conservative who had lately been a Liberal; a Liberal who for forty years had been a Conservative; a Socialist who condemned the policy of the existing Socialist government; an Independent Conservative who divided his allegiance between high tariffs and Lady Mercy Cotton; and a Scottish Nationalist who was apparently at odds with many other members of his party—for whenever Magnus was questioned about a policy for India he adopted an Imperialist attitude, while Beaty Bracken and Hugh Skene hotly denounced Imperialism and said that India would be far better off if the Brahmins and Mr Gandhi and the Untouchables and the Pathans were left to work out their destiny for themselves.

Lady Mercy did what she could to clarify the issue, for the *Morning Call* roundly asserted that the only candidates who need to be taken seriously were Mr Emerson and Mr Hammerson. With singular broad-mindedness the *Call* praised Mr Hammerson for his pure-souled advocacy of Liberalism, and reported his meetings in a very flattering way. But the electors were always reminded that, however much they might admire Mr Hammerson, their duty was to vote for Mr Emerson. And the electors—many of whom sat on chairs presented as free gifts by Lady Mercy, and patronized her chamber pots—thought in the solitude of their homes a broad Scotch thought that might be construed in the universal tongue as *Timeo Danaos et dona ferentes*, and decided to vote for neither. So Lady Mercy clarified the issue despite herself.

Now as Nomination Day approached, and hourly the atmosphere grew more hectic, a rumour spread that the Nationalists, whom everybody despised, were making converts by the thousand. And promptly, the other four candidates, who had a proper notion of their function as politicians, simultaneously declared that they too favoured the idea of Home Rule for Scotland—if the people of Scotland desired it—and heartily promised to promise the electors anything else they wanted; for such was the plain and simple duty of democratic candidates.

The rumour of Magnus's progress originated in the fishing villages, where he had held a couple of unusually enthusiastic meetings. This success had come just in time to rescue him from complete depression. The adoption of Mr Hammerson had filled him with disgust at having to compete for power among such a crowd of pot-hunters; he was bored by the necessity of repeating the same arguments night after night—for was not the tongue's ability to range from cockle-shells to Saturn, from madrigals to buccaneers, the only excuse for its employment? Parrots might be content with a pair of phrases, but the talking of men should be variable as the wind; and he felt ashamed of himself because of an experience that was the reverse of his dismal Pitsharnie meeting: he had gone to another village, ill-tempered, and addressed a small audience in hectoring tones, telling them that Scotland's plight was their own fault, and they should sleep in shame to think of it; then he had looked more closely at his listeners, and seen nothing but kindly faces, sad and noble faces, faces made grave by years of toil, lined with sorrow, and sweetened by virtue, or faith in God, or their perception of winter's transience and summer's kind return; and he had been filled with remorse to hear himself blaming these simple, helpless, and lovable people for what was far beyond their power to alter.

In these moods of depression the incompetent ebullience of Captain Smellie was very hard to endure. The Captain pretended that Magnus's success with the fishermen had been due to his organization of the meetings, and now he was eager to concentrate for a few days on the mining district. But Magnus thought it wiser to establish himself firmly with the fishermen, and told Smellie to arrange a meeting in one of the coast villages for the eve of Nomination Day.

The ceremonies of that day were important, for it was then that the candidates were each required to deposit, by the hands of their agents, the sum of one hundred and fifty pounds as a guarantee of their serious intentions, their honourable behaviour, and their ability to poll at least one-eighth of the total votes cast.—Should any candidate fail to attract that small percentage of suffrages, then his deposit would be forfeit.—On the preceding morning Mr Macdonell came through from Glasgow to confer with Magnus. Owing to the unfortunate back-sliding of Lord Sandune the Party was almost bankrupt, and they were quite unable to find the deposit money. Magnus had previously been assured that he would not be asked to find this sum himself, for his personal expenses in the election would be considerable and he had already generously contributed to the Party's funds. And he had explained to Mr Macdonell that, despite some semblance of prosperity in his behaviour, he was far from being a wealthy man. But now Mr Macdonell was compelled to seek his help: if Magnus could not produce a hundred and fifty pounds, then no one could, and his candidature would come to an untimely end: and as there was no risk of forfeiting the deposit . . .

'Oh, none,' said Magnus.

'Smellie tells me that you're doing very well indeed,' said Mr Macdonell.

'I am, in spite of what he says.'

'Then perhaps . . .?'

'Yes,' said Magnus, 'I'll pay the deposit myself.'

Mr Macdonell expressed his gratitude, and Magnus went

to a bank where, after telephoning to Edinburgh for authority, the manager cashed his cheque for a hundred and fifty pounds: for according to the regulations governing the conduct of an election the deposit must be paid in actual cash.

Captain Smellie, who had accompanied Magnus, said very cheerfully, 'Well, that's your duty done, Merriman. Now I must do mine. You won't see this money again till the Sheriff gives it back to you: I'll take charge of it now, and I'll pay it in tomorrow. That's my part of the job, so you needn't lie awake tonight listening for burglars. Ha-ha! I'm the watch-dog, and I don't think many burglars would care to tackle me.'

Captain Smellie stuffed the notes into his pocket-book and regarded Magnus with an amiably converging stare.

The fishermen's meeting that night was a great success. Hugh Skene first woke them to enthusiasm, and Magnus maintained it by outlining a scheme for the protection of Scottish seas and fishing-rights, that, he declared, would be the first duty of an independent Scottish parliament. No longer would their inshore waters be invaded by English trawlers and foreign trawlers; no longer would they suffer the destruction of their gear, the ruination of their fishing grounds, the neglect of their harbours; but when Scotland had asserted her sovereignty then Scotland would protect their livelihood and her seas, and foreign pirates would be treated as they deserved.

It was a fighting speech that he made. He was inspired by the sight of the three hundred fishermen who faced him. There were no women in the audience. The men sat close-packed in sombre rows. They were dark and keen of face, blue-jerseyed, solid and strong. They smelt of the sea, and like the sea they could break to storm. He quoted case after case of trawlers that had been sighted in inshore waters—pirates and poachers—and the listeners growled like the sea when the wind is waking. He spoke of the cruisers that were supposed to protect the fishing-grounds, and the fishermen laughed in savage scorn. Then he said, 'If the English government won't do their duty and protect our seas, we must take matters into our own hands. We fought for England in the last war: we'll fight for ourselves in the next one—and God help the first foreign trawler that puts a nose into the Forth, or the Minch, or the Moray Firth!' Then the storm broke, and the fishermen rose in their excitement like the sea on a winter's night.

As if on a wave Magnus was borne on their enthusiasm, and the meeting became a Scottish triumph. Nor was he disappointed when he returned to his hotel in Kinlawton, for all the other speakers who had been out had come back with stories of success. His camp had filled, for the last few days of the battle, with Nationalist supporters from Edinburgh and Glasgow and elsewhere. Beaty Bracken had addressed an out-door audience in Kingshouse and led them down the street singing *Scots Wha Ha'e*. McVicar—still in Meiklejohn's evening trousers—and Mr Macdonell reported good meetings in several villages. Two or three enthusiastic young men from Glasgow swore they had been asked to give their speeches all over again from the beginning, so enamoured had been their listeners of their eloquence and fine arguments. Sergeant Denny and McRuvie had made a score of converts by the simple process of assaulting them, and Mrs Dolphin, who had been energetically canvassing for a couple of days, declared she had helped to cook fifty dinners in Kingshouse and Kinlawton, and taken Nationalism into every kitchen she visited.

'Do you know this,' she said earnestly, 'there's scarcely a woman in Scotland knows how to cook a piece of beef. They roast it till every bit of colour and flavour's gone out of it. I found half a dozen of them spoiling good joints today alone. And do you know why? Because they think it looks indecent if you put it on the table when it's nice and red. Now that's a fact, though you mightn't believe it. But Scotland is so full of bloody Puritans—excuse my French—that they're frightened even of a piece of beef when it looks in any way naked and like real flesh. I told that to some of the women I was talking to today, and I said, "Now you vote for Mr Merriman, and when we get a government of our own you'll be taught to cook a decent dinner, not like that brown bit of leather there. And you won't be frightened to look at a sirloin of beef because it's red and juicy and naked, so to speak," I said. "You won't be frightened of anything, whether it's naked or not, because we're going to have a lot of fun when we've got a government of our own, and fun's worth having, so be sure and vote for Mr Merriman, and for God's sake take that joint out of the oven before it's burnt to a cinder," I said.'

With all this encouragement Magnus grew very cheerful and began to think that he was winning indeed. Had it not been for the presence of Captain Smellie he would have been perfectly happy, sitting in the midst of his supporters and supplying them with a handsome variety of drinks. He called to a waiter: 'Three large whiskies, a crême de menthe, a benedictine, two bottles of Bass, and a gin and ginger.'—How mellifluous an order, and how delightful to gratify the desires of one's friends with entertainment so robustious and multi-coloured! But it was exasperating to waste good money on buying a drink for Captain Smellie. The Captain was displeasing, in that company, as a penny whistle in a suite for strings. He drew his chair closer to Magnus's, and said, 'Well, Merriman, I've worked hard for you, and now you're reaping the benefits of my work. You're winning, as I always said you would. It wasn't easy to organize a constituency like this, but I think you'll admit that I've done it pretty well. If I hadn't foreseen the various difficulties that have risen . . .'

'Oh, go to hell,' said Magnus, and wondered if it was worth while to explain to Smellie exactly how incompetent, boring, and mendacious he was. But the Captain gave him no opportunity to say anything more.

'That's all right, Merriman,' he said in a kind and purring voice. He stood up and smiled down at Magnus. 'You're tired, I know you're tired. I'm tired myself, but my job doesn't permit me to say so. Now you go to bed and get a good sleep, and you'll feel a lot better in the morning. I'll call for you at half past ten. Good-night, Merriman. Good-night, everybody! I'm very pleased indeed with the work you've been doing. Keep it up! And don't let the candidate sit up too late: he's very tired, and we must nurse his strength. Good-night, good-night!'

On the following morning, shortly after ten o'clock, Mr Boden arrived at the hotel. Magnus was reading the papers.

They discussed the news of the day and admired the accomplishment of Nelly Bly in describing the behaviour of a hostile audience with such ambiguity that readers of the *Morning Call* might easily imagine that Mr Emerson had been accorded a unanimous vote of confidence. At half past ten Captain Smellie had not yet arrived. At twenty minutes to eleven Mr Boden went to the front door and said there was no sign of him. Five minutes later Magnus suggested they should walk round to his lodgings: perhaps he had overslept.

They walked briskly, for the nomination papers and the deposit money—both of which were in Captain Smellie's possession—had to be in the hands of the Sheriff in Kingshouse, the county town, before half past twelve. And Kingshouse was ten miles away.

Mr Boden knocked at Captain Smellie's door. His landlady came and said that he was out.

'When did he go?' said Magnus.

'I couldna rightly say,' she answered, 'for I was late in getting up this morning, and he was away before I came down. So I thought maybe he'd gone to the Committee Rooms, and I put his breakfast on the table to be ready for him when he came back. But there's been no sign of him, and I doubt his porridge'll be cold by now.'

'Go along to the Committee Rooms and see if he's there,' said Magnus. 'I'll wait here. And hurry.'

Mr Boden, travelling so fast that his waistcoat leapt up and down, ran along the street. Magnus went into Captain Smellie's sitting-room and looked about him. In a pigeon-hole in a desk he found the bundle of nomination-papers. A thought struck him, and he called to the landlady.

'I suppose Captain Smellie slept here last night?' he said.

'And why shouldn't he?' said the landlady.

'You heard him come in?'

'Well,' said the landlady, 'I was that tired last night that I went to my bed at the back of nine, and I couldna just say that I heard anyone come in later than that, or go out either for that matter.'

'Where's his bedroom?' asked Magnus.

The bed-clothes were thrown back in disorder, the pillows were crumpled.

'Apparently he slept here,' said Magnus.

'Like enough,' said the landlady. 'Though now that I think of it his bed wasna made yesterday. I was that tired all day.'

Mr Boden returned with the news that Captain Smellie had not been seen at the Committee Rooms. 'Perhaps he's gone to Kingshouse,' he said. 'He's daft enough to forget whether he promised to meet you there or at your hotel.'

'Perhaps,' said Magnus doubtfully.

They hurried back to the hotel. A car was waiting for them, and they drove to Kingshouse. A small crowd of reporters and press-photographers waited outside the Townhouse. Magnus did his best to look cheerful. He went in and inquired if his agent had arrived. But Captain Smellie had not been seen. A reporter overheard his question and said light-heartedly, 'Hullo! has Smellie skipped with the deposit?' 'No,' said Magnus, 'the deposit's all right.' He asked for an interview with the Sheriff, and told him what had happened. The Sheriff said, 'It's a quarter to twelve. You still have time to send your other man back to Kinlawton to make further inquiries. But he'll have to hurry.'

Mr Boden returned to Kinlawton in the motor car, and Magnus defended himself against the reporters, who were now pressing him to admit that Captain Smellie was a welsher and had said good-bye to politics with a hundred and fifty pounds in his pocket. Half an hour later Mr Boden telephoned to say that he had examined Smellie's bedroom and found none of his possessions except a suit of pyjamas and a tooth-brush. There was no suit-case there. He had evidently packed and gone. He was a welsher: there was no other explanation.

Magnus returned to the Sheriff, who listened sympathetically. Magnus said, 'Here are the nomination-forms. Will you take a cheque for the deposit?'

'I can't do that,' said the Sheriff. 'The deposit must be paid in currency.'

'Then give me time to go to the bank, and I'll cash a cheque there.'

'That will make three hundred pounds altogether,' said the Sheriff. 'I have no desire to influence you in your decision, but are you sure that you are acting wisely in continuing the contest after this set-back?'

'I'm winning all along the line,' said Magnus, 'and I'm damned if a welsher's going to stop me now.'

The Sheriff played with his finger-tips a little tune on the table. 'Perhaps my watch is fast,' he said. 'At any rate, I shall give you the benefit of the doubt.'

Magnus hurried to the bank and the reporters followed him. The bank-agent telephoned to Edinburgh. The Edinburgh bank replied that Magnus's credit balance was twenty-three pounds and some shillings. Magnus spoke urgently and assured his Edinburgh bankers that his publishers owned him a vast sum of money that was due to be paid on June 1st, and that meanwhile he could obtain advances up to five hundred pounds without difficulty. Somewhat reluctantly the bank authorized its Kingshouse branch to cash his cheque, and Magnus returned to the Sheriff, ten minutes late, with a hundred and fifty pounds in notes of various denominations. Then he informed the police of Captain Smellie's disappearance.

Before evening the news had spread throughout the constituency that the Nationalist Party's agent had absconded with his candidate's deposit, and the sound of laughter dominated every other noise of the election. Magnus and his assistant speakers were all asked, at question-time, 'Can the speaker tell me where Captain Smellie is?' Not an audience in the country would take them seriously, and to mention national finance was fatal, for immediately someone would inquire, 'If you can't look after a hundred and fifty pounds, how can you look after the National Debt?'

It was useless to answer, as Magnus did, 'It would be a very good thing to lose that too,' for the joke was against him and the Kinlucians would not let him side-step or forget it. The *Morning Call* and the other newspapers reported the mishap with gravity or hilarity according to their temper, and though the Edinburgh *Evening Star*—of which Meiklejohn was Editor—eulogized Magnus for his heroic payment of a second hundred and fifty pounds, that aspect

of the case proved less attractive than its comic side, and it became evident that the Nationalist cause was lost.

Magnus himself threw away his last hope a day or two later. In the moment of stress he had been able to make a magnificent gesture, and he had paid his second deposit without a qualm. But in a little while he began to think more soberly about his three hundred pounds, half of which he had already lost, and of which the second half now seemed in considerable danger. For electors who laughed at a candidate would certainly not vote for him. Three hundred pounds represented the sale of several thousand copies of *The Great Beasts Walk Alone*. It was more than he had made by all his other books. It was a large sum of money, and the prospect of losing it made him both angry and sorrowful. Nor, when he thought of the electors of Kinluce, whose stupidity in not voting for him would be the cause of his impoverishment, could he think of them so amiably as he had done.

He spoke in Kinlawton about the general advantages of small nationalism, and foolishly said that it would encourage individualism. 'That,' he said, 'should prove a welcome state of affairs in Scotland, where every man is at heart an individualist. It is the individual, not the mass of the people, who is responsible for progress, for beneficent invention, and for the production of works of art. It is the duty of a nation to encourage the gifted individual, but in the vast political systems of today the claims of the individual are forgotten in a machine-like conception of the whole. The majority of people are incapable of contributing to the good of humanity, and so it is manifestly absurd to increase the mass and legislate for its benefit: but that is the democratic tendency of the modern world.'

A score of hecklers rose, noisy and indignant. 'Does the candidate believe in democratic government?' cried one of them.

'Less and less,' said Magnus.

'Then what are you doing here?' bellowed half a dozen irate but logical electors.

'Wasting my time,' said Magnus.

'And your money!' shouted a fellow at the back of the hall.

The audience, its anger diverted, roared with laughter, and Magnus, who had plumed himself on the urbane percipience of his reply, was disconcerted by this crude reminder of a distasteful fact. But he made an effort to appear good-humoured, and said, 'After all, it's my own money. . .'

'It was. It's Smellie's now,' shouted the jester at the back, and the audience laughed again.

It was impossible to control them, and the few remaining meetings that Magnus addressed were similarly unresponsive to anything but unintended occasions for laughter. Magnus made heroic efforts to save the Nationalist bacon at the last moment, but his nerves were so frayed that he again forgot, on more than one occasion, the democratic rules under which he was fighting, and propounded unwelcome theories of privilege and individualism. His followers were openly disheartened, and went glumly about their work without hope of winning another vote. The other parties finished the campaign with a series of demonstrations so spectacular that all four candidates appeared to be victors, but the Nationalists concluded with two or three subdued little meetings that had the air of relatives gathered together to say good-bye to an only son who was departing to some distant fever-stricken shore.

On Polling Day Magnus attended the final ceremony, and watched the unhappy process of counting votes all cast for his opponents. He derived some amusement from the pallor and nervous sweating of Mr Buchanan, Mr Emerson, Mr Hammerson, and Mr Nimmo, and their determined efforts to appear bluff, genial, and careless of the result; but that was poor compensation for his own defeat. It soon became evident that Mr Buchanan was the winner by a very large majority—in their perplexity the electors had clung to Conservatism like limpets to a stucco Rock of Ages—and that Mr Nimmo was the runner-up with about nine thousand votes. Mr Hammerson and Mr Emerson had a couple of thousand votes apiece, and Magnus had six hundred and eight.

*

CHAPTER TWENTY

Two days later there was an unpleasant scene in his flat in
Queen Street. Frieda, who had a key of her own, arrived
with a bleak expression and the barely concealed intention
of creating a row. She found Magnus still in a dressing-gown,
though it was three o'clock in the afternoon. He had neither
shaved nor washed. He had abandoned his recently-acquired
habit of snuff-taking—its virtues now seemed illusory, it
appeared to be unlucky, and in his disgust with the world
he despised it as an affectation—and he had returned to the
pernicious practice of smoking: as if by some grey fungus
his dressing-gown was discoloured with tobacco-ash, and
the charred ends of many cigarettes lay in the fireplace. A
suit-case, half-unpacked, filled the sofa. A large tumbler of
whisky and soda stood on the floor by his side, and he was
reading an American detective-novel.

Frieda stood and looked at him. 'Well,' she said, 'you're
a fine politician, aren't you?'

'Sit down and have a drink,' said Magnus.

She pushed the suit-case off the sofa. Falling, it emptied
its remaining contents on the floor.

'Be careful,' said Magnus. 'There's a flask in there, and
a couple of rather valuable books.'

'So you're in a bad temper, are you? Well, I don't wonder,
after the exhibition you've made of yourself.'

'I'm not in a bad temper,' said Magnus. 'I merely asked
you to avoid, if possible, breaking my flask and so spoiling
my books.'

'Well, you ought to have unpacked your suit-case and put
your things away. My God, you look like a hobo, sitting
there!'

'If you came only with the idea of making yourself
unpleasant . . .'

'Oh, that's your line, is it? And I thought you said you
weren't in a bad temper! There doesn't just seem to be honey
dripping off your tongue now, does there? But I suppose you
want to work off your spite on me: I'm to suffer because
Kinluce wouldn't vote for you. Is that the idea?'

'What do you want me to say?' asked Magnus wearily.

'What do I want you to say?' Frieda repeated. 'I want

you to say what you're going to do to get me out of the
mess I'm in. I can't go on living in Rothesay Crescent.
I told them I was engaged to you, and they raised hell.
Hell's been simmering ever since, and now it's burst again.
Aunt Elizabeth says you're a gaol-bird, and Uncle Henry
says you're an unsuccessful mountebank.'

'I don't give a danfn what your Uncle Henry says,' said
Magnus indignantly.

'No? But it's true! You just made a fool of yourself in
Kinluce. You let that guy Smellie levant with your hundred
and fifty pounds, you make everybody laugh at you, and
then you lose your second deposit. Didn't I tell you from
the beginning there was nothing to this damned Nationalism
of yours? How d'you expect people to vote for a crazy notion
like that? Uncle Henry says. . .'

'I've no desire whatever to listen to your Uncle Henry's
opinions.'

'Well, I've got to listen to them, so I don't see why you
shouldn't. I got to listen to them till I'm sick to death of
them, even though I know that half of them are true. And
I've got to stay in his God-damned house because there's
nowhere else for me to go, unless I go on the streets—even
then I couldn't keep myself in coffee and decent stockings
in this darned tight-wad country of yours.'

Magnus said, 'I suppose you want me, first of all, to take
the blame for seducing you. Then . . .'

'Go on!' Frieda interrupted. 'Now say that I seduced
you!'

'I wasn't going to say . . .'

'Well, I did! And you fell mighty easy and you fell mighty
hard. But that's all right. Then I fell in love with you, and
that wasn't all right. Oh, God, I wouldn't mind what Uncle
Henry says if only you hadn't made such a God-awful fool of
yourself! He could have told me to break off my engagement
and I'd have told him to go chase himself round the block.
But how can I say that now? Don't you see what you've
done? I can't even trust you myself now. You made such
a mess of things in this darned election that you may go
on and make a mess of everything you ever do all through
your life.'

'Yes,' said Magnus, getting up and facing her in a towering rage. 'That's probably the case. I'll make a mess of things, but a handsome mess and a lively mess. I'm going to be a grandiose, multiple, and consistent failure. And I don't care! I don't want to be successful and damned for success by smugness, impercipience, spiritual arthritis, and jaded appetite. You'd like me to put on success as though it were a coffin, and write *Respectable* over my life for an epitaph to show I'm done with life. Well, I'm not going to! I'd rather have my ambitions ripped up every year, as if by a plough, and then they'll sprout again, and grow again, and be green through time. I'm going to be a failure, am I? But I'll be alive, really alive, able to make a fool of myself and get drunk as I please, when your successful men are limping around three-parts dead under the weight of their success. A failure, by God! Failure can't kill me: simply what I am will keep me alive.'

'That's a lot of hooey,' said Frieda.

'It's the soundest sense you ever listened to,' said Magnus.

'Anyway, it doesn't help me.'

'It wasn't meant to. I don't see what you have to grumble at. Apparently you want comfort, security, and a settled home. Well, you've got them so long as you stay with your uncle. What else are you looking for?'

'I want you too! Didn't I tell you I was in love with you? Do you want me to go on saying it again and again?' Frieda's voice was shrill. Her loveliness was stormy: the clouds threatened rain: and Magnus grew acutely uncomfortable to think there might soon be tears. He answered her in a mild and pleasant tone.

'As a politician I'm obviously a failure,' he said. 'As a poet I shall probably be a failure too, because for the life of me I can't remember how I was going to handle *The Returning Sun*, and for weeks I haven't felt a single metrical impulse in me. But I don't feel disheartened. I feel curiously confident, partly, perhaps, because cigarettes are much more satisfying than snuff, but also because I've got rid of some more serious affectations. Now if you care to link your life with mine on an unofficial and possibly immoral basis—in a word, to be my mistress—I shall be delighted indeed, so long as you

behave in a reasonable manner and try to keep your temper.
We shall see the cabbage-stumps and the ash-bins and the
broken bottles of failure gilded by the self-same glorious sun
that gilds. . .'

'Oh, can that,' said Frieda viciously.

'I take it, then, that you have fallen out of love with
me?'

'I don't want to marry a guy that's going to make a mess
of his whole life and mine too.'

'I wasn't talking about marriage,' said Magnus. 'However,
have it your own way.'

There was silence for a minute or two, and they heard a
newsboy calling loudly in the street below. Magnus leaned
out of the window and shouted to him.

'I'm going down to get a paper,' he said, and left her. He
returned with a copy of the *Evening Sun* and looked carefully
through it.

'They haven't caught Smellie yet,' he said.

'I guess he was the only guy in your whole darned Party
who'd grey matter between his ears. He got something out
of the election.'

'He won't get very fat on a hundred and fifty pounds,'
said Magnus.

'Neither will you on your cock-eyed philosophy of failure.'
Frieda rose abruptly. 'Well, I'm going,' she said. 'I guess I'll
be back some time or other, though God knows what's the
use of coming.'

A great weariness descended on Magnus when she had
gone, for the election had exhausted his strength and he
felt his nerves like worn fiddle-strings. Such large pity for
himself afflicted him that it overspread its original object and
included Frieda too. For all his brave contempt of success he
could not yet, except in the heat of excitement, contemplate
his political failure without unhappiness, and the loss of his
three hundred pounds was the heaviest grief of all. But
seeing himself as Fortune's waif, he saw Frieda as another.
He forgave her rudeness and her violence, beholding, in the
tearful mirror of his mind, the bitter disappointment which
had inspired them. He drank some more whisky, and was
moved by such sympathy for her, such a vivid picture of

her beauty, that his thoughts considered and his eyes dwelt upon the telephone. Then he heard footsteps on the stairs outside. Someone was coming to the flat, and in half-panic he wondered if Frieda had returned. He waited in miserable anticipation.

The bell rang, and he heard something fall into the letter-box. The footsteps retreated. It was only the postman who had called.

Then he realized how strongly disinclined he was from seeing Frieda again. Another quarrel was more than he cared to endure, and a sly infant fear assailed him that, should Frieda grow reconciled to his capacity for failure and again want to marry him, he might even submit to being married rather than face more brawling and its aftermath of pity and remorse. At that he fell into a half-panic, and finished his whisky at a gulp.

Then a blissful thought occurred to him. He picked up the evening paper he had bought, and turning to the shipping advertisements discovered that the steamer *St Giles* would sail from Leith, at eleven o'clock that night, for Kirkwall in the Orkneys. He immediately decided to follow Captain Smellie's example and levant.

He was aboard with all his belongings by half past ten, and as the *St Giles* faced the strong easterly wind that blew up the Forth he found an exhilarating illusion of escape, and strode about the dark and lonely deck with such contentment that he began to sing the metrical version of the Twenty-third Psalm in its ranting tune of *Covenanters*.

But presently the sea turned rough, and for most of the voyage he lay in his bunk and was either actively or passively sick.

CHAPTER TWENTY-ONE

Magnus's surviving relatives in Orkney, in near degree of blood, were only two in number. He had a younger brother, to whom he was not greatly attached, who was a school-master in the island of South Ronaldsay, and a sister who was married to a farmer in the West Mainland. A score of cousins in the first degree, and many others at remoter stages of consanguinity, lived in different parishes of the Mainland;

a paternal uncle was a banker in Stromness; and a maternal aunt owned a small hotel in the island of Westray. But it was his sister Janet's house that he considered his home.

Janet was a woman of forty-two or forty-three years who had inherited her father's somewhat dry and executive disposition, and the deceased schoolmaster's not very distinguished collection of books. The latter she kept, carefully dusted, in the bedroom, and in the winter months occasionally selected one, quite impartially, and read it through without giving any indication as to whether she enjoyed it or not. Magnus's books—those that he had written—she kept by themselves in a glass-fronted cabinet that contained pieces of supposedly valuable china. She had no children.

Her husband, William Isbister, was a shrewd easy-going man with an eye for a good cow and a disinclination for hard work. He was one of the many peerie lairds in the West Mainland, and his farm of Midhouse was as good as any in the parish. He kept a married ploughman, whose son, a tall strong boy, also worked for him, and there was a servant-girl in the house. Though far from being wealthy, he had money in the bank and was in easy circumstances.

His half-brother, Peter Isbister, who owned the farm of the Bu in the same parish, was a more energetic, ambitious, and talkative man. He was constantly experimenting with new seed, with new kinds of potatoes, and buying cattle of a superior and usually unprofitable strain. But what he lost in breeding he recouped in dealing. He had a large family and his house was a lively place. On his last visit to Orkney, about seven years before this, Magnus had spent almost as much time at the Bu as he had at Midhouse.

His arrival now was unheralded. He hired a car in Kirkwall: his sister's home was some fourteen miles away. It happened that he came to Midhouse just as the cows were being driven in for the evening milking. There was a great deal of noise, for a young collie dog had entirely misunderstood his orders, and so far from shepherding the cows round to the back of the steading, and so to the byre, was vigorously opposing their progress and trying to turn them into the road. The collie, obviously enjoying himself, was barking; Johnny, the ploughman's boy, was shouting to the collie; and Janet was shouting to Johnny. Two of the more determined cows menaced the dog with massive heads held low, but the rest of the small herd turned into the road at a lumbering trot, their full udders ponderously swinging, and Johnny running to overtake them. Magnus, getting out of the car, stood right in their path.

Janet saw him, recognized him at once, and immediately made use of him. 'Turn the kye for me, Mansie!' she called. 'Don't let that red one get by you, or they'll all be gone.'

Magnus shouted and waved his arms. The red cow shied and stopped. The others stood still, breathing heavily, their fat sides rising and falling, their huge dark eyes glaring in sombre suspicion.

'Shoo!' he cried. 'Get back there. Get back! Here, Glen, Glen!'

The other dog came to him. Magnus had never seen it before, but the dogs at Midhouse were always called either Glen or Boss.

'See a haud, boy,' he cried. 'Get on there. Here, Glen! *Glen!* Come in ahint, man.'

So, making more noise than Johnny and Janet put together, he drove the cows back to the steading and was greatly pleased with himself.

Janet said, 'Well, Mansie, you've been long in coming, but you came at a good time after all.'

'I meant to write to you,' he said, 'but I've been very busy lately. I was so worried and uncertain about my plans that I couldn't decide, till just before leaving Edinburgh, whether I was going to leave it or not. I scarcely had time to catch the boat to Leith—we had a rotten crossing—and so. . .'

'All right,' said Janet. 'I suppose you're not going back tomorrow, so there'll be plenty of time to tell us why you came and how you came. Wait till I see to the kye, and then I'll listen to you.'

They followed after the cows to the farmyard. The steading was built on three sides of a square, the middle of which was almost filled by a rich and abundant midden. A few hens, their feathers shining in the sun, were pecking at the dark-stained yellow straw. All but two of the cows had disappeared into the byre: one showed its huge stern in the doorway: the one behind it looked round, raised its head, and bellowed softly.

Willy Isbister came out of the stable with a bottle of Condy's Fluid and a roll of lint in his hand. He was a slow-moving, red-faced, round-shouldered man of about fifty. For a moment he looked hard at Magnus.

'Mansie!' he said. 'Welcome home. It's a denty while since we've seen you here. And now you're a famous man, they tell me.'

It was seven years since Magnus had been called by the Orkney diminutive of his name, with its soft sibilant [it rhymes with *fancy*] and homely sound; it was seven years since he had smelt this farmyard smell, the acid air mingled with perfume of sweet grass from the stable, the warm odour from the byres; it was seven years since he had turned, as now he turned, to look westward and see the shining loch that lay below Midhouse, two small fields away, and held in its vast mirror the brightness of the sky. But suddenly the interval of his absence was foreshortened, time closed in upon itself like a telescope, and to be in Orkney again seemed as natural, as proper to him, as though he had left it only the week before.

He pointed to the loch: 'Is anyone catching any fish nowadays?'

'There's no fish left to catch,' said Willy. 'Man, I mind the time when there was that many they came ashore of their own free-will at the burn-mouth just below Waterha', and we took them away in cartloads. I was a boy at the time, but I was down there with a graip, and me and my father loaded two carts ourselves. Ay, there was fish in the loch then, but that time's past.'

Magnus had heard this famous story from his early youth, and to hear it again was like greeting an old comrade. Willy followed it, as he always had done, with a discussion of the various causes that had led to the decline of the trout population, and Magnus listened, still on familiar ground, to his division of the blame between eels, the killing of the otters that had fed upon the eels, and the widening of contributory burns to drain the neighbouring fields.

They looked into the stable: it's only occupant was a

filly, bright-skinned but dejected, showing a swelling like a tea-cup on her side that Willy had been dressing. 'The other horses are lying out,' he said, and patted the filly who stood with her ears laid back.

They visited the byre. The ploughman's wife and Maggie Jean, the servant-girl, sat milking. Their heads were pressed against the flanks of their cows, and quick streams of milk shot hard into the resounding pails. The air was hot with the grass-fed smell of the animals, and two ginger-furred cats mewed in thin greedy tones for milk.

Willy stood regarding his beasts in silence. Then he said, 'But you'll be tired, Mansie? Come into the house and rest you. Janet'll have the tea ready, but we'll have time for a dram first.'

Magnus went into the kitchen, the living-room, the dining-room of the house. The dog, lying under a horse-hair sofa, barked, and then came out and wagged his tail. Janet had laid the table: there were a pile of white bannocks on it, a pile of bere bannocks, a mound of thin oatcakes, a great round cheese; there were boiled eggs, a grocer's cake, pancakes, shortbread, a huge square lump of yellow butter, dishes of jam, a gigantic tea-pot; and Janet was bending over a pot that hung on the open fire, skewering out of it a fat boiled hen.

Willy poured glasses of neat whisky for himself and Magnus. 'Welcome home,' he said again. 'By God, I'm glad to be back!' said Magnus. They drank, and then sat down to their tea.

'So you're a politician now?' said Janet. 'You'll be able to tell us how much of what we read in the papers is true, and how we all ought to behave, I suppose?'

Magnus told them at great length about the election in Kinluce, and explained exactly how he had lost it. They were greatly interested by Lady Mercy's part in it—her share in Mr Hammerson's candidature had become common gossip in Kinlawton—and though Janet was inclined to be angry with her, Willy chuckled and said she must be a fine clever woman with a good head on her. But they were both very sensibly shocked by Magnus's loss of the three hundred pounds, and Willy said he would like to have

Captain Smellie there, in the kitchen of Midhouse, for just five minutes.

Then the ploughman came in, to ask about the morrow's work, and he was introduced to Magnus, and sat down to listen to the conversation. The ploughman's boy Johnny, and the servant-girl Maggie Jean came in, and they sat down too. Presently a neighbour-man came in. He had seen Magnus's car arrive, and he wanted to know who had been in it. He remembered Magnus, and he also said, 'Welcome home!' So they all sat in front of the peat-fire, and Magnus talked about India, and about Persia, and about America, and one after another of his audience asked sensible shrewd questions, or made sensible shrewd comments on the more notable and unexpected things that he had to say. And when it grew late the neighbour-man said, 'Weel, man, thoo's seen a great part of the world, but I doot there's no piece of it would please thee better than Orkney.'

The great lands with their palaces and mountains vanished over the rim of the world, and Magnus said soberly, 'I believe you're right.'

Then he and Willy walked part of the way home with the neighbour-man, and slowly came back to Midhouse. It was early June, and there was no darkness on that northern land. The sun had set, but the north-west sky was stained with a rich afterglow. A twilit veil hung over the still fields. The wind had gone, and there was no sound but the lazy booming, muted by distance, of waves on the Atlantic shore.

Magnus slept late into the morning. The kitchen was empty when he came downstairs, for Janet was busy with her hens, and he heard from the back-house a rhythmical *chunka-chunk* that told him Maggie Jean was churning. He made tea for himself and boiled a couple of eggs. Then, still without seeing anyone, he went out and walked through the calves' park and a long field of grass to the loch, and sat by its edge and contemplated the rippling water.

The loch stretched north and south, indenting the land with wide bays. A few small islands broke its surface. On the far side of it the land rose to a low ridge, a small hill or two with smoothly flowing lines. The island was treeless, and every contour showed clear and unbroken. The fields were bright green or plough-land still naked brown, and the heather-brecks were dark. To the south-west rose the great hills of Hoy, twin domes, dark blue, and a stark barrier running south. Magnus lay on the lapping shore all morning, and was conscious of little but the changing sky, a placid and irrelevant current of minor thoughts, and a growing beatitude.

For several days he lived in idleness and hardly went out of the farm-lands of Midhouse. Janet said, 'You'll be going to the Bu, to see Peter?' But Magnus answered, 'Not yet. I've been seeing too many people and talking too much for the last few weeks. It's a relief to have no one but you and Willy to think about.' He walked through the fields with Willy: they would stand for an hour, leaning against a dyke, and discuss the grazing horses. Willy had a fine bay mare with great feet, proudly feathered, and a little sorrel foal running beside her waving his flax-fair mane and tail. There was another mare, an older one; a tall black gelding; and a young two-year-old horse that promised to be a champion. Or they would walk to other fields that bordered a small reedy loch, where the cattle grazed, and where black-headed gulls were nesting, and native snipe, and coots were noisy in the rushes.

There was not a great deal of work to be done on the farm at this time of year. The ploughman was sowing turnips. The early swedes were showing green lines of close-sprouting leaves, but they were not yet ready for singling. The cows had to be milked, the calves fed, the hens fed, and their eggs collected. One day Willy and Magnus, the ploughman and his boy, went in carts, a slow easy progress, to the peat-hills and set up the new-cut peats to dry. But all this could be done without hurry or bustle, and fine weather gave to their work an air of graciousness and ease.

Magnus found his old trout-rod, and took Willy's boat and went fishing on the big loch. Now as though he were in the middle of a saucer the country made a rim about him. The bare slope of the hills drew delicate lines against a clear pale sky, and the mild bright colours of June made a gay and pleasant pattern. In spite of Willy's pessimism he caught some good trout: and he caught something more important.

He caught a mood, clear-sighted and detached, and in the light of that mood he saw how to write his poem, *The Returning Sun*. The romantic vision that had first inspired him returned and was clarified; the indignation that had fired his conception of the early satirical part lost its extravagance and acquired form and discipline; and the bitterness he had felt in Kinluce was now transmuted to a bland ironical perception of politics' vulgar intrigue and perverted folly. That evening, in the swept and garnished ben-room at Midhouse, he returned to work, and for some days worked with happy concentration.

He destroyed much of what he had already written, and recast the harsh ebullience of other passages. He was still embarrassed by the abundance of matters meet for satire in modern life, but his new-found mood enabled him to review knavishness and stupidity from a distance and limn in bold outlines that which, in his earlier attempts, he had attacked in furious detail from too-close range.

He drew an excellent picture of Lady Mercy and her endeavour to govern Britain by the distribution of newspapers and free gifts. He ridiculed the idea of Socialism, that offered to build a perfect state on human foundations immeasurably remote from perfection—as though one should endeavour to construct a mansion house of unfired clay—and he derided the new Tory Bankocrats with mordant contempt. He talked, with genial mockery, about compulsory education, and suggested that wisdom lay elsewhere than in spending public money to educate, by the medium of teachers themselves not educated, children whom no power on earth could educate; and he questioned the sagacity of the democratic state that put governing power in the hands of those whom it had thus forcibly miseducated. He concluded this part of the poem with the following lines:

> Nor's it the worst of this benevolence
> That it should melt its pounds and waste its pence
> To make silk purses out of plain sow's ears—
> Yet if the schools took only volunteers,
> Eager, book-hungry youth, and sanely spent
> On them the wealth poured now incontinent

On dullard conscript benches: spread the fare
Of ripe and various instruction where
Good appetite awaited it; not threw
Vast scattering of crumbs, but gave a few
Lucullan banquets so each guest might sup
On the full course of knowledge, and his cup,
O'er-brimmed with art, inflame and fill his soul:
Thus fed, true wisdom, radiant and whole,
Might talk in golden though but single notes
Above the land that now a myriad throats
Fills with such senseless and harsh stammering
As frogs in chorus in the marshes sing—
Yet waste is not the worst: what grows from waste
Is poison that's already killed our taste
For poison, so we take more unwittingly,
Grow weaker day by day, and know not why.
The penny wisdom of our schooling's taught
All men are capable and all men ought
To frame the rules of their own governance,
And choose as rulers rulers who will dance
To suit their piping who elected them!
Freedom, it teaches, freedom, the fairest gem
In our bright national diadem,
Shines on the lid of every ballot-box:
Choose your own whore!—We choose; and get the
pox.

One evening while he was working with undiminished
energy Janet came through to say that Peter Isbister had
come to see him. Magnus, with some reluctance, put down
his pen and followed her to the kitchen.

Peter was three or four years younger than Willy, taller,
and better-looking. He had brown hair, a brown face, deeply
lined, that was constantly changing its expression. He was
rather more smartly dressed than Willy, for he wore a collar
and tie.

He said, 'Well, Mansie, have you forgotten your old
friends, or got too old to walk up-hill, that you haven't
been to the Bu yet?'

Magnus made a few amiable remarks, and said that he
had been busy.

'Man, it canna be good for you, working with books
and papers all day,' said Peter. 'It's maybe no so bad in

the winter, but in this grand weather a body needs to be outside.'

'It's his own work,' said Janet, 'and he'll need to do it. He can't be idling all summer when he's just lost three hundred pounds. He'll want to make that up.'

'I heard tell of that,' said Peter. 'It was an awful pity to lose all that. But there's many a man lost more than his money through getting mixed up with those politicians, and maybe Mansie won't miss a few pounds nowadays.'

Peter cocked an inquiring eye at Magnus: Janet and Willy listened intently: and the servant-girl paused unobtrusively in the doorway. None of them was greedy, none was dominated by a desire for wealth, but the financial worth of one's acquaintances was a matter of the liveliest interest, and since Magnus's appearance as a Parliamentary candidate it had been said in the countryside that he must have grown very rich.

Magnus grinned at Peter's pointed suggestion. 'I'm not ruined yet,' he said. 'But I'd rather have kept the money than lost it.'

Janet and Willy nodded and murmured sympathetically. 'Just so, just so,' said Peter. And the servant-girl vanished from the doorway. Magnus's answer had satisfied them: it seemed that he was not foolishly rich, but as he could lose three hundred pounds without apparent distress he was plainly a sound man: and they could still speculate on the precise degree of his soundness.

The conversation turned to other subjects. Peter was a good talker, full of genial gossip, and the whole parish came to life in his stories. Magnus listened to his tales of good fortune and ill-fortune, of crops and cattle, and found no desire to break in with reminiscences of India and America. Most of the people whom Peter mentioned were known to Magnus, and the names of their farms—Buckquoy, Nistaben, Northbigging, Settiscarth, Overabist, and the like—conjured familiar pictures of snug steadings and brown hillside and fat beasts in the yard. There was enough close-woven interest here to make a man independent of the outer world. And Peter had the Orkney lilt in his voice more noticeably than Willy or Janet: a light and lively cadence very different from the Scottish tongue, a cheerful unsentimental cadence, a lilt that gave point to the half-ironical flavour of Orkney humour. Peter, he decided, was a fine fellow: full of schemes and gossip: he told a story for the interest or amusement inherent in it, not because he had a grudge against the man of whom he told it: and his busyness was due to a restless desire to make use of all his faculties.

The following afternoon Magnus paid his long-delayed visit to the Bu. Peter's farm lay on the hillside a couple of miles east of Midhouse. Magnus walked across country to it. He went by the north end of the small reedy loch, where the coots and the black-headed gulls were nesting, and came to a narrow road leading uphill. Primroses grew thickly in the deep ditch beside it, and smaller flowers in the long grass made circlets of colour. The wind blew lightly in a field of young corn, rippling into faint blue shadows its gay and tender green. Starlings were busy in a clump of gorse-bushes and about an old loose dyke. A herd of black cattle stopped their grazing and looked sombrely at Magnus as he walked among them. In a field some distance away half a dozen men and women were singling turnips: they stood in a line diagonal to the long parallel drills: their movement down the field was scarcely perceptible.

In a paddock below the Bu there was a brisk and lively scene. A girl was struggling with two calves that plunged and kicked at the end of their tethers. They ran in opposite directions and she stood with her arms at full stretch and shouted to them. The calves turned inwards, met, and set off on a new line, prancing side by side. The girl pulled against them. She was lithe and slender, and her body arched like a bow. Now the calves turned stubborn and would not budge. The girl hauled like a bargee on a rope, and her breasts showed their firm and pleasant shape under her blouse.

Magnus came near, laughing. 'Hallo,' he said. 'You're Rose, aren't you? There's none of the others could have grown so lovely.'

'Oh, stow!' [an expletive: it rhymes with *plough*] she said. 'Here, take hold of this tether.'

Magnus took the dirty rope and hauled the nearer calf

to the other side of the paddock. Rose followed, and they knocked the stakes of the tethers into the ground with a heavy stone. Magnus wiped his hands on the grass.

After her first brusque demand for help Rose appeared to have become shy. She stood awkwardly for a moment or two, and then, as if striving to make conversation, said, 'That's the first time for many a year you've had sharn on your fingers.'

'I suppose so,' Magnus answered without paying much attention to what she said. She had been a nice-looking child, he remembered, but not so nice-looking as to promise prettiness so uncommon as this. Her hair was black, curling and untidy in the breeze, and her face was flushed by her struggle with the calves. She was of medium height and slim. Her features were fine, her teeth perfect, and her eyes a curious blue-green under long dark lashes. Her cheeks were delicately coloured, and the texture of her skin—her arms and neck were bare—was flawless. Magnus found it difficult to look away from her.

But Rose did nothing to encourage his admiration, for she grew embarrassed under his stare and said nervously, 'You'll be coming in, won't you?'

'Yes, I'm coming in,' said Magnus, and followed her into the house.

Mary Isbister, Rose's mother, was in the kitchen, baking. She welcomed Magnus with floury hands and immediately began to gossip with great animation. Rose left them and went upstairs. Presently other members of the family came in: there was a tall strong silent boy called Alec, a girl called Peggy, a couple of younger ones. The family had diminished since Magnus had last been there, for one of the sons had gone to Canada, one to New Zealand, and the eldest girl was married in another parish.

Peter arrived when tea was ready and said, 'Well, Mansie, you've found your way here at last, have you?' Mary Isbister continued the theme, and said she had been thinking that maybe Magnus had grown too grand to come and see them now, but, 'Faith,' she said, 'he hasna changed so much after all. I took a look through the window, and there he was flitting the calves with Rose, and a sharny old rope in his hands as though he'd been wont with nothing else.'

Rose came down to tea and sat so quietly that her mother made some remark about her silence.

'Say nothing to rouse her,' said Peter. 'Let sleeping dogs lie.'

Alec and Peggy and the younger children laughed as if at some private joke, and Rose flushed uncomfortably. She had brushed her hair, and looked very pretty and neat despite her working clothes. She scarcely spoke throughout the meal.

After tea Peter took Magnus out to see his beasts. He bred pure Aberdeen-Angus cattle, and he looked with a lover's eye at their broad flat backs, their square sterns, the tail hanging like a whip-lash, the silky hide, and the short straight legs. Magnus caught his enthusiasm and discovered for himself the beauty of good breeding, and became aware of the delectable quest for perfection of breeding. His peasant ancestry came to life in him, and he felt their urgent desire for land of their own, for beasts of their own. To have black cattle like Peter's, moreover, would give him an aesthetic satisfaction almost as great as the peasant-satisfaction in possessing land. He saw himself breeding a bull—broad of head, mighty of dewlap, shouldered like Atlas—such as the islands had never seen.

As if divining his thoughts Peter said, 'Man, you should buy a farm of your own and settle down in Orkney. You've seen as much of the world as you need to, and you've made some money: you could buy a fine tidy farm, stock it well, and be your own master. You won't make a fortune, but there's a lot of satisfaction in breeding a good beast now and then, and getting your harvest in. And there's always something newcome in a farm. Look at that field there: I drained it the year afore last and there's grass in it now to feed twice the number of kye.'

But Magnus was hardly ready yet to admit his new and delicate imaginings. They were still dreamlike and vague. They would not support details so material as field-draining. He answered, 'I'm writing a poem, a long one, and that must be finished before I can think of anything else.'

'There'd be time enough for your poetry in the winter, in

the long evenings,' said Peter. 'Summer's no time at all for writing books.'

CHAPTER TWENTY-TWO

But Magnus was filled with the fury of working, and in the morning he returned to his poem with eagerness undiminished. The excitement of composition made his pulses beat as though, in some street-scuffling, he had been challenged to fight. And by midnight he would be drained of strength and weary to the bone.

He added half a dozen political portraits to the first part of his poem. One was of the Prime Minister:

> McMaster, that great Socialist, a Scot:
> His creed was fashioned by his boyhood's lot
> Of poverty among the striving poor,
> Whose honesty, whose courage to endure,
> Whose kindliness, and strength on land or sea,
> Made virtue seem to inhere in poverty.
> Seeing these merits in poor men, his friends,
> Poor men have all the merits, he contends,
> Thinking because a man is strong and kind
> He must have logic and a prudent mind.
> For sixty years McMaster thought like this,
> And then behold a metamorphosis!
> McMaster grew to power and lived among
> The rich whom he'd despised when poor and young:
> Whose charm of speech, whose tact and *savoir-faire*,
> Whose butlers, and whose heavy-lidded stare
> Convinced him that the virtues in Debrett
> Excelled all others he had ever met;
> And having found that peers and plutocrats
> Now walked in piety as well as spats,
> He faced facts boldly, and—*memento mori!*—
> Prepared to seek the Lord—or Lords—a Tory.

The satirical half of *The Returning Sun*, then, was when finished a fine gallimaufry. The body of it was the dismal and lifeless condition of Scotland, but its limbs stretched out in all directions. Here, resounding as a slap in the face, was a passage on modern love; and there, loud as a guffaw, were twenty lines on modern religion. The League of Nations, armament firms, newspaper advertisements, Soviet

Russia, Mr Gandhi, and international tennis tournaments were saluted with a catcall and dismissed with derision. Yet, tempting as these diversions were, they never obscured the principal theme: Magnus's general iconoclasm was only a frame for his Scottish satire, and his excursions abroad were no more than chapter-headings for his denunciation of Scotland's insufficiency. He avoided the tone of a Jeremiad by the gusto of his satire, and all his raiding and spoiling he did with unfailing pleasure.

But when he came to write the second half of the poem he found many obstacles: for the latter part was to be constructive, and constructive criticism is regrettably more difficult than detraction and the buffeting of robust disapprobation. He began with an evening vision of the western sea: the poet, standing on a cliff, was watching the great orb of the sun drop down the sky with all its company of roseate clouds and golden mists, draining the firmament of colour like a tyrant's court that bleeds an empire for its finery; down to a handsbreadth from the stiff horizon came the sun, and the wall of the cold sea was ready to obscure it: but like some aureate bird, fat, and with feathers of flame, the sun perched on top of the wall, its circle flattening somewhat with its weight, and then, rebounding slowly, rose again, and the chorus of pink-breasted clouds and the mists with their golden wings applauded it, and the sky grew bright once more to welcome it. Now that vision was intended to symbolize the returning pride and vigour of Scotland, but how to fulfil the vision and equip it with practical details gave Magnus no little trouble. That renascence should come from the west suggested, of course, a Celtic character for it, and the Celtic ethos was a fine opponent to the decadent commercialism of Scotland and the world at large. But as an Orkneyman Magnus did not wholly trust the Celtic spirit, and was resolved that his renascence should be stiffened by certain Norse characteristics. And this cross-breeding, this mixture of the spiritual and the practical, presented several difficulties.

One afternoon the conflict between the two ideas grew so disturbing that he could not sit still, but went walking at a great pace over fields till he came to the main road, and down that with long strides and a scowl on his face, muttering odd lines and half-made phrases, and striving to see consistency in a crowd of inconsistent images. He was interrupted by a voice, intoning its words in a very different fashion from the Orkney style, that asked him what o'clock it was.

He looked round and saw, in an old grass-overgrown quarry by the roadside, a tinker's camp. The man who had spoken to him, a tall dark-faced fellow, stood beside a little black tent, and at his feet a thin unhappy-looking dog was rubbing its stern on the ground. Magnus told him the time. A buxom woman with rusty-red hair and a child in her arms came out of the tent. 'It's a fine day,' she said in a high-leaping voice. Magnus fell into conversation with them. 'Do you know anything that will take worms out of a dog?' said the man. Magnus said there were certain pills for that purpose, but he could not remember the name of them. 'I've heard that if you grind up some broken glass and put it in the dog's food, that will do good,' said the woman. Magnus doubted it. The man suggested other remedies, and the dog lay down, and looked mournfully at them. 'It's a poor thing of a dog anyway,' said the woman.

The topic died and Magnus continued his walk. The tinkers were old acquaintances: their name was Macafee. He remembered with sudden delight a conversation in Edinburgh, in Rothesay Crescent, and Mrs Wishart's asking if he knew the So-and-so's and the What's-their-names in Orkney—the eminent So-and-so's and the very dignified What's-their-names—and he had countered, in the same tone of social inquisitioning, 'Do you know the Macafees and the Newlands?' Tinkers all, and 'charming people', he had said. He imagined himself introducing Mrs Wishart to the woman with rusty-red hair. The tinker woman would not be disconcerted, but Mrs Wishart would be sadly ill-at-ease, especially if she had to listen to the description of the worm that had once been driven out of a greyhound—so the tinkers said—by a dose of chopped horsehair.

Unfortunately from thinking of Mrs Wishart his thoughts took an awkward turn and Frieda stepped into the picture. Ten days after his arrival in Orkney a letter had come from her, addressed to him care of his publishers and forwarded by them. It was an unpleasant letter, full of upbraiding and sorrow. He had torn it up immediately after reading it and sought refuge in work from her wounding phrases and more painful reiteration of affection. He had meant to be brutal and ignore her letters. But his resolution had wavered and weakened when he could find no peace in his work, and that night he had replied to her at great length, offering in his own defence nothing but a distaste for marriage—incurable, he said—and protesting his remorse for the unhappiness he had caused her. He endeavoured to word his letter so that it would minister to her self-esteem and restore her self-respect, and at the same time he contrived to give it a tone of finality. Since then he had not heard from her, and the importunate demands that his poem made upon him gave him little time to think of her. Instead of whipping himself with contrition, as in idleness he would have done, he had been contentedly whipping the abuses of the day with satire. But occasionally unwelcome thoughts penetrated the armour of his preoccupation, and now, with the day so fine about him and the fields so greenly prosperous on either side, he felt the weight of Frieda's unhappiness, and swore again that he would traffic no more in love, since love always came with unbidden guests to wish it ill, like witches at a christening.

He walked to Dounby, the nearest village, and stayed to talk with the blacksmith, who was shoeing a big white-footed mare. He leaned against the wall of the smithy and watched the paring of the mare's feet. Presently he saw a cyclist on the road, and when she came near he recognized Rose, and was aware of a little surge of excited pleasure. She smiled as she passed, and a hundred yards further on he saw her dismount at one of the village shops. Ten minutes later she returned, and would have ridden by. But Magnus called to her to stop.

She had a heavy basket on the handlebars of her bicycle. Magnus said good-bye to the blacksmith and walked back with Rose. At first he found it difficult to make her talk, and when her initial reserve was broken down she still spoke shyly, with sidelong glances to see if her conversation was approved. It was family stuff, domestic matters, and country topics she spoke of. She had no wit and only the most elementary appreciation of humour, but her voice was young and her shyness engaging. Magnus, without deliberately intending a comparison, found himself contrasting her with Frieda. He had never reconciled himself, wholly and with comfort, to Frieda's background of too-lavish experience, and in Rose's simplicity he found the freedom of relief. The timid bait of innocency attracted him—that May-fly on the stream of time—and the longer he looked at her the more he was convinced that she was uncommonly pretty. In particular his admiration was captured by her complexion, and in a little while he was unwise enough to interrupt her story of what her mother had said to James of Buckquoy's wife, and tell her so.

Rose fell silent immediately, and charmingly blushed, and Magnus never heard what James Buckquoy's wife had said in reply.

But having started to talk about her prettiness he found the theme engaging, and enlarged on it till Rose grew patently unhappy and begged him to stop.

'But I'm only telling you the truth,' he said.

'You're not,' she answered. 'It's nothing but a lot of lies. I think you'd better give me the basket now: you've come far enough.'

They had reached the farm-road leading to the Bu. Rose, flushed with embarrassment, reached for the basket that Magnus had been carrying, but Magnus, who was enjoying himself, said, 'Think of your nose, for example . . .'

'I won't,' said Rose, and snatched the basket from him.

'All right,' said Magnus. 'If you don't believe me, look in the mirror and see what it has to say.'

That night he could make nothing of Scotland's renascence, and added not a line to *The Returning Sun*. But he thought of Rose, and the more he thought of her the more she excited him, till at last he wrote, quick-fingered, a set of verses that might very well do for an autograph-album, and they gave him even more pleasure than the stabbing couplets of his satire:

Fine yellow flags in the tall green reeds,
Wild white cotton on the heather-brown hill,
Lovely things growing on the moor, in the meads,
    And you are lovelier still.

A sorrel foal with a flax-fair mane,
A puff-ball cloud in the noonday blue,
And a great gull sitting on a weather-vane—
    Is there nothing lovely as you?

The plover's black bib has a new renown,
For your sweet blowing hair is the same proud hue,
And the sun's so glad that your hands are brown—
    'Be quiet!' said Rose of the Bu:

'I won't listen longer and I won't stay here
If you flatter me like, for your flattery is lies.'—
But I said: Could I flatter the spring of the year
    Or the flighting of northern skies?

There's a trio of things I can truly declare:
That young corn's green, and the tide will turn,
And you are lovely beyond compare—
    Look in your glass and learn!

So early next morning, jumping from bed,
Into the mirror looked Rose of the Bu,
Frowned, and was puzzled, and sulkily said,
    'You must be flattering too!'

CHAPTER TWENTY-THREE

The Returning Sun became more and more unmanageable, and Magnus's vision of a resurgent Scotland was elusive as a unicorn when he strove to describe it in compact lines and detailed phrase. He toiled and sweated and chased his fleeting thoughts as unsuccessfully as an old sheepdog in pursuit of a young hare. He cursed his empty wrestling with shadows, his vain huckstering with words that only a merchant-prince like Milton, a royal spendthrift like Shakespeare, a fortuned favourite like Shelley, could dare to throw on the counter, and he swore he would abandon poetry for ever and be a farmer instead, as Peter urged him to be—and the more he cursed and abominated his craft the more he bent his shoulders in its service.

But when the time came that hay was ripe, and Willy of

Midhouse had had his reaper-knife sharpened, and yoked his horses for cutting, Magnus felt the compulsion of the seasons more cogent than the perennial claims of poetry, and put away his manuscript and took instead a hayfork, excusing his recusancy with the misquotation—that none but himself appreciated—*Poetam furca expellas, tamen usque recurret.*

For a day he worked stoutly, coling the cut hay, and found that he remembered how to make the coles weather-proof and fit to run the rain. Then he was allowed to drive the reaper, and took a vast delight in its straight progress down the field, in the steady falling of the grass, the hard stammering sound of the knife, the rhythmical forward-lurch and backward-thrust with which he pushed off the gathered swathes.

A steady breeze blew, drying the harvest, and the hay was hardly cut and coled before it was ready for carting. Then Magnus worked mightily, forking huge trusses to the waiting carts and sweating prodigiously as the loads grew higher, and each forkfull—ponderous, shaggy in the wind—had to be thrust up as far as he could reach, turned inwards, and released from the prongs with a last jerk of the wrist. Hay-seeds stuck to his sweating forehead, hayseeds descended his sweating back and chest, but the sweet smell of the hay filled his nostrils, the blue loch lay below him, the strong horses strained to the load, the larks rose singing to the sky. He found contentment and laughter in his companionship with Willy and the ploughman, with Johnny the ploughman's boy and Maggie Jean the servant-girl, and happily shared with them the ale of Janet's brewing that was brought down to the field and passed from mouth to mouth in a blue quart-mug.

They built their hay at Midhouse before carting began at the Bu, and Magnus, pluming himself on the strength that he had scarcely used for years, took his fork and went to help Peter. Peter had all his family in the field, and Magnus contrived to work beside Rose. She wore an old shapeless hat tied under her chin with a scarf to keep the hayseeds out of her hair; her frock was dingy and soiled; her stockings were thick and her boots course country leather. She was strong, and she hoisted aloft great loads of hay with tireless vigour. 'Have you looked in the mirror yet?' said Magnus, and Rose, with simple percipience, answered, 'I think you're silly.' But she was conquering her shyness, and presently she asked, 'What have you done with all your fine clothes?' For when she had first seen him Magnus had been dressed in smart tweeds, finely tailored, and now he wore a grey flannel shirt and old corduroy trousers. The sun had given a rusty light to his dark hair, his face was red, and two days' stubble of beard was on his chin. 'Fine clothes are a vanity,' said Magnus. 'I'm a son of the soil, dirty and virtuous, shining with simple piety and sweat. I'm going to buy a farm and breed black cattle, and every Saturday night I'll change my shirt and shave my beard and come and make love to you.' 'You'll find the door locked,' said Rose, no longer so shy, and led the horse to the next cole.

At one o'clock they went in for their dinner, and sat crowded round the table. Mary Isbister put plates of thick broth before them, untidy ends of mutton and boiled pota-tqes, and bere bread and rhubarb jam. Then they went back to the field. Unclouded and bright, the sun shone down, and the west wind, blowing over meadowlands below, carried the smell of grass and wild honey. Peggy brought ale to them and Magnus drank thirstily. He and Rose forked up another cole, and Alec, who was building the load, cried that was enough. Magnus undid the ropes from the back of the cart and threw them up to Alec, who passed them diagonally over the load. Magnus caught hold of the ends, heaved and strained, and tied them to the shafts. Alec slid down and led the horse away, and the unwieldy load went jolting and swaying over the brig-stones.

Magnus and Rose sat down beneath a cole, and now Magnus, yielding to his inclinations, to the heartiness of the day, and indeed to common sense, put his arm round her shoulders and leaned over to kiss her. But Rose thrust him away and would have nothing to do with embraces. For a moment it seemed that now her shyness had gone indeed and that she was going to be most unbashfully angry. But the little flame of temper sank, and she held him off with pleading instead. After they had loaded another cart Magnus tried again, and now, though still she would not suffer to be kissed, she did not seem offended by the attempt to kiss her. And when they had piled-high yet another cart they sat beneath a haycock that overleaned the burn—running brown with silver streaks between meadowsweet and reeds—and now Rose resisted less strenuously, and was kissed, not wholly complaisant but uncomplaining, upon the nose and brow. So for the rest of the day they worked, lifting great loads and kissing under the haycocks, heaving on the binding-ropes, and holding each other's hot and blistered hands.

For some time Magnus lost interest in his poem and became so rustically-minded that Janet found his presence in the house embarrassing. He cleaned the stables and smelt strongly of dung, he spoke with an Orkney accent, he discussed the rotation of crops and talked lengthily of manures and wild white clover, he inquired into the pedigrees of cattle and horses till often the kitchen at Midhouse seemed full of leaping stallions, philoprogenitive bulls, and amorous tups, and the whole countryside opened wide in ceaseless fecundity. When the sow farrowed it was Magnus who sat up with her and helped her in her labour, and presently he took to eating with his knife. Then Janet spoke harshly to him, and told him that was no way to behave, and said that if he wanted to live in her house he must mend his manners. But Willy was delighted with his new-found enthusiasm, for Magnus worked so hard on the farm that there was little left for Willy to do but to stand and watch, and contemplate the increasing girth of his stirks, the rising height of his corn, and the burgeoning of his turnips. And that suited him very well indeed.

After the hay had been built there were peats to be brought from the hill. The carts set out in the early morning, a slow procession, creaking on the road. The hill-tracks were rough with boulders and deep ruts that sent the carts lurching from side to side. Sometimes they startled a covey of young grouse, sometimes a leaping hare. Then they came to the peat-banks, and loading began. The upper peat was dusty and brown, but that dug deeper was solid blue-black, solid and heavy. With full loads in the carts the men had to walk the five miles back to Midhouse. From early morning till evening they came and went, and slowly the Midhouse peat-stack grew to a proper size for winter fires.

On the second day Magnus deserted and left the peat-banks to climb farther up the hill. In a high lonely place he sat down and looked at the country spread beneath him, the chequered fields, the lochs, the low moors to the west that here and there were broken into by the sea, and beaches made by the waves' invasion. In three places the sea was visible, bright blue, but the rest was moorland and tillage, and every year the ploughed fields were marching farther into the moors and the island grew more green. It was a land cultivated and kindly and secure, a little land in the midst of the sea, treasuring its comfort because of the storms that were its familiar neighbours, prizing its small prosperity because three thousand waste Atlantic miles broke on its threshold. Its contours were graceful and strong, swept smooth by the wind, unbroken by trees. Cattle, tiny at that distance, moved slowly in the fields.

Magnus thought: Here is my home and here is where I shall live. We're virtually independent here and a man can live on the products of his own labour. When that is possible there's no need to think of politics, and it will be a relief not to think of them, for the more I consider political theories the less I can believe in them and the less I can wholly dismiss them. If I had lived in 1890 I would have been an Imperialist, and if I were living in London today, and were unemployed, I would call myself a Communist. But between those blissfully positive poles there's a world of twilit muddle and quarter-truths, and I'm damned if I can find a label to suit me, or any other reasonable man. How pleasant would be a democracy were demagogues forbidden to cross its frontiers; how excellent an autocracy with a philosopher for king! And peace would be infinitely desirable if all the world were wise and witty; but to go to war with Napoleon or Hannibal or Montrose must have been a splendid adventure. I would like to believe whole-heartedly in something, but such belief is impossible in this disgusting ant-hill of a modern world, where nothing is clean-cut, nothing simple and whole. I would believe in God—sometimes I nearly do—if it were not for the abominable suggestion that He made man in His own image: if God is like an out-of-work miner from South Wales, or a fox-hunting stockbroker, or Smellie, or even me, then thank the sceptics for atheism. Perhaps man was God's Frankenstein and destroyed Him with the stink of the cities of the plain. Lord, what a stench goes up from the chimneys! And the cities are drugging themselves with the bedside comforts of their civilization so as to be unaware of their death when it comes. But I shall escape that destruction— perhaps, like Lot, I shall beget a new race on my daughters if they can make me drunk enough to forget my manners— and when all the nations have laid themselves waste, like clockwork cats from a mechanized Kilkenny, humanity will still survive in the quiet islands of the sea, in Orkney, in the Outer Hebrides, in the Paumotus and Fiji and the granite islands of the Aegean. And we shall trade with each other, bartering dried fish for olives, and exploring together the ruins of London and the broken walls of Berlin.

His speculations having reached this visionary stage, Magnus lay back on the heather and fell asleep. He dreamed of marrying Rose and fathering on her a huge family who worked three hundred acres of good land for him, while he sat at the table-top, a patriarch, and thundered his commands to sons and serving-maids and dogs and children. A curlew, crying loudly, woke him, and he yawned awhile, and then lay down again. Now he dreamed that the heather was growing into his armpits and overgrowing his legs, that the moss was yielding and the hillside making him its own, one soil with its soil, till the wild bees found honey in his hair and whaups made a nest in his navel.

The sun was far down the sky and a cold wind blew when he woke again. He stretched himself slowly and scratched his armpits, that felt itchy when he remembered his second dream. It was either a death-wish, he thought, or else he had visualized the earth as Demeter and was re-entering the womb. And as he walked home he composed a bawdy poem about psycho-analysis.

No sooner were the peats brought in than it was time to prepare for an event of social importance, the West Mainland

Cattle Show. For this congregation of animals, competing in beauty for the pride of their masters, Willy selected a calving cow, three stirks, the bay mare and the sorrel foal, the black gelding, and the promising two-year-old horse. On the eve of the show Magnus and the ploughman washed the horses' legs, scraped and combed them, and scrubbed and oiled the black hides of the cattle. Willy, leaning on his stick, stood wisely watching them, and debated what price he could ask for the stirk and the gelding should buyers present themselves.

On the following morning the household was early astir, the cattle were washed again, and the horses were groomed again, and coloured straw was woven into their manes and tails. The animals had the bright aspect of holidays about them when they set out for Dounby, but Magnus, who was leading the black gelding and the two-year-old, wore a serious look. His enthusiastic interest in farming matters gave the occasion a somewhat exaggerated importance, and he was deeply concerned lest the dusty roads should mar the gelding's toilet.

Similar small processions of men and their animals were converging from all directions on the village of Dounby, where the show-ground lay. The wealth of the country was on the roads: tall Clydesdale horses, satin-skinned, feathered of fetlock, trod in their pride; fat sheep, their wool tight-curled and clean, were foolish and eager to go any way but the right one; and heavy cattle followed with an air of resentment that their dignity, so notable in repose, should be lost in movement. There were men who led a lonely cow, and others who drove a small herd. Here were half a dozen horses together, and there a shy yearling filly, the single entry from a little hillside farm. The beasts in the fields, the commoner kinds fit only for work and beef, came to the roadside fences to see their more handsome cousins pass. And in every house the morning's work was quickly done, so that all who could might come to the show: but the goodwife or a servant-girl must stay at home to feed the hens and boil a pot for the calves.

By eleven o'clock the show-yard was full. The young horses stood in a long row on one side; the mares and

their frightened wild foals were in stalls farther on; the
stirks, the cows in milk and the cows in calf, standing
quieter than the horses, were closely ranked; a few bulls
regarded the world with insolent and sleepy eyes; and among
the silly sheep, packed closely in their pens, was insolence
as lordly as the bulls' where the Leicester tups with their
great Roman noses sniffed the rich air. The owners of this
wealth had no such conceit of bearing as they walked about
and met their friends and exchanged their news: they were
good honest men who worked too hard to show a front of
pride, and all their swaggering was in their beasts. They
stood round the judges' ring like little shabby sculptors
who carve giant limbs that mock their own, and watched
impassively the massive beauty they had bred compete for
pride of place.

Magnus, in his shirt-sleeves, was still at work on the toilet
of the black gelding and the younger horse. He brushed
them anew, and washed their legs. He rubbed sawdust into
the long silky hair that grew from their fetlocks, and he
re-tied the straw bows on their tails. Mere spectators who
walked by, or paused perhaps to make some comment on the
gelding, he regarded with a certain contempt: his busyness,
his more intimate concern with the animals, raised him
above their meagre stature. But to the men and boys about
him who were also in charge of horses, and who, like him,
were curry-combing and finicking with the last details of
show-yard finery, he spoke as an equal and entered himself
as a full member of their society.

When the time came for him to lead his charges into the
ring his manner was dignified and remote. He obeyed the
judges, trotted the horses up and down, and stood with an
air of grave detachment till the awards were made. Each of
his horses took a first prize in its class, and he accepted
the decision and the red tickets with composure that pol-
itely indicated his concurrence with the judges' views. He
returned to the picket-line to wait for his reappearance in
the championship classes.

Now many people came to talk to him—friends of his
father, cousins of his own—and his manner grew more
genial. The strain of his début as a show-yard groom was

over, and he had been gratifyingly successful. There were many jokes made about his appearance in the ring, and in the conversation of his friends there appeared a genuine undercurrent of surprise that he—who was now a famous man, so they had heard—should accept this menial task. But Magnus put on his Orkney accent and did his best to prove that all his ways and all his interests were more rustic than their own.

Then he caught sight of Rose in the crowd, and left his horses in charge of Johnny the ploughman's boy. He walked round with Rose, and gave her his impressions of the judging and of the more notable animals they saw. She listened obediently and gently agreed. Sometimes he stopped and passed his hand sagely down the leg of a horse, and knowingly felt its fetlock. Rose took him to see her father's cattle: Peter of the Bu had done well, and one of his young calving cows was reserve for the championship. Magnus was filled with admiration for its sleek and solid beauty: his devotion to his horses weakened: his admiration for the cow and his affection for Rose mingled, he held her hand, and almost asked her to marry him on the spot. He was determined to be a farmer.

Willy's horses were not so fortunate in the championship classes. One took a Third Prize and the other was Very Highly Commended. Magnus was a little cast down by this, till Willy told him he had expected no better, and was indeed very well pleased by an offer he had received for the black gelding. Magnus left Johnny to take the horses back to Midhouse, and went off to look for Rose.

He found her in the village, where the crowd, coming from the show-yard, now gathered about the cheap-jacks, the shooting-galleries, the swing-boats, and the fruit-sellers who filled the village-green. It was a lively and diversified spectacle. The vulgar simplicity of those who purveyed thick slices of melon for twopence apiece was in sharp contrast to the art of the man who sold gold watches: this was no dull shop-counter trading, but with a ceaseless flow of words the watch would be wrapped up in a ten-shilling note, half a crown and a pocket-knife added to it, and the parcel offered for a pound; or else the cheap-jack would start the bidding at a pound, add cuff-links, studs, and second a watch when there were no takers, and sell the whole collection for thirty shillings; sometimes he would seem to give money for nothing: and sometimes a puzzled purchaser would find himself the possessor of a lady's wristlet watch for which he had mysteriously paid double the price he intended. He was an artist in words, a juggler, a psychologist, and a lightning calculator, and Magnus stood fascinated by his accomplishments while Rose was impatiently waiting to ride in the swing-boats. They lost some money to a foxy man who ran a modified roulette wheel and kept an anxious eye lifting for the police—but the police were remonstrating with a pugnaciously drunken farmer—and they shot with untrue rifles at spotty targets for the glittering prize of a clock. Then they consulted Madame Vanda, the palmist. Rose came out of her tent laughing and blushing and would not say what she had been told. Magnus went in, and Madame Vanda, in a perfunctory way, said there were two women in his life, a fair one and a dark one; he must beware of the tall fair one, but the dark was trusty and true and would make a good wife for him. She looked at the signs of labour on his hands, and possibly smelt a little smell of horses on them. She said, 'You'll be going a journey soon, but only a short one, for your life will mainly be spent in the country, and you'll be successful at farming or some such occupation. March is your lucky month, and you should think twice before starting any new kind of business on a Thursday. . .'

Magnus went out and said that Madame Vanda had talked a lot of rubbish, but secretly he was gratified by her prediction that his métier was farming. He asked Rose to go to the dance with him that night. Shyly she answered that she would love to, and they went home for supper and to change their clothes.

The dance began about ten o'clock. An hour later the village hall was full of a lusty, perspiring crowd, and the walls resounded to a magnificent tumult of noise. Here was no listless ambling to a drawling orchestra, here was no walking of the spineless two-backed beast to a melody deep-drowned in sweetness: but the fiddles kept racing time, and the dancers trod lightly, and girls were whirled off their feet. Slouching lads who followed the plough were neat and nimble in their dancing shoes, and fat red-faced girls kept easy time with them. Now the whole company made a score of arm-linked circles, and the circles became swift-turning wheels, and the floor shook to a wild quadrille. Then, man and girl, they jigged and lifted their knees and turned most deftly in a schottische. Now with a roar an eightsome reel began, fast-weaving, high-stepping, and loud with the skirling cries of the dancers. Nobly the fiddlers led them, sweat on their brows and their bows like arrows flashing. The air was furnace-hot and the lamps were yellow and small like the sun in a winter fog. The dancers were stout and strong, the music was fast and fierce. 'Be God,' said the dancers, 'that was fine.' And the fiddlers wiped the sweat from their foreheads and reached for the ale-mugs that stood beside them.

Magnus led Rose through the crowd at the door and took her outside to breathe cool air. The night was moonlit and serene. A few clouds like soft old sails, loosely furled, floated in the sky and the full moon was lambent silver. Behind them they heard the parley of the dancers and the fiddlers re-tuning for a waltz. But Magnus said, 'We've had enough dancing. Come and do pooja to the moon, and I'll tell you stories about moon-nymphs and goblins and lunacy and love.'

They found their bicycles by the doctor's wall, and rode away. 'Come out and be rich with the moon,' he said again. 'I'll make a poem for you, Rose, by God, I'll make a poem, and a damned fine poem, before we get to the loch.

> The moon is a silver penny,
> And the sun is a golden pound—

There's the first couple of lines. What shall we do with the penny? Get rich with it. What shall we do with the pound? Throw it away. There's lots of them. For there's many a day in the year—there's another line, or something like it. For the sun has a common ground, a daily round, a milkman's round, anything you like. So squander the day without fear: that rhymes with many a day in the year. But damn the days, I want to get on with the moon, the silver penny, the wishing moon, the kissing moon, luckpenny moon, lovepenny, what the devil shall I call it? Wait a minute, I've got it now.'

Magnus rode on muttering to himself, pedalling hard. Then he sat upright, let the bicycle run free, and declaimed loudly:

> But take care of the silver penny,
> I'll buy you a ring with it soon—
> Shall we keep it for wishing or spend it on kissing?
> Come out and be rich with the moon!

'There now: that's the last verse. What do you think of it?'

> Shall we keep it for wishing or spend it on kissing?
> Come out and be rich with the moon!

'I think it's lovely,' said Rose.

The road was white and hard beneath them, the sky was a vast enclosing dome. They were in a moonlit and finite world. Their movement was swift and silent. A glowing pallor transformed the fields, and before them lay the quick-silver loch.

They came to the shore and walked over lush meadow-grass towards the ruins of an ancient broch. The pallor of the moonlight now discoloured Magnus's thoughts, and his excitement turned the corner from exhilaration into a hushed expectancy. The shining surface of the loch dazzled him, and when he turned away from it the mild darkness seemed to recede and return more dark. A delicate trepidation assailed him, as though the lunar virus had coldly touched his nerves.

The ruined broch rose before them, a little steep knoll thrust into the water. A hundred yards beyond it the moonlight rippled on a shoal, and in the shivering gleam lithe bodies, touched with argent, slipped out to play and slid again beneath the surface.

Magnus, bewildered, stopped stock-still, and Rose, with a little gasp of fright, stood still beside him. The lithe bodies in the water, moonlight flowing on their shoulders, swam to and fro, and lay, moonbright and slender, on the shoal. They played a shimmering game of touch and go, and smoothly dived between the ripples. They made no louder sound than the lapping of the water on the shore, and the leaping of their slender bodies seemed to be without effort, like the ruffling of the water on the rippled path of the moon. The water on the shore made a little tune of three soft notes, and the swimmers played in time. Their silver sides were ruffled with shadow when they turned, but sometimes they shone more brightly than the moon, and the water was dusky beside their quicksilver leaping.

Gently, so as not to frighten them, Magnus went a little nearer. 'I almost thought they were mermaids come in from the sea,' he said.

'I didn't know what they were,' Rose whispered. 'But they're otters, aren't they?'

The fallen stones of the broch were thickly overgrown with grass, and grassy banks buttressed the walls and like a broken basin closed in a central space of turf. For another minute or two Magnus and Rose, leaning on the soft wall, watched the otters at their play. It seemed to be a family party, for two were larger than the others. Then something frightened them. With a last bright-shining dive they vanished, and the shoal, untenanted, lay more darkly in the ripples.

With that silver picture lingering in their minds Magnus and Rose made no movement for a little while. Then they turned, and lightly, tentatively kissing, appetite grew by what it fed on, and they held more closely.

Rose said softly, 'It's lovely being here with you.'

Magnus told himself that it was time to go home, but he lay too warm and comfortable to move. Some time later he thought again that they had better go before it was too late: but the music of the fiddles had not left his memory, and the moonlight was a white foe to resolution, and Rose clung so close that still he stayed.

Now Rose sat up, and stared awhile at the bright loch, and then, troubled and ashamed, said, 'Mansie, I want you so much.'

The sky grew darker, and presently they walked back to the road and found their bicycles. Magnus took Rose home to the Bu. She kissed him good-night, and lingered awhile, unwilling to go in.

Clouds had come up when the moon went down, and now a drizzle of rain was falling. Magnus rode back to Midhouse feeling too tired to think clearly, but unpleasantly aware that a certain trepidation was displacing the pleasure in his mind; as when the tide runs out and leaves behind it a shore of uneasy sand.

CHAPTER TWENTY-FOUR

The weather had been fine for so long that Magnus had forgotten the abominable ugliness that could descend on Orkney when the skies pressed close and through a dirty light the rain fell sullenly on sodden fields. But on the morning after the Cattle Show the country was dismally transformed. The fields had lost their brightness, grey mist obscured the firm contours of the land, and cold damp air filled every house. Willy and Janet came in with wet clothes and made the dark kitchen comfortless. The chimney would not draw, and the dog, its coat drenched with rain, stank miserably. Runnels from the midden overflowed the farmyard, and the cattle trod the wet earth into mud. August had come with its usual freight of broken weather. Janet said philosophically, 'It's the Lammas spoots: what other can you expect?' But Magnus found this seasonable philosophy insufficient to console him for discomfort and the spoiling of his fine pastoral picture.

For three weeks there was nothing but transitory relief. A northerly gale drove off the rain and the heavy clouds, swung round to the south-east, and blew them back again. A patch of blue sky would show itself, and flee before the stormy rain a west wind brought from the Atlantic. Iceland exported southward-driving gales, and the clouds sucked their skins full of moisture from the abundant sea and discharged it on the darkened islands. The lochs rose to winter level, the burns, dark brown, ran bank-high, and every low-lying meadow became a marsh. The cattle huddled together in the fields, hens fluttered their discomfited feathers at the house-doors, and the ducks quacked joyfully in over-flowing ditches.

Magnus's farming enthusiasm waned in this weather. Willy and Janet and the others possessed a happy indifference to the rain, and would go all day in wet clothes without a sign of discomfort. But Magnus grew ill-tempered when the skies wept down his neck while he sat in a slow-moving cart or scythed a load of sodden grass, and he took no pleasure in tramping through the farmyard mire. He returned to his poem and laboriously reconstructed, in verse, a Scotland untroubled by its present discontents and even by its present climate.

But he could not recapture the gusto with which he had attacked so much of the world's evil and folly, nor could he devise a really convincing method of reform for industrial conditions and the distasteful appearance of Glasgow, Motherwell, Dundee, and other important cities. He suggested rebuilding them in a style between the modern Viennese and the American, and pictured the Clyde displaying on one side a façade that resembled the lake-front of Chicago, while on the other public playgrounds smiled and tuneful fountains murmured. But the economic complications of this transition were not unravelled, and though poetry is ill-adapted for economic exposition and poets may be excused a ledger-like calculation of their theories, Magnus was uneasily aware that his new Scotland was borrowing the unsubstantial foundations of Utopia. His rural improvements were outlined with more firmness though perhaps with scarcely more practicability, for he proposed a return to the odal laws of the Norsemen, and described a community of sturdy odallers each in his own township dispensing household justice and reaping in peace that which he had sowed. But even here Magnus was not quite satisfied with his writing, for he detected in it that faint wistfulness which is so hard to keep out of any picture of *le beau temps de jadis*, and wistfulness, he knew, was a poor basis for reform. He endeavoured to correct it by the insertion of some good hearty passages, and imagined his odallers drinking, as had their Orkney forebears, the starkest ale in Albion: but he could not stress too much this favouring glimpse, for the brewing of much stark ale is an economic flaw in the structure even of Utopias. But he did what he could with the beneficent rays of his returning sun, and was conscientious about the structure of his verse.

The bad weather gave him an excuse for staying away from the Bu. He had intended to go and see Rose on the day following their misadventure in the moonlight, but the weather had been so bad that he postponed his visit. The next day and the day after that had been equally unpleasant, and the situation was complicated by the fact that except in fine weather he had little chance of speaking to Rose alone: there was no hope of finding privacy in the farmhouse. If the skies were propitious they might saunter out of doors and converse with a field between them and their nearest neighbours, but to ask Rose to go for a walk while the heavens discharged abundant rain and the wind howled in anger was to invite general suspicion of the most pointed kind. So Magnus argued—and most reasonably argued—and stayed at home till the weather should mend. But the weather did not mend, and as day after day intervened between the misadventure and his resolve to discuss, frankly and honourably, its possible consequences, his resolve weakened and he felt a growing embarrassment at the thought of meeting Rose again. He pacified his conscience by arduous work on his poem, and by thinking that the misadventure might very well have no consequences. He remembered that an old friend of his, a medical student in Inverdoon, had often remarked upon the infrequency with which effects resulted from the initial or, as it were, the exploratory cause. It was absurd, thought Magnus, to take too sentimental a view of the occasion: for though he had day-dreamed of settling back in Orkneys with Rose in his kitchen and fine black cattle in his fields, he felt curiously indisposed to accept such responsibilities when it seemed possible that he had actually incurred at least one of them: and the weather was still abominable.

But one day sentiment or conscience got the better of him, and he went to the Bu. It was still raining, and the Bu was as damp and uncomfortable as Midhouse. The blue flagstone floor of the kitchen was sullied with muddy footprints, and the air was heavy with the smell of wet clothes. For two or three minutes Magnus and Rose were left alone together, and Magnus anxiously considered several ways in which to introduce the topic that was uppermost in both their

thoughts, but before he could decide on one Mary Isbister
came in with a long story of a hen that had laid far afield
and hatched a misbegotten brood, and now brought them
home to be cared for, and the chance was gone. But Rose
gave no signs of uneasiness. She was quiet as usual and
shy as usual, and there was no new warmth in her voice
when she spoke to Magnus, no indication in her manner
of the significant possessiveness that on other occasions he
had unhappily observed in other young women. He went
home persuaded, or almost persuaded, that he had no cause
to fear an embarrassing sequel to his indiscretion.

Nothing happened to revive his agricultural ambitions.
The corn grew higher for harvest, but to Magnus it seemed
unlikely that it would ever ripen, and even the handsomest
cattle were so bedaubed with mire that he could feel no
affection for them nor desire to own their like. His poem
approached completion, and a restless desire for change of
scene grew in him. He considered the possibilities of going
abroad again, and spent an hour in debate with an atlas,
turning its coloured leaves to find a winter home with some
melodious name and the promise of a blue sky.

But one day towards the end of the month he received
a letter, forwarded by his publishers, from a wholly unexpected source, and almost immediately he abandoned his
questing thoughts of South America, Ragusa, and the Malay
Archipelago. His correspondent was Nelly Bly, the gifted
special reporter of the *Morning Call*, and one of the most
favoured members of Lady Mercy Cotton's staff. Magnus
had met her several times during the election in Kinluce,
and despite her cynical opinions and the flagrant dishonesty
of her reporting he had conceived a liking for her: she was
pretty, clever, and full of vitality. She wrote now to say that
the post of dramatic critic on the *Morning Call* was vacant,
and would Magnus care to accept it on probation? It was
she herself, she explained, who had suggested his name to
Lady Mercy, and though Lady Mercy had held the lowest
opinion of him during his Nationalist candidature, she had
read *The Great Beasts Walk Alone* since then and had come
to the conclusion that he was a very clever young man in
spite of his political opinions. 'I don't suppose you know

anything about dramatic criticism,' said Miss Bly, 'but that, of course, will be no hindrance to you. The *Morning Call* doesn't want learned disquisition: three jokes are better than the three unities any day, and a little butter will make up for no bread. I think you would find the job amusing, so you had better come along and try it. If we don't like you we shall say so fast enough, and if you don't like us you won't be unique.'

In his mood of rural disillusion this proposal appealed very strongly to Magnus. It was true that he had castigated newspapers such as the *Morning Call* with the utmost severity in his poem, and that he had supposed they were among the most pernicious phenomena of the day. But now he began to wonder if they were really so pernicious as he had thought. They were at least amusing. They were clever and lively. And even if they had a pernicious influence, what of it? If civilization was in truth rotten, then pernicious influences were surely laudable in so much as they would help destroy it. In any case, in a world so crazy and out of joint as this, the sanest mood was cynicism, and if Nelly Bly could be cynical, so could he. Magnus grinned a dog-tooth grin at the mirror in front of him and contemplated the twisted image with satisfaction. He would be a cynic, not a farmer, and in more parlous individualism than ever he would navigate alone the chaos of the time, believing in nothing but the rectitude of making hay—not real hay, thank God, but hay metaphorical—while a metaphorical sun was shining. He would pick apples when they were ripe, take the tide at the flood, and wear a set sardonic smile. He remembered Autolycus and quoted aloud: 'How blest are we that are not simple men!'

He sent a telegram to Nelly Bly saying he would arrive in London in a few days' time and was prepared to accept Lady Mercy's offer. But on his way back from the post-office he temporarily forgot his cynicism and determined to become the foremost dramatic critic in London. It was a pity that Walkley was dead, he thought. He would have only Agate and Brown to compete with. And how absurd of Nelly Bly to suppose that he knew nothing of criticism! Had he not read the whole corpus of it from Aristotle to Burke? Coleridge,

Hazlitt, Morgann, Boileau: he knew them all, and upon that base of erudition he would erect the liveliest of new structures for the delectation of the registered readers of the *Morning Call*. He began to compose an imaginary *critique*, on no particular drama, in which he made fine play with modern instances and wise saws from Longinus and Dionysius of Halicarnassus. He was going to be a dramatic critic of no mean order.

He finished his poem on the following day with a twinge of conscience for such hasty work: but the returning sun was in partial eclipse and would soon darken altogether, he feared. Then he made known his new plans to Janet and Willy. The latter was sorry to hear of his departure. 'You've been a real help,' he said. 'Man, could you no bide with us till harvest's over? You'd do fine at forking sheaves after your practice with the hay.' But Janet said, 'I thought you'd soon be tired of farmer's talk and pleitering in the gutter all day. You'll be better off in London, for there's bound to be more there to write about than you'll find in Orkney. But there's a home for you here when you want it: I'm not sorry to see you go, but I'll be blide to see you back.'

Magnus went to say good-bye at the Bu, and Peter was regretful as Willy had been to hear that he was leaving. 'I fairly thought you were going to settle down here,' he said. 'There's a good farm over by Stromness that'll be coming into the market, with entry at Martinmas, and it would suit you fine.'

But Magnus was unmoved by Peter's enthusiastic description of the Stromness farm. He was going to be a dramatic critic, and as the theatre, as well as Scotland, was degenerate, there lay before him not only the goal of a magnificent reputation, but the arduous and shining task of reformation. He was, moreover, going to combine reformation and the search for fame with a cynical philosophy: his mind was well occupied, and farming had small hope of entering now.

Rose did not appear to understand the nature of his new occupation nor to realize that he was finally turning his back on Orkney. She seemed to think that he was going away for a little while only, for she said, when he shook hands with her, 'You'll be coming back soon, Mansie, won't you?'

There was nothing in her voice to give her question more significance than ordinary friendship, but Magnus's conscience suddenly made a coward of him, and he answered cheerfully, 'Yes, I'll be back before long, Rose.'

The balloon-like exuberance of his mood was pricked, however, and for the rest of the evening his spirits drooped. Even cynicism would not come to his aid: it was useless as a crowbar to a drowning man.

But he felt better in the morning, for at last the weather had mended and the sun shone brightly on grass all pearled with dew. He sailed from Scapa on the *St Ola*. The morning was windless and the air was crystal-clear after the rain. The islands lay like jewels in a blue sea, a circlet of entrancing colour. No one could be sad on such a day, but Magnus felt like a fool to leave such loveliness behind him.

CHAPTER TWENTY-FIVE

On the day following his arrival in London Magnus had lunch with Nelly Bly at Simpson's in the Strand. He had called for her at the offices of the *Morning Call*, and in that huge building he had felt again the excitement he had first experienced in the *News-Sentinel* building in Philadelphia: there was a busy coming and going in the corridors, there were signs of great activity, typewriter noises, messengers hurrying, voices heard in quick discussion—all that, however, might be observed in offices of any kind if their dimensions were comparable with this one: but the air was charged with a special quality, there was a tension, there was, it seemed, an awareness of fleeting time that bore on its swift tide an argosy of news, and here were pirates to take its cargo of a murder in Tooting, a famine in China, war in Bolivia, crisis in Berlin, divorce in Mayfair, falling aeroplanes in America, and a bishop's view of immortality in Birmingham—no other walls contained an air so quick as a newspaper office, no other workers under the earth's sky so bore themselves with the brow-furrowed pride, as of doctors at the lying-in of a queen, that came from intimacy with the first hours of the world's greatest affairs and most poignant small affairs; and Magnus, who had breathed the air in America, though only as a Literary Editor, who has little concern with news, snuffed it again like a semi-authentic war-horse, and felt that he had returned again to his own country.

He said something of this sort to Nelly Bly. She asked him what he had been doing since the election in Kinluce. He answered that he had written a poem.

'Only one?' she asked.

'It's a long one.'

'Why did you write it? No one will read it.'

'It's rather a good poem, in parts,' said Magnus.

'I don't believe you. No one can write a good long poem nowadays, because nowadays no sensible person can believe in any one thing or set of things for long enough to compose more than twenty lines under his original inspiration. I never believe in anything—except Lady Mercy—for more than three days.'

'Not even in your own ability?' said Magnus.

'Yes, in a relative way. In the country of the blind the half-canned man is king. But it would take a full-time hundred per cent genius to write a poem under the single inspiration of his own ability, and nowadays a genius doesn't want to write poetry: he makes a multi-million fortune and suffers delusions of omnipotence.'

'Like Lady Mercy?'

'Lady Mercy's a great woman: make no mistake about that.'

'But quite unscrupulous?'

'My God,' said Nelly, 'who was ever great without being unscrupulous? I seem to remember hearing you say, in Kinluce, that you believed in individualism: well, what's individualism but going your own way without scruples till somebody with fewer scruples and an axe gets up and stops you?'

Magnus finished his Niersteiner at a gulp. 'I've just been delivered of a theory,' he said. 'I grant all you suggest about greatness and unscrupulousness cohabiting with the regularity of those whom God hath joined. Now it's a demonstrable fact that the arts most conveniently flourish under a despotism—take medieval Italy or Elizabethan England, for example—but in such circumstances the mass of the people

have a pretty thin time. Therefore the arts are anti-social, or
at least the symptom, when they flourish, of an anti-social
policy. Now I'm anti-social, because I believe that society—
and I don't mean *le beau monde* only—has become rotten.
Therefore I can serve my principles by serving Lady Mercy,
because she, being great and unscrupulous, is potentially a
despot, and so anti-social, and so, to balance things, a nurse
to the arts. But unfortunately you say the arts—or, at any
rate, the art of poetry—is dead. So what is there left for her
to nourish?'

'Journalism,' said Nelly Bly.

'My God,' said Magnus.

'And talking of journalism,' said Nelly, 'I'm afraid you'll
have to wait a little while before starting your dramatic
criticism. Solomon Tite, the furniture man who furnishes
our free-gift houses for registered readers, and who's our
heaviest advertiser, has a nephew just down from Oxford
who's been looking for a job, so he's taking care of the
national drama at present. But he'll get the sack before
the new autumn shows come on, and you'll be appointed
then. Barney Wardle, the editor, wants to see you and talk
things over with you, so you'd better give me your telephone
number. I'll have to be getting back to the office in a few
minutes.'

Nelly Bly insisted on paying for their lunch. She would
debit the cost of it to business expenses, she said; and this
was only the first of a series of meals that Magnus ate at
other people's expense, for in the course of the next week
or two he twice had lunch with his publishers, twice with
Mr Barney Wardle, with Nelly Bly again, and with Lady
Mercy herself.

His publishers' entertainment was more modest than
that paid for by the *Morning Call*. Newspaper profits,
it appeared, enabled a man to use the Savoy Hotel as
his chop-house, but the publishers of more permanent
literature had to be content with Soho. Mr Cassock, the
publisher of Magnus's works, was not moved to enthusiasm
by the information that the author of *The Great Beasts Walk
Alone* had written a poem in succession to that very popular
novel. He told Magnus that poetry was unprofitable stuff,

and that although publishers with literary as well as commercial ambitions—such as Cassock and Abel—occasionally
accepted a volume of verse, verse was accounted merely as
an ornament to their catalogues, like holly in the shops at
Christmas. Magnus, he said, must on no account write any
more poetry for a long, long time, or he would assuredly lose
the public whose precarious favour had been gained by his
novel. Mr Cassock's tone was so grave that Magnus had no
heart to defend his poem, and ate his spaghetti and drank
his chianti in a shameful silence, and felt as though he had
been detected in some abominable misdemeanour.

Two days later he lunched with Mr Abel, Mr Cassock's
junior partner. Mr Abel adopted a more sprightly manner
and behaved as a broad-minded man who does not summon
the police when he finds a burglar in his dining-room, but
gave the fellow a cigarette and lets him go. 'So you've been
writing poetry, have you?' he asked. 'Well, well. Hardly
a wise thing to do, you know, but I suppose you wanted
to. Eh? It won't sell, of course. Not a penny in poetry
nowadays. We've lost heavily on every book of verse we've
ever published. Still, I like to see a little variation in our
winter list especially, and when a man's done fairly well
for us with one book, I believe in letting him have his fling
with the next—within reason, of course, within reason. So
I've persuaded Cassock to publish your poem, though, in
confidence, he wasn't very keen about it. We've decided to
take it, however. But this is my advice, Merriman: stick to
novels after this. Modern novels, of course: historical ones
are almost as bad as poetry. And now, what are your plans?
Are you going to settle down in London?'

Then Magnus had lunch with Mr Barney Wardle at the
Savoy Hotel. The task of editing the *Morning Call* had given
him a far more prosperous appearance and commanding
manner than the publishing of novels—and a little poetry—
had bestowed on Mr Cassock and Mr Abel. He was large
in size and pink in colour, and he was dressed in excellent
taste with here and there a touch of sartorial exuberance that
gave him the air of perpetually enjoying a holiday. In his
company Magnus entirely regained the cheerful confidence
with which he had come to London, but which had been

somewhat obscured by his conversations with Mr Cassock and Mr Abel.

In the Grill Room of the Savoy Hotel Mr Barney Wardle was so much at home that he resembled a professional guest at a house-party. He knew everyone there and told Magnus their names, peculiarities, sources of income, and extra-marital attachments. The meal was frequently interrupted by people who came to engage Mr Wardle in conversation, and Magnus was introduced to a well-known actress, a well-known novelist, a well-known motorist, and a financier not then so well-known as he became when he was arrested. Ostensibly Magnus had been invited to lunch in order that he and Mr Barney Wardle might discuss the various aspects of his appointment as dramatic critic to the *Morning Call*; but there were so many other things to talk about that they did not arrive at this topic until the time came for Mr Wardle to return to his office, and then, in a great hurry, he said: 'Well, you're going to cover the theatres for us this winter, aren't you, Merriman? But I don't want you to start yet. There's nothing very interesting being produced just now, and as a matter of fact we're in a little difficulty about this nephew of Solomon Tite's: his uncle's our largest advertiser, and we feel it would be advisable to keep him on for another two or three weeks before giving him the sack. But you'll take over from him as soon as he goes, and meanwhile you can amuse yourself well enough, I suppose? There's always plenty to do in London.'

And Mr Barney Wardle said good-bye very warmly and expressed the hope that they would meet again quite soon.

Magnus accepted this postponement of his dramatic duties with equanimity. In reaction against his rural enthusiasm of the summer he now discovered London to be the source of true delight. At first he pretended, as he had promised himself, to regard his surroundings with cynical eyes, but he forsook the affectation when he found that he could enjoy the metropolitan scene without it. London, indeed, in September sunlight, wore a mellow look that suited most admirably its careless dignities and gave its large untidiness a benign autumnal ease. Slowly the comfortable flood of the river ran seaward, and the hospitable red buses navigated the crowded streets with a cheerful mien. The country was in the throes of a political crisis, but the good easy people pursued their way without apparent fear or manifest concern: Melvin McMaster had told them that if they trusted him they would weather the storm, and George Pippin, the Conservative leader, had broadcast a message to the effect that Englishmen were at their best in a crisis: the honest Londoners cheerfully acquiesced, and took the morning's news of impending calamity—but for the efforts of Melvin McMaster—as a titbit for their breakfast plates. Their visible sense of security, that would have been insolent had it not been so comfortable, gave Magnus such pleasure that he almost forgot his Scottish Nationalism and declared himself a Cockney.

He had returned to his flat in Tavistock Square. He had failed to sub-let it. It was ready for him—somewhat dirtier than it had been—and paid for till the end of the year. He felt much more at home than he had while Margaret Innes was visiting him there. He called on several friends and acquaintances, and discovered that Nelly Bly was an admirable companion for the theatre or the supper-table. He was perfectly idle and well contented.

Then one day he received a telephone message from the *Morning Call* and was informed that Mr Barney Wardle desired Mr Merriman to lunch with him at the Savoy Hotel. Magnus obediently accepted the invitation and found Mr Wardle sprucely attired as ever but more serious of demeanour. This time their lunch was less interrupted, for Mr Wardle, having a great deal to say, selected a comparatively obscure table and refrained from waving his hand to all his friends.

He began by saying, 'I suppose you realize, Merriman, that we are in the midst of the most momentous crisis we have been called upon to face since the conclusion of the War? And in our opinion McMaster is the wrong man to be in command at this juncture. We don't trust him and we don't think very highly of his ability. Lady Mercy doesn't trust him, and a woman's intuition is sometimes more valuable than a man's most careful reasoning. We rely a great deal on Lady Mercy's intuition, and she never lets us down.'

Mr Wardle hurriedly selected a few dishes from the menu, and returned to his political topic.

A crisis of considerable magnitude had indeed occurred. It was primarily financial in its nature, and very few people understood it. But the Bank of England was said to be in danger, and Mr McMaster had declared that the Bank expected every man to do his duty. Mr McMaster had already done his by sacrificing his Socialist principles and forming a National Cartel consisting mainly of himself and the Conservative Party. Because the bankers had insisted on speed he had dispensed with the formality of a General Election: the House had simply played General Post, the Socialists had gone into Opposition, and the Conservatives occupied the government benches. And Mr McMaster was prepared to outline an economic policy that would safeguard the Bank from whatever danger might be threatening it.

Lady Mercy, however, was unconvinced by Mr McMaster's pleading. With one of those rapid changes of front for which she was famous, and for which her intuition was doubtless responsible, she had ranged herself with the Socialists and by her command the *Morning Call*, showing great hostility towards McMaster and the Bankocrats, was hotly denouncing their proposed policy of increased taxation and reduction of expenditure in the social services. Lady Mercy declared that these economies were the condition imposed by the American bankers to whom the British Government had applied for a loan of £40,000,000, or £100,000,000, or some such amount. 'And who are the Americans,' she rhetorically demanded, 'that they should dictate our policy? And what is the Bank of England, that it should negotiate on our behalf? The Bank may rule its ledgers, but Britannia rules the waves!'

'To put it briefly,' said Mr Wardle, 'Lady Mercy is convinced that McMaster's so-called National Cartel is not serving the interests of the country, and she is accordingly resolved to destroy it. Now this is where you come in: we invited you here to be our dramatic critic, but all the world's a stage, and at present the most enthralling dramas are being played outside the theatres. Therefore I suggest that instead of interpreting "dramatic critic" in its narrowest sense we should consider its broader implications, and we are prepared to commission you to do a series of articles on various aspects of the present political crisis. You go to Parliament, for example, and give your impressions of a debate: you attend a football-match, a night club, a fashionable church, a workmen's club, and describe the manner in which people of all kinds are facing up to the crisis. A roving commission, in fact. Lady Mercy had read that novel of yours and she was very favourably impressed—as I was myself—by your faculty of satirical description and forceful invective. We believe you would be the ideal man for the job: you're interested in politics and you won't be afraid to say what you think—or what we think—of McMaster and his new colleagues. And, of course, as a featured writer for the *Morning Call* you would instantly become famous. Your name would be a household word throughout the country: our average net sale for August was 2,163,000 copies. Now, Merriman, what do you say?'

Magnus said yes. To an offer so alluring there was no other answer. Before Mr Wardle had finished speaking Magnus was busily composing satirical descriptions of McMaster and the Bankocrats and improvising happy invective for their policy. He was on fire to begin work, and now Barney Wardle was equally in a hurry. On the following day the *Morning Call* published a photograph of Magnus and announced that this brilliant young novelist had joined its staff; while Magnus sat in the Press Gallery of the House of Commons and listened with considerable interest to the debate on the second reading of the Great Economy Bill.

Mr Melvin McMaster was speaking. His manner was grave, his verbiage abundant, and his accent sufficiently Scotch to give the proceedings an air of piety: one thought of *The Cottar's Saturday Night*, the lugubriously metrical version of the Psalms, and the slow passage of the collection-plate. Mr McMaster said that as responsible and clear-thinking men they were prepared to face the facts. And what were the facts? They were overhung by the clouds of insolvency and confidence was oozing out in every direction. They must stem the tide by setting up machinery to investigate every problem. They were in danger of national shipwreck and they must find a formula to avert it. They had already mobilized the goodwill of the nation, and now— it would be untrue to say that little remained to do, because a great deal remained to do—but goodwill was all-important, and if they could find a formula their task of rebuilding Britain on the solid foundations of prosperity would be made much easier. He wanted sympathy, not carping criticism, and he appealed for the co-operation of all parties. He then referred to the *canard* that some of their economy proposals had been forced upon them by the dictation of American bankers and the directors of the Bank of England. 'That,' he said, 'is a monstrous allegation. It is true that we consulted the banks before formulating our programme of economies, and it is true that the banks gave us their expert advice and indicated what economies were essential to our acquiring of a suitable loan. But to say that the banks dictated those economies is an insult to my Government and to our country.'

Here there was prolonged applause interrupted by prolonged vilification from the Opposition.

Mr McMaster said that the proposed reduction of Unemployment Benefit was just and desirable. 'It would be grossly unfair to the unemployed,' he said, 'if they were not given a chance to share in the common sacrifice of the nation in this time of common crisis. The vast majority of them are eager, nay, clamouring, to have the dole reduced and so to do their part in the great struggle that confronts us.'

At this point the warm commendation of the Conservative benches was obscured by cat-calls and other vulgar noises emanating from the Opposition.

Mr McMaster concluded by saying that it was the duty of himself and his colleagues to remain in office until the crisis was past and the Bank of England—that precious stone set in a silver sea—should be herself again, glorious and unafraid. 'And in this respect,' he declared, 'we are ready to do our duty though it should take us three years, five years, or even ten or twenty years.'

By this time both members of the Government and prominent members of the Opposition were anxious to reveal their share in dealing with the crisis, and the debate continued on the orthodox lines of spacious generalization and intrusive personal details.

Magnus returned to the offices of the *Morning Call* and with great gusto composed a description of the proceedings. His article was so lively, so nearly libellous and yet not libellous, so bitingly accurate in certain details and of others so cleverly omissive, that Lady Mercy read it with large approval and for a sign of her favour invited Magnus to lunch with her in her house in Charles Street.

CHAPTER TWENTY-SIX

Magnus was familiar with many stories of Lady Mercy's eccentricities and kindness: of her charm of manner that made devoted friends of her most embittered enemies, and of her mordant censure that reduced all to silence: of her intense interest in everyone she met, and her conflicting and alternative interest in herself alone. He went to her luncheon-party feeling somewhat nervous but still keenly desirous of meeting this remarkable woman. To his great disappointment the party was a fiasco.

Lady Mercy was tall and dignified. She had a long, greyish, horsy-looking face, and her black hair was streaked with white. She had a very mobile mouth and she talked rapidly. Her guests included Lord Faloon; a Member of Parliament addicted to her service; a lady newly returned from exploring some remote part of Brazil; a lady who wrote detective stories; and Lady Martha Moran, whose ladyship depended on no extrinsic activities. While they drank their cocktails Lady Mercy expended her benigner gifts and made the occasion agreeable to all. But as time passed and the remaining member of the party did not arrive—who was Professor Birdwhistle, the well-known Inflationist—she began to show signs of impatience, and a little acerbity invaded her conversation.

Presently one of her secretaries entered and spoke to her in a low tone of voice.

'What?' she exclaimed indignantly.

'This is the telegram,' said the secretary.

Lady Mercy snatched it from him and read aloud: 'Regret my inability to be present. Am sailing for New York at noon today.' 'Sailing for New York!' she repeated. 'But I asked him to come to lunch!'

Her secretary agreed.

'And then he goes to New York. New York! What's New York compared with me? I wanted him to come to lunch. Couldn't the fool realize that I wouldn't have asked him if I hadn't wanted him? New York, indeed!'

Lady Mercy was now in a tremendous rage, and her guests drew back a little from the spectacle of her wrath. 'You can't depend on anyone nowadays,' she said bitterly. 'This man Birdwhistle's a currency expert, and I wanted him to come here and formulate my new policy of Currency Reform. It must be done today—it's got to appear in the morning paper—and now he's gone to New York!'

She turned to her secretary. 'Get Wardle,' she commanded. 'Get everyone you can. Get Cole, Stamp, Withers, Douglas, anyone you like. We must have that new policy for tomorrow whatever it is. And I must go and think what else is to be done.'

Without apology she marched from the room, and her guests were left in silent embarrassment till Lord Faloon said cheerfully, 'Well, we'd better have another cocktail. A little water layeth a great wind, and gin's more effective still.'

It was Lord Faloon who insisted they should have lunch despite the absence of their hostess, and it was Lord Faloon who made the only respectable attempt to maintain cheerful conversation. The others were still overawed by the thunder and lightning of Lady Mercy's wrath, and more than a little nervous lest it should again descend on them. They took an early opportunity to leave, and hardly felt safe till the breadth of Berkeley Square was between them and her ladyship's house.

One of the results of the publicity thrust upon Magnus by his new employment was a visit from Margaret Innes. It would be an overstatement to say that he had made up his mind not to see her, but he had refrained from communicating with her and sedulously resisted the temptation to consider the consequences of their meeting. When Margaret, however, saw in the *Morning Call* that he had returned to London, and inferred from the prominence given to his articles that he was occupying a position of importance, she wrote to him a pleasant letter that made no reference to their previous disagreement but merely asked, as one old friend to another, when he was coming to see her.

Magnus replied that he was still living in Tavistock Square, and invited her to tea. She arrived quite punctually, and he found that she had wholly lost her power to excite him. She fell between two stools: she was older than Rose and duller than Nelly Bly. Even with the most skilfully applied cosmetics her complexion could not compete with Rose's, and her costume, admirably tailored though it was, lacked the dashing air of Nelly Bly's clothes, while her conversation was painfully without interest in comparison with Nelly's. She put on her brightest manner, and Magnus felt sorry for her—because he had ceased to love her he naturally thought she was in need of pity—and behaved very pleasantly. He would have been kinder still had not their past love stood like a ghost between them.

They talked of various matters, and even discussed the political situation: for both desired to avoid the embarrassment of silence.

Margaret said, 'I suppose you know everything that's going on? You must have lots of news that we ordinary people never learn.'

'I've heard a good deal of gossip, of course,' said Magnus, 'but nothing you could honestly call news. I believe that everybody from the Prime Minister downwards is completely mystified as to what's going to happen, and while some say we've turned the corner, others say we haven't yet come in sight of the corner.'

'I see what you mean,' said Margaret very seriously.

The crisis, in truth, appeared to be extending into a series of crises. In spite of Mr McMaster's efforts on behalf of the Bank of England the gold standard had been suspended and the pound sterling had depreciated abroad by one-fifth. But although this was one of the several calamities about which Mr McMaster had spoken so gravely, and to fight against which the country had mobilized its sentiment and its Old Age Pensions, no one seemed any the worse now that it had happened. There were indeed many people who hailed the suspension of the gold standard as a great triumph, and foretold new health for the pound sterling since it had been lopped of four redundant shillings. It was all very puzzling, and whether the financial experts had been mistaken—in which case they were no experts—or Britain had risen from bankruptcy, as from the azure waves, by Heaven's command, was very hard to determine.

Magnus related some Fleet Street rumours to which Margaret listened attentively, and then, with sudden compunction for not having remembered before, he asked how the children were getting on.

Both Nigel and Rosemary, it appeared, were progressing favourably in physical growth and mental development. Rosemary's morbid preoccupation with religion had given way to enthusiasm for dancing, which she was beginning to learn, so that worry had disappeared, said Margaret. But Nigel's interest in the day's news was keener than ever. He read both morning and evening papers now, and asked more difficult questions than ever.

'He came to me yesterday,' said Margaret, 'and said "Mummy, how is it you can still get two hundred and forty pennies for a pound when a pound's only worth sixteen shillings?"'

'Did you tell him?' asked Magnus.

'Well, I explained that other countries had different kinds of money, and that a pound was really only a pound so long as everybody agreed that it was one. And this morning he broke open his money-box and spent all his pennies, and when I asked him why he had done that he said, "Well, people think they're pennies now, so I thought I'd better use them while they still seem good."'

Margaret continued to talk about the children and thoroughly enjoyed herself. But when on the point of going she hesitated a little, and said tentatively, 'I've missed you a lot this summer, Magnus.' Magnus answered lightly, 'That's flattery, Meg. Well, I suppose we'll see each other again before long.' And after she had gone he thought: I should have asked her to dine with me, or to come to a theatre. I behaved meanly to her. Oh, hell, hell, hell! But I don't want to make love to her again, and after a good dinner I might, and then the same old trouble would start again. Poor Meg. But she's making a good living, and she's got Nigel and Rosemary to think about. She's all right. But I should have asked her to dinner . . .

For two or three weeks Magnus continued his work for the *Morning Call*, and wrote with great exuberance about a variety of subjects. In his poem, *The Returning Sun*, he had discovered how much easier it is to invent destructive criticism than to elaborate constructive plans, and now, to his satisfaction, he found that the former rather than the latter was what both Lady Mercy and Barney Wardle required of him. According to his instructions he visited football matches and the places where greyhounds raced; he went to fashionable night-clubs and to the House of Commons; and everywhere he learnt what Lady Mercy and Barney Wardle wanted him to learn: that the heart of the people was sound, but the leaders of the people were twisted and rotten.

It would be unfair to Magnus to suppose that he discovered these facts merely in obedience to his employers. One of his several weaknesses was a quality of shifting enthusiasm, and it often happened that sympathy for his immediate environment blinded him to all its faults and aggravated the frailties of everything external to it. If he stood in the cheapest enclosure at a football-match, surrounded by out-of-work engineers and veteran dole-men, and was momentarily captivated by their enthusiasm for the game they were watching, then all his sympathy would overflow upon the unemployed and let loose his most rancorous scorn against the Government that proposed to cut a slice of their weekly charity. And, for the present, Lady Mercy and Barney Wardle were well pleased that he should indulge this temper. But if he had dined with Melvin McMaster and George Pippin and the Bankocrats he might have discovered an equal sympathy for them, and turned his invective upon their enemies. Fortunately for the *Morning Call*, however, no chance of hob-nobbing with these personages came his way.

In late October he found that his more exuberant animadversions on Government policy were being watered down or even deleted from his printed articles. Then he was instructed to write on less controversial topics, and somewhat unwillingly he composed an appreciation of Mr Edison, the American inventor, who had just died; a disquisition suggested by a record-making flight from England to South Africa; and a review of a popular author's latest work on astronomy. But he took little pleasure in work of this kind, and he was worried to find that his political essays were no longer to the liking of Lady Mercy and Barney Wardle. It occurred to him that Nelly Bly might be more in Lady Mercy's confidence than he was, and he decided to ask her opinion of his position on the *Morning Call* and, if possible, to discover from her the inner facts of the whole situation.

He telephoned to her and asked her to dine with him that evening. But Nelly answered she would be working till nearly ten o'clock: if, however, he cared to call for her then she would be delighted to eat a sandwich and drink some beer with him at the Café Royal. Magnus readily agreed to do this, and wasted most of the day speculating on the result of his inquiry.

A little before nine he was surprised by the arrival of Margaret Innes. He concealed his lack of pleasure behind a mask of cordiality, and for some time she conducted herself as though this unheralded visit were nothing that called for special comment or explanation. She told him that she had been very busy, and when she talked of professional matters she spoke in a cold common-sensical voice. A glimpse of her surgery manner appeared. But when she reverted to personal affairs she seemed less sure of herself.

After a short silence, during which Magnus looked at the clock and wondered when he should tell her that he was pledged to go elsewhere that evening, Margaret said, 'Perhaps I shouldn't have come so unexpectedly, but I was feeling terribly lonely tonight. The children were in bed, and I'd nothing to do. I've been hoping all the time that you would ring me up, but I suppose you're terribly busy nowadays.'

'Yes, I've been busy,' said Magnus.

'I began to think about you and to remember some of the

things you told me about India and New York and all sorts
of places. They were terribly amusing. I've never met any
one who could talk so well as you—you know such a lot of
interesting things—and the more I thought about you the
more I wanted to see you. So I just came.'

Margaret smiled appealingly, and Magnus, despite his
perception that the situation was going to be embarrassing,
could not help feeling pleased by her flattery. To show that
it was not unjustified he began to speak about nothing
in particular, advanced by easy stages to a discussion of
human nature, and after ten minutes' traffic in mixed ideas
concluded his monologue with a pleasant little paradox that
he had used already in his review of the popular astronomer's
latest work.

'Isn't it charming,' he said, 'that in this age of astronomi-
cal knowledge, this age that's aware of man's littleness and
eccentricity in the universe, people should still say, quite
happily, "The sun is trying to break through the clouds"?'

'Yes,' said Margaret with a start, 'it is, isn't it?'

Magnus looked at her suspiciously. 'Were you listening?'
he asked.

'Of course I was! It was terribly interesting.'

Magnus controlled his temper with difficulty. He was very
angry that his paradox should have crashed itself to death
against the blank wall of her inattention.

'Are you cross with me?' she asked.

'No,' said Magnus, 'but I've just remembered I must go
out tonight. I've an appointment at ten o'clock.'

Margaret looked troubled. She leaned over and put her
hand on his knee. 'Have I made you angry? I was listening,
really I was, but then I began to think of something else and
I didn't quite hear what you said. I've had such a tiring day,
and though I try to forget all about patients and things when
I go out, it's not easy, and I keep remembering them. But
I'm sorry if I've offended you.'

'I'm not offended,' said Magnus, 'and I'm not angry. But
I have to go out; I'm meeting someone at ten o'clock.'

'Then why didn't you say so? I believe you're only making
an excuse to get rid of me. Oh, Magnus, why are you
so changeable? You took a sudden dislike to me before,

and now you've done it again. I've tried to be nice to you: I haven't bored you by talking shop, or about the children—'

Magnus grew impatient. 'I'm telling you the simple truth,' he said. 'If you don't believe that I have an appointment, come with me and see.'

'Who is it that you're going to meet?'

'A woman called Nelly Bly.'

'Honestly? The Nelly Bly who writes for the *Morning Call*? Oh, I should love to meet her! Can I really come?'

Magnus had not the slightest desire to add Margaret to the party, but having in some sort invited her he found difficulty in explaining this. He hesitated before replying.

'But I suppose I should only be in the way,' said Margaret. 'You don't really want me, do you?'

She looked so pathetic—or so it seemed to Magnus—that his heart melted and he answered, 'Of course I want you to come. I shouldn't have asked you otherwise. And Nelly will like to meet you too.'

He went to put on his coat and thought ruefully that now he would have little chance to extract any information from Nelly, and wished that he could arrange his affairs more cleverly.

In the taxi that carried them to Fleet Street, Margaret sat silent for most of the time, but as they turned into Aldwych she said brightly, 'I knew I couldn't have offended you really, because I hardly said anything at all. It was you who were talking all the time, wasn't it?'

'Yes,' said Magnus. 'I talk too much.'

'Then perhaps you offended yourself?'

'I habitually do,' said Magnus.'

In the *Morning Call* office he told Nelly that an old friend of his had visited him just as he was about to leave, and for politeness' sake—mere politeness, that frailty in human intercourse—he had brought her with him. 'She's a doctor,' he said. 'I hope you don't mind her coming?'

'That's all right,' said Nelly. 'Bring the whole harem, if you want to. I always like to see what sort of girls a man gets hold of.'

They drove to the Café Royal and found a table in the

crowded *brasserie*. Margaret was delighted and talked to Nelly Bly with great animation. She referred to Nelly's work to show that she was familiar with it, and casually mentioned her own profession. Nelly was interested and asked several questions that Margaret answered with some authority. Then Margaret called her attention to a somewhat remarkable hat worn by a woman at a neighbouring table, and, growing more friendly still, they discussed the bonnet with common interest. One hat led to another, and then to such matters as tulle and georgette. They described their past, present, and future wardrobes to each other, and Magnus, who had thought a witty cynicism was the invariable staple of Nelly's conversation, was surprised to hear the simple enthusiasm with which she discussed what seemed to have been an ordinary green frock. He had expected that Margaret would be the unwanted guest, and now it seemed that he was playing that distasteful part. He listened with great boredom and displeasure to the interminable rigmarole about shops, prices, blouses, furs, bonnets, and whatnots.

After a long time Margaret leaned back in her chair with a sigh of satisfaction, and said, 'Oh, I do love a good talk about clothes!'

At this moment two people, looking for a table, halted beside theirs to survey the over-populous scene. One of them was a tall young man in evening dress, a handsome haughty young man who might be in the Guards; the other was a tall girl in a white velvet cloak with a fine collar of ostrich feathers, a handsome rose-and-tawny girl at the sight of whom Magnus's heart leapt like a shot rabbit.

She chanced to look down, and saw him. 'For the Lord's sake,' she said, 'look who's here!'

'Hullo, Frieda,' said Magnus, and stood up somewhat awkwardly.

'Don't get worried,' said Frieda, 'we shan't intrude on your simple ménage. Do you see a table anywhere, Jimmy?'

'No,' said the young man. 'I told you there was no use in coming here. It's always crowded.'

'But I like a crowd,' said Frieda. 'Get hold of that waiter and see what he can do.'

'You'd better stay here,' said Magnus. 'There's plenty of room.'

'Well, that'll be quite like old times. You don't know Jimmy, do you? This is Jimmy French.'

Mr French submitted to the introduction with a marked indifference. Magnus introduced the others and ordered more drinks. He felt very uncomfortable. Nelly Bly sat with an expectant smile of a playgoer waiting for the curtain to rise. Frieda looked at Magnus with a sardonic smile. Margaret looked at him and at Frieda with open curiosity. And Mr French, looking at nobody, appeared to be thoroughly bored and displeased by the circumstances in which he found himself.

Magnus asked Frieda, 'Have you been long in London?'

'Oh, a few weeks,' she answered. 'Uncle Henry didn't send you his love, if that's what you're wanting to know.'

Nelly Bly looked at Magnus with frank inquiry. Margaret looked at him with growing suspicion. And Mr French glanced at him with chill displeasure.

'Well, that's a pity,' said Magnus, endeavouring to deal lightly with the situation. 'Did you see anything of Frank Meiklejohn during the summer?'

'No, I got tired of politicians,' said Frieda. 'I got tired of Scotland, too.'

'Are you not going back?'

'Not till the Jews go back to Egypt.'

Now Margaret looked inquisitively at Frieda; Nelly Bly regarded her with interest; and Magnus feverishly wondered which of the dozen questions in his mind would sound discreetest and yet elicit the most information.

Frieda drank some beer. 'That's good beer,' she said. 'What are you drinking, Jimmy?'

'Er, brandy,' said Mr French.

'Why, that'll just rip the lining right off your stomach, Jimmy. You've got a delicate stomach: you know you have!'

Mr French frowned slightly, but offered no other comment on this accusation.

'Perhaps Mr French might usefully consult Dr Innes about his stomach,' suggested Nelly.

'Oh, these aren't surgery hours,' said Margaret brightly. 'Anyway, I don't think there can be anything seriously wrong with Mr French. He looks perfectly healthy.'

Mr French's frown deepened perceptibly.

Margaret, welcoming her release from silence, leaned forward and said, 'Look at that awful old man over there with the lovely girl.'

Everybody except Mr French turned and regarded with interest a ferrety wizened old man with a grey moustache and an excited leer on his face who was eagerly talking to a girl, young but opulent in beauty, red-haired and boldly dressed.

'I shouldn't think he could handle her,' said Frieda.

'I shouldn't think he could do anything else,' said Nelly Bly.

Frieda laughed loudly. Margaret laughed a little shyly. Magnus, because he was anxiously wondering why Frieda had left Edinburgh, laughed somewhat half-heartedly. Mr French surveyed them with cold astonishment.

'That was pretty good, Nelly,' said Magnus.

'Pretty good!' exclaimed Frieda. 'Why, it was just perfect!'

Magnus, as host, felt the necessity of entertaining his guests. 'You know the awful difficulty of maintaining conversation with a stranger?' he said. 'The first five minutes are easy: you talk about a play or two, the weather, what-do-you-think-about-New-York, anything at all: and then the easier springs dry up and you begin to wonder what the other person is really interested in, so that the topic won't fail after the first gush. I remember dancing with a girl in Philadelphia once and this difficulty cropped up. I had just been introduced to her, and somehow it happened that we had to dance together for a long time. And I couldn't find anything to say. But while I was hunting for a subject it occurred to me that there was one thing that everybody was interested in, so I said quite innocently, "I've been trying to think of something to talk about that you would enjoy: but there's only one thing in the world that's guaranteed to interest everybody, and perhaps I don't know you well enough to discuss that." Well, she was evidently both Puritanical and frightened, for she suddenly stopped dancing, looked at me in the most hostile manner, and left me without a word.'

'That was just too bad,' said Frieda. 'I guess you don't usually get rebuffed?'

'I know just what you meant, Magnus,' said Margaret kindly, 'and how you meant it. I wouldn't have been offended, and I don' see why she was.'

'Oh, he was right enough,' said Frieda. 'Everybody *is* interested in it. Even Jimmy is. You're interested, aren't you, Jimmy?'

'In what?' asked Mr French.

'Why, in love!' Frieda made a histrionic *moue*, and winked dramatically.

'We need something more to drink,' said Mr French. 'Waiter!'

'I seem to remember that the philosopher Zeno had to do with a woman only once in his life,' said Nelly, 'and then he says, it was simply out of politeness on his part.'

'I don't call that philosophy,' said Frieda. 'I call that dumb.'

'Philosophy may be exclusive as well as inclusive,' said Magnus.

'I know what philosophy is. I had a boy-friend from Iowa once—I guess I told you about him—and he knew the whole line-up from old man Plato to Bergson. And I've done some pretty tall thinking of my own. I was telling Jimmy my girlish thoughts the other day, and if he'd only listened he could have built up a right smart system of philosophy out of them. One that works, anyway. But he doesn't seem interested in my mental processes.'

'Only in your motor impulses?' suggested Nelly.

'Say, what the hell do you mean by that?' demanded Frieda.

Nelly looked at her with a tolerant smile.

It was Margaret who averted the impending breeze. She giggled. She leaned forward and said, 'I don't know if I ought to tell you this, but it's terribly funny. I read it in a medical book. It said that Acton, who was once regarded as the chief English authority on sexual matters, had declared that "happily for society the supposition that women possess sexual feelings can be dismissed as a vile aspersion." That was a good many years ago, of course.'

'You certainly discovered an interesting subject,' said Nelly to Magnus.

'There's still politics,' he answered.

'Oh yes!' exclaimed Margaret. 'Do tell us about the election in Kinluce! I read everything I could find about it at the time, but I've always wanted to hear what really happened, and why you only got—how many votes was it? I'd have voted for you if I'd been there.'

'Kinluce!' said Frieda. 'My God. I never want to hear that name again in all my life.'

Margaret and Nelly Bly looked at her with renewed inquiry. Had it not been for curiosity Margaret would have been definitely hostile. And though Nelly Bly was more impersonal there seemed little amiability in her regard. But Magnus was troubled by the reminder of the election's consequences, and his sympathy went out to Frieda, and he hated Jimmy French, and was irrationally jealous of him, and felt thoroughly unhappy. He had never before seen Frieda dressed so magnificently or seeming so handsome.

Mr French looked wearily at Frieda and said, 'I think it's time we were going.'

For a moment Frieda stared bitterly at Magnus. Then rudely she blew a draught of cigarette smoke over the table, shrugged her shoulders, and said, 'Just whatever you say, Jimmy. Wheresoever you go I go also.'

She stood up and gathered her white velvet cloak about her. Mr French coldly inclined his head. Frieda said, 'Well, good-night everyone. Good-night, Magnus. Two heads are better than one, but three's a crowd on the pillow. Sleep well!'

'She doesn't seem to like us,' said Nelly.

'How terribly rude!' said Margaret. 'Where did you meet her, Magnus?'

'In Edinburgh.'

'And that man she was with was even ruder, though he's terribly good-looking. I wonder who he is?'

'He's in the Guards. His father had a bicycle-shop in

Birmingham and made a fortune during the war by turning it into a munition factory,' said Nelly.

'Do you know him?' Magnus asked.

'I know who he is. I know who everybody is who's got enough money to be news or potential news. And he seems to have a fancy for American girls. He was keeping one a year ago, a nice girl, though she wasn't as good looking as this one.'

Magnus was unpleasantly affected by this unequivocal reference to Frieda's position. He had realized she was French's mistress: it was impossible to suppose anything else. But to hear it stated as an actual and ostensible fact was painful indeed.

'Did you know her well?' asked Margaret.

'I saw a good deal of her when I was in Edinburgh,' said Magnus. 'She'd had a very rough time in America—her parents died and left her completely destitute, I believe—and then she came to live with an uncle and aunt who were very difficult and unsympathetic. She hasn't had an easy life.'

'I wouldn't worry about her if I were you,' said Nelly. 'She seems able to look after herself all right.'

'Magnus was always far too ready to believe in people,' said Margaret.

'Rubbish!' said Magnus.

'Every animal walks in its own way,' said Nelly, and finished her drink, and picked up her gloves and her bag, and suggested it was time to go.

Magnus told the taxi-driver to go first to Manchester Street, where Nelly Bly lived very comfortably. On the way there she said to him, 'You'll be hearing from Barney Wardle in a day or two, I expect. There's going to be a change of policy, and you'll have to get new instructions.'

'Has Lady Mercy had another intuition?'

'Yes, and it's a good one, as usual,' said Nelly faithfully.

In Manchester Street she said good-by to them, and the taxi continued its roundabout route to Tavistock Square. Margaret, as had been her custom before, had left her car there. Magnus did not ask her to come in.

She stood for a moment on the pavement. Then she said,

'I do understand how a girl like Frieda can attract a man, but honestly she wouldn't be good for you. She knows too much, and she's dangerous.'

'Frieda?' said Magnus. 'She means nothing to me, Meg.'

He opened the door of her car and said good-night.

The darkness of his mood intensified when he sat alone in his flat, for he could not absolve himself of responsibility for the change in Frieda's circumstances and he could not believe that she was happy to be living with French. He supposed that she had left the Wishart's house after a quarrel of which he might well have been the cause: or perhaps she had grown reckless, flouted their authority, and abandoned their smug dwelling in a flare of impatience. But even so he was partly responsible, for he had refused to marry her and so by frustration increased her recklessness. It was true, he reflected with meagre consolation, that none but a saint could be expected to marry a girl to save her from ruin: but then a saint would not have made Frieda his mistress to begin with. And every moralist averred that such indulgence was a new milestone on the road to ruin. The road to ruin! A good melodramatic phrase, long out of fashion, but still truth-telling and significant. The whore's progress, he thought. Her feet go down to death, her steps take hold on hell. And he thought of Frieda's beauty, her courage, her gaiety, her love, that he had thrown away, and now, it seemed, they were to be wasted in common harlotry.

He fell into a passion of despair and cursed alike his self-indulgence, his cowardice, his instability, and his luck. The Pelion piled itself on Ossa and both toppled over, for he remembered there was Margaret too: she had been his mistress, and he had grown tired of her also. His conscience could bear and be miserable under the burden of one cast lover, but to have two hanging on it was more than it could support. His conscience collapsed and wearily, as if from a distance, he contemplated himself and Frieda and Margaret and saw them as tiresome and unnecessary puppets absurdly posturing on an overcrowded stage. The world was full of tiresome and unnecessary people. The image of himself, however, seemed more important than the others: he disliked it more. He wondered if he bore seeds of destruction with him, the germs of failure, like a moral typhoid-carrier. If that is so, he thought, I ought to commit suicide. That is the only logical and honest thing to do.

He got up to look for a drink. The siphon was empty and he went to the pantry for another. The passage was dark and the door stood ajar. He hit his forehead hard against the edge of it, and flew into a rage.

'Good God damn and blast the bloody fool who made that door to everlasting hell, the lousy bastard!' he shouted, and kicked the dumb wood with all his strength. He took a siphon and went back to his sitting-room. He used the siphon so injudiciously that half the whisky he had poured was splashed out of the glass. He drank what was left, and in his anger forgot that he had been meditating suicide.

Slowly his ill-temper vanished, and now he felt less sympathetic with the victims of his romantic ardour. He had not been the first to sleep with Frieda, and if she had not fallen in love with him she would have fallen in love with somebody else. She had confessed that celibacy didn't suit her. She was hardy and restless and inflammable, and he wasn't responsible for her character. He remembered that Nelly Bly had said that every animal must walk in its own way. That smelt of determinism, and determinism was a detestable heresy, but there might be a grain of truth in it. Perhaps, like a deer park, free-will was circumscribed by the tall fence of one's character, temperament, and individual nature. Perhaps every human being was a kind of specific magnet, drawing to himself only incidents and fortune of a particular kind. Perhaps, thought Magnus, nothing happens to a man except that which is intrinsically like him.

This thesis occupied his attention for a long time. He succeeded in persuading himself that it was neither determinism nor behaviourism, for he hated any infringement of personal liberty or diminution of the soul. He reconciled it, however, with the admirable spirit of Norse fatalism, that was active, not passive, and full of energy and ego even in the very face of doom. He discovered an analogy in the universe and saw man as a miniature earth attended by his specific planets, yet travelling freely in space. The more he thought of it the more he was convinced that his thesis was true.

'Nothing happens to a man except that which is intrinsically like him,' he repeated.

It accounted for Frieda's rakish progress, and if, as he had often thought, there was something indomitably clownish in his own character, it accounted for his frequent misfortunes. And what did it predict for his future? Magnus spent a wakeful night in this vain speculation.

CHAPTER TWENTY-SEVEN

Two days later Barney Wardle invited Magnus to lunch with him in the Savoy Hotel. The magnificent environment of Mr Wardle's entertainment impressed Magnus less as he grew more familiar with it; and while he listened to Mr Wardle's gossip about their neighbours, and observed Mr Wardle's familiar acquaintanceship with half the occupants of the room, and even overheard tattling fragments of talk from the nearby tables, it occurred to him that all this was remarkably like Orkney. Here as there one's social horizon was comparatively narrow. Mr Wardle's acquaintances, despite their wealth or notoriety, lived a life as circumscribed in its interests as that of an Orkney farmer, and though they spoke in a different accent they spoke of comparable topics: the profits of a new play and the profits of a harvest; the peculiarities of a marquis and the idiosyncrasies of the village post-mistress; the conviction of a financier and the capture of a ploughman riding his bicycle without a lamp on it—there was no great difference between such things as these. The smart, fashionable, and notorious people in London made for themselves a village society, as did the literary people in Hampstead, the more specifically or assertively intellectual people in Bloomsbury, the theatrical people wherever two or three of them were gathered together, the suburbanites in the brick-and-acacia amenities of their own garden city, the soldiers in their clubs in Piccadilly, the costers here, the Civil Servants there, the dockers by the river, and the wives of £300 a year clerks in that station whither God had pleased to call them. Probably, thought Magnus, the human mind is essentially a village mind, unfitted and unwilling for a wider life, and so, whatever its circumstances, it constructs for itself an horizon between the duck-pond and the Squire's ancestral walls.

Mr Wardle's voice broke in upon his thoughts, and he was startled to hear him saying, 'So Lady Mercy has decided to give absolute support to McMaster's government. With the revelation of his new attitude towards tariffs, and after the firmness he has shown to both the Liberals and his former Socialist colleagues, she is convinced that he is the right man to lead the country. And I myself feel that with our support he will be able to do a great deal of good. Now you have attracted a lot of attention by your denunciation of McMaster and your witty and sarcastic comments on his policy, and we feel that we could make a very telling gesture by publishing your new and revised opinion of the National Cartel.'

'But I haven't any new opinion of it,' said Magnus. 'I never did like it, and I don't like it now.'

'Nonsense,' said Barney Wardle. 'I tell you that Lady Mercy is putting forward a new policy, and so we have all formed a new opinion of McMaster. Now what I want you to do is this: you'll write an article entitled "I am a Convert", and you'll describe your conversion to the policy of the National Cartel in a mood of glowing enthusiasm. No sarcasm or irony, remember! Write simply but fervently. Say that you have seen the light, that you realize McMaster is the only man who can save Britain from bankruptcy and ruin, and that you bitterly regret your previous strictures on him. Don't be afraid of a pious note. After all, the welfare of the nation is a sacred charge. So let yourself go—quote the Bible or Shakespeare if you like—and give us something red-hot. "I am a Convert". It will do a lot of good if you bring it off properly. About twelve hundred words: let me have the article tomorrow, will you? And now I must get back to the office.'

Before Magnus could collect his thoughts Mr Wardle had paid the bill, given friendly greetings to a couple of friends, advised another to buy dollar securities, and was gone.

Magnus walked home. He lingered awhile in Charing Cross Road and bought the Loeb translation of Lucretius'

De Rerum Natura. He crossed Oxford Street and continued slowly up Tottenham Court Road. He felt that the successive displays of second-hand books and cheap new furniture were vaguely symbolic of something or other, but he had not the patience to consider what. Indignation against Mr Wardle and his proposals, that grew stronger as he walked, was obscuring all other thoughts. At first he had been too surprised to feel any definite emotion. Then a small and fleeting temptation had assailed him to accept the offer and vindicate the theatrical cynicism he had packed with his suits and shirts for the journey to London. But he soon discovered that this was impossible. He was not a conjuror to swallow his words and regurge their antonyms. He was not a circus-clown to turn somersaults whenever the ringmaster cracked his whip. He was not in truth a journalist, who might save his conscience by serving his paper: he was—he suddenly remembered it—a poet. 'A poet, by God,' he said loudly on the west pavement of Tottenham Court Road. And a poet, he thought fiercely, is not to be bought: he is neither merchandise nor a whore, but master of his own kingdom or an outlaw in another's.

Now he walked rapidly, head high and frowning. As soon as he reached his flat he sat down and wrote to Mr Wardle briefly but forcibly, and resigned his temporary position on the *Morning Call*. He felt better for this exercise and re-read his letter with great satisfaction.

He found waiting for him the proof-sheets of *The Returning Sun*, and, since he was now under no compulsion to remain in London, he decided to go to the country for a few days and revise them carefully and at leisure. He recalled a brief holiday spent some years before in a farm-boarding house in the Mendips, and wired to engage a room. He left town on the following morning and stayed a week in Somerset. He revised his proofs with meticulous care, read Lucretius, and took solitary pleasure in walking over the winter-pale hills in an air too mild for winter.

He returned to London without any definite plans for the future, and found his future had already been dictated. Among the letters that had arrived during his absence there was one addressed in a neat, unformed, school-room hand. He opened it and read:

> Dear Mansie,
> I think you had better come back to Orkney soon now. I didn't want to worry you before it was necessary, but I think it is time now. You remember that night down by the loch after the Market? Well, I am going to have a baby. I hope you are not doing anything that will keep you from coming back soon. I am quite well, and hoping to see you before long. I hope you are well too.
>
> With love from
> Rose

His first feeling was panic. He had long ago persuaded himself that his moonlight escapade had been inconsequential as moonlight, and to learn that it was shortly to have very lively consequences was an overwhelming shock. But after the initial dismay he had no doubt as to what he must do. He suddenly felt a tremendous necessity for hurry and wished most ardently that he could marry Rose within the next half hour. It was not that he wanted to be married. He contemplated his approaching state with dull foreboding. But he thought of Frieda and of Margaret, and that Rose should be added to them, and they should hang round the neck of his conscience a triple burden, was more than he could stand. And Rose was infinitely more defenceless than they, Rose had been innocent, and Rose with a child in her womb had no chance to forget him and find consolation in other love. Remorse and pity clamoured in his mind, and pity goaded him to make instant reparation. He left his other letters unopened and began to pack his clothes with feverish haste.

Then he looked at Rose's letter again, and discovered from the postmark that it must have been lying in his flat for nearly a week. Here was new cause for unhappiness. He pictured her watching every day for the postman, watching for his own arrival, and slowly, despairingly coming to the conclusion that he meant to desert her, to leave her to her shame. He tortured himself with vain imagining of her fears and misery.

He could send a telegram to say that he was coming

immediately, but that would tell her family, tell the whole parish even, the plain unvarnished story of their love. Should Rose receive a telegram saying that he was returning at once, everyone would at once know why. There could be only one reason. Even a letter would provoke inquiry, and a telegram was open for the world to read. It was impossible to reassure her by anything but his own return, and to put a stop to her fears he must go without delay. It was too late to travel that night, but he would take the morning train to Glasgow.

He made such arrangements as were necessary, and once again left his flat in charge of the caretaker. But this time, he said, he would not be coming back.

In the train he re-read Rose's letter. Compared with his own mood it was calm and serene. She seemed in no way to doubt the honesty of his intentions, and to think of such confidence, of her trusting innocency, redoubled Magnus's desire to maintain the former nor disabuse the latter. How touching was her belief! He grew more tender towards her with every mile, compassion became twin-sister to love, and he vowed he would repay her faith with loving kindness.

The long journey made him restless and weary with continued excitement. He slept a little between Glasgow and Inverness, but no more than an hour or two. Through the sombre magnificence of Sutherland and the great heather-deserts of Caithness the train ran slowly northwards. The Pentland Firth lay cold and dull-hued as lead. The little mail-steamer picked her way between the tides and the roosts, and came into the calmness of Scapa Flow. The early darkness of a winter evening was falling when he went ashore.

CHAPTER TWENTY-EIGHT

Not till Magnus had actually landed in Orkney did he consider the many difficulties that confronted him. No one expected his arrival, except Rose presumably, and he would have to explain his sudden reappearance to his sister and to Willy at Midhouse, to Peter and his family at the Bu, and to many other people who, while not openly inquisitive about it, would certainly expect to be told the reason, or some reason, for his return. So great was his anxiety to see

Rose and bring her the comfort of his presence that for a minute or two he thought of going straight to the Bu. Then he reluctantly decided that this was impossible, for to appear at the Bu with such sign of haste would inevitably cause suspicion. And he very naturally shrank from facing Peter and his wife in the character of their daughter's seducer: they would discover the truth before long—there was no need to suppose they had learnt it already—but once he was safely married to Rose it would matter little though all the world knew what had gone before. He must combine discretion with haste, and Rose would have to wait another two or three hours for reassurance until he had established himself at Midhouse and invented some explanation for his presence in Orkney.

He hired a car in Kirkwall and was driven into the West Mainland. In the darkness of the car he considered various stories he might tell his sister to account for his return, and for some time played with the idea that he could pretend to have suddenly discovered he was in love with Rose and to have come home hot-foot to marry her. As, in a very short time, he was going to marry her, that would obviate renewed explanations prior to the wedding, but he found it difficult to reconcile such a romantic declaration with Janet's essentially rational and practical understanding. A romantic declaration requires a sympathetic ear, and Janet, though kind as she could be and very hospitable, was not built for romantic confessions whether true or fictitious. To say, 'I have suddenly been overwhelmed with love for Rose' would ring like a false coin in the sensible shrewd kitchen of Midhouse—and Magnus began to think of a better story to tell.

At the sharp corner by the dykes of Binscarth his car slowed down to let another come past in safety. Magnus looked out and saw that the approaching car was the ambulance from the County Hospital. A moment after it had disappeared a terrifying thought occurred to him. Perhaps it was Rose who lay in it. There might have been an accident. She might have been working too hard, she might have slipped and fallen—when was a woman most likely to suffer miscarriage? Was it late or early? Magnus did not know, could not remember if he had ever heard, and feverishly tried to remember. Or perhaps it was even worse than that. Perhaps she had despaired of receiving an answer to her letter—it had lain a week in his flat—and in despair had done herself some injury, had found some household poison and swallowed it, had yielded herself to misery and called for death to relieve her. A catalogue of horrors unfolded itself in Magnus's imagination. He was tempted to bid the driver turn round and chase the ambulance back to Kirkwall, but the fear of making a public fool of himself inhibited such decision, and instead he sat still and let fears of every kind prey upon his mind.

He found his sister alone. She had simultaneously been knitting a sock for Willy and reading a book from her father's exiguous library, but when she had heard a motor car stop outside the house she had put down her knitting and her book and gone to the door. She peered into the darkness.

Magnus said, 'Hullo, Janet! I've come back rather sooner than I expected.'

'Mansie!' she answered. 'What's the meaning of this?,

Magnus carried his suit-cases into the kitchen and stooped over the peat-fire to warm himself. 'It's cold,' he said, 'but you know how to make yourselves comfortable here.'

'Were you not comfortable in London, that you couldn't stay longer there?' she asked.

'I disagreed with the editor of the *Morning Call* about what I should write,' said Magnus, 'so I resigned. And as there was nothing else to keep me in London I thought I would come home. For Christmas, you know.'

'It's a while till Christmas,' said Janet. 'But I'm real glad to see you again, though I didn't expect you to be back so soon.'

'It was a matter of principle,' said Magnus. 'I've been attacking McMaster and the National Cartel . . .'

'I know. We've been reading the *Morning Call* ever since you began to write for it.'

'And then they wanted me to turn the cat and support him. And I wouldn't do it.'

'They'd be paying you a good salary?' said Janet.

'Yes, fairly good. But I wasn't going to eat my words whatever they paid me.'

'It seems a pity,' said Janet, and there was a short silence. 'You'll not have had your tea?' she asked, and began to make preparations for a meal.

Magnus's thoughts recurred to the ambulance. 'Are you all well?' he asked.

'Well enough,' she answered. 'Willy's away to Dounby, but he'll be back before long.'

'And all the folk at the Bu?'

'They were all fine the last I heard of them. Peter's bought a new quey at some price that's just fair ridiculous, they say.'

'We passed the ambulance on the road,' said Magnus tentatively.

'It'll have been to Northbigging,' said Janet. 'There's one of the bairns there got scarlet fever. The whole family's had it now.'

Magnus was comforted by this news, and took his tea with a good appetite. He told Janet a great deal about his work in London, and after a decent interval said he thought he would go for a walk.

'There's no use going to the Bu,' said Janet, 'for Peter and Mary are away to Birsay to see her sister, and they won't be back till late. You'd better stay here and rest you.'

'No,' said Magnus. 'I want to go out. I won't be able to sleep unless I get some exercise first.'

'London's done you no good if you feel like that,' she said, and began to clear the table.

Magnus found the ploughman's bicycle and rode swiftly to the Bu.

He left his bicycle by the peat-stack and walked round to the back of the house. As he passed the kitchen window he heard the sound of angry voices, a girl shouting, and somebody laughing. The blind was drawn and he could not see in. Then he went to the backdoor and entered quietly. He stood in the darkness of a short passage, and listened awhile. But the voices were confused. Two people were speaking at once and his ear could not disentangle their words. He opened the kitchen-door, and the quarrel died into silence as the participants turned to see who was coming in.

Rose and Peggy stood with the table between them, and from the way in which Peggy held on to it she seemed to be using it as a barrier and defence against her sister. Rose was bright with anger and Peggy was red with more than that, for one cheek was coloured by a blow, and tears swam out of her eyes and trickled down. Alec, their brother, sat in a chair laughing, and the two younger children were together on the sofa, a little frightened, but not too frightened to enjoy the squabble.

'Hullo!' said Magnus, 'what's the matter?'

He came forward half expecting that Rose would run to him, throw her arms about his neck, weep, and beg him for comfort and protection. He was prepared to be strong, compassionate, and wise. But Rose gave no sign that she wanted the comfort of his bosom. She was too angry even to show her surprise at seeing him, and when she looked at him her expression still wore the indignation it had assumed for Peggy.

She turned to Peggy again, and in a voice still wrathful, said, 'Let that be a lesson to you, and don't come thieving my things again.'

Then abruptly she left the kitchen by the other door and slammed it behind her.

Alec got out of the armchair and offered it to Magnus. 'You've got back?' he said genially.

'Yes,' said Magnus. 'What's the matter with Rose?'

'There's nothing wrong with Rose,' said Alec. 'It's Peggy that's not feeling very well.' He chuckled over his joke.

Peggy picked a heavy wooden spoon off the floor. 'She hit me with this,' she said, sniffing her tears, 'just because I borrowed a pair of stockings without telling her.'

'She'll hit anyone within reach of her when she loses her temper,' said Alec appreciatively.

Magnus, though surprised by this revelation of Rose's character, was not long in finding an explanation for it. Clearly, he thought, she was in a very excitable condition. Her nerves were strung taut by anxiety. Her state of health would easily account for a certain amount of irritability.

Pregnant women, he knew, were often the prey of irrational
desires and strange antipathies: they craved exotic fruit, they
turned from their husbands in disgust, they were quarrelsome, unpredictable, and exigent. Obviously he must treat
Rose with even greater tenderness, more patient care, than
he had meant to, and he grew almost as indignant as she had
been to think that her brothers and sisters should behave so
heartlessly towards her, quarrel with her, and laugh at her.

'I think I'll go and speak to Rose,' he said. 'She's probably
feeling very sorry about it all now.'

'Not she,' said Alec.

'There's a poker in the ben-room,' said Peggy. 'Take care
she doesn't hit you too.'

Magnus went through to the other end of the house and
found Rose sitting in dim lamplight, her hands folded in her
lap, a frown on her forehead, and her lips closed firmly in a
sulky line.

'Rose!' he said. 'Are you feeling better now?'

'*Me* feeling better? There's nothing the matter with me!'

'I know, I know,' he said soothingly, and stroked her
arm.

She jerked away from him. 'It was a good pair that I'd
newly washed,' she said. 'And I'd told her before what would
happen if I caught her wearing my stockings again.'

'You're feeling tired,' said Magnus. 'Why don't you go
to bed?'

'Bed?' exclaimed Rose. 'What would I want to be going
to bed before nine o'clock for?'

'I thought you might be tired.'

'Stoop!' [a very rude expletive] said Rose.

After a brief silence Magnus said, 'I came as soon as
I possibly could. I was out of London when your letter
arrived, but immediately I found it I packed up and left.

Rose moved restlessly in her chair.

'Does anybody know yet?' asked Magnus.

'Know what?'

Magnus lowered his voice: 'That you're going to have a
baby.'

'Who should know that? Do you think I've been fool
enough to tell folk?'

'No, but I thought someone might have suspected something, and asked you. Your mother, for instance.'

Rose made an angry noise and pulled her dress straight. 'Then you're wrong,' she said.

'Well, soon it won't matter though everybody knows,' said Magnus. 'We'll get married as quickly as possible.'

He paused, expecting that Rose would melt at this, and come to his arms in a fervour of gratitude.

But Rose only said, 'We can't be married till I get my clothes.'

Magnus, though somewhat surprised that she should want to delay the ceremony for so trivial a reason, remembered that he must humour her, and agreed that it would be advisable to wait till then.

'And where are we going to live?' asked Rose.

'I don't know,' said Magnus. 'I haven't had time to think about that yet.'

'You'll need to hurry then. I'm not going to live in a tent like a tinker.'

He assured her that he meant to find an abode more comfortable than that, and a little later, still solicitous about Rose's health, and fearing to overtire her, he rose to go.

'I'll come and break the news to your father tomorrow,' he said.

'You'll need to be careful what you say then, for I'm not wanting anybody to know about the bairn yet.'

'I'll be very careful,' said Magnus, and patted her head. Rose showed no desire of a stronger demonstration of affection, and he left feeling a little disappointed. He talked for a few minutes with Alec and Peggy, and then went back to Midhouse.

The interview had been very different from what he had expected, and the feeling of anti-climax was unpleasant. He had anticipated returning from the Bu in a spirit exalted by his own nobility and touched by Rose's gratitude. He had imagined the relief of her anxiety and his own relief as two rivers that, joining together, should spread their generous flood and lave them both in healing waters. He had behaved in a manly, honourable, and selfless fashion, and he had hoped for some reward for his virtue. But Rose had treated his return, his promise to marry her, in the most off-hand way, as though she had expected nothing else. It was disappointing, to say the least of it.

But presently Magnus decided that her off-handedness, her certainty of his return, were merely proof, if more proof were needed, of her innocence and simple faith in him. And how dear a thing is innocence! His heart was touched again, and he thought tenderly even of her rudeness. She had looked very lovely, sitting in the lamplight, and very young. It was his fault that her temper was irritable, her nerves dangerously taut, and he determined to be long-suffering with her though she should demand apricots in January and turn him out of doors in March.

Willy was at home when Magnus came back to Midhouse, and the tale of the disagreement with the editor of the *Morning Call* was told again. Willy also thought it was a pity that Magnus should have resigned simply because he had wanted to say one thing and Barney Wardle wanted him to say another. Surely it didn't matter very much what was written in a newspaper? But Magnus maintained that it mattered a great deal, and Willy, seeing that he was in earnest, pretended to agree with him.

Magnus said nothing about his affairs at the Bu that night.

CHAPTER TWENTY-NINE

The next day, on his way to the Bu, Magnus met Peter and Alec coming down the farm-road beside a cart loaded with barbed-wire and fencing-posts. Peter let Alec go on alone and stayed to talk with Magnus.

'Man,' he said, 'I was just delighted to hear you were back. I've been expecting nothing else. After all that interest you showed in farming, and in the kye particularly, I knew fine you wouldn't long be happy in London. I said to the wife more than once, "You'll see Mansie back before the New Year. He'll no be satisfied till he's got a farm of his own and breeding his own beasts." I saw that you'd taken a notion for it, and I knew it was just a question of time before you made up your mind. Man, you should have let me know you were coming home. That farm near Stromness, that I told you about in the summer, was bought no more than a week ago. But we'll find something else for you, if you're wanting to start at once.'

'That's very good of you, Peter,' said Magnus. 'I was hoping that you'd help me. But I haven't quite made up my mind as to what I want yet.'

'Just so, just so,' said Peter. 'But there's two or three places in the market, and—let me see: this is the 18th—you've got ten days till the term, so if you're in a hurry you'll maybe find something to suit you before then, and you can get to work right away.'

Magnus, who had been thinking that perhaps Peter might be able to tell him of a cottage he could rent for the winter, was somewhat taken aback by the instant assumption that he intended to buy a farm. He had almost forgotten his enthusiasm of the summer, and now, while they stood in a cold wind that brought with it recurrent showers of colder rain, and the sky loomed black above them, the prospect of being a farmer was less attractive than it had seemed in the sunny spacious days of July. But Peter talked of a farm in the East Mainland, of another in Evie, and a third in the island of Stronsay, as though it were concluded that Magnus was going to take one of them. Peter had a quick and energetic nature. Where others would pause and consider the idea for weeks or even months, Peter would make up his mind in the morning and go off to buy his cow or sell it between dinner-time and tea. And sometimes his initiative paid him, and sometimes it did not. Now he was convinced that Magnus would be well advised to buy a farm at once, and he was already calculating, at current prices, the cost of stocking it.

That happened which had happened before, and as he talked Magnus, despite the weather, gradually became infected by his enthusiasm. The more he thought of it the more he became persuaded that if he was going to live in Orkney—and Rose elsewhere would be unhappy and ill-situated as Pocahontas at the court of James VI—the only sensible thing to do was to become a farmer. He remembered Peter's black cattle, the shining and magnificent Clydesdale mares at the Dounby Show. And

Rose would make a splendid wife for a farmer, though a poor and awkward one for a suburban author. Peter, moreover, would be well disposed to him if he agreed to buy such-a-place in Evie or what's-its-name in Stronsay, and he earnestly desired Peter's goodwill before telling him that he proposed to marry his daughter in something like an improper hurry. He grew light-hearted to think of the gamble that was offered him—opportunistic it might be, but still it was a gamble: a double gamble: a wife and a farm together, good Lord!—and whenever he became light-hearted his mind was made up.

'Very well, then, Peter,' he said, 'we'll go round tomorrow and look at the two places on the Mainland, and if neither suits me we might take a trip to Stronsay.'

'That's fine, man,' said Peter. 'Man, I couldna be more pleased though you made me a present of all three of them.'

'And now,' said Magnus, 'I've got a surprise for you. I want to marry Rose.'

Peter looked at him for a long time in silence. 'Ay,' he said at last, 'that is a surprise.'

Magnus waited.

'You're sure of yourselves?' asked Peter.

'Yes,' said Magnus, 'we both want to get married, and we want to get married soon. Almost immediately.'

'She's young,' said Peter thoughtfully, 'but that's a mending fault.'

Then he said, 'You'll not have spoken to her mother yet?'

'Not yet,' said Magnus.

'It'll fairly be a surprise for her. But you'll get settled in your new farm before you think of marrying?'

'I don't see why we should wait for that.'

'You're surely in an awful hurry,' said Peter, and his voice grew a tone less friendly.

'Perhaps I'm being selfish,' said Magnus, 'but Rose has agreed with me that there's nothing to be gained by waiting.'

'And this is what brought you back from London?'

'Well, partly.'

'You'd better come up to the house and see the wife,' said Peter, and walked in silence back to Bu.

Mary Isbister took the tidings as a joke at first, and cried, 'My mercy! Mansie's far too bigsy [Conceited] nowadays to marry a lass from hereabout!' But when Magnus assured her that he was in earnest she became too flustered to be coherent, and talked of this and that, and called Rose to come and tell them what it was all about, and scolded her for no reason, and again said that Magnus was having a joke at her expense, and began to speak of a sale of furniture that was advertised, and finished by laughing heartily and saying it was time indeed she had some more grandchildren, for her married daughter had only two bairns and James Robert in New Zealand, though married a year, had none at all.

Peter sat in his chair without speaking during all this discussion, and Rose stood almost as silent. But her aspect was more friendly than it had been on the previous evening, she smiled at Magnus, and though in some degree her shyness had returned, her affection for him became evident enough before the end of the parley. Magnus's spirit mounted high, and when at last an opportunity arrived to take Rose, without undue ostentation, to the empty ben-room, he found to his delight that she was almost as lovingly disposed towards him as she had been on that moon-lit night in the ruined broch. She told him, too, how glad she was that he had come so promptly in answer to her letter, for though she had never doubted his coming she had feared that business of some kind might delay him. Magnus told her that nothing on earth could have kept him from her, and won the reward of virtue that he had hoped for in vain on the night before.

He faced the necessity of telling Janet about his impending marriage with scarcely a qualm, but he was hard-pressed by his sister's arguments, and found it difficult to persuade her of the wisdom of his intention. Janet was ambitious for him, and though she was fond of Rose she did not think her good enough to marry Magnus, and she did not hesitate to say so. She talked of his books and of the name he had made for himself, and she spoke with such emotion that Magnus feared she was going to cry over him. He had never seen his sister in tears, and tears so foreign to her nature that he became acutely embarrassed by the prospect of her weeping, and argued with the greatest eloquence about the prudence and sagacity and acumen of his decision. Willy came to his rescue with a series of questions about the farms that Peter had recommended, and the subject of the wedding gradually disappeared in the larger topic of agriculture.

On the following day Magnus hired a car from the garage in Dounby and drove with Peter to inspect the farm in Evie and that in the East Mainland. Both were large, as farms go in Orkney, and Magnus felt a proleptic pride of ownership as he walked the boundaries and pretended to be knowing about the condition of the land, the steadings, and so forth. A fleeting doubt assailed him that he could hardly afford a place so large as one of these, for when the cost of stocking it was added to the purchase price it made a total but little short of his entire capital. But farming was still a fairly profitable occupation in Orkney, no matter what it was in other parts of the country, and Peter had sold a hundred lambs for a good price only a few weeks before. So why should he hesitate at sinking his whole capital? He would be making a sound investment, and the larger the investment the larger the profits. Though Magnus was by no means an authority on financial matters he knew that that was a fundamental axiom.

Rose, however, had other ideas. She was indignant when she heard that Magnus was contemplating the purchase of so large a farm, and she declared that no power on earth would make her live either in that in the East Mainland or the nearer one in Evie.

'But why?' asked Magnus.

'Because you know nothing about farming, and you'd be ruined in a year if you went to a place of that size.'

'I know a great deal about it,' said Magnus. 'I don't pretend to be an expert, but I've a fairly good idea of the general principles and your father says that I'm a useful judge of cattle already. And he would help me if I were in difficulty about anything, and I daresay you know a lot about animals yourself.'

'So you're depending on me and my father to do the work for you?'

'Not at all. But I don't deny that I may want help occasionally.'

'Why don't you take a small place to begin with, and then if you do well in it you can find a bigger one later on?'

Magnus admitted there was something to be said for this suggestion, but maintained that for several reasons the ownership of a large and handsome farm was preferable to possession of a small and narrow one. But Rose was not to be persuaded. Peter and her mother joined the discussion, and Rose revealed such decision, such knowledge of her own mind, that Magnus was amazed to find this wealth of determined character behind the front of shyness that was almost all he knew of her. He was compelled to admire her firmness, but he could not wholly exclude from his mind a small and vague feeling of uneasiness about it.

It appeared that Rose already knew the proper place for them. There was a little farm called Mossetter on the hillside no more than a mile from the Bu. It also was for sale. The man of Mossetter had died, there were no children, and his widow was going to live with her sister in Kirkwall as soon as she could dispose of the farm. Mossetter would suit them very well indeed, said Rose.

'You didn't tell me about it, Peter,' said Magnus.

'It's too small a place for my father to think about,' said Rose. 'He's got grand ideas, the same as your own.'

'Man, man,' said Peter, 'Mossetter's not the place for you at all. There's no more than twenty-five acres of arable, and a small bit of outrun for sheep. You'll do no good at all there.'

'It's Mossetter or nowhere,' said Rose.

After a great deal of argument Rose had her way, and a week later Magnus bought the little farm for £400. The widow had already sold off the stock except for a cow, a couple of sheep, and the hens. Magnus bought these and also such of the farm implements as Peter recommended. Peter relented when he saw there was no hope of fruition for his own ideas, and helped Magnus in the purchase of suitable stock. He sold him a good cow in calf and a yearling beast at a fair and even generous price.

But Rose's industry far surpassed Magnus's. She refused to have anything to do with the widow's furniture, and, taking her mother with her, she spent day after day in

Kirkwall buying chairs and lamps and linoleum and pots and pans and all the other things for which there is room in even the smallest of houses: and the dwelling-house of Mossetter was little enough. But for major articles of furniture she relied on the catalogues of greater firms than existed in Kirkwall. She had sent for these catalogues weeks before, and knew exactly what she wanted. She took no little pride in ordering a bed from London, and though she had insisted on Magnus being economical in his purchase of the farm, she proved somewhat extravagant in the purchase of furniture, and Mossetter had a rather crowded appearance when she had bought all she wanted.

It was Rose, too, who made arrangements for their names to be cried in the parish church, and though preparations for the wedding were mainly in her mother's hands, Rose directed them. Magnus proposed that the wedding should be as small and quiet as possible, but Rose declared she did not mean to be married as though she were ashamed to be seen in a veil, and proceeded to invite friends and relations from far and near.

Because of this bustle and busyness Magnus found few opportunities for private conversation with Rose, and even when he was alone with her she generally had some problem to discuss that interfered with the display of affection. She was clearly very fond of him, and well pleased that she was going to be married to him, but she appeared to treat her feelings with less indulgence than Magnus showed to his. She seemed, in fact, to believe that frequent embracing was a sign of moral weakness, and was often impatient with herself for yielding to an amorous temptation.

CHAPTER THIRTY

A few days before his wedding Magnus had the misfortune, while shaving, of cutting off a small pimple on his upper lip. The tiny wound became infected, and on his wedding morning he observed with extreme disfavour that the small but objectionable sore was no better. He felt far from well. He had slept poorly and he had a sour taste in his mouth. He considered the approaching ceremony without enthusiasm.

The postman brought him a few letters forwarded from

his London address. There was an invitation to dine in Kensington, an invitation to speak on *Modern Criticism* at a literary luncheon. A press-cutting agency sent three reviews of *The Returning Sun*, which had just been published. One was tolerant, one was severe, and the third endeavoured to be amusing at his expense. In the opinion of these three, at any rate, *The Returning Sun* was a failure.

There was also a copy of the *Morning Call*. Janet was responsible for its presence. She had carefully studied Lady Mercy's scheme for the distribution of free gifts to registered readers, and discovered that a year's subscription carried the bonus of a cottage-piano. It soon occurred to her that by paying a year's subscription in Magnus's name she could give him a very handsome wedding-present at a very trifling cost to herself, and being of an economical turn of mind— though generous in the acts of hospitality, that did not cost ready money—she took advantage of Lady Mercy's kind offer and Magnus now possessed a piano, somewhat damaged in transit, that neither he nor Rose could play. He was also assured of tidings from the outer world for twelve months to come. And as though for a marriage greeting the present copy contained a news item of particular interest.

On the back page there was the photograph of a newly-wedded couple with the caption below: Mr J. J. Chamberlain French and Miss Frieda Forsyth, of New York, after their marriage yesterday at the London Register Office. A brief paragraph on an inner page repeated the information that Miss Forsyth was an American, and added that Mr French had resigned his commission in the Guards, and the bride and bridegroom were sailing in the *Empress of Britain* on its third luxury-cruise round the world.

Among a variety of minor sensations Magnus's predominant feeling was amusement: not, however, the robust after-dinner merriment of bachelor-parties, but something akin to the weak laughter of a convalescent. Frieda had got her man, and even if she failed to keep him he could not desert her without proper compensation. And Frieda, whose fate had so troubled him, was going round the world in luxury, while he was about to settle himself in a small farm in Orkney. It was clearly an occasion for laughter, and had he been feeling better he might have laughed more heartily. But owing to his *malaise* there was a certain frailty in his amusement.

Magnus's brother Robert, the schoolmaster in South Ronaldsay, had come to be his best man. It was Janet who had insisted on his being asked to perform the service, for Magnus had no great friendliness towards his brother, who was a dull and disagreeable person. But Janet maintained that it was his privilege to be best man, and Magnus's duty to ask him to accept the office. So Robert had arrived and Magnus found his company not the least of his burdens.

In the early afternoon Robert discovered the press-cuttings and read them. 'These people don't seem to think much of that poem of yours,' he said.

'No,' said Magnus.

'It's a pity,' said Robert.

'I don't care a damn what they say.'

'But they form public opinion, don't they?'

'To hell with public opinion.'

'Well, perhaps you can afford to say that now. I don't suppose public opinion matters much to a man farming twenty-five acres of land in the middle of Orkney.'

'No, and your opinion doesn't affect me either.'

'If you had asked it earlier,' said Robert, 'I would certainly have advised you against this absurd idea of becoming a farmer. However, I suppose it's too late to say anything now.'

'Look here,' said Magnus, 'will you mind your own business? I know perfectly well what I'm doing, and I'm doing it because I want to, and for no other reason.'

'Oh,' said Robert. 'I assumed you were marrying Rose because you had to.'

Magnus lost his temper. 'I've never done anything in my life because I had to do it,' he shouted. 'I do as I please and I always have done as I pleased. Because you're one of nature's conscripts you think that everyone else must act as though circumstances were a sergeant-major and the whole world a Prussian parade-ground. But I'm not a conscript: I'm a volunteer and I always have been!'

Magnus paused. His rodomontade was growing dangerous. The military metaphor might be extended and his marriage be said to resemble confinement to barracks. But Robert failed to observe his opportunity.

'You're a dull fellow,' said Magnus.

'I'm quite content to be what I am.'

'I know you are. Let's have a drink, and forget it.'

But Robert refused to drink, so Magnus took his own dram and that which he had poured for Robert as well, and felt more cheerful because of them.

The marriage ceremony took place in the ben-room at the Bu, and the number of people who contrived to be present in that little space was remarkable. Yet they were only a small proportion of the guests. Others filled the passage outside or stood in the garden and peered through the windows. There were more in the kitchen, and still more in the barn that had been cleared for dancing. And through the gathering darkness late-comers were approaching the Bu from all directions, some on foot and some on bicycles, some in motor cars and a few in old-fashioned gigs. Rose was to be gratified in her desire for a large and popular wedding.

She made a charming picture in her bridal array, and bore herself with such dignified composure that, in comparison, Magnus's behaviour seemed to be merely an improvisation of the bridegroom's part. Rose received congratulations as one accustomed from early childhood to a multiplicity of compliments, but Magnus endeavoured to minimize the seriousness of the occasion by a jocular acceptance of all the well-wishing.

The marriage service was but a minor part of the celebrations. The minister left before the last guest had arrived, and feasting and dancing continued till the tardy dawn. Mary Isbister and her assistants had prepared such vast quantities of food as might have served for a siege. Sheep had been killed, poultry slaughtered without ruth or counting, puddings made, bread baked, ale brewed enough to drown a horse, whisky bought, cakes and biscuits had been bought, and the bride's cog prepared with such heat, richness, potency, and savour that the mere perfume, as it was borne from mouth to mouth, fortified the senses and was carried in a sweet breeze of intoxication to the barn where the fiddlers waited.

Except for the busy women who filled and replenished the tables, a fine air of leisure characterized the early behaviour of the guests. The night was before them, and while they waited their turn to eat they stood in little groups in the barn, at the house-end, in the yard—for the night was fine though cold—and gossiped and drank the ale that was brought to them. But a richer atmosphere enfolded them when dancing began, and the fiddlers' music quickened their blood, and the ale came faster.

Rose danced as vigorously as though she were already lightened of her child, and Magnus, who had drunk liberally and often, forgot his *malaise*, and threw off his coat, and clasped whatever girl was nearest, and felt that a wedding was the finest way of spending a night he had ever found. Then he grew thirsty and went indoors. Peter was sitting with half a dozen men of his own age and three or four stout, brisk, and talkative women.

'Come away, Mansie,' he said, and made room for him, and gave him a glass of whisky. 'Man, we were just talking about the old days and the hard drinking there was in Orkney. My father used to tell about a wedding in Hoy when they brewed far stronger ale than they do nowadays, and some time after their tea all the men went outside together to settle an argument about which of them were fou' and which were still sober. And some said the moon was rising in the east, and some in the west. And they werena fou'. And some said there were two moons in the sky. And they werena fou' either. But one man said there was no moon at all, and *he* was fou': he was damn fou', fair fou', fine fou', skin fou', blin' fou', and fou' altogether.'

'He must have been like Peter o' Taing,' said an old man with blue eyes and a white beard. 'He's dead now, but he lived to a great age. I mind him saying once—and he was fou' at the time—"Man, I've only got one vice, but it's given me more pleasure than all my virtues".'

Then someone remembered that Peter o' Taing had once been asked at what age a woman would no longer take a man, and he had answered, 'So long as her shin will bleed I wouldna trust her.'

The conversation grew Rabelaisian. A succession of ripe

anecdotes followed this story, and all the dead worthies of the country were remembered, their eccentricities recalled, their quips and the quirks of their robust independence recited with deep relish. A new ambition revealed itself to Magnus while he listened to these tales, and he thought how enviable was a rustic immortality. His mind leapt forward and he greatly desired that in time to come his jests and the oddities of his behaviour would be remembered and woven to a legend. He would cultivate a humorous eccentricity; he would be unorthodox and witty; in his old age he would be a notable figure in the country and his conversation would bristle with memorable remarks; he would, in fact, prepare to become a tradition. But while he was meditating how to set about it, and when he had but finished his second dram, Rose came in to look for him, and said that she hoped he hadn't been drinking too much, and took him away to dance again, and was no sooner dancing with him than she complained about the odour of whisky on his breath.

'It'll be worse by morning,' said Magnus, and lifted her briskly round in a Highland Schottische.

The barn was now like the inside of a smoky lamp on a summer evening when the moths, maddened by the light, have come to dance in the round globe. It was hot as a lamp, noisy, full of ceaseless movement and a smoky yellow light. Red faces shone with sweat and the girls' bright frocks were creased and crumpled. But the fiddlers played with a tireless spirit and ale was there for all who wanted it.

Magnus went outside to cool himself and met a man called Jock of the Brecks whose wife, some little time before, had taken him home and put him to bed thinking he had drunk enough and might disgrace her if he were allowed to drink more. But Jock was a shrewd fellow, amiable in his temper yet not easily discouraged. He had agreed to go to bed, and then, as soon as his wife had left him, he got up again, and dressed himself, and took his bicycle and put a bottle of whisky in his pocket and returned to the wedding as fast as he could. Now Magnus took a drink from his bottle and told him he had done well. And Jock had a drink himself and invited some other men, dimly seen in the darkness of the yard, to join them and drink also. The party grew and

Jock's story induced such merriment in them that a witty fellow called Johnny Peace began to make a song about it, and declared that with another dram or two to help him he would make a very good song indeed. Then Magnus said that he would sing a song, and gave them the scandalous ditty of *Reilly's Farm*. This jocular noise attracted more people, and presently there were almost as many men listening to him as there were dancing. So Magnus sang, for an encore, the dolorous but robust ballad of *Samuel Hall*, and the sonorous notes of its vindictive refrain echoed magnificently about the yard.

During the penultimate verse Rose interrupted the recital. She thrust her way through the audience and taking Magnus firmly by the arm bade him to come with her.

'Do you think that's the way to behave at a wedding?' she demanded.

'It's my wedding as well as yours,' said Magnus, 'and I'm going to enjoy myself.'

'You've had your last drink for this night,' said Rose, 'except a cup of tea.'

But already the full darkness of night was fading, and sombre grey was creeping into the sky. Rose went to change her dress and Magnus to make ready for their journey. A honeymoon is not usual among the Orkney farmers, but Magnus had determined to take Rose to Edinburgh for a week. He was not ashamed of his bride, and he was going to show that he wasn't ashamed of her. They were to cross the Firth that morning.

The remainder guests were breakfasting when they left. A short distance from the house their car stopped beside a man, one who had lately been dancing and drinking most vigorously, who now was faring homewards, slowly but resolutely, on his hands and knees. Magnus got out and asked if he needed help.

'Is this the road to Birsay?' asked the crawler.

'Yes,' said Magnus. 'But you've six miles to go.'

'It's early yet,' said the crawler, and plodded on.

CHAPTER THIRTY-ONE

The sea was calm but the wind was cold, and long before

they had crossed the Firth Magnus had lost the night's exhilaration, and its queasy aftermath was aggravated by the *malaise* he had felt on the previous morning. The small unsightly sore on his lip was no better, and his tongue was furred with a richer fur than whisky and tobacco, even in the largest quantities, should bestow. It appeared to be somewhat swollen and clumsy in its movements. He shivered violently in the cold wind, and when he went below felt hot and feverish. Rose made an unfavourable comment on his miserable appearance, and said, 'This'll be a lesson to you, I hope. If your stomach won't stand whisky, you'll need to stop drinking it.'

To Magnus, who prided himself on a hard head and capacity for huge potations, this was a bitter reproof. That he, who so often had drunk out the night with strong men, should be called a weakling in drinking by a mere girl, this child of twenty-two, his shy and simple bride! But he did not defend himself. He said, 'I think I'm sickening for something. I'm afraid I'm going to be ill, Rose.'

'Come up on deck and you'll feel better,' she answered, and Magnus, obediently following her, walked the deck and felt the wind come cold-fingered under his clothes, and tried to talk in a honeymoon way though his teeth were chattering and his tongue seemed too big for his mouth.

They landed at Scrabster in the early afternoon, and drove to a small hotel in Thurso for lunch. But Magnus had no appetite. He went out and found a chemist's shop, where he bought a thermometer, and returning to the hotel hid himself in the lavatory and took his temperature. It was rather more than a degree above normal. He felt worse immediately, and finding Rose in the lounge told her the news with a certain feeling of satisfaction.

'You've caught a cold, I suppose,' she said. 'Standing out in the yard drinking with Jock of the Brecks, with your coat off, and you all hot from dancing! Well, we'd better stay here for the night, and maybe you'll feel better in the morning.'

Magnus engaged a room and went to bed. Rose, in a brusque, matter-of-fact way, made him comfortable with a hot-water bottle and extra blankets, and then left him. She spent the afternoon in the lounge, reading a magazine that she had bought. In the evening Magnus's fever increased and Rose borrowed a couple of aspirin tablets from a maid. He suggested, half-heartedly, that she should sleep in another room. But Rose was scornful of that proposal, and said that if he was really ill, which she doubted, she must stay there to look after him; and if he wasn't ill, then there was no need to go the expense of taking another room.

She turned his pillow and remade the bed. She undressed very modestly and quickly, put out the light, and got in beside him. For a minute she lay still. Then she turned and threw her arms round him and kissed his cheek and forehead, and whispered endearments, not pleading for love, but giving it. Magnus restrained his answering tenderness and said mournfully, 'How the hell can I kiss you as you ought to be kissed, with a damned sore on my lip and a mouth like a heron's nest? Rose, I swear I'll never get drunk again. I'll work hard, I'll be a damned good husband to you, I'll. . .'

'You'll go to sleep now,' she said, 'and you'll feel better in the morning.'

She patted his shoulder, moved to the far side of the bed, and in a few minutes was comfortably sleeping. Magnus, drowsy already, silently repeated his good resolutions and followed her example. He woke in a heavy sweat some hours later, and, without waking Rose, got out of bed and changed his pyjamas. In the darkness of the night he grew pessimistic, and felt sure that he was seriously ill. He was cold now, his tongue was dry and swollen, and his throat was sore. A sore throat, he knew, might be the symptom of grave disorder. Perhaps he had diphtheria. Typhoid fever, perhaps, or paratyphoid. He knew a man who had caught rheumatic fever after a drinking bout. Pneumonia was another possibility. He had seen a man die of pneumonia, but that was after an operation. He also had been a heavy drinker. And someone he had known in India—he could not remember his name—had died of enteric fever. There were so many fevers, and probably they were all heralded by a sore throat. He shivered. That was a rigor, he thought, and wondered if he should put on the light and take his temperature. But drowsiness held him, and reluctance to face the coldness that lay beyond the blankets. He was tempted to seek warmth by creeping nearer to Rose, but heroically he resisted the temptation lest she by contact should be infected with the grave disease, whatever it was, from which he suffered. Eventually he fell asleep again, but with such gloomy thoughts of a choking death from diphtheria, of the racking pains of rheumatic fever, that he dreamt of torture and the scaffold and midnight cemeteries.

In the morning his throat was worse and his temperature was 102 degrees. He tried to inspect his tonsils with a hand-mirror, and what he saw frightened him severely. For now his tongue was not merely furred but spotted like a leopard-skin. He regarded the horrid image with the utmost consternation. Morbid fears possessed him. He put out his tongue again, and again the mirror reflected the leopardish spots. Perhaps he had brought home from India the germs of some oriental disease that, stirring at last, had now come to awful life. It might even be leprosy. He wakened Rose and bade her get up and go for a doctor.

'Are you worse?' she asked.

'Much worse,' said Magnus. 'I'm really ill, Rose. I don't know what it is, but it's serious. It may be typhoid, or something like that, or it may be some fever I was infected with in India. I don't know. There are some tropical diseases that don't show themselves for a long time. I don't want to frighten you, but you must get a doctor at once.'

He spoke with difficulty owing to his swollen tongue, and Rose, now also alarmed, dressed in all haste. 'I don't like to leave you,' she said when she was ready to go.

'I'll be all right,' said Magnus, and smiled bravely. 'Don't be frightened, Rose.'

'I'll be as quick as I can.'

Magnus nerved himself to make a fine gesture. 'You'd better have your breakfast before you go out,' he said. 'I can wait a little longer, I expect.'

'I'll do no such thing!' said Rose indignantly, and shut the door behind her.

She returned with a doctor in less than half an hour.

She had found him at breakfast, and been very ill-pleased because he would not come with her till he had finished eating. The doctor was a tall stout young man with an air of great assurance. He felt Magnus's pulse, took his temperature, examined his tongue, and asked when the little sore on his lip had first appeared.

'Four or five days ago,' said Magnus. 'I cut myself shaving.'

The doctor nodded contentedly and began to write a prescription.

'What's wrong with him?' asked Rose.

'What's the matter with me?' asked Magnus in the same moment, and waited nervously for typhoid, enteric, or even leprosy.

'Thrush,' said the doctor.

'*What?*'

'Thrush,' repeated the doctor.

'But that's something that only children get. And dirty children at that,' said Magnus, who was even more taken aback than he would have been had the doctor said 'leprosy'.

'That's generally so,' agreed the doctor. 'But other people get it occasionally. You are a very good example. Your mouth was probably infected from the sore on your lip.' He turned to Rose. 'He'll have to stay in bed for a few days, Mrs Merriman. Light food only till his temperature goes down. No, it's nothing serious. You have nothing to worry about. I'll look in again. Good-bye!'

'Thrush!' said Rose disdainfully when he had gone. 'And you saying it was typhoid or worse!'

'Anyway, it's damned painful. I feel damned ill,' said Magnus.

'When I was at school,' said Rose, 'there were two bairns that no one would sit near to, because of their heads. And I mind one day they said they were sick, and it was thrush they had. I saw their tongues myself.'

'I don't care though every foundling, orphan, and tinker's brat in the kingdom has had it,' shouted Magnus, and choked on his words, and coughed, and choked again.

'If you'd shown me your tongue I'd have known what was wrong with you. Let me see it now.'

'I will not!'

'Pull it out. Right out. It would have been better if you'd done that before, instead of frightening me with your stories of typhoid and I don't know what!'

'I didn't mean to frighten you.'

'Well, you did!' said Rose. 'And now what do you want for your breakfast?'

Magnus lay in bed for three days and submitted to Rose's nursing. She was efficient in the sick-room and unfailingly attentive, but only at long intervals did she reveal any sympathy. On the third day she admitted that she did not like invalids, and having admitted it she grew more cheerful and appreciably fonder. But Magnus, whose spirit was still rueful at the thought of having been stricken down by so trivial a disease, was again humiliated. He was aware that in these three days of nursing Rose had acquired a moral advantage over him. She had found that his wisdom was impeachable and his judgment liable to error. She had been in command of the situation, and her manner had shown that she was aware of her power. He admitted his admiration for her capability, and perceived in himself a growing inclination not only to rely on her but also to enjoy such reliance. Now and again, in small matters, her maiden shyness reappeared, but generally she behaved as though she had been married for years, and though she had only once before travelled out of Orkney the fact of living in a strange hotel did not appear to disconcert her. She had, indeed, as many Orkney people have, a slight feeling of contempt for foreigners, and she could not believe that the actions and opinions of those who dwelt elsewhere had very much significance.—Magnus discovered that his reputation as a novelist, his modest fame in both England and America, impressed her only in the smallest degree.—This parochialism sometimes annoyed him, but on thinking it over he came to the conclusion that it was only an extreme example of the small nationalism he had been preaching earlier in the year, and that he had no logical complaint against it.

It was Rose who suggested they should abandon their honeymoon and go back to Orkney as soon as Magnus was able to travel. She said, very sensibly, that he was in no condition to enjoy himself, and that a holiday without enjoyment was mere waste of money. After a little argument Magnus agreed with her—as she had made up her mind there was nothing else he could usefully do—and a few days before Christmas they slept for the first time in their new home at Mossetter.

To his amazement Rose's shyness reappeared when her friends came to visit her, and though she was efficient in other ways it was difficult to believe that she was so accomplished an actress as to present this perfect simulation of bashfulness and innocence but newly surprised. Her shyness was real, but it was no more than a blind over the window of a room, small indeed, but well-lit and furnished most orderly.

CHAPTER THIRTY-TWO

Their child was born in April after a labour that was more enervating to Magnus than to Rose. She indeed had gone about the whole business of motherhood with calmness and ease. She had worked hard and without sign of distress until the very eve of her confinement, and only once had she betrayed that instability of mind which, so Magnus had feared, was inevitably and always concurrent with pregnancy. She had never demanded strange exotic fruits, she had never turned him out of doors, nor shown a frenzied antipathy to familiar furniture. But once she did behave unreasonably, and suddenly declared, 'I've nowhere to put my things.'

'What things?' said Magnus.

'All sorts of things,' said Rose irritably. 'I must go and buy a chest of drawers.'

'There's no room for another one.'

'Then you must make room.'

'But why? You have two already, and a wardrobe, and cupboards, and a wooden chest. . .'

'I tell you I need a new chest of drawers,' said Rose, and took a bus to Kirkwall and bought one at an auction-sale of which she had seen the advertisement. It arrived on a lorry the next day and proved too big to go through any of the doors. It was an article of stupendous size, a monument rather than a piece of furniture. The drawers were as big as coffins and must have been excessive even for the bed-linen of the Victorian family for whom it had been designed. With great difficulty it was carried into the barn, and Rose spent the rest of the day there looking at it. In some distress Magnus went to Peter of the Bu and told him what had happened. Peter bade him not to worry.

'She's nesting, that's all,' he said. 'Her mother was the same at first, only it was sofas she wanted. She bought three of them.'

And when a day or two had passed Rose no longer worried about the chest of drawers, and presently Magnus found it very useful for tools and hens' food and odd pieces of harness.

The child that was born after this model or nearly model pregnancy and this easy labour was a well-made boy weighing almost ten pounds. He fed well, slept well, and soon began to display considerable energy. He was christened Peter after Rose's father, and Magnus was extremely proud of him. As soon as he had forgotten the anxiety—his rather than hers—of Rose's confinement, he decided to have a very large family as early as possible, and become indeed the patriarch of whom, lying drowsily on the heather, he had once dreamed.

He found farming less easy than he had thought it would be. His small stock of animals had been delivered to him within a day or two of his return from the unfortunate honeymoon, and as he had bought Mossetter with the previous year's crop in the yard there was no difficulty about feeding, except that he was not quite sure how much food to give to the different beasts. But he had engaged Johnny the ploughman's boy from Midhouse to work for him, and by watching Johnny he soon learnt a great deal. He had a pair of horses—a rough, strong, ten-year-old gelding, and a mare two years younger—a cow in milk, two in calf, three yearling cattle, a couple of fostered calves, and three ewes. He bought a young sow, and Rose had her own hens. The cattle did not improve much on a diet of turnips and straw, but they seemed healthy.

Magnus took a great delight in ploughing and did it all himself. To follow the straining horses, and keep a straight furrow, and watch the sheared earth fall, lightly crumbling, in long broken turves, was a constant pleasure. A little cloud of gulls would keep him company, and the north-east wind blew coldly, and the plough leapt like a live thing when its nose struck stone. At first his arms ached with the labour and his fore-arms were hot with pain, but in a little while his muscles strengthened and the plough seemed to run more easily and almost of its own accord. Had farming consisted merely of ploughing, hay-cutting, harvesting, and leading fine animals to the Dounby Show he would have done very well at it. But there were a hundred details to attend to, and of many of these he was, not wholly ignorant perhaps, but possessed of a merely casual knowledge.

Even when ploughing he was not always certain that he was ploughing what should be ploughed. He knew that the rotation of crops was a fundamental principle of modern agriculture, but apparently there were different systems of rotation. Peter of the Bu advocated a six-year shift, and had pointed out that his farm could be nicely divided into twelve acres of grass, four acres of cleanland crop, four acres of lea crop, four acres of turnips and potatoes, while the remaining acre would make a useful little paddock. That was all very well, but it seemed to Magnus that there were still a good many possible per-mutations and combinations in his acres, and as he was naturally averse from parading his ignorance he was com-pelled to spend considerable time talking to Peter in such a way that Peter would be led to supply the necessary information without being directly asked for it. In this he was ultimately successful, and his fields were at last ploughed, harrowed, sown, rolled, or left alone in perfect orthodoxy.

He showed a regrettable tendency, however, to buy unnec-essary implements. Rose had yielded to the lure of furniture catalogues and filled the house to overflowing with chairs and tables; and Magnus was unable to resist the temptation to buy more turnip cutters, disc harrows, manure distribu-tors, horse rakes, and mowers than he really needed. Yet these were not wholly wasted, for his neighbours borrowed them, and as he was always willing to lend what they wanted they thought well of him and frequently helped him in return, pleasantly and unobtrusively.

By early summer he was feeling very well satisfied with himself. He had spent a lot of money and so far there had been no return except a small steady income from poultry.— Rose looked after the hens.—But that did not worry him. He was prepared to lay out more capital still before he looked for profits, and there were already masons at work extending and improving his byre and making some small additions to the house. He had decided gradually to replace his cattle with better ones, for only the cow he had bought from Peter was a really well-bred animal, and to house good beasts in a poor byre was clearly foolish. And Rose had taken advantage of the masons' presence to demand a back-kitchen and a small room where Johnny could sleep more conveniently than in the kind of cupboard which he occupied at present. Magnus offered no objection. Rose deserved well of him: she had borne a child who grew in strength from day to day, she worked hard and well, and she looked prettier than ever before. Rose could have her back-kitchen if she wanted it. Perhaps, said Magnus, she would also like a porch added to the front of the house? Rose said she would indeed. So the masons, having finished the byre, set to work and built a porch.

With all this activity to speed them the first seven or eight months of Magnus's married life passed with the semblance of unusual rapidity, and when he cut his hay in July it seemed there had been no more than a handsbreadth of time since he had yoked his horses, that now paced strongly in a ripe and yellow field, to the plough that sheared stiffly through a field all cold and black. He surveyed the neat cocks of hay, he considered the additions to his house and steading, he bent in fond admiration to tickle the fat ribs of his son: and everywhere he saw the evidence of achievement. The result of this self-satisfaction was that he began to cast about for an excuse to take a holiday: between haytime and harvest time there was little work to be done, and he felt that he required some relaxation and that his work deserved celebration.

In this mood he received an invitation that otherwise he would have ignored, for he was done with politics. The invitation arrived in a letter from Francis Meiklejohn and consisted of a request to address the people of Scotland—or as many of them as cared to attend—on behalf of the National Party and in memory of the death of Sir William Wallace, the Scottish patriot. In the hands of the National Party, said Meiklejohn, this pious exercise had become an annual event of great importance, and this year, on the six hundred and twenty-seventh anniversary of his death, they hoped to attract even more interest than usual. Cunningham Graham and Compton Mackenzie had promised to speak: Hugh Skene, Macdonell, and other people whom Magnus knew would be there: and it was earnestly desired that Magnus himself, who had contested the by-election in Kinluce with gallantry undiminished by misfortune, would also be present. 'Come back, like Cincinnatus from the plough, and help us once more,' said Meiklejohn. The date of the celebrations, he added, was August 23rd.

Coinciding with his holiday inclinations this request might have been successful in whatever words it had been couched, and the felicitous allusion to Cincinnatus made it irresistible. Magnus felt an impatient desire to meet again the man who could make so happy a comparison. Meiklejohn was in truth the ideal companion for his present mood. He went to Dounby and telegraphed acceptance of the invitation. Then he returned home and told Rose.

Rose was not pleased at all. She said he was a farmer now and had no time for nonsense about Sir William Wallace or anybody else who had been dead so long as that. But Magnus said that even a farmer might take an interest in the affairs of his country and told her the whole story of Cincinnatus to convince her of this. On discovering that Cincinnatus had been dead even longer than Wallace, however, Rose refused to be convinced, and for the next few days went about her work in a very bad temper. She made an unnecessary noise in the handling of pots and plates, her voice grew harsh, and, most illogically, she referred unpleasantly to the extravagance that Magnus had shown in the enlargement of his house. 'And now you're going off to spend more money,' she said, 'though there's not a penny coming in except what I get for my eggs and butter!'

But disregarding her anger Magnus made preparations for his journey and, when the time came, embarked for the mainland.

Scarcely had the mail-steamer left Scapa Pier when he fell into conversation with a stout, red-faced, comfortably dressed man with watery blue eyes and a slight smell of whisky around him that was far the more perceptible because of the early hour. He said he was a farmer in Caithness. His name was Carron. It soon became evident that his farm was considerably larger than Magnus's. He seemed to own wide acres, to breed only cattle of the finest sort, and to employ a large number of men. Yet he complained bitterly that farming did not pay and that unless prices grew much better than they were—and there was little hope of that, he said—then he would assuredly be ruined in a few years' time. At Thurso he and Magnus took lunch together and grew more friendly still. Mr Carron had his motor car in Thurso, and presently he suggested that Magnus might care to come and inspect his farm. 'You would see Jupiter,' he said.

'Jupiter?' asked Magnus.

'The bull,' explained Mr Carron.

'Do *you* own him?'

'Yes, at present,' said Mr Carron. 'But I can't afford to keep him much longer. I'd sell him tomorrow if I could get a proper price.'

Both in Midhouse and at the Bu Magnus had seen photographs in farming journals of Jupiter, and he remembered the devout words with which Peter and Willy had praised him. Jupiter was a bull of superlative virtue. He had taken the Championship Cups at the Highland Show and the Royal Northern Show. He was perfect in his kind. But though Magnus had remembered all this he had forgotten the name of the owner, and now he regarded Mr Carron with increased respect. He said that he would be very pleased to visit him and see his notable herd.

Mr Carron found his motor car and they drove a long way through the spacious melancholy of Caithness till they came to the southern part of the county and reached a farm whose magnificence could be discerned from a great distance. Magnus was impatient to see Jupiter at once, but first he was taken into the house, which was large and cheerless, and there he and his host had another drink. Then they walked through the fields and viewed the comely black herd, every one of which filled Magnus with envy. But Mr Carron, though obviously proud of them, constantly remarked in a gloomy voice that he was sure to lose money on them. Complete gloom had descended on him, indeed, at the very moment they came within sight of the farm, and the liberal dram he had taken had done nothing to lift it. They inspected the large and handsome steading, and Magnus, thinking of Mossetter's tiny byre, marvelled exceedingly.

'It cost far too much,' said Mr Carron. 'I'll never be repaid for what I spent on all this.'

At last they came to Jupiter, and Magnus was silent before his glory. Never had he seen such a bull. His black hide shone like silk, his broad head and generous nostrils bespoke virility, his tail hung like a whip-lash. He was enormous and his enormity was cast in a perfect mould. From square quarters to massive shoulder he was without blemish, and the ponderous pride of his head was superb. Nor was his pride a vain thing. There was sapience, there was even benignity, in those heavy eyes. They stood a long while in admiration of Jupiter.

Then Mr Carron said it was time they went in for dinner, and when Magnus protested that he must continue his journey added, 'You'd better stay the night here. You're not in a hurry, are you?'

'I must get to Edinburgh tomorrow night,' said Magnus.

'You've got plenty of time to do that.'

Magnus felt a strong disinclination to remove himself from the vicinity of Jupiter. He was fascinated by the male beauty and bred perfection of the bull, and to be able to return and gaze a little longer at this nobility he agreed to postpone his southward journey and become Mr Carron's guest.

They returned to the house and Magnus was introduced to Mrs Carron, to her daughter, to an elderly Miss Carron, and to a Mr Beith. The meal was solid and the conversation dull.

At the first opportunity he proposed to Mr Carron that they should revisit Jupiter. His host agreed, but suggested that, as there was no hurry, they might have a little whisky before they went. They had drunk whisky during dinner and some more after it, and by this time the mere emptying of a glass seemed a good excuse for refilling it. When they returned to the byre that housed Jupiter Magnus's imagination was expanded to bursting-point, tight as a Christmas balloon, with a splendid extravagant notion.

Jupiter *couchant* was more impressive than ever. His bulk seemed to overflow the surrounding floor, and his shoulders rose from the straw like a flank of the Himalayas. Mr Carron began to recite his pedigree as though it were an obituary notice. Pessimism and whisky infused his voice as he spoke of Jason of Ballindalloch, Belle of Candacraig, Victor of Ballindalloch, Electra, Mosstrooper, Black Begonia, Montargis, Pride of Mulben, and other cows of price and bulls of great privilege and pride. The black-polled aristocracy of Scotland were Jupiter's ancestors, and Jupiter was their proper scion.

'How much would you sell him for?' said Magnus suddenly.

'Two hundred and fifty guineas,' said Mr Carron.

'That's a lot of money.'

'I couldn't take a penny less.'

'I'll give you two hundred guineas,' said Magnus, and his voice cracked as he said it.

Mr Carron was surprised. 'I didn't know you were a breeder,' he said.

'I'm not.'

'Then why. . . ?'

'I mean to become one.'

'What sort of herd have you?'

'It's a very small one.'

'Well, two hundred and fifty guineas is my price,' said Mr Carron.

'I can't afford more than two hundred. Will you take that?'

Mr Carron fingered his chin and emitted a little belch. 'Yes,' he said and led Magnus back to the house.

CHAPTER THIRTY-THREE

Two days later Magnus returned to Orkney and took Jupiter with him. He had wired to Meiklejohn saying that circumstances prevented him fulfilling his engagement at the Wallace celebrations, and having established *bona fides* he had given Mr Carron a cheque for two hundred and ten pounds. Mr Carron had celebrated the sale in lavish style and Magnus was but imperfectly sober until the winds of the Pentland Firth expelled the last fumes of Caithness whisky. But sobriety did not impair his satisfaction in possessing a champion bull. His excitement, when he looked at Jupiter, was now of a more delicate kind than the robust confidence that had sailed on whisky, but he would not have resold the bull though Carron had offered three hundred guineas for it. He was inexpressibly proud and glad with a kind of tremulous joy. He could still hardly believe that he owned this marvellous animal.

In Orkney Jupiter created a major sensation. Such a bull had never been in the island before. From far and wide people came to Mossetter to see him, and applications for his services were immediate. On his father-in-law's advice, however, Magnus considered these requests very carefully and agreed to admit to this desirable union only such cows as were eminently worthy of it. His own best animal, the cow that came from the Bu, being happily in season, was Jupiter's first mate.

Even Rose admitted the bull's superlative qualities and was proud that her husband should own him though she had been profoundly shocked by his recklessness in buying him.

'How much did you pay for him?' she asked.

'A hundred pounds,' said Magnus.

Rose was appalled and Magnus congratulated himself on forgetting to fill in the counterfoil of the cheque he had given Carron.

'A hundred pounds!' she repeated. 'Best forgive you, that's more than my father ever paid for two beasts, and there's not many in Orkney buys as dear as he does.'

But the longer she looked at Jupiter the feebler grew her criticism, for his beauty disarmed her. He was gentle, moreover, and peaceful despite his strength. His nature was mild as his loins were mighty. Rose and Magnus both spent a lot of time talking to him and making much of him, and work was neglected on his account. Still his visitors came inquisitive and went home envious, and still, when they had gone, Magnus returned to his shed and contemplated him with unabating joy.

For three weeks Jupiter was the pride of the house and bestrode his cows with potent dignity. Then came the tragedy. He slipped and fell, and rose again slowly. They took him to his shed and, scarcely daring to suggest it, hoped that he was not hurt. But in the morning he seemed uncomfortable and Magnus called in the veterinary surgeon, who was uncertain as to what had happened, but optimistically applied a blister. Jupiter did not improve and the vet declared he must have injured one of his vertebrae. Jupiter found more and more difficulty in getting to his legs, for his weight was vast and hung grievously on his damaged spine.

The day came when he could not rise at all, but lay in mournful bewilderment on the straw. Now and again he would struggle and thrust out a forefoot. The huge muscles under his smooth black hide would tremble, and gather their strength, and the foreleg, absurdly small for so great a body, would stiffen beneath the weight put on it. But always the effort was too much. There would be a groan, a dull moaning sound that seemed to come from the depths of his being, and Jupiter would fall back helpless. Sometimes he would raise his head and piteously low. But his head sank lower and the strength of his head acquired an infinite sadness. Between the frontal ridges, thick and jutting, on his massive forehead there was a depression over which the skin was corrugated, and those deep wrinkles appeared to grow more deep. Save when he struggled to get up his brown eyes were patient, but late in the afternoon huge tears ran from them and his head went from side to side in a vain questing for help. Seeing this, Rose wept openly, and Magnus hardly restrained his grief.

They sat with the dying bull all night, and in the morning Magnus went to Bu and asked Peter to come and shoot him.

CHAPTER THIRTY-FOUR

Harvest came and Magnus sold a few animals for little more than the price he had paid for them. His corn was only moderately good and the pessimism he had felt after Jupiter's death recurred and darkened the coming of winter. Neither he nor Rose had readily recovered from the loss of the bull. He had admitted that the purchase of such an animal was senseless—extravagance—and Rose, in her occasional fits of temper, did not hesitate to accuse him of senseless extravagance—but it was not the loss of two hundred guineas that chiefly afflicted him. Jupiter had represented his loftiest ambitions in farming, and by his gentleness and semblance of benignity he had excited not only pride but, despite the incongruity of such emotion, love. The memory of his death pains was a permanent memory, and his grooved and puzzled forehead, his piteous eyes, were a picture not to be erased from the mind.

In his autumnal unhappiness Magnus did what he seldom had the inclination to do and studied his finances. He found to his dismay that he had spent over £1,250 since the previous December, and made nothing but a boy's pocket-money. *The Great Beasts Walk Alone* was still selling slowly, but his receipts from it would rapidly diminish now, and of *The Returning Sun* a bare five hundred copies had been sold. He had a thousand pounds in War Loan stock, but clearly he must begin to make money out of the farm or that modest capital would quickly vanish. In reaction against the expensive purchase of Jupiter he bought a foal for eight pounds and a shabby-looking cow in calf for ten. And in the comparative idleness of winter he began to think once more of writing.

He had no clear conception of the new book he contemplated, but vaguely he desired to write about Orkney. He filled a note-book with scraps of local description. He remembered the colour and figuration of the sky on a summer morning or at the setting of the sun, and described with care and selection the flocculence of little clouds, the grass-green peninsulas that escaped the fiery splendour of the sun's descent, and the quiet pallor of the unripened moon. He recalled the minute but lavish wealth of meadows in June, and discussed the flight of mating lapwings, the coming of the terns, the buccaneering of hen-harriers and black-backed gulls. He took notes of Mary Isbister's conversation, of Peter's, and of the stories that Johnny Peace the shoemaker and Jock of the Brecks had told him. He read the Orkenyinga Saga. And out of all this he hoped, some day and somehow, to make a story. But the intention, form, and style of the story as yet eluded him.

He re-read familiar books with increasing pleasure. He had a library that to Rose seemed wantonly enormous and was indeed big enough for a whole community of farmers. He had gathered it in various places and at various times. Tod's *Annals and Antiquities of Rajasthan* and some volumes on Mogul painting recalled his residence in India, and first editions of Ernest Hemingway came from America. His taste was catholic: Jane Austen, Tchehov, and Rabelais stood shoulder to shoulder on his shelves, and *Don Quixote* was neighbourly with Doughty and *Extraordinary Women* and *Revolt in the Desert. The Thousand and One Nights*, in four green volumes, jostled Bradley's *Shakespearean Tragedy*, and several copies of *Transition* were curiously placed between Webster and Wodehouse. His bookshelves occupied an unfair proportion of the benroom, and from the bedroom, that opened off it, Magnus could see the sober variegation of their rows and delight in the proximity of so much wisdom and wit, life caught in the act, and poetry, and prejudice, and incongruity. How charming to have the Icelandic sagas next door to *Conversations in Ebury Street*, and Froissart leaning friendly on *Mrs Dalloway*!

And he had discovered all his old school-books at Midhouse, and having taken them home he perceived a strange desire to re-educate himself. At one time, apparently, he had been able to read Greek texts of such varying difficulty as the *Anabasis* and *Prometheus Bound*. He examined them and found that even Xenophon presented difficulties nowadays. This was regrettable, he thought, and he recalled a poem he had opportunely remembered

once before, that was called *The Princess of Scotland* and
contained the lines:

> Poverty hath the Gaelic and Greek,
>   In my land.

In pursuit of this visionary state he decided to relearn the
language of Plato and Euripides, and began to study a bat-
tered red-covered grammar-book called *Greek Rudiments*.

The habit of much reading persisted even after the turn
of the year, and grew untimely when the days lightened
and work became more urgent. Rose was often ill-tongued
when he sat indoors with a book on his knees, but having
grown more familiar with the routine of farming Magnus
discovered that Johnny could do much of it, especially in wet
weather, without his help, and continued his studies. In the
spring he was greatly cheered by selling for no less than nine-
teen pounds the foal he had bought for eight. And the ten-
pound cow had given birth to a surprisingly handsome calf.

In June Rose followed suit and bore him another son,
who was christened Magnus and known as Peerie Mansie.
He seemed healthy enough, but he was a noisier child than
Peter had been. Peter was now a boy that any parents might
be proud of. He was big and strong, he was already trying
to walk, and according to Rose already successfully experimenting with speech. Magnus began to transfer his own
ambitions to Peter, and found in the child's high forehead
a clear indication of intellectual strength.

The mobility on which Magnus had for long depended for
enjoyment and vital interest was now completely lost, and
he was settled fast in Orkney. His guerrilla days were over
and he did not regret their passing, for he had little time to
remember them. He had been used to think that if a man's
life was static then time around him was correspondingly
slow; but now he discovered the hours slid by with the easy
movement of a rich man's car. Time no longer rattled past,
but like a Rolls-Royce purred sweetly and devoured day
after day, swiftly and with no sound of haste. April led to
summer, and harvest came, and winter followed. The year—
his second as a farmer—was full of interest and devoid of
excitement.

He grew somewhat stouter and his clothes were shabbier. His face reddened and he became indifferent to cold winds and muddy roads. He learned a little more about farming and studied with pleasure the Greek texts he had scamped and yawned over and detested at school. He was friendly with all his neighbours and, whenever he remembered, he continued to record in his note-books the racier fragments of their conversation beside his descriptions of the plover's black bib and the shaking of reeds in the wind. His second harvest was much better than his first, and the bull-calf which the black cow had borne to Jupiter was a dainty model of his great father. He bought Rose a gold bracelet to mark the second anniversary of their wedding, and she rated him soundly for his foolishness.

Magnus had now lived for a long time in soberness and respectability, for not since buying Jupiter had he been really drunk. And now, though the season of joy and drinking was upon them, he behaved with the decorum befitting an honest farmer and the father of a family. Christmas passed and New Year came, when there was meat and ale in every house and every traveller after the fall of darkness had a bottle in his pocket. Yet Magnus conducted himself with virtue, and whenever he was offered whisky in a friendly house took a little cheese with it to mollify its effects, and from his own bottle drank only the merest sip for courtesy's sake. When he went visiting with Rose he did not forsake her and join company with the wild young men who passed round their little flat bottles in the stable, but sat with her and the other married people and contributed his proper share of the gossip. Christmas passed and New Year followed it: Magnus's virtue remained unspotted, Rose's temper woke only to trivial expression even though she found him studying *Greek Rudiments* when he should have been suppering the horses: and they lived together in happiness and content.

But late in January he fell from grace.

A winter storm broke on the islands and wrought destruction beneath its wings. In the cold light of day it began with a mutter of wind from the north-west, and the wind grew towards night, and in the darkness it came to its strength and roared madly under a maddened sky. The sea in never-ending waves broke on the cliffs and poured its salt cascades on their bald and sodden shoulders. Out of the Atlantic desert came the black battalions of the waves, rearing in the darkness their ruffled hides, shaking their tattered manes, falling in ceaseless fury on the stubborn shore. They broke a trawler and drowned her crew by the Kame of Hoy: they drove another, borne like Mazeppa on a giant horse, hard ashore in a Westray geo. They shook their saltness over the unseen fields, and the noise of their attack—trundling huge boulders up a narrow beach, thundering on the rocks—sounded like gunfire through the yelling chorus of the winds. In the landward parishes chimneys were blown down, ricks fell flat and strawed their broken sheaves about the fields, and wooden sheds were toppled over with wanton buffets. Women lay sleepless in their beds and wondered if their roof would, on a sudden, crack asunder and leap apart and leave them naked under the howling sky. Men, hastily booted and dressed, thrust open resisting doors, and staggered to and fro in the darkness and the wind to make fast all that was loosely founded or frailly built. And shrieking round a gable the wind would fill their throats as though to drown them.

At last, like a black and ragged plaster, the night was torn from the sky and left a grey distress behind it. Now could be seen the ruins of the gale: here were ricks fallen sideways and there, as though clawed by gigantic tigers, were others with their round tops torn off; here a wooden henhouse lay upside down beside a dyke, and where the hens were no one knew; and there, capering across the fields, a large tarpaulin flounced and faltered, and filled its belly with wind, and sailed awhile, and shook a flapping corner, and finally wrapped itself round a telegraph post and flew there like a monstrous grey banner.

Magnus spent most of the night outdoors. At first the wind had daunted him, then it had angered him, and at last it had filled him with joy. As he worked to make fast all that could be made fast he fought with the wind and beat it, and having beaten it he derided it, and like a twopenny Lear shouted his mockery against it.

'Blow, wind!' he cried. 'Smack with a bold robustious hand the broad backside of the buffoon world! Puff and blow, boy! Rip the blankets off the bed and smack the bare dowps you find, you bellowing fool, you winter spasm, you burst balloon!'

By shouting such nonsense as this he added to his enjoyment of the storm, and went indoors with a very restless feeling, a feeling of superfluous energy, and a desire to spend it recklessly on any activity that offered. He made love to Rose, who had been frightened by the wind, and got up again, and rebuilt the fire, and set the table for breakfast.

Presently Rose went to the door and very cautiously opened it. But no sooner was it half-open than the wind tore it from her grasp and flung it wide. The household cat had followed her, and, foolishly inquisitive, crept over the doorstep. Immediately the wind bowled it over. Picking itself up the cat turned tail and ran, and once running could not stop.

'My cat, my cat!' cried Rose. 'She's blown away, Mansie!'

Magnus followed, and past the corner of the house saw the cat turned tail over head, and find its feet again, and leap like a toy kangaroo, all its fur brushed the wrong way, and powerless to halt or turn. It was a big yellow cat and the wind used it like a yellow football. He followed it to the road. It was blown through a barbed-wire fence and somehow succeeded in steering itself between the barbs. Then it fell into a ditch on the other side of the road, and lay there secure. Magnus carried it back to the house, struggling against the wind, and Rose fondled it as though nothing she owned were more precious to her.

The boy Peter wanted to know what had happened, and Magnus, all out of breath but pleased by the second chance to try his strength against the storm, took him on his knee and began to tell a fantastic story of a ginger cat that was blown all round the world, and a giant followed it, and the giant trod cities out of sight as he ran, and tripped over St Paul's, and fell in the Channel with such a splash that three steamers sank, and got up again and ran through France and Spain. But a mouse came out of the Prado and the wind changed and the cat followed the mouse, that was going to help an African lion but was unsure of the way to Africa, so they ran eastwards along the Mediterranean and crossed the Greek islands like stepping-stones, and came to the desert, and at last after running for a long time—and the wind was changeable—they reached the Equator. And there the ginger cat took a great leap into the sky and became a comet with a ginger tail. But the giant stayed where he was and undid the Equator and used it for a skipping-rope and lived happily ever after.

Peter understood practically nothing of this story, but Magnus thought it an excellent tale and wished he had made the journey more complicated so that it might have lasted longer. He found the routine of farm-life very dull that morning, and impatiently desired that something would happen to engage his attention in a livelier way.

By eleven o'clock the storm had passed, leaving a dead calm behind, and the country, windless and almost breathless it seemed, lay under the still sky with an odd look of dishevelment. It was a cold stillness. The sky was white and cold, and in the afternoon the air held a chill suspense.

Magnus was uneasy and excitable all day, and at tea-time he said he was going to the village with a pair of shoes that needed mending. Rose, who had observed his restlessness, appeared suspicious, but Magnus had found a pair of boots so badly worn that a visit to the cobbler seemed reasonable indeed. He mounted his bicycle and rode away. But when he came to the main road he turned, not towards the village, but to Kirkwall. Having ridden the fifteen miles thither he bought a bottle of whisky and rode back again and took his boots to the cobbler.

Johnny Peace, the village shoemaker, was a witty fellow who could make rhymes and who knew all the gossip of the country. He was a young man and lived alone. His shop was a favourite gathering-place, and rarely an evening passed there without debate of some kind. He was, however, alone when Magnus went in, and readily agreed to have a drink. Johnny Peace already knew everything that had happened during the storm for several miles around, and he himself had had an adventure, for on his way to one of the village shops he had encountered the schoolmistress coming down-wind like a full-rigged ship. 'If she'd had a bone in her mouth the picture would have been complete,' he said. 'But God! she ran aground. She came full-speed against me and flung her arms round my neck. "It's the wind," she said, "I can't help it, Mr Peace; I give you my word I can't help it!" But from the way she hung there—and she's no lightly made—I doubt she was just waiting for the opportunity, and the next time there's a hurricane I'm staying safe at home till she's safe in the school.'

Jock of the Brecks arrived while they were talking, and after having some of Magnus's whisky he related his own experiences in the storm, and took another drink. The topic was hardly exhausted when it was found that the bottle was empty, so Johnny Peace shut his shop and they went to the village inn, where they drank beer till closing-time. It was Saturday night and the shops were still busy. Under the gable-end of one of them a little group of men and boys stood sheltering from the snow that now was falling. Before the lighted windows the flakes descended in a thick but gentle flurry. After the inn had closed its doors Magnus and his friends talked awhile with the casual bystanders, and then Johnny Peace proposed they should return to his shop. They added the blacksmith to their number, and Johnny produced another bottle of whisky.

After an hour or so the blacksmith went home. Half an hour later Jock of the Brecks went home. But Magnus stayed where he was, for Johnny Peace was a fine congenial soul, and by now Magnus had reached that state of mind in which talk seems infinite and infinitely desirable. He wanted to tell Johnny about the War and about India and about America; about the books he had written and the book he was going to write; about love and death; about women he had known and about his plans and hopes for Peter and Peerie Mansie. And Johnny, though a gifted talker himself, was sympathetic and a patient listener. Long after the bottle was empty Magnus talked on, and Johnny agreed when agreement was required, and deprecated that which it was politic to deprecate. At last he fell asleep, and Magnus bore him no ill-will, for the load of speech was almost off his mind and he felt free of a great burden.

He went out, and saw that the world had turned white. A virgin landscape lay before him, starlit and placid. The air was clear and the fallen snow was faintly luminous. It had raised the dykes to a new level and smoothed the rough ground with gentle undulations. Magnus beheld that blanched serenity with drunken ecstasy.

The cobbler's shop was a little distance from the road and a little higher than the road. Sheltered by a wall the down-hill path from its door was but thinly covered with snow, and Magnus mounted his bicycle. At the corner he ran into a drift and fell heavily, striking his chest on the upturned grip of the handle-bar. When he got up he felt sick and there was a dull pain under his heart. He stood for a moment or two, swaying slightly, and the odd determination of drunkenness took him: he had started to go home and he would continue to go home. But the snow lay deep on the road, it was nearly a foot deep, so he left his bicycle where it had fallen and began to walk. He moved slowly, for his feet sank at every step and the pain in his side made it difficult for him to breathe. He walked on, head down and half-dazed. Presently, despite the pain, he felt curiously happy. His heavy plodding walk became a slow rhythm and he took a childish joy in crunching through the snow. A part of his brain was sleepy and inactive, but another part was intensely alive to a multitude of small impressions. He perceived the shape of the snow-filled ditches with singular delight, and the lurching rhythm of his own walk seemed enchanting. He looked at his feet, rising and falling, sinking and reappearing, with great amusement, and the dark gable of a cottage, neatly roofed in white, held him for a minute of exquisite pleasure. The countryside appeared to fall away from the road in endless folds, and the suave and simple lines were delicious to see.

In time—he did not know how long—he came to the farm-road to Mossetter, and slowly climbed uphill. He stopped to rest awhile, and turned and saw beneath him a starlit maiden land, stained with the star-twinkling darkness of the great loch, spreading in dusky whiteness to the white round breasts of Hoy. Twin hills they stood, snow-clad, round as the buxom breasts of a girl, and flatly before them lay the

white map of Orkney. And now a new drunkenness came
to Magnus, but whether of his belly or his soul he did not
know. Tears sprang to his eyes to see such loveliness, and
perception like a bird in his breast sang that this land was his
and he was one with it. As though his tears had flooded it his
mind was filled with knowledge and he knew that his life was
kin to all the life around him, even to the beasts that grazed
in the fields, and to the very fields themselves. Live was the
flowering of a single land, and love of country was no virtue
but stark necessity. Patriotism and the waving of flags was
an empty pride, but love of one's own country, of the little
acres of one's birth, was the navel-string to life. His life, as
the life about him, was the vigour of his blood, and life could
not be whole save in its own place. Now he knew why, in far
parts of the world, he had often felt the unreality of all he saw
and descried a foolish artifice in his own business there. The
far parts of the world were fine roving for pirates who had
a secret island whither they might bring back their booty,
but to roam the world without a haven or a home was to be
lost as a star that fell to nothingness through the ordered
ranks of heaven. Now he knew why, in late months, time
had passed so simply and untroubled. This soil was his own
flesh and time passed over him and it like a stream that ran
in one bed. Here indeed he was immortal, for death would
but take him back to his other self, and this other self was
so lovely a thing, in its cloak of snow, in the bright hues of
spring, in the dyes of the westering sun, that to lie in it was
surely beatitude.

His thoughts grew feebler and more diffuse. He shivered,
and felt the cold. The pain in his side was a dull aching. He
turned homewards and wearily climbed the hill.

Rose was waiting for him. She had sat by a dying fire,
anxious and angry. She came to the door, and her voice was
hard enough to shatter any dream less firmly set and safely
guarded than Magnus's. But Magnus's dream of knowledge
was now like a bubble of pearl in the depths of his mind,
and girded round with sleep.

'Do you know what time it is?' she demanded. 'What have
you been doing till now?'

'Talking,' said Magnus. 'Talking and seeing the world.'

Rose came nearer him and sniffed. 'You're drunk!' she said.

'Not drunk, but sleeping,' said Magnus, and stumbled indoors.

CHAPTER THIRTY-FIVE

Like the storm of the preceding night Rose's temper gathered strength in the darkness and as soon as daylight came Magnus was wakened by her angry voice. Had he been guilty of treason, regicide, and all infamy she could not have assailed him more bitterly. Drunkenness was to her the blackest of sins, and her tongue lashed him like scorpions. Hearing her so loud the children began to cry, and the house was filled with the noise of wrath and weeping. But Magnus lay and said nothing till the worst seemed over.

'Well, are you going to get up or do you mean to lie in bed all day?' asked Rose, a little breathlessly.

'I think I'll stay in bed,' said Magnus.

'You'll do no such thing!' said Rose.

'All right then. I'll get up. I fell and hurt myself last night and I'm pretty sure I ought to stay in bed; but if you don't want me to, I shan't.'

Magnus sat up and threw back the clothes. Then he began coughing, and coughed up a little blood.

'There!' he said. 'I told you I had hurt myself. I've broken a rib, I think.'

'Stoop!' [The rude imprecative.] said Rose. 'You've spoilt your stomach with whisky, that's all.'

Magnus lay down again. 'I think I'll stay in bed however,' he said.

'All right,' said Rose, 'then you can mind the bairn till I'm ready for him.' And she planted the still wailing child in Magnus's arms and left them to go about her work.

Although it was Sunday she worked with great vigour all day and made as much noise as possible. Nor did she cook any dinner, but some time in the afternoon brought Magnus a cup of tea and a slice of thick bread and butter, saying, 'There's no use cooking anything, for you couldn't eat it anyhow, after drinking like that all night.'

'As it happens I'm feeling very hungry indeed,' said Magnus.

'You don't need food when you lie in bed all day,' said Rose, and went away to make a great clattering noise by rearranging all her pots and pans in the kitchen.

And Magnus lay and remembered his beatific vision of the world washed white and unified by snow, and the bubble of pearl in his mind was unbroken by the clatter of pots and his wife's anger. Peerie Mansie slept in his arms and Peter played on the floor at the bedside.

On the following morning the pain in his side was worse, and Rose consented to send Johnny for the doctor. The snow had frozen hard and the roads were passable now. But scarcely had Johnny gone than Peggy of the Bu came to tell of a great and splendid scandal in the country, and this news put Rose in a worse temper than ever.

The snow on Saturday night had played falsely with a hundred lovers. In Orkney it is the habit to go a-wooing on Saturday night, and to court your girl not in cold corners but warmly, yet with circumspection and restraint, in her bed. But though everyone knows of this practice, and, if they are young enough, looks forward eagerly to the week-end's darkness, there is a certain decorum used and the custom is not openly talked about. And now the heavy snow had betrayed what convention would fain conceal. For the Saturday lovers, arriving when the sky was clear or merely a flurry of snow was falling, had stayed longer than Magnus had stayed with Johnny Peace, and risen to find the snow deeper then he had found it.

Many had come long distances, and now their bicycles and motor bicycles were useless to take them home again. Sometimes indeed they were hard to find, for if they had been left at the weather-side of a wall the banking snow had covered them. So the lovers had to walk home, and the motor bicycles, too heavy to push through the snow, had to be left behind as evidence against their owners.

Sunday morning was bright and sunny, the snow had

stopped falling, and over its smooth fields the deep tell-tale footprints led from every house where lived a comely or a kindly girl. Far across country they stretched, and everyone could tell at a glance that Jessie and Jean and Molly and Minnie had slept with their boys beside them. And it was worse still for the boys, for some of them had so far to go that when respectable folk set out for church they met them still slowly trudging homewards, some with their bicycles on their shoulders and others with embarrassing memories of where their bicycles had been left.

This was the story that Peggy of the Bu, laughing and delighted, told to Rose, and Rose's anger mounted with every sentence. For her man had also been out on Saturday night, and left his bicycle in the snow, and it would be said that he, a married man, had been running after the lasses, and so her pride would be shent and her name sullied beyond redemption.

When Peggy had gone—she had not been allowed to see Magnus—Rose came ben and fiercely told him all this. It was in vain that Magnus declared his bicycle had been left outside the shoemaker's shop and that no one was likely to think he had been sleeping with Johnny Peace. She would not be comforted. She was sure that scandalous tales would be told, and how could she deny them when it was clear that Magnus had been out so late? Her distress was genuine and she vented it in anger.

Nor was her wrath diminished when the doctor came and said that Magnus had indeed broken a rib and must stay in bed for several days. She contained herself while the doctor was present and listened to his instructions with grim politeness, but when he had gone she told Magnus that it served him right and he need expect little care and less sympathy while he lay abed.

'I've got my work to do,' she said, 'and you could be doing yours if you'd had the sense to behave yourself and keep away from the drink. And keep away from Johnny Peace too, after this! Johnny Peace, indeed! It's all right for him if he likes to spend all his money on whisky, for he's a single man and has only himself to spoil. And

a fine name he has through the country for his talking
and drinking! But you're married and you've a family
forbye, and the thought of you drink, drink, drinking
with Johnny Peace fair makes me mad. And you haven't
the stomach for it, I say! You fall off your bicycle and
break your ribs and let everyone know you were out past
midnight when a decent man should be at home in his
bed, and God knows where they'll say you were, for there's
lasses about that would let anyone in, married or no. But
heaven help you if you get drunk again, for there's never
any knowing what you'll do when there's a dram in you.
You were drunk, I'll warrant, though you never admitted it, when you bought Jupiter, and what use was he
to you? Nothing but the waste of a hundred pounds—
bringing a bull like that into a peerie farm like this!—
and that's more money than you'll ever make again, for
you're getting lazier every year, and so long as you have
a book to read there's little enough work to be got from
you. Have you mended that harness yet? Not you, faith.
But you'll read your books whatever happens, and never
a thing they'll do for you in return, no, no more than
Jupiter did.'

Magnus waited patiently till her tirade was done and she
had gone. The harder she talked the harder she would
work, he thought, and there was comfort in that. Then
he reached under his pillow and brought out *Candide*,
Pride and Prejudice, and *Madame Bovary*. *Candide* he put
aside: some disturbing association clung to it, though he
could not think what it was nor discover whose memory it
nearly evoked. And after turning a few pages he put away
Madame Bovary, for the account of Hippolyte's operation
had always made him unhappy, and, with his ribs newly
strapped, he did not care to read about tenotomies and
the like. But opening *Pride and Prejudice* he chanced to
read Mrs Gardiner's query, 'Pray, how *violent* was Mr
Bingley's love?' and Elizabeth's reply, 'Is not incivility
the very essence of love?' Rose, he concluded, must still
be very deeply attached to him, for she had carried incivility to its extreme, and he rejoiced to find so appli-
cable a sermon in the smooth tones that underlay the

running brook of Jane Austen's silver fluency. He read
for an hour and thought how much pleasanter it was to
read fine writing, to note the coolness of others' wit, than
to write unhandily a book of your own and thrash your
wits till they brought forth at last a mouse of wit that
might be written down. And he thought with satisfaction that although his wealth was only a few hundred
pounds he had more books than many a richer man. He
had enough to last him. He would not need to buy any
more.

On Tuesday Rose was in no better a mood and Magnus
decided that her ill-humour would endure for the week at
any rate. She contrived new ways to make him uncomfortable. She took away his cigarettes, and found the books
under his pillow and took them away also.

'You've wasted enough time reading,' she said sourly.

'Well, I can't do anything else at present,' said Magnus.

'You can mind the bairn,' she said, for Peerie Mansie was
crying loudly. She put the child in Magnus's arms. 'If you
can manage to keep him quiet you'll be clever enough, and
you'll have no time for books,' she said. 'And keep an eye
on Peter, he'll be getting into some mischief or other if you
don't. I've my washing to do.'

While Rose scrubbed clothes in the back kitchen Magnus
endeavoured to pacify his younger child. But Peerie Mansie
had taken a dislike to the world about him and would not
be quiet. So Magnus thought of the principle by which a
great pain may drive out a less and a large noise subdue
a small one, and began to sing. And the first song he
remembered was the disreputable ballad of *Samuel Hall*.
Peerie Mansie evidently enjoyed it, for he stopped his
crying almost at once. Magnus came to the third or fourth
verse, and, though it hurt his side somewhat, sang louder
than ever:

> Then the Parson he will come, he will come,
> And the Parson he will come, he will co-ome!
>   The Parson he will come
>   And he'll look so bloody glum,
>   And he'll talk of Kingdom Come,
>   Damn his eyes, blast his soul!

The comminatory refrain he sang in fine full-throated fashion, and before the last note had died the door was thrown open and Rose stalked into the room.

'What's that you're singing to my bairn?' she cried. 'That's no a song for a bairn to hear, no, nor any decent body either!'

'Why, have you been listening?' asked Magnus.

'Yes, I've been listening, and I wonder you're not feared of a judgment, singing a song like that, and to a bairn.'

'Mansie thoroughly enjoyed it. He stopped crying at once.'

'Poor wee bairn, my poor wee bairn,' said Rose, and rocked Peerie Mansie in her arms. The child immediately began to cry again.

'Give him to me,' said Magnus. 'I can keep him quiet.'

'Poor wee bairn,' said Rose again, and still without effect. She grew impatient. 'Here, take him then,' she said, and gave him back to Magnus. 'But mind and not let me hear that song again, nor any other like it!'

When she had gone Magnus sang once more, but softly now, the ballad of *Samuel Hall*, and Peerie Mansie fell sound asleep.

Magnus called to his elder son: 'Come here, Peter. I want you to do something for me. I want you to get me a book. A book, do you understand? Any book you like.'

Peter obediently went to the shelves in the ben-room and brought back a tattered red volume. It was *Greek Rudiments*.

'Well,' said Magnus, 'I had hoped for something of a more definitely literary interest than this: something more finished, more accomplished, and so more entertaining, if you take my meaning. But if you think I should continue to polish up my Greek I suppose there's little use in asking you to go back for a novel. No? One book's enough, is it?'

Peter tried to climb on to the bed and Magnus lifted him up and settled him against his knee.

'Would it amuse you to hear the Athenian tongue?' he asked. Καίπερ χρήματ' ἔχοντεζ οὐ βουλόνται μεταδοῦναι τοῖζ πένησιν: that means, "Though they have money they will not share it with the poor"; and that shows you the benefit of a classical education, for you discover by it that human nature doesn't change much. "Share my χρήματα with the poor?" said the Peloponnesian War profiteers. "Not bloody likely!" And so say all of us, Peter, yet not knowing—unless we have had a classical education—that that sentiment, like all notable or worthy sentiments, was already a commonplace on Athenian pavements some two thousand five hundred years ago.' And Magnus solemnly repeated the Greek sentence.

'Pen-aysin,' said Peter.

'What?' said Magnus.

'Pen-ay-*sin*,' said Peter.

'My God,' said Magnus, 'he's talking Greek! I've sired a prodigy.'

He read other sentences and asked Peter to repeat the words, but Peter preferred the one he had learnt for himself, and stubbornly reiterated 'Pen-ay-*sin*.'

'All right,' said Magnus, 'then we'll start at the beginning, as a rational education, which means a classical one, should be started. Now say this after me.'

He repeated the alphabet and Peter made many of the simpler sounds with reasonable accuracy.

'That's magnificent,' said Magnus. 'My dear fellow, you're going to be a scholar of the first magnitude. You have the intonation of a professor, the fine high forehead, the voracious appetite of a researcher—stop chewing it, confound you!—and I'm the man to direct your infant feet to the academic grove and the foothills of Parnassus. Now let's try the verbs, which are very difficult and extremely numerous. Indeed from the appearance of a Greek grammar you might imagine that Greek conversation consisted solely of verbs, and the Athenians were exclusively interested in moods and tenses. But that is not so. They weren't nearly so moody and tense as we are.—That's the kind of joke that will be useful to you when you're a professor, Peter.—And so we come to λέγω, which is a very good verb: λέγω, I say; λέγειζ, says you. Now then, Peter, after me: λέγω!'

'Leggo,' said Peter.

'λέγειζ.'

'Leg-*ice*.'

'λέγει.'

'Leg – I'

'Full marks,' said Magnus. 'What Ben Jonson—who was a great man, Peter—once called his boy Benjamin, that I may certainly call you: "Magnus Merriman his best piece of poetry." Peter, my lad, you're going to be a great man!'

Peter played with the grammar-book and Magnus lay back on his pillow and pondered the charming humour of the scene. But in a little while the joke became a serious thing, and presently he saw Peter as Professor of Greek at Oxford University, a scholar who should expound Aeschylus in the very tones of Aeschylus, a towering figure in the schools whose voice, loud and passionate in debate upon Mycenae rich in gold, would yet meander in grave love-liness about the Platonic dialogues, or leap in a riot of Aristophanic scorn upon his critics. To know, to be a scholar: what loftier aim had man? Yet why should Oxford be his goal? Would he not do better to live in his own country and by his virtue inspire new greatness in it? Here in the islands where Hakon had died, whose first earls were the elder issue of the family that fathered Eng-land's Norman conqueror, whose cathedral of St Magnus was built before Oxford was built, whose people were yet sturdy and shrewd and independent, here was the boy's domain, and with his gardening Orkney might flower most brightly. True, it was a small place, not rich, but what virtue was there in bigness? Athens in its prime was not large and Rome in its heyday was a little town. Iceland, the home of heroes, was but a fringe of people in a northern sea, and Gloriana's London a pair of vil-lages at the ends of a bridge. Greatness was not measured by the mile, and the world might yet hear of Magnus Merriman's best piece of poetry though he never stirred from home.

Enchanted by this, the newest, the finest, and the most far-off of his ambitions, Magnus lay blissfully content.

In the back kitchen Rose was washing his dirty clothes, angry still, but deft and careful in her work. The cattle in the byre crunched their turnips and straw. Peerie Mansie slept. Leaning against Magnus's knee, happy as his father, Peter sucked a red corner of the grammar-book. And the country that was to share his greatness lay dark and warm beneath the snow, and meditated nothing but the year's new grass.